# CRITICAL ACCLAIM
# FOR JAMES HOUSTON TURNER'S NOVELS

**"Ludlumesque!"**
*—The Dallas Morning News*

**"Jason Bourne meets The DaVinci Code meets Tom Clancy."**
*—LA's the Place Magazine*

**"Masterful."**
*—Who Magazine (Time Inc)*

**"One of those searing cliffhanger books that simply
defy you to put the thing down."**
*—The Advertiser*

**"Pulsates on every page."**
*—BookPleasures*

**"Unputdownable!"**
*—The Sunday Mail*

**"Unlike any spy hero you've encountered before."**
*—NewsBlaze*

**"Starts fast and picks up speed!"**
*—San Francisco Book Review*

**"Hits the ground running!"**
*—IndieReader*

**"Absolutely riveting!"**
*—Midwest Book Review*

**"Don't start this book in an airport. You'll miss your plane."**
*—News Ltd*

**"James Houston Turner and his Talanov thriller series
. . . definitely one of our favorites!"**
*—The Mystery Tribune*

## BY JAMES HOUSTON TURNER

FICTION
The Search for the Sword of St Peter
The Identity Factor
Department Thirteen
Greco's Game
November Echo
Dragon Head


NON-FICTION
The Earth of Your Soul
The Spud Book
The Recipe Gal Cookbook (photographs)

# JAMES HOUSTON TURNER

# DRAGON HEAD

## AN ALEKSANDR TALANOV THRILLER

REGIS

Published by Regis Books
*An imprint of Ruby Rock Films LLC*

First edition, 2020

For more information about James Houston Turner,  visit
*www.jameshoustonturner.world*

To follow James Houston Turner, visit his official Facebook page:
*@officialjameshoustonturner*

Cover design by Frauke Spanuth

Author photo by Bill Rich

ISBN: 9780958666497

Manufactured in the United States of America

*For Wendy*

# ACKNOWLEDGMENTS

This book has been a long time coming since its announcement in 2011. During that time, many of you helped Wendy and me through some difficult periods of personal loss. At times we were on the verge of being crushed, but we endured those losses and challenges and here we are, and here this book is . . . finally! Thank you for supporting us along this journey.

The person I want to thank most is my wife and best mate, Wendy, who endures with grace and humor the highs and lows of being married to this idealistic, determined writer. I could not have done this without you.

And because books *are* judged by their covers, I would like to acknowledge the graphic arts genius of Frauke Spanuth for yet another spectacular cover. Thanks also to my editor, Flo Selfman, who helped make this book shine.

I would also like to thank all of the young men and women who contributed to my "Team Talanov" creative writing competition. In brief, I asked students to submit names and character profiles for the three orphaned kids you will meet in this book. Due to storyline changes, I was not able to use the winning character names, although the profiles received from these talented young writers helped me frame three spunky young personalities whom you will soon meet. I would therefore like to applaud winners Taylor Johnson, Daria Dragicevic, and Susan Sullivan, and finalists Rylan Brown, Ashley Chen, Fulton Costa, Taylor Doxey, Rebecca Ford, Morgan Garrett, Zoe Brigid Gray, Adam Grumman, Mollie Hobensack, Montana Holman, Christina Imboden,

Caoilfhionn Illes-Hall, Devin Johnson, Makayla Kemper, Adrienne Mabry, Rose Richter, Abby Rimer, James Seely, Haley Sheets, Bridget Short, Brooklyn Small, Tiffany Tyers, Jake Villies, and John Walker, Jr.

An extra shout also for Rebecca Ford, whose emails brought laughter and support during those dark times mentioned above.

Thanks also to Cheryl Masciarelli for her invaluable help with publicity.

A special thanks also to Ricardo Valerdi, for his expertise on cyber crime, Sylvia Rowland, for her awesome graphics, and Matt Peterson and Mike Bernardo, for their help with cyber lingo.

A huge thanks also to Walker Hanson, who has traveled many years with me on this roller-coaster journey, and to Taylor Hanson, for reminding me to value what I do.

In closing, I want to thank the incredible people who have worked faithfully to bring Talanov's story in *Greco's Game* to film audiences around the world: Thomas B. Fore, Ross C. Hartley, Jeffrey Bowler, and Bret Saxon.

Speaking of *Greco's Game*, I would like to express enormous relief that my longtime friend, Bill Rich, did not get arrested while taking book setting photos for me in Los Angeles. I am *so* glad I do not have to visit you in prison, Bill!

# DRAGON HEAD

# CHAPTER 1

Wu Chee Ming looked anxiously behind him. Where were they? *Who* were they? When would they strike? An attack in a crowded street like this would be over in seconds. A silenced pistol. A knife. A needle. Death would be quick and the assassin would vanish. One face in an ocean of faces.

He was not even sure they were onto him. In fact, they probably weren't. He had taken extreme care over the last few months to make sure his movements went undetected.

*One does not seek what one does not see.*

It was a proverb that guided his every move.

And yet, in spite of his meticulous planning, he had to proceed as if they *had* noticed, which was why he had chosen Lan Kwai Fong, a small, bustling tourist district in the heart of Hong Kong, to make his escape. The narrow streets of Lan Kwai Fong were perfect for what he was planning. Flashing neon. Music. Thousands of people surging in and out of nightclubs and restaurants. The perfect place to disappear.

*The perfect place to be killed.*

The proverb, however, held the secret to his survival; namely, that the best place to hide is often in plain sight . . . that people usually do not notice what is right in front of them. Hence, his choice to pass through Lan Kwai Fong each night on his way home from work, so his being here tonight would not attract any undue attention.

Suddenly, an elbow caught him in the chest and knocked him into a group of Chinese girls texting one another. They were holding their phones so close their eyes glistened with light from the tiny screens.

"*Kàn tā!*" one of them barked.

Wu Chee Ming pushed on.

Ahead, the street bent ninety degrees and sloped downhill

for a short block before meeting D'Aguilar Street. Wu Chee Ming turned at the corner and threaded his way uphill along another street filled with partygoers. Within minutes, he reached a short flight of steps that branched away from the street. Taking the steps two at a time, he reached the top and began running along a darkened walkway that angled between a pair of highrise office towers. Before long, the sounds and smells of Lan Kwai Fong had receded into the distance.

Wu Chee Ming knew he would miss those sounds and smells. But at least he would be alive to remember them. He glanced behind but saw no one.

*One does not seek what one does not see.*

His survival hinged on the truth of that proverb, and yet if he truly believed it, why was he running? Why was he not relaxed in the knowledge that he was but another face in an ocean of faces?

Under normal conditions, Hong Kong was the perfect city in which to vanish. But these were not normal conditions. He was running from a crime boss who knew every inch of the island. A crime boss with eyes and ears everywhere. A crime boss so skilled in the art of death that some people considered it an honor to die by his hand. Dexter Moran was his name, although no one dared address him that way. To everyone in Hong Kong and the New Territories, he was known as Dragon Head, and he was the supreme leader of the *Shí bèi* organized crime society, which was based in the Zhongzhen Martial Arts Academy.

The name "Dragon Head" was actually a title that had been seized by Moran in the same manner a lion becomes the alpha male of his pride: by defeating or killing his rivals. And not just known rivals, but anyone suspected of being a threat. Which was why Wu Chee Ming had chosen to run. He wanted to make sure he was not among them.

Ahead, beside a tree, was an old bicycle. Wu Chee Ming had purchased it from a repair shop with instructions that it be placed beside the tree this afternoon. It had a basket above the front fender and a tiny dome bell on the handlebar. Lifting the bike onto the path, Wu Chee Ming walked it to an intersecting walkway, where he turned left, jumped on, and began pedaling. In less than a minute he emerged onto a busy street.

Like New York, Hong Kong was a city that never slept. Even at this late hour, cars filled the streets and the sidewalks were gorged with people. A few dings on his bell caused pedestrians to stop long enough for him to bicycle across the sidewalk and into the bicycle lane, where he turned left and began pedaling with the flow of traffic. He kept pace for two blocks, then cut across to the other side of the street, where he began pedaling with the flow of traffic in the other direction. He bicycled past noodle bars, restaurants, and retail outlets offering everything from designer clothing to electronics, phone cards, and cosmetics. Before long, he turned down a side street and raced to the next corner, where he turned right and raced to the next corner, where he turned again. The zigzag pattern took him away from the neon madness of the tourist district and into Hong Kong's shadowed side streets.

Within twenty minutes, Wu Chee Ming had made his way to a four-story apartment building in a rundown part of Wan Chai. Unlike the glamour and polish of the financial precinct where he worked, this part of town was stained with the gloom of poverty. There were no gleaming office towers of tinted glass. No stepped terraces with architectural flourishes. The buildings were rectangular and squat. Rust and soot were the predominant colors.

Leaning his bicycle against a metal roller door, Wu Chee Ming entered a darkened stairwell and dashed up a flight of steps. There were no lights in the stairwell because Wu Chee Ming had broken the bulbs. No one must remember his face to anyone asking questions. And there *would* be questions, and Dragon Head would be asking them. By that time, however, he would be long gone, which meant Dragon Head would have no choice but to hunt down the only other person who could give him answers. That person was former KGB colonel Aleksandr Talanov. Talanov, of course, would have no answers because he would not know what had happened. Torture would be employed, and Dragon Head would be merciless, but Talanov would not be able to reveal what he did not know. Yes, Talanov was a walking dead man, while he, Wu Chee Ming, was about to become a ghost.

# CHAPTER 2

With sweat dripping from his brow in a basement in Cedarville, Maryland, Talanov cranked the jack-post higher and paused to check its stability. The adjustable steel post was supporting one end of a two-by-twelve floor joist that supported a kitchen floor. Over the last few years, the floor had suffered water damage from a leaky dishwasher and Talanov had just replaced the rotten joists. The new joists of freshly cut Douglas fir made the basement smell like Christmas.

"Are you sure that's going to hold?" asked Dr. Pam Monahan. Dressed in a navy blue skirt suit and heels, Monahan's honey-blonde hair had been pulled back in a ponytail that hung to the middle of her back.

"I'm sorry, doctor," said Talanov, "but I still don't get why you're here."

"Bill said you needed some help."

"With these joists, yes, I do, and with the ton of sheetrock I've still got to put up. No offense, doctor, but you're not exactly dressed for the job."

"None taken," replied Monahan brightly. "Is that coffee fresh?"

Talanov followed her line of sight to a French press on the workbench. It was full of dark-roast coffee that had been steeping for twenty minutes. Beside the carafe was an empty mug. Monahan walked over to the bench and peered inside the mug. She recoiled at the sight of coffee stain that had turned the inside of the mug brown. She then brightened when she saw a shiny porcelain mug holding a selection of large nails. After emptying the mug of its contents, she blew out the dust and filled it with coffee. She then looked at Talanov and gestured inquiringly with the carafe.

With a sigh of resignation, Talanov dismounted the ladder

and stepped over to the workbench to watch Monahan fill the stained mug.

While she poured, Monahan looked Talanov over and smiled at what she saw. Leather tool belt, sweaty tank top, cargo shorts, clunky work boots. *Definitely a man's man,* she thought, glancing at his hair, which was standing upright in places from caked-on sawdust. His face was likewise covered with dust, except for an outline where protective goggles had shielded his eyes and a dust mask had covered his nose and mouth. "Here you go," she said, handing Talanov the mug.

While they each took a sip, Monahan let her eyes roam the basement. On the wall above the workbench was a large panel of pegboard. On it was a wide variety of hand tools on hooks. To her right was a stack of lumber on a pair of handmade sawhorses. Across the floor were some bundles of insulation, and to the right of those, leaning against the wall, was a stack of drywall sheets. At the far end of the basement was a miter saw on a metal stand. On the floor beneath the saw was a pile of sawdust and some scraps of wood.

"This is quite a man cave," Monahan remarked. She looked at the pegboard and removed an adjustable wrench. "What's this?" she asked.

Talanov took the wrench from Monahan and put it back on the hook. "You're not here to assist me with joists and drywall, are you?"

"Of course I am," Monahan replied.

Talanov raised a skeptical eyebrow.

Monahan pulled a wooden stool over to the workbench and sat. "Bill thought it might be easier for you to talk in an informal setting." She scooted aside some galvanized steel brackets and placed her coffee mug in the clearing.

"No disrespect, but I'm reinforcing the kitchen floor of Bill's house, which has been rotting for several years because of a water leak. I don't need to talk. I need to work. No offense."

"None taken, and, please, call me Pam. Doctor sounds so formal."

"And you want this to be informal?"

Monahan smiled and took a sip of her coffee.

"I don't need to talk," Talanov said again. He downed the remainder of his coffee and grabbed one of the brackets.

"Are you certain about that?" asked Monahan.

"I'm certain," Talanov replied, returning to the ladder.

"Bill thinks differently."

"Which is why he drafted you."

"Sometimes, friends see what we don't want to see."

"Sometimes, friends don't listen very well."

"Are you certain you don't need to talk?"

"I don't need a therapist, Pam. I need an extra set of hands. No offense."

"None taken. But are you certain that's all you need?"

Talanov repositioned the stepladder beneath the far end of the two-by-twelve joist he had just installed.

"Do you find it difficult accepting help from other people?" Monahan asked.

"Not if it involves sheetrock."

"Do you think Bill misled you?"

Talanov paused with one foot on a rung. "I appreciate what Bill's trying to do. He's a good friend who's concerned about my well-being."

"He said you took quite a hammering in yesterday's hearing."

"He told you about that?"

"Only in passing. He said both of you were involved in a congressional hearing and that he was giving testimony today – which is why he had to leave early – and that you addressed the committee yesterday, but that it was a hard day, although he didn't say why."

"And he thought I might want to talk about it?"

"That and other things."

"What kind of other things?"

Monahan shrugged and took another sip of her coffee.

Talanov scrutinized Monahan's expression but she remained

noncommittal. "Are you referring to my wife or Larisa?"

"Is that something you want to talk about?"

"I don't want to talk about anything, Pam. I want to finish this job."

"Then why did you bring them up?"

Talanov growled and shook his head.

"Are you certain you don't want to talk?" asked Monahan.

"I'm certain," answered Talanov.

"Are you certain, I mean, *really* certain? Sometimes, we think we're certain but we really aren't."

"You like using that word, don't you? Yes, I'm certain."

"You don't have to talk about anything you genuinely don't want to talk about. If, however, you do want to talk, then whatever you tell me is private and protected."

"Like a priest in a confessional? Or a lawyer?"

"I prefer doctor-patient, and, yes, if we're being honest, Bill did send me instead of a construction hand because he cares more about you than he does his floor. He says you're the best friend he's ever had – his only friend, he's joked on several occasions – and, yes, he did brief me on the tragedy of your wife getting killed."

"She wasn't just killed, Pam, she was *assassinated,* on stage, standing by my side, and then died in my arms, with her blood squirting through my fingers from a bullet that ripped through her neck."

Monahan winced then nodded somberly.

"And that's after dozens of people were murdered at our home in Sydney and we were hunted mercilessly across Australia, Vanuatu, and Switzerland. And for what? An old KGB bank account opened in my name years ago."

"By the same people who murdered your wife?"

"No. A different mob, which was, literally, the mob – the Russian mob – who also tried killing Bill. They gunned him down, Pam, and I was in the room when it happened, and he would have died had Larisa not stopped the bleeding and helped me get him to the hospital. I take it Bill mentioned

Larisa?"

"He said the two of you became . . . involved."

"Which Bill thought was a good thing."

"But you didn't."

"No, I didn't."

"Why do you think that is? You were a widower. She had affection for you, and, according to Bill, you felt the same."

"Because death and violence follow me, and the same people who killed my wife and tried killing Bill would one day come for her. I couldn't let that happen. That's why I got her a job in Australia."

"Figuring she'd be safe on the other side of the world?"

"Safer than she would be around me. Look, I realize I can't keep living in fear of what might happen. That's what Bill keeps saying. He thinks the danger has passed. I know it hasn't, which is why I won't risk the safety of people I love."

"Are you saying you love Larisa?"

"I'm saying I won't allow a target to be placed on her back."

"You didn't answer my question."

With another growl of frustration, Talanov climbed the ladder and began nailing the bracket in place.

"Did Larisa have a say in that decision?"

Talanov looked down at Monahan. "Ever had someone die in your arms?"

Monahan shook her head.

"I did what had to be done," Talanov said.

Monahan did not reply. The seconds stretched.

"Okay, yes, I was probably too hard on her," Talanov admitted, feeling the need to explain further, "and maybe I shouldn't have pressured her into taking that job, but I absolutely could not bear something happening to her, okay? She deserves a good life and happiness, not . . . this."

"This?"

"The kind of life that Bill and I lead."

"Again, wasn't that a decision Larisa should have made? From what I hear, she's tough and resilient."

Talanov did not reply.

"Does Bill agree with your decision?"

"I think you know the answer to that. Otherwise, he wouldn't have asked you to stop by for this little chat that we've been having."

Monahan smiled.

"Bill is stubborn," Talanov continued. "And refuses to listen to reason."

"Remind you of someone else?"

"He knows I'm right, and I told him so – numerous times – but of course he didn't want to hear it, which is typical. And, no, he hasn't forgiven me for sending her away. He keeps telling me how rare it is to find someone who truly – "

Talanov hammered in another nail to avoid finishing his sentence.

"Who truly what?" asked Monahan.

Talanov drove in another nail.

Monahan repeated her question, but Talanov avoided answering it by driving in two more nails, and once he had climbed back down, Monahan repeated her question.

"As much as I've enjoyed our talk," Talanov said, "I think our session is over. I have a water line to reconnect before I can take a shower."

"You're not going to answer me, are you?"

"Like I said."

"Okay, well, is there anything I can do to help?" asked Monahan, then stammering momentarily before quickly adding, "As in helping you reconnect the water line, not helping you take a shower. I mean, you certainly don't need help taking a shower – obviously – so I wasn't referring to that, which would be *totally* weird and creepy – so I wanted to be clear on that. Are we clear?"

Talanov responded with a look of amusement.

"Okay, yes, I talk too much when I get rattled," said Monahan, "and you rattled me – okay? – so I wanted you to be clear on what I meant so there would be no misunderstanding."

Talanov grinned. "Okay."

"Stop it, you're doing it again."

"Doing what?"

"Stop it!" said Monahan, waving Talanov away. "Go do whatever it is you need to do before you do whatever it is you need to do. I'll wait in my car, then drive you to the hearing."

"So you're my chauffeur as well?"

"Bill asked me to help with that, too. In case you needed to talk."

And this time, Talanov laughed.

# CHAPTER 3

Across the street from Wu Chee Ming's apartment in the Wan Chai district of Hong Kong, a woman named Xin Li stood in the shadows of a recessed doorway. Standing six feet tall, Xin Li was lean and muscular, with short black hair streaked with gray. Although she looked unmistakably Chinese, many of her features were sturdier, including her height, which she inherited from her Russian father, Valentin, a dashing naval officer who had been stationed at the Soviet Union's torpedo testing facility at Lake Issyk-Kul, which was a remote saline lake in northern Kyrgyzstan, near the Chinese border. Xin Li's mother, Xin Hualing, had been a strikingly beautiful Chinese girl of sixteen who had hiked across the border with a stream of other illegal immigrants, where she began wait-ressing in a nightclub near the facility. After meeting Valentin, who had just defeated six challengers in arm-wrestling contests for drinks, Xin Hualing seduced him with the single purpose of bearing the child of a Soviet military officer, which she figured would give her a much better life than the poverty-to-waitress existence she had been living. At least that was the story told to Xin Li by the owner of the nightclub, where her mother had worked. The owner was an old woman with a face like a tortoise, with whom Xin Li ended up living after her mother died during childbirth, and her father a few years later from radiation poisoning.

The tenacity of her mother and the strength of her father. Those were the only two personality traits she knew about her parents, which, in truth, was all she needed to know. Tenacity and strength had brought her to this moment. That and instinct, which Dragon Head seemed to lack. Otherwise, he would not have ordered her to stop following Wu Chee Ming.

"He knows something. I'm certain of it," Xin Li remembered

telling Dragon Head after being given the order to quit following Wu Chee Ming.

"A guilty man wears his guilt," Dragon Head responded. "This man wears nothing."

"Which is why I think he knows something," Xin Li replied. "His behavior is *too* routine, *too* contrived, too absent of variation."

Xin Li had come to this conclusion after the death of Wu Chee Ming's boss, Ling Soo, at Sun Cheng Financial Group Limited. Authorities investigating the death, which occurred over a year ago, had ruled it a suicide based on Ling Soo's written confession. Xin Li was not so sure. Ling Soo was a thief and a womanizing pig who would steal from his mother, so a suicide note apologizing for the shame he had brought on his family made no sense. Which was why she began following his associate, Wu Chee Ming. Something about him did not smell right.

During the ensuing months, she recorded which routes Wu Chee Ming took to work, how punctual he was, where he drank tea, and with whom. She also recorded which routes he took home, where he ate dinner, when he ate dinner, noting that he never deviated beyond the parameters of this routine. Same way to work. Same way home. Same mealtimes every day. Wu Chee Ming was a creature of habit. Even on weekends, his routine was predictable. Same restaurants. Same grocery store. Same kind of movies, which were cheap martial arts films made somewhere on the mainland. Bad acting. Bad fight sequences. Bad in every way, like the old Godzilla movies.

Two months ago, however, Wu Chee Ming began varying his routine by taking a different way home. At first, it was nothing more than a two-block variation. But it was enough to catch her eye. Then he was back to normal. Then came a three-block variation, then back to normal, then a five-block variation that included Lan Kwai Fong, and from there, an even wider variety of routes. The question was, why? What was going on? Why was he varying a routine that he had worked so hard to establish . . . a routine he'd maintained so fastidiously for many months? Obviously, these eccentricities were to disguise something between Point A – work – and Point B – home, and not on his way to work, which remained consistently the same, but on his way home.

Careful surveillance confirmed he was not meeting anyone for drinks. He was not even drinking by himself. Or visiting prostitutes. Or purchasing drugs, or selling them. Why, then, was he taking different and elaborately circuitous ways home each night?

She soon found out. Wu Chee Ming had rented a second apartment from a shady realtor willing to accept a sack of cash left for him along a walkway in Lan Kwai Fong. The apartment was on the second floor of a rundown block of apartments in Wan Chai, where prostitutes roamed the streets and gaudy neon lit up the night. A quick look inside the apartment, however, generated more questions than answers.

Unlike Wu Chee Ming's classy residence on the thirty-third floor of an upscale building across town, the Wan Chai apartment was empty except for a small suitcase containing six energy bars, two bottles of water, some toiletries, a paperback novel, and three changes of clothes. Otherwise, the apartment looked uninhabited. No bed, no furniture, no food or utensils. Furthermore, the windows were filthy and so was the floor. Wu Chee Ming's highrise residence, by contrast, was organized and clean. In his closet was a selection of expensive clothes, on hangers and arranged by color and style. Beneath the hangers were his shoes, all carefully polished and placed neatly on an angled shelf. His bed was fastidiously made, with folded hospital corners and decorative pillows placed symmetrically, almost to the millimeter.

But Wu Chee Ming's anal tendencies didn't end there. The living room was likewise an exercise in disciplined order. Near the sliding door were four antique Chinese panels, hinged and tall and standing in a zigzag pattern, with cherry blossom designs inside cream-colored frames. Next to these was a bamboo plant in a ceramic pot. On the walls were expensive pieces of art. In front of a marble fireplace was some Scandinavian furniture, efficient and cold. And clean. Not a speck of dust anywhere. Even the leaves of the plant had been dusted. Same with the kitchen. Tidy pantry. Expensive cookware in compartmentalized drawers. Dishes precisely stacked. Spotless glasses positioned in rows. Yes, indeed, Wu Chee Ming was meticulous.

*Unfortunately for him, not meticulous enough,* Xin Li thought with a wicked smile just as three black SUVs sped toward her.

# CHAPTER 4

Screwing a silencer onto her pistol, Xin Li stepped out of the recessed doorway when Dragon Head's SUV screeched to a stop in front of her. Wearing a tank top and black cargos, Dragon Head was the first to jump out. Standing several inches shorter than Xin Li, he had intricate patterns of tattoos covering his shoulders and arms. Next to get out was Dragon Head's daughter, Chin Chi Ho, who went by the title Straw Sandal. In her thirties, petite and strong, she was dressed in a fitted black jumpsuit. She had the white skin of her father but her mother's delicate Asian features, and coal black hair. Piling out of the second and third cars were twelve of Dragon Head's *Shí bèi* martial arts fighters, all lean and strong.

Straw Sandal glanced sharply at Xin Li. She had never liked her father's lover and the feeling was mutual. In fact, Straw Sandal suspected Xin Li of poisoning her mother, who died of a mysterious blood toxin shortly after Xin Li began working for her father. Within a year of her mother's death, Xin Li and her father had become lovers.

After a dismissive sneer at Straw Sandal, Xin Li led the way up the darkened stairwell. The entire group moved as one, like shadows, barely making a sound. At the top of the stairs, Xin Li nodded toward the door on their left.

"I want him alive," instructed Dragon Head, and taking a leaping hop, he kicked open the door.

*The apartment was empty.*

Xin Li ran to an open bedroom window and looked out. The adjoining flat rooftop, the size of a small parking lot, had been recently tarred, and a trail of footprints was visible on the tacky surface. "He's onto us," she said as Dragon Head came to her side. She pointed to a rusting fire escape on the far side of the rooftop.

Dragon Head commanded one of the *Shí bèi* fighters to follow the footprints.

The fighter sprang nimbly from the window.

Dragon Head led the way back downstairs and was just sliding behind the wheel of his SUV when his cell phone rang.

"Red taxi, end of the block," the *Shí bèi* fighter reported.

"Which way did they go?" asked Dragon Head.

"North."

"Toward Hennessy Road," said Dragon Head, his implication clear. An MTR station was on Hennessy Road.

The MTR – Mass Transit Railway – could transport Wu Chee Ming to any of thirteen other stations spread across the densely populated heart of Hong Kong. If Wu Chee Ming reached one of those stations, he would vanish forever.

"Text his photo to our men," Dragon Head instructed his daughter. "I want that station covered."

"He will not go to there," Xin Li remarked while Straw Sandal began working her phone.

"Why else would the taxi go north?"

"To divert us into thinking he is heading to that station."

"What makes you so sure?"

"Because I have been studying his movements and methods. He will assume we saw him get into the cab. In fact, he may well have planned it that way. But even if he did not, he will respond as if we had. Which means he will go elsewhere."

"And if you're wrong?" demanded Straw Sandal.

"I am not."

"He has already escaped you once – just now – so he obviously knew you were following him."

"Impossible. I was here waiting when he arrived."

"Then he saw you across the street. If he escapes, the fault will be yours."

"Enough!" snapped Dragon Head.

"Wu Chee Ming has been anticipating this moment," Xin Li explained. "He is devious and methodical. He would not do something so obvious."

Dragon Head scrutinized Xin Li. Since appearing on his doorstep many years ago, Xin Li had demonstrated a prowess that both impressed and worried him. She barely slept and possessed impressive speed and alarming strength. In the middle of the night, he would sometimes hear her practicing sparring techniques on one of the *muk yan jongs,* or wooden dummies, stationed in his gym. Her aggressive cries would awaken him, even though their penthouse bedroom was on the floor above.

He was aware of Xin Li's violent past by the scars on her face and back, of which she rarely spoke and he had learned not to ask about, for asking only provoked a glare of bitterness about some distant memory. He had tried discovering what had happened, but each time he asked, she steadfastly refused. And while her flesh had long since healed, her emotional wounds were still as raw as ever. Thus, while he had come to trust her instincts, he was still wary of her dark side, which, admittedly, added to her sexual attraction.

"Then where, if not the Hennessey Road station?" Dragon Head asked.

"Kowloon," Xin Li replied.

Dragon Head understood the implications of Wu Chee Ming reaching Kowloon. Hong Kong was an island, and if Wu Chee Ming wished to truly disappear, he needed to get off the island. That left him with one choice, Kowloon, which lay across a narrow stretch of water known as Victoria Harbor. Unlike Hong Kong, Kowloon was attached to mainland China by way of a sprawling peninsula known as the New Territories. If Wu Chee Ming made it to Kowloon, a larger variety of escape routes became available.

The first was the airport on Lantau Island, which was reachable by taxi, and since Wu Chee Ming was already in a taxi, it would be an obvious choice.

But there was also the huge train terminal at Hung Hom, which served both the West and East Rail Lines. If Wu Chee Ming chose the West Rail Line, he could travel to the densely populated cities on the western side of the New Territories peninsula. If he chose the East Rail Line, he could travel north all the way to Shenzhen, where more than ten million people lived.

Dragon Head asked Xin Li which choice Wu Chee Ming would make.

"Not to the airport," she replied.

"Why not?"

"Airports mean cameras and security, and he knows you have many friends. He will take the route of least exposure."

"Which is?"

"The East Rail Line to Shenzhen."

Large enough in itself, Shenzhen was also gateway to the massive Pearl River Delta Economic Zone of Guangzhou – the old "Canton" – with a population of over forty million people. Finding Wu Chee Ming there would be impossible.

"Once again, how can you be sure?" asked Dragon Head.

"I can't," Xin Li replied. "But I offer this deduction based on his behavioral patterns. It is what I would do."

Dragon Head glanced at Straw Sandal for confirmation but she was noncommittal. "All right," he said, "Kowloon. And you had better be right."

# CHAPTER 5

Talanov had been placed in a lone chair in the center of the small windowless viewing theater in Washington, DC. Behind him were four Federal agents, all big guys, with coiled ear wires and suit jackets concealing .357 Sig Sauer pistols. It was overkill, to be sure, but the government was taking no chances with their number-one enemy, which is what the late CIA Director, William Casey, had once called Talanov. To this day, Talanov smiled at what he still considered to be the ultimate compliment.

Mounted on the wall was a mammoth flat-screen monitor, on which Talanov could see his longtime friend, Bill Wilcox, addressing the United States House Permanent Select Committee on Intelligence, otherwise known as the House Intelligence Committee. In appearance, Wilcox was everything Talanov was not. Where Talanov was lean and tall, the five-foot-nine Wilcox weighed in at a solid two hundred and twenty pounds. Where Talanov possessed a full head of dark hair that was salted at the temples, Wilcox possessed a rim of wiry gray hair around the base of a mostly bald cranium. Where Talanov was clean-shaven, Wilcox sported a short salt-and-pepper chin beard, or "Friesen roan," as he liked to call it. Where Talanov was dressed in a tailored light gray suit, Wilcox was dressed in an ill-fitting blue sports jacket, patterned red tie, and baggy gray slacks.

As a CIA station chief in the American Embassy in London during the Cold War, Wilcox had recruited Talanov away from the Soviets, and as his former handler and now longtime friend, was regarded as the one person who knew Talanov better than anyone. As such, his testimony was vital as to whether or not Talanov would be allowed to officially consult for the CIA.

Talanov had already spent more than three hours yesterday answering questions posed by the committee. Representative Warren Levin, the sixty-three-year-old ranking minority member, did not believe Talanov's services were needed by the CIA. He believed the CIA was more than capable of functioning on its own, even though Casey believed the KGB had laid the groundwork for virtually all of today's terrorism tactics, and that former KGB officials like Talanov would be invaluable in identifying agents once trained by the KGB. Levin did not agree. Citing official records obtained from Moscow, which showed the KGB to be clumsy and antiquated when it came to assassination and sabotage, the white-haired Levin believed the KGB's role in training today's terrorists had been grossly overrated.

"Are you aware of these reports, Colonel?" Levin had asked yesterday from the paneled dais, where all of the committee members were seated.

"Indeed I am," Talanov had replied. "I wrote them."

"Are you saying those reports substantiate what I just said? That the KGB was clumsy in its methods and overrated in its effectiveness?"

Talanov laughed. "Of course not. I wrote those reports and their conclusions so that we could leak them to gullible people like you. It's called disinformation and we pioneered the concept."

After rebuking Talanov for his lack of respect, Levin then asked, "Have you ever been a member of the Communist party or any party advocating a violent overthrow of the United States?"

Talanov shook his head with disbelief. *You really are stupid,* he thought, and started to offer a sarcastic reply but noticed the ranking majority member, Diane Gustaves, glaring at him. It was a warning not to make things worse than they already were. Dressed in a power suit of bright yellow brocade, Gustaves, who chaired the committee, was Talanov's only firm ally in the room right now. In her sixties, she was one of the most powerful congressional leaders on the Hill.

After a calming breath, Talanov politely asked Levin if this wasn't the primary reason he had been asked by the CIA to serve as a consultant, which was to identify agents trained by the KGB, how they had been trained, and where they were now.

"How are we to know you are still not a communist who is committed to the violent overthrow of the United States?" pressed Levin.

"I believe Colonel Talanov's record speaks for itself," answered Gustaves.

"Perhaps," responded Levin. "But if Colonel Talanov was once a communist, not to mention the youngest colonel in KGB history – a rank earned, no doubt, by his contributions to communist principles and ideals – then how are we to know he is still not sympathetic to those ideals and in fact may *still* be committed to the violent overthrow of the United States?"

"Aside from my Cold War service as a spy for America," answered Talanov, "which would have resulted in my being executed had I been discovered, I've identified and stopped no less than seventeen terrorists and embedded agents operating within the United States. Those individuals had all been trained by the KGB."

"How are we to know that you simply identified what I would call the low-hanging fruit, while leaving the much more dangerous agents tucked safely out of sight?"

"Then let's compare records," answered Talanov. "In addition to what's already been mentioned, I also tracked down and pinpointed nine KGB-trained terrorists operating within Europe and the Arabian Peninsula. Special Ops teams were able to kill two of them, four are still at large, while three others were captured and taken to Guantanamo Bay. You then voted to release those terrorists, who are on record as having stated their hatred toward America by advocating its overthrow and destruction. So, thanks to you, they are now safely back home, where they are recruiting and radicalizing more terrorists to attack American interests. I also recall you arguing for an open-border policy for the United States, which would allow those very same terrorists get-back-into-America-free cards. So you tell me whose record of common sense and loyalty speaks loudest to us here today?"

"Thank you, Colonel," declared Gustaves with a whack of her gavel while Levin's face flushed red with fury. "This committee will recess for lunch."

The thought of Levin storming out of yesterday's hearings brought a brief smile to Talanov's face while he watched Wilcox raise his hand and swear to tell the truth, the whole truth, and nothing but the truth.

Levin skipped the courtesy of thanking Wilcox for his service and jumped right into a blistering tirade about Talanov's irreverent behavior toward congressional authority.

"You're right," confessed Wilcox once Levin had finished. "Talanov is annoying, pugilistic, flippant, arrogant, and dangerous."

"That's kind of harsh," remarked Talanov inside the viewing theater. He glanced around at the semi-circle of big guys, who looked back at him but said nothing. Talanov shrugged and looked at the monitor again, where Wilcox was scanning the faces of each committee member. All were startled by Wilcox's remark and none of them knew what to say.

"Are you surprised by that statement?" asked Wilcox.

"Frankly, yes," answered Gustaves.

"Don't be," Wilcox replied. "He was trained by our enemies. He kicked our asses on numerous occasions." He then smiled and leaned forward for emphasis. "Which is precisely why I recruited him. We needed him on our side."

"Are you certain he's on our side now?" Gustaves asked with a drilling stare.

"You know my answer to that."

"For the record, you need to say it."

"He's absolutely on our side," said Wilcox. "I staked my career on it then and I'm staking my life on it now."

Once the morning session had adjourned, Talanov was ushered out of the building by two of the big guys, where Wilcox was pacing back and forth on the sidewalk with his cell phone to his ear.

"That's good news, Charlie, thanks," he said, hanging up just as Talanov came down the steps. Charlie – Charunetra Suri – was Wilcox's twenty-six-year-old technical analyst at Langley. Originally from India but having moved with her family to Texas when she was two, Charlie, who doubled as Wilcox's executive assistant, had mocha skin and long, thick raven hair.

"What's good news?" asked Talanov, approaching Wilcox.

"Walk with me," Wilcox replied.

"Where are we going?"

"To meet someone."

"Who?"

"A friend."

Talanov stopped abruptly on the sidewalk. "If it's Dr. Monahan, forget it. I've had enough therapy for today."

Wilcox laughed. "That Pam, she's quite a kick, but, no, that's not who we're meeting."

"Then, who?"

"A friend. I told you that."

"Does your friend have a name?"

"A friend, that's all I can say," answered Wilcox, glancing discreetly around before continuing along the sidewalk.

"And I have a plane to catch."

"We have time."

"We *don't* have time. My flight leaves in two hours. That's two hours to get back to your house, grab my things, then *hope* there isn't traffic on the way to the airport."

"Don't worry. I had Charlie change your ticket."

They had just started across the lawn of the Capitol grounds when Talanov jumped in front of Wilcox and stopped him. "You did *what?*"

"Had Charlie change your ticket," answered Wilcox matter-of-factly, "which will be waiting for you at the gate, along with your new seat assignment . . . in first class, of course. I also sent an agent to get your suitcase, which will be waiting for you at the counter. Feel free to thank me later."

"How about I strangle you later?"

"You crack me up," said Wilcox with a laugh. "Now, come on, we need to keep walking."

Wilcox stepped around Talanov and continued on while Talanov remained standing in place. After a few steps, Wilcox realized Talanov was not beside him, and after glancing around nervously, returned to where Talanov was standing. Behind them now was the gleaming dome of the Capitol.

"Alex, we need to keep moving," Wilcox said quietly but emphatically.

"I'm not going anywhere until you tell me what's going on."

"Nothing is going on."

"Then why do you keep glancing around?"

Wilcox did not reply.

"Have you forgotten what I do?" said Talanov. "I notice things. People, patterns, irregularities, inconsistencies, and subtleties. And what I'm noticing right now is making me uneasy. So either you level with me or I'm gone. What's it going to be?"

Wilcox bit his lip in frustration.

Talanov turned to leave.

"All right," announced Wilcox. "You win. But we really do need to keep walking. Now, come on, there's no time to waste."

# CHAPTER 6

The red and white taxi emerged from the harbor tunnel in Kowloon and stopped at the brightly lit toll booth. The expressway was jammed with traffic and there were headlights and taillights everywhere.

Wu Chee Ming glanced anxiously out the rear window of the cab. It was impossible to tell if he had been seen or if he was now being followed. He knew Dragon Head would try to anticipate his next move by thinking logically and then acting on that logic.

But Dragon Head was also a linear thinker. Logic to him was different than it was to Xin Li. He remembered peeking out through the slatted blinds and seeing Xin Li across the street, standing in the shadows, watching and waiting. He hadn't seen her when he arrived, and it was simply a stroke of luck that he had seen her when he did. How on earth she had managed to locate his Wan Chai apartment, he had no idea. But she had. And that meant she knew how to anticipate. It also meant she thought laterally, which both terrified and encouraged him.

It terrified him because if anyone could calculate his next move, it would be her. It encouraged him because lateral thinkers were generally not linear thinkers, which meant she may well be looking so far to the side that she would miss what was right in front of her. Plus, she would already be divided in her focus by their one and only backup option, Talanov.

From his knowledge of the former KGB colonel, he knew most people tended to underestimate him. Several attempts had been made on his life and failed, although one attempt, by the Russian Mafia, saw Talanov's wife slain at an awards ceremony in Los Angeles. He remembered reading about it last year in the news. But when he tried locating Talanov's address, no amount of internet searching could provide him with that information, which meant Talanov was skilled at concealment. News reports then surfaced about him saving the life of a government agent named Bill Wilcox, whom he learned worked for the CIA. So he renewed his search to locate Talanov by tracking Wilcox, and once again failed. That left Congresswoman Diane Gustaves as his remaining means of locating Talanov. Gustaves was a longtime friend of Wilcox who recently brought Talanov to Washington to undergo questioning before a subcommittee.

Which meant if he could locate Talanov through Gustaves, so could Xin Li.

He knew she had been trying because of an algorithm he created that tracked keyword searches – in this case, Talanov's name – as well as which IP addresses had been conducting those searches. To his surprise and relief, Xin Li's address topped the list, which meant she was already anticipating the need to locate Talanov which he, Wu Chee Ming, would make certain occurred.

The thought of being captured by Dragon Head made Wu Chee Ming shudder. No one could endure his torture. His only chance was outsmarting him. That meant he had to think as Dragon Head would think, or, more accurately, as Xin Li would think, and not simply doing the opposite, but the oblique.

*One does not seek what one does not see.*

Wu Chee Ming hoped it would be enough.

Fifteen minutes later, his taxi arrived at Kowloon Tong, which was a much smaller station than the larger terminal at Hung Hom, where concealment would be easy because of its enormous size and popularity. Kowloon Tong was an illogical choice, which was why he had chosen it. There would be far fewer commuters on the platform, which was open and relatively small. That meant concealment would be much more difficult than at Hung Hom, where anonymity among the masses was virtually guaranteed. Hung Hom was the logical choice for a person wanting to disappear.

After paying the driver, Wu Chee Ming took the escalator down to an underground concourse. At the other end of the concourse, he took another escalator back up to the long, narrow platform that divided the north- and southbound tracks.

The platform was unusually busy, with hundreds of people – commuters, students, and shoppers – carrying backpacks, briefcases, suitcases, and shopping bags. Which was a better situation than he had hoped, because one more person carrying one more suitcase would be impossible to spot.

*One does not seek what one does not see.*

Mingling with the crowd, Wu Chee Ming allowed himself a smile for the first time tonight. He was actually going to escape. He was actually going to live.

All of that would change within thirty seconds.

# CHAPTER 7

With Talanov glaring at him suspiciously, Wilcox led the way toward the Russell Senate Building, where people were leaving after a long day at work.

"Okay, Bill, start talking," said Talanov.

"Not here," Wilcox replied.

With a shake of his head, Talanov followed Wilcox through the crowd and along a sidewalk that ran beside the building. To their right, four stories of windows rose to a smooth ledge of marble that cut a clean line against the sky.

"Okay, start talking," said Talanov again.

"Do you remember what you once told me?" Wilcox replied.

"I've told you a lot of things."

"We were in Berlin during the winter of 'eighty-seven. Crummy little coffee shop, colder than hell, snow gusting out of the north. That shop is where you gave me the name of a Soviet mole in one of our embassies."

"You said the idea was preposterous."

"That's because your information didn't check out, and I had my people run a background check through every database we had."

"And yet . . ."

"And yet, in the end, you were right. The person in question was a mole who was buried so deep she would have done irreparable damage had you not provided me with her name."

"Is that what we're dealing with here?"

"No, it's not," answered Wilcox, "and I bring it up here only to remind you of what you told me that day. Do you remember what it was?"

"I asked if Arthur M. Anderson meant anything to you."

"And I asked if that was a codename for one of your

espionage programs."

"And I laughed outright."

"Yes, you did, in my face," said Wilcox, "whereupon you proceeded to tell me how the Arthur M. Anderson was a Great Lakes cargo ship built by the American Ship Building Company of Lorain, Ohio, which got caught in the same storm on Lake Superior that sank the Edmund Fitzgerald."

"In 1975."

"Which Gordon Lightfoot memorialized the following year in his hit song, *The Wreck of the Edmund Fitzgerald*. Unlike the Edmund Fitzgerald, however, the Arthur M. Anderson survived that storm, which to this day I do not know how you knew. But it led you to look me in the eye and say, 'Only in a storm do you appreciate the kind of ship you're on.' When I asked what you meant, you replied, 'You tell me.' I remembered staring at you for the longest time until I realized you were talking about yourself, and that your performance in the storms we'd gone through together spoke louder than any words you could have said about your character and loyalty."

"It usually takes a storm for us to realize what we're made of," said Talanov. "Storms reveal character. Which is the advantage of studying history. We look back so that we can look forward, either with confidence or concern."

"Exactly. Which is why I'm asking you to look back at *our* history so that you can look forward right now with confidence."

"In other words, you're not telling who we're meeting."

"No, I'm not, and I need you to trust me on this."

Talanov thought for a moment, then nodded.

"By the way," said Wilcox, "I checked, and the Arthur M. Anderson is still in operation."

"Then I guess you two have a lot in common. Old and rusty, but still sputtering along."

"Hilarious. And to think I was actually going to spring for the first round of drinks."

"Oh, we are *way* beyond drinks, my friend. We're talking

lobster for what you and that ridiculous subcommittee put me through."

"How about a little gratitude? If you recall, I was the only one standing up for you in there."

"Pugilistic, flippant, arrogant, annoying, and dangerous? You call that standing up for me?"

"I was under oath. I couldn't lie."

The two men laughed and took a sidewalk that cut through the trees of Lower Senate Park, which flanked the rear of the Russell Senate Building. In the distance was Union Station.

"By the way, I heard from Larisa," remarked Wilcox. "She loves her job as a nurse in Adelaide."

Talanov did not reply.

"She said to give you her love."

Talanov did not reply.

"She asked how you were."

Talanov did not reply.

"Will you please say something?" asked Wilcox.

"What's there to say?" answered Talanov.

"That maybe you're a little interested in how she's doing since you're the one who got her that job?"

"And you know why I did."

"I know you're trying to convince yourself that it was the right thing to do."

"It was the right thing to do," stated Talanov.

"I disagree. Larisa should have had a say in that decision."

"Okay, so maybe she should have. I suck at relationships and you know it."

"And that's a flimsy excuse and *you* know it."

"And you're not the one who gets people killed, Bill. I was married once – remember? – to a woman I didn't know how to love. And she got killed for it, and died in my arms. And so I spun out of control for a while, and then Larisa came along and I began to feel things I knew I couldn't allow myself to feel, or she'd be the next person to die."

"You don't know that."

"Yes, I do."

"No, you don't, and I live in the same world of shadows and secrecy that you do. So don't go trying to convince me of something you're not even convinced of yourself. Larisa loves you. Don't you get it?"

Talanov stopped in the middle of First Street and looked directly at Wilcox. "Don't *you* get it, Bill? It seems you don't, so allow me to repeat myself. The mob killed my wife, and they tried killing Larisa – and her family – and they nearly killed you. Which means you, of all people, should understand what I'm talking about here. Larisa needs to be someplace far away. It's the only chance she'll ever have at a normal life."

"It's a decision she should have made."

"I couldn't take that chance."

"You really can be a jerk."

"No argument there. Now, come on. Let's go meet whoever it is you won't tell me who we're meeting."

# CHAPTER 8

Dragon Head paused at the top of the escalator and a hushed murmur rippled through the crowd of people waiting on the platform, which was a long, concrete island between two sets of tracks. Flanking him were Straw Sandal and the *Shí bèi* fighters. Straw Sandal took half of the fighters and began combing her way south. Dragon Head took the other half and began working his way north.

*North toward him,* thought Wu Chee Ming as a wave of panic swept over him. How Dragon Head managed to find him, he had no idea, but he could not think about that now. The only thing that mattered now was staying alive.

He had, at most, a minute before he was seen. His only chance was getting off this concrete island. Across the tracks to his left was an impossibly high wall. Across the tracks to his right, however, was an embankment topped with a much smaller wall. If he timed things just right, say, at the approach of a northbound train, he would be shielded from pursuit. That would allow him enough time to climb the embankment, scale the wall and steal a bicycle, which would give him an advantage over anyone chasing him on foot.

Wu Chee Ming's heart began to race. This just might work.

An announcement sounded against the metallic keening of an approaching train and Wu Chee Ming stepped to the edge of the platform as the northbound train emerged from the tunnel and began to slow. With adrenalin pumping and hopes soaring, he heard the train screech to a stop. He then heard the hiss of its doors as hundreds of passengers inched slowly forward. The nose of the train was directly in front of him now, and through the large glass windshield, he could see the bored conductor.

Suddenly, from his left came the rhythmic clacking of an

express train as it emerged from the other tunnel. It was speeding south, toward the Hung Hom terminal. Wu Chee Ming instinctively glanced toward the noise, and what he saw made the blood freeze in his veins.

On the northern tip of the platform was Xin Li. Taking long, powerful strides, she was headed straight for him, her eyes fixed on him like a panther moving in for the kill. He turned to run just as Dragon Head pushed his way through the crowd and saw him from the other direction.

He was cut off. His life was over. And not in a peaceful way, either. Dragon Head would make him talk before ending his life in some horrific, unimaginable way.

A horn blast from the approaching express train startled him, and in a moment of clarity, he saw his ultimate escape. And with a quick glance toward the open sky above, he turned and ran.

"*No!*" Xin Li shrieked when she saw Wu Chee Ming dive in front of the train.

With a loud thump, Wu Chee Ming's body bounced off the locomotive before being run over and crushed. Brakes began screeching and passengers began shouting and pointing. Many used their cell phones to record Wu Chee Ming's body being dragged beneath the undercarriage. Clothing and debris from his suitcase swirled along in the wind.

Xin Li ran to the edge of the platform and stared angrily at the scene. She had calculated every option but this.

Dragon Head stepped to her side. "I presume you know what this means," he stated rather than asked.

Xin Li's face hardened.

"Are you sure you can handle it?" asked Dragon Head.

Xin Li turned to leave but Dragon Head seized her by the arm.

"Alive, do you understand? I want Talanov alive."

Xin Li tried twisting away but Dragon Head held firm.

"*Do you understand?*" Dragon Head repeated emphatically.

"I understand," Xin Li snarled bitterly. "But he is mine once this is over." She glared at Dragon Head for a long moment before he let go and she stormed away.

"Go with her," Dragon Head told his daughter.

Straw Sandal nodded and followed.

By now, the train had stopped and station officials were rushing to the site of the trapped body. Sirens could be heard in the distance, and loud-speakers were warning spectators to stay clear of the tracks. Other announcements advised people that all southbound trains were being diverted.

When Dragon Head turned to leave, he saw a man in a sports jacket watching him from across the platform. Shorter and heavier than Dragon Head, the man, whose name was Chao Lin, had a full head of peppered gray hair that hung down over his forehead.

The man turned to leave but Dragon Head blocked his exit.

"What are you doing here, Chao?" Dragon Head demanded.

Six of Chao's men surrounded Dragon Head just as the *Shí bèi* fighters surrounded them all.

Chao glanced around. With odds clearly not in his favor, he bowed deferentially to Dragon Head, then pushed his way through the circle of *Shí bèi* fighters and vanished down the escalator.

# CHAPTER 9

Wilcox led the way across a parking lot full of cars toward the green canvas awning of the Monocle Restaurant. The iconic Washington, DC watering hole was actually a conjoined pair of two-story cream-colored brick buildings, with flat roofs, green shutters, and French windows on pop-out extensions. Behind the Monocle was a Cadillac SUV. It was silver and was parked in a reserved space beside the back door.

*Someone important,* thought Talanov, noting the laminated permit hanging from its rearview mirror.

Talanov followed Wilcox inside. On their right was a polished bar with a brass foot rail, where groups of government workers were unwinding from a long day. To their left along the wall was a row of small tables, most of which were occupied by young bureaucrats sipping drinks and working their phones. At the last table was a young Chinese woman sipping from a glass of white wine. She had a fitted turquoise top and a bulging Hermès handbag in the chair across from her. Talanov would not have taken any special notice were it not for the look she gave him. Most glances were casual and brief. Hers was different. A flash of recognition. A stiffening of her posture. A quick grab of her cell phone, as if checking for messages.

With a thoughtful frown, Talanov followed Wilcox into one of the Monocle's two dining rooms. It was paneled in blond oak and was buzzing with quiet conversation, as was an adjoining dining room off to the right, which was separated from the first dining room by a waist-high pony wall. When Wilcox and Talanov passed through the first dining room, many people looked but paid no special attention.

The second dining room had a brothel-like decor, with framed photos of celebrities and politicians on the salmon-colored walls. Large inset panels were covered with patterned yellow-and-orange wallpaper. The carpet, a similar color, both clashed with and complemented the rest of the decor. White tablecloths added elegance.

In the back corner of the room was a small table where Diane Gustaves was seated. She had changed out of her yellow brocade and was now wearing a slack suit and jacket. She stood when Talanov and Wilcox approached.

"Congresswoman Gustaves?" said Talanov, surprised. "You're the reason for this top-secret meeting?"

"One can't be too careful with someone so pugilistic and dangerous," Gustaves replied with a smile. "And, please, call me Diane. I believe you know Grady and John?"

Talanov glanced at the neighboring table. Seated there were two of the big guys who had guarded him earlier. Talanov nodded but they remained deadpan.

"I'm surprised you beat us here," Talanov remarked.

"I move quickly when tequila's involved."

Talanov laughed.

"Speaking of which," Gustaves said, gesturing for him and Wilcox to sit, "I took the liberty of ordering the first round."

Their waiter, Henry, approached with a silver tray. On it was a bucket of ice, a bottle of red wine, a bottle of Don Julio tequila, a bottle of frosty Chopin vodka, several glasses, and two small bowls. One bowl contained slices of lime; the other contained ribbons of orange zest. After placing the items on the table, Henry said, "Shall I pour for you, ma'am?"

"I've got it, Henry, thank you."

Henry bowed and left the table.

Gustaves handed the wine to Wilcox. When he looked at the label, his mouth fell open. It was a bottle of La Tâche, from the Burgundy region of France, which was Wilcox's favorite wine from his favorite wine region in his favorite part of the world. La Tâche had also been Wilcox's codename while he was working undercover for the CIA in the American Embassy in London.

"Diane, I don't know what to say," Wilcox said, knowing the premium price tag of such a label.

"You deserve it, Bill," Gustaves said. She watched Wilcox gaze at the bottle for a long moment before filling his glass one-third full, which he then swirled several times before reverently savoring its bouquet.

Gustaves then smiled at Talanov. "Colonel, I understand you prefer your vodka at fourteen degrees, Celsius, correct?"

Talanov replied with a nod that said he was both impressed and guarded about where this was leading.

Gustaves poured three fingers of Chopin into a tumbler and handed it to Talanov. She then poured herself three fingers of tequila and held up her glass in a toast. "To the future," she said.

While taking a sip of his drink, Talanov noticed Turquoise Girl, as he found himself calling the young woman in the fitted turquoise top, walking quickly to the rear corner of the restaurant, where the bathrooms were located. Her stride was tense and she was clutching the shoulder straps of her bulging handbag tightly. Before entering the bathroom, she glanced his way.

Talanov thought about her for a moment. Had she been in yesterday's hearing? He didn't remember seeing her, not that he would have noticed, with his attention on the committee members who had been grilling him. He thought about the glance she had given him just now, which, when he thought about it, was not so much aimed at him as—

"So, Alex, what do you think?" Gustaves asked.

Talanov looked at Gustaves, then back at Turquoise Girl, who was hurrying through the dining room toward the bar, but without her handbag.

*Who leaves a Hermès handbag in the bathroom?*

"Excuse me," said Talanov, standing.

And with Gustaves and Wilcox watching curiously, Talanov hurried up the steps and through the dining room in time to see Turquoise Girl drop some cash on her table and make a beeline toward the front door.

Talanov ran to the rear corner of the restaurant and into the women's bathroom, where he made a quick search of the toilet stalls. He then looked inside a large metal trashcan with a swing-top lid.

And that is where he found what he hoped he would not find.

# CHAPTER 10

The bomb inside the handbag was two bricks of C-4 explosive duct-taped to a cell phone. Inserted into each brick were six rod-like blasting caps. All of them were connected by wires to an electronic motherboard that had been wired to the phone. C-4 did not require that many blasting caps, so it was obvious that some were real and some were fakes. But which? Other wires ran from the C-4 to a small metal box. Was the box a battery pack? A movement detonator? A timer? The whole assembly was a dizzying array of wires so that no amateur would know what to do.

Running out of the bathroom, Talanov ran to Gustaves and Wilcox.

"Diane, you need to get out of here," said Talanov. "There's a bomb in the women's bathroom." To Wilcox: "Call the bomb squad and clear the restaurant." To Grady: "Give me your gun. I saw who planted that bomb and I've got to stop her from detonating it."

"That's a job for the Capitol Police."

"We've got a minute at most before she stops to dial a number that will blow this place to hell. Now, give me your gun!"

"He can't; take mine," Gustaves said, retrieving a Glock 19 from her handbag. "Don't use it unless you have to," she said, handing Talanov the gun. "And I mean that."

"When you're clear of this place, call the Capitol Police. Tell them who I am and that I'm in pursuit of a young female. Chinese, black hair, turquoise top."

With Grady leading the way, John rushed Gustaves out the back door while Wilcox began shouting for everyone to move toward the exits.

After pushing his way outside, Talanov began scanning the crowd. No Turquoise Girl. He then ran into the parking lot, where people were running in all directions. No Turquoise Girl.

To his left, he saw Gustaves climb into the backseat of her silver SUV, which had been parked near the rear of the restaurant. John shut the door behind her, then jumped into the front seat and the SUV squealed away.

With Gustaves out of danger, Talanov continued scanning the parking lot. Where was Turquoise Girl? It was possible she had changed tops to avoid being seen, and she knew she had been seen when he and Wilcox had entered the Monocle. She also knew she had been seen entering and leaving the bathroom, so a change of tops made sense. Still, a pretty woman changing clothes in public would attract attention and he was not sure she would take the risk. She had to be hiding somewhere.

*Time to change perspectives,* thought Talanov. He leaped up onto the hood of a car, then up onto its roof, where he saw her kneeling between a pickup and a sedan, looking in the direction of Gustaves and her SUV.

And she was smiling.

Talanov glanced in the direction of the SUV, then back at Turquoise Girl, who began dialing the cell phone in her hand.

*My God, there's a second bomb.*

"Put it down!" shouted Talanov, taking aim with the Glock.

Turquoise Girl spun toward him and froze. Several seconds passed and Talanov wondered what she would do. Would she surrender? Would she attempt to finish dialing? How many numbers had she dialed? She was no more than twenty feet away, and if she tried dialing, he could easily put a bullet in her head. He could see her deliberating.

"Last time, put it down," Talanov commanded from the top of the car.

Turquoise Girl slowly held out her hand and showed Talanov the phone. Then, stepping from between the vehicles, she slowly swung her outstretched arm toward Talanov, which enabled him to see the screen.

*Why was she moving so slowly?*

Talanov heard someone shouting about a man with a gun but he did not take his eyes off Turquoise Girl. He motioned for her to lay the phone down, and Turquoise Girl bent slowly forward, as if placing the phone at her feet.

An instant later, a deafening blast ripped the Monocle apart.

Talanov saw the flash of the explosion a millisecond before the shock wave punched him off the roof of the car and down onto the hood of a neighboring car, where he tumbled head-long down onto the pavement, where he lay dazed and blinking, his ears ringing, unable to comprehend what had just happened. Each passing second sounded like a kettledrum in his head until finally, with debris floating in the air around him like confetti, he groaned and rolled onto his side, picked up the Glock, and climbed unsteadily to his feet. Behind him, what was left of the Monocle was a raging inferno.

Talanov looked to where Turquoise Girl had been standing. She was gone. Stepping into the main aisle of the parking lot, he turned a full circle looking for her. Which way had she run? Hearing sirens in the distance to his left, he instinctively began searching to his right, where many car alarms were blaring. Two rows ahead, he saw her, leaning against the side of a van, her eyes on her cell phone, dialing.

Talanov raised the Glock to shoot just as Turquoise Girl saw him and froze. They locked eyes, Talanov with his finger curled around the trigger and Turquoise Girl with her finger poised over her phone.

*Don't use it unless you have to.*

Talanov knew he should fire, but Diane's words kept running through his mind.

The seconds stretched.

Suddenly, another explosion from the Monocle sent a fireball thundering into the sky. When Talanov ducked to his knees, Turquoise Girl sprinted away.

Climbing to his feet, Talanov ran after her.

Turquoise Girl sprinted across the street into Lower Senate

Park, where crowds of spectators and cyclists had gathered beneath the trees to watch the burning restaurant. Police had now arrived at the Monocle, and a fire truck was not far behind. Sirens and horn blasts filled the air.

Running up to a group of women cyclists, Turquoise Girl punched one of them to the ground, grabbed the woman's bike, jumped on, and began pedaling toward Union Station, where four lanes of traffic coursed like a swollen river around the Columbus Circle fountain.

Talanov paused in the street to shoot, but there were too many spectators in the way. Several of them saw him raise his gun and ran the other way.

Lowering the Glock, Talanov sprinted over to the group of cyclists, who were now gathered around the woman Turquoise Girl had punched to the ground. "Federal agent," he said. "I need one of your bikes to chase down that woman."

An athletic brunette in an aerodynamic helmet handed Talanov her Cannondale. "It's pink but it's fast," she said.

Talanov stuck the Glock near the small of his back and hopped on the bike. It had a lightweight frame that was angled and sleek.

He handed the brunette his phone. "Find the icon of a pig and dial it," he said. "It's a speed-dial button that will connect you with a man named Wilcox. Tell him to phone Diane and warn her about a second bomb under her vehicle. Tell Wilcox I'm in pursuit of the woman with the detonator." To one of the other cyclists, who was wearing a Bluetooth earpiece. "You with the Bluetooth, follow me." To the brunette: "Give Bluetooth's number to Wilcox and tell him she'll feed him live updates on where we are."

"You got it," said the brunette. She touched the icon of the pig and put Talanov's phone to her ear.

"Okay, Bluetooth, let's go," said Talanov. "When Wilcox phones—"

"Live updates. I got it."

Cutting across the park, Talanov and Bluetooth raced after

Turquoise Girl, who reached the sidewalk and turned left. When Talanov reached the sidewalk, he heard Bluetooth call out, "Wilcox is on the line. He'll track us on GPS. Said a chopper was on the way."

Talanov waved and raced across Delaware Street, gaining on Turquoise Girl.

Up ahead, Turquoise Girl saw a small break in the oncoming traffic and used it to cut across both lanes to the other side, where she merged in with traffic flowing along Massachusetts Avenue. Increasing her speed to match that of the traffic, she threaded her way between cars until she reached the right-hand side of the street.

The maneuver caught Talanov and Bluetooth by surprise and they had to slow down and wait for a similar break before they could do the same.

Ahead was a busy intersection. The light was green and Turquoise Girl raced through. The light changed to amber but Talanov and Bluetooth raced through after her.

Suddenly, Turquoise Girl swung left into the flow of traffic again. The car behind her honked and reluctantly made room. Two cars back, Talanov and Bluetooth did the same. Turquoise Girl raced between the lanes of cars, inches away from the vehicles on each side of her before cutting right into the bike lane again. Talanov and Bluetooth did the same. Increasing her speed, Turquoise Girl waited for a break between cars, then cut back into the narrow gap between both lanes of westbound traffic. Talanov and Bluetooth did the same.

All three bicycles were racing single file between the two lanes of traffic on each side. Cars on their left and cars on their right, just inches away. Turquoise Girl was out of her seat now, hunched over, pedaling furiously.

*How long can she go on like this?* Talanov wondered. He was keeping up with her for now, but she was showing no signs of letting up. *Push harder,* he told himself while his legs burned and sweat ran down his face.

Ahead was a low median that divided eastbound from

westbound traffic. The median was low and no wider than a sidewalk. Before reaching the median, Turquoise Girl cut between two cars at the last moment and shot across all lanes of oncoming traffic. The result was a massive pileup of cars that skidded and crashed into one another.

Caught between the two lanes of westbound traffic, Talanov was unable to follow. So he increased his speed, merged left between the moving cars to the inside edge of the street, then yanked up on his handlebars and with a pump of his legs, jumped his bicycle over the median. He bounced hard when he came down, wobbled and almost fell, then regained his balance before weaving his way through the pileup and back the other way, head down, pedaling as fast as he could.

But when he looked up, Turquoise Girl had vanished.

Talanov looked left, across the street. No Turquoise Girl. She wasn't straight ahead of him, either, which meant she had to have turned right down a side street.

The first street he came to angled back at a forty-five degree angle. When he passed by it, he looked. No Turquoise Girl. A reverse angle like that would have meant a significant slowing, so instinct told him she had gone to the next corner, which was a ninety-degree turn to the right.

Following his instincts, he turned where he hoped Turquoise Girl had turned. Straight ahead was the Capitol towering majestically against the sky.

Talanov's heart sank at what he saw, or, more accurately, at what he didn't see.

No Turquoise Girl.

But if his instincts were right – and that's all he had right now – then she had to have turned onto this street and found a place to hide and catch her breath and then dial the number she knew she must dial.

Skidding to a stop, Talanov jumped off the Cannondale. His heart was pounding and he was on the verge of collapse. *Where was she?* Across the street was a parking lot, with plenty of cars and plenty of people. And while a person dialing a cell phone in a parking lot would not attract attention, a winded woman crouching behind a parked car with a bicycle would, and Turquoise Girl would not risk that. She would choose another place of concealment. But where?

He looked to his right. There were two brick buildings on the corner that had been renovated into what looked like apartments, then an alley, then another building of glass panels.

Talanov approached the alley, which was a descending concrete ramp that accessed the rear of a brick building. Parked at the bottom of the ramp was a black pickup truck, after which the alley took a ninety-degree turn to the left. If he were Turquoise Girl, he would choose an alley like this.

When Bluetooth pulled up beside him, Talanov put a finger to his lips, and using hand signals, told Bluetooth to remain in the street while he checked the alley.

Pulling out his Glock, Talanov crept down the ramp to the black pickup and peeked inside the cab. No Turquoise Girl. He then crept alongside the pickup until he saw her sitting with her back against the wall, arms on her knees, panting, her cell phone in one hand, her bicycle laying on the pavement nearby. When Talanov stepped into the open, Turquoise Girl jerked with surprise.

She hurriedly began dialing her phone.

Talanov lifted the Glock and fired.

Shock was the first look on Turquoise Girl's face when the bullet tore through her shoulder. Then the pain hit and she screamed and dropped the phone in order to grab her shoulder. Seeing Talanov coming toward her, she grabbed for her phone.

Talanov arrived first and kicked it away.

"Who paid you to kill Gustaves?" asked Talanov, kneeling beside her.

Turquoise Girl glared at him but said nothing.

Talanov grabbed her wounded shoulder and squeezed. Turquoise Girl cried out.

"Who paid you to kill Gustaves?" Talanov asked again. "I know she was your primary target because you placed a secondary bomb beneath her vehicle. In fact, you wanted me to notice you in the Monocle, didn't you? You wanted Gustaves in her car."

A defiant glare was Turquoise Girl's reply.

"The question is, who paid you? Who told you we would be there?"

Turquoise Girl spat in Talanov's face.

With a thoughtful sigh, Talanov stood and wiped his face. "I'm sure they promised you protection," he said. "I'm sure they told you they had sympathetic judges and prison guards on their payroll, and maybe they do, not that I think they had any intention of letting you live once Gustaves had been assassinated. But, hey, if you want to take your chances with people you know are killers, that's fine with me. If, on the other hand, you'd rather cooperate with me, I'll make sure you get a new identity in a secure facility beyond their reach."

Turquoise Girl did not reply.

"Gustaves is safe," Bluetooth called out from the street. "They found the other bomb and it's been disabled. The police will be here shortly."

Talanov waved, then looked back at Turquoise Girl. "What's it going to be?"

Turquoise Girl did not reply.

"Suit yourself," said Talanov as the wail of sirens grew louder. "But I can tell you right here and now, you will not last a week in prison. Whoever recruited you *will* have you killed, to keep you from talking, and once the police have taken you into custody, my offer is gone." He looked toward the approaching sirens, then back at Turquoise Girl. "Last chance."

"How do I know you're telling the truth?"

"Because you're still alive."

Turquoise Girl thought for a moment. "He said you noticed things," she said, scooting over to the wall and leaning against it. Blood was oozing through her fingers and her turquoise top was covered with blood. "He said you would find the bomb and rush Gustaves from the restaurant."

"Who said that?"

"Some guy on the phone."

"Who?"

"I don't know. He never said."

"What's your name?"

Turquoise Girl hesitated.

"Do you want my help or not?" asked Talanov.

"Saya Lee."

"How do you spell it?"

Saya told him.

"How did he first make contact with you?"

"At a young socialists rally at NYU. He slipped a cell phone into my purse, then called me that night to say he saw me at the rally and wanted to talk about changing the country. So we talked a while and he asked if I was from China. I said my parents were but that I was born here. He then asked if I still had family in China, and I said I had some cousins and some uncles and aunts. He seemed really interested in that, which I thought was weird. Anyway, he then asked if would be willing to help a group of progressives create a better America, so I said sure. He then said to keep the phone with me at all times, that he would call me again soon with more information."

"And you dutifully obeyed," said Talanov, "which is how he discovered where you lived and who you were, plus all kinds of other details. He then called a few days later and recited personal information about you and your family, after which he made a series of threats that he said he would carry out unless you agreed to do what he said."

By now, Turquoise Girl was staring at Talanov with disbelief. "How do you know this?" she asked.

"Do you still have that phone?"

Turquoise Girl pulled it from the pocket of her jeans and

handed it to Talanov, who stuck it in his pocket.

"When the police take you into custody," said Talanov, "tell them your lawyer is on the way and that you're not saying anything until she is present."

"So you really are going to help me with a new identity in a secure facility?"

"Don't mistake this for kindness," answered Talanov. "You're a killer as far as I'm concerned, and if I had my way, you'd be dead right now. But I gave you my word that I'd help you if you helped me, and I'll keep my word. Provided you continue to cooperate. If you don't, I will make sure you're put back in the system, where they *will* kill you."

"Who are you?"

"Your only hope of staying alive," answered Talanov, pulling Turquoise Girl to her feet and leading her into the open. "Remember, talk to no one except your lawyer. She will know what to do."

And after laying the Glock down on the pavement in plain sight for the arriving officers, Talanov raised his hand in the air and walked Turquoise Girl out of the alley.

# CHAPTER 11

Three hours later, after furnishing statements to the police and the FBI, Talanov was seated in the back seat of a limousine speeding along George Washington Memorial Parkway, headed south. Sitting across from him were Gustaves and Wilcox, with Grady and John in the front seat.

"No casualties, thank God," said Wilcox. "The Monocle will need a major facelift, but at least nobody was killed."

"Thanks to you, Alex," added Gustaves. "I didn't get a chance to say it before, but thank you for saving my life. I shudder to think what would have happened if that second bomb had gone off."

Talanov smiled and nodded.

"Witnesses are calling you a hero," said Wilcox, reading from a list of social media posts. "Others are calling you a cowboy, a badass, an old dude, and I especially like this one: the Bicycle Bandit. But get this: Amy 61691 thinks you look like Hugh Jackman. Are you kidding me? You don't look anything at all like Hugh Jackman, not that I'm jealous that people think you're the badass even though *I* was the one who got people out of the restaurant while you fled the scene on a bicycle."

"In pursuit of the person with the detonator," said Talanov, "who happened to have stolen a bicycle and would have gotten away had I not chased her down . . . *on a bicycle!*"

"You chased her on a girl's bike. And a pink one at that."

"Bill!" Gustaves broke in. "Let's focus here, okay?"

"It's all right, Diane," said Talanov. "Joking around is how we let off steam after something like this."

"It was still a girl's bike," muttered Wilcox with a smirk of satisfaction.

"What tipped you off about the bombs?" asked Gustaves.

"Instinct and vibe," answered Talanov.

"How did you leap from something as subjective as 'instinct and vibe' to a bomb in a trashcan?"

"Instinct and vibe. Which I then tested by looking in the bathroom."

"And the second bomb? How did you know about that?"

Talanov responded with one of those you-know-what-I'm-going-to-say smiles.

"Instinct and vibe," said Gustaves with a chuckle. "You do realize there is no way to quantify any of that? No way to come up with some kind of an advanced training technique in the science of detection that we can circulate to our people?"

"That's because detection at this level is an art. We study and train – yes – the 'science' part – but human behavior and observation of that behavior – especially the little things and how to accurately interpret those little things using instinct and vibe – is not something you can teach. It's part instinct, part experience, and part gift, like the inbuilt navigation of migratory birds that cross oceans without ever having done it before."

"See now why I recruited him?" said Wilcox. "He talks in metaphors that none of us understands but which we know says something important, even if we don't know exactly what that is."

"So, no clue as to who hired the girl?" asked Gustaves. "She didn't give you a name?"

"No, and even if she had, I wouldn't have trusted what she said. Drones like her seldom possess information so important. She did, however, give me this." He fished out the cell phone Turquoise Girl had given him and handed it to Wilcox.

"Did you withhold that from the police?" asked Gustaves.

"No, I saved it for Bill. It's a burner – obviously – with a call history that's connected to what is no doubt another burner, although we may get lucky by tracing the number and finding where it was purchased, which may give us something, such as a credit card receipt, surveillance footage, or a counter clerk remembering something. Search for any traces on that number, too. Someone tracked its movements to find out who Turquoise Girl was, where she lived, and everything about her. That implies sophisticated hardware and software."

"So by running a search on whoever was tracking that phone . . ."

"We may get lucky and get a name. However, to me the real clue lies in the fact that she knew about our meeting, who I was, and that I 'noticed things,' as she put it. You were their main target, Diane, but whoever was behind this was counting on me noticing her and finding the bomb in the trashcan, which meant you would be rushed from the restaurant and into your SUV, where the real kill was set to take place."

"So the first bomb was a decoy?" asked Gustaves.

"Unless they got lucky, but, yes."

"This implies meticulous planning."

"Indeed it does," agreed Talanov. "How many people knew about our meeting?"

"Only a handful," Gustaves replied.

"Look into who those people were. But there's one more thing. Turquoise Girl said her contact asked if she was from China and if she still had family in China, which she thought was strange."

Gustaves and Wilcox exchanged uneasy glances.

"Does that mean something?" asked Talanov.

"Who do you know in China?" Gustaves asked in return.

"No one," answered Talanov. "Why?"

"Do any of your former colleagues live there? Any old contacts? Any enemies?"

"None that I know of."

"Have you ever been to China?"

"I was trained there in martial arts as a boy, but nothing since. Mind telling me what this is about?"

"Someone in China has been trying to find you and we need to know who it is, and why."

"They also ran searches on Diane and me," added Wilcox,

"with those searches daisy-chained and phantom-replicated through a series of anonymizers and proxy servers that made it impossible for us to trace or identify the source. And that same source tried hacking our server. They got nowhere, of course, but they tried."

"I don't know what any of that that means."

Wilcox worked the screen of his phone until a recorded video began to play, which he held up for Talanov to see. The screen showed a pretty Chinese woman in her forties, with friendly eyes, clear skin, and long black hair pulled back in low ponytail at the base of her neck. Dressed in a light blue uniform with dark blue epaulets on the shoulders, she was seated at a desk in an office, with file cabinets in the background.

"Hi Bill, this is Alice," the woman in the video began.

Wilcox paused the video to explain, "Alice is Alice Ti, who is with the Hong Kong CIB, which is their Criminal Intelligence Bureau, which is part of the Crime and Security Division of the Hong Kong Police Force. Alice is a longtime friend that I met back in the day . . . not long after I met you, in fact, when she was on vacation in Italy and we quite literally ran into one another outside this magnificent little winery."

Gustaves discreetly cleared her throat.

"Sorry," Wilcox said, touching his cell phone screen again, which recommenced the video.

"As you know," Alice continued, "we, like you, have a monitoring agency that catches certain keywords used in internet searches and communications. Our software vocabulary includes the names of important people from around the world, including our own political leaders, as well as yours. Your name is on that list, Bill, as is the name of Congresswoman Diane Gustaves. Obviously, this is not because you're a threat, but because we would want to know if you're in any potential danger. Your names came up several times in connection with a focused search for a man named Aleksandr Talanov. We do not know who Mr. Talanov is, or why someone would be looking for him, but the search was intense and the connection with you and Congresswoman Gustaves was unmistakably clear. We attempted to trace the search, but the signal had been daisy-chained and phantom-replicated through a series of anonymizers and proxy servers that made it impossible to identify the source, although we know it originated in China."

Hearing the same computer jargon again, Talanov glanced at Wilcox, who grinned sheepishly and shrugged.

"Bottom line," said Alice, "we were not able to determine who was looking for Mr. Talanov, or why, or what his connection is with you and Congresswoman Gustaves. In any case, I thought you should know. In the meantime, we will keep looking, and if I hear anything further, I'll let you know."

Wilcox stopped the video and he and Gustaves both looked at Talanov expectantly, waiting for him to comment.

Talanov looked back and forth between them before saying, "I wish I could add to what Officer Ti just said, but I have no idea why someone in China would be looking for me. I don't know anyone who lives there."

"Isn't Turquoise Girl, as you've been calling her, Chinese?" asked Gustaves.

"What's one got to do with the other?" asked Talanov.

"After what you just heard about someone in China conducting a search on you, don't you think that's relevant?"

"Maybe."

"I think it's more than a maybe. After what happened today, I think someone in China is behind the assassination attempt and was trying to get to me through you or Bill. This is supported by what you just told us, that I was their primary target, so, again, we need to find out who that person is and why they want me killed."

"Correlation does not necessitate causation."

"What do you mean?" asked Gustaves.

"Whistling drives elephants away."

Gustaves responded with a reprimanding scowl.

"I whistle all the time," said Talanov. "See any elephants around?" He looked out the window of the limousine as it sped along. "Correct me if I'm wrong," he said, "but I don't see any of them running around out there." He sat back and looked at Gustaves. "Okay, yes, I just used an absurd example to make a point, which is, the correlation of no elephants running around does not mean my whistling drove them away. Correlation does not necessitate causation. Which means, we can't assume a single point origin of someone in China looking for me and a Chinese girl trying to kill you. There is obviously a correlation, but it may be nothing more than that. There may be causation, but there may not be. At this point, we simply don't know."

"I don't believe in coincidence," said Gustaves.

"Which is a great line for a TV cop show, where scriptwriters have to link everything together because it's part of the formula. But if you assume a single point of origin, then you blind yourself to the fact that we may have two separate, coincidental, points of origin. Unless, of course, there's something you're not telling me, such as why you brought me to DC in the first place. You told me it was to furnish testimony about an individual whose name you couldn't reveal. I thought that individual might have been Bill, that maybe he was being awarded some kind of a medal. But the individual in question was actually me, and it required me to sit through some of the most intense interrogation I've ever experienced. So, again, why am I here?"

Gustaves thought carefully about her words. "A lot of people want you gone from the intelligence community," she said. "They think we've allowed a Trojan Horse into our ranks. That you're colluding with the Russians, and, now, the Chinese. In short, they think you're a spy."

"Me? After all I've done for this country?"

"Easy, Tiger," said Wilcox. "That's why we made you sit through that subcommittee hearing. It gave us an official record – and documentation – of your outstanding service to this nation. For the record, no one on the committee could find any evidence against you, and believe me, they tried."

"Do you honestly think that matters? If they can't find evidence, they fabricate it. It's how they work."

"Which is why we need to find out who in China was conducting that search and what their connection is to the people who tried killing Diane."

"And I'm telling you there may not be a connection."

"Except there *is* a connection," said Gustaves.

Talanov scrutinized Gustaves for a long moment before realizing what she was saying.

"Me," he said before looking out the window bitterly. "They're blaming this on me, aren't they?"

"Without a shred of evidence," Gustaves was quick to respond. "While you were chasing down Turquoise Girl, my assistant, Amber, phoned to say Levin was already asking suggestive questions to the press about your Chinese connections, saying that you had trained there as a boy. How he got a copy of your KGB records, I have no idea, but he did, and, now, with someone in China trying to locate you, and with someone from China trying to kill me . . . well, you can guess the innuendos he's making."

"They'll say I was part of the operation," said Talanov, "that the trashcan bomb was simply a diversion so that you would be rushed out of the Monocle and into your SUV, where the actual kill would take place. And that I knew it all along."

"I've already told Amber to issue a statement that you chased down the assailant and stopped her from detonating a second bomb. If you'd been complicit, you would have allowed it to go off, then shot Turquoise Girl to keep her from talking. Instead, you prevented her from setting off that bomb and turned her over to the police. Your actions speak louder than Levin's words."

"Unless it was to ingratiate myself in order to prove my loyalty so that I would be accepted more deeply into your ranks." Talanov shook his head. "I just don't know if it's worth it anymore. I honestly don't need the grief. I don't need any of this."

"Maybe not, but I need you," Gustaves replied. "I need you working behind the scenes to identify our nation's opponents and verify the accuracy of intelligence data coming my way. I need you watching my back and helping me see what I don't see. What happened today is a perfect example. You neutralized a threat that no one else noticed. Please. I'm asking you to weather this storm and stay on to work with me in a closer capacity. I need people around me I can trust, and I hope you believe me when I say, I trust you, Alex. Help me find out who's behind this. Who in China wants me dead."

"If I do, and I'm not saying that I will, you may not like what I find. Because I don't think the Chinese are behind what happened today. Why someone over there is looking for me, I have no idea, but what happened today has the smell of something closer to home. Some*one* closer to home."

"Why do you say that?"

"Because whoever tried killing you knew about our meeting at the Monocle, and there is no way someone in China would be able to plan an assassination attempt on something as last-minute as that. Look, I'm not saying you don't have enemies abroad, or that some radical faction in a far-flung corner of the world doesn't want your head on a stick. But other countries are not your worst enemies. For the most part, they respect you because you're strong and forthright. Your enemies, and I'm talking about the real ones, are those who hate you because you *are* strong and forthright, and those people are right here in your own backyard, smiling at you each and every day in the corridor."

"But everything points to China."

"If that were the case, why would Alice have contacted Bill? China is not your enemy."

"But Turquoise Girl is Chinese."

"And she may have been chosen for that fact, to get you looking in the wrong direction, especially if whoever's behind this knows someone in China is looking for me, which means they planned to blame me for the assassination and get rid of two birds with one stone. Except they failed, and I'm going to find them, and when I do—"

"We're here, Madam Congresswoman," Grady announced, stopping the limousine outside the departure concourse of the airport. He lowered the dividing window briefly to make the announcement, then closed it again.

"We'll talk more when I get back," Talanov said. "For now, I need to get away."

"Where're you headed?" asked Wilcox.

"San Francisco. To see an old friend."

"Anyone I know?"

"Actually, I'll be visiting Zak."

Wilcox lurched forward in his seat. "Babikov? You're going to see *him?* I didn't know he was even alive."

"He is," said Talanov, "and that information goes no further than the back seat of this car. I mention it now only because you and Diane are the only people *I* trust. So the fact that Zak is alive and living here in the United States remains totally confidential. Understood?"

"Alex, we're talking *Babikov.*"

"I mean it, Bill. Otherwise, it's goodbye on me telling you anything ever again."

"Who's Babikov?" asked Gustaves, looking back and forth between the two men.

"A longtime friend," answered Talanov.

"As innocuous as that sounds," explained Wilcox, "at one time, Zakhar Babikov was one of the most feared agents in the KGB . . . a Spetsnaz major who became the drill instructor and mentor of Alex when he joined the Soviet military as a teenager. Later, as a team, Alex and Zak gave us fits when they were running around Europe on the loose."

"Ancient history," said Talanov. "These days, Zak runs a community center in San Francisco."

Wilcox's mouth fell open. "Babikov runs a *community center?*

You've got to be joking."

"Nope. Zak found God, or should I say, God found him. Zak's a lot older, wiser, and a lot different than he was in the old days. I've been driving up to see him for the last few months. He's been helping me work through some things."

"What kind of things?"

"Things."

"As in?"

"Personal things."

"How come you never said anything?"

Talanov checked his watch. "I need to go."

"And you can take another two minutes to tell me what's going on. Alex, we're talking *Babikov*. You saw what it was like in that hearing. If word gets out that Babikov is here and you two have been hanging out . . . how did he get into the country, anyway? Is he here illegally?"

"Who cares? He's doing a good thing among the Chinese community in San Francisco."

"The *Chinese* community? Are you flippin' *kidding me?*"

"His wife is Chinese."

"No one will care about that! If word gets out—"

"Quit worrying, he's been here for years. If word was going to get out, it would have gotten out already."

"Quit *worrying?* Worrying is part of my job description, especially when it comes to you. Now, how did Babikov get into the country? When did he arrive? What kinds of things have you two been talking about?"

"Let it go, Bill," said Gustaves. "We'll discuss this if and when Alex is ready. In fact, I think you need a vacation more than Alex does, and if you worked for me, I'd order you to take one, which I've a mind to do anyway or your funding may get cut."

Wilcox grumbled and looked away.

"I know you've got a plane to catch," said Gustaves, "so, go, enjoy yourself. I'll give you a call tomorrow."

"Can't. I'll be keeping my phone switched off."

"You're not serious?"

"I need a break, Diane. A break from all of this."

"What if I need to reach you?"

"Isn't the purpose of vacation to get away from people trying to reach you?"

"And if the same people who tried killing us decide to try again? I need to be able to warn you. At least give me the name of the community center."

"If Bill didn't know about Babikov, the bad guys don't, either. No one can try to kill me if they don't know where I am or who I'm with. I'd like to keep it that way."

"And I respect that," Gustaves said. "But I really do need to know where you'll be. If something does happen, or if we get updated information that affects you, I need to be able to reach you. Those details will remain strictly confidential."

"Since when has anything in this town remained confidential?"

"Eyes only. Mine and Bill's. Emergencies only."

Talanov assessed Gustaves for a moment. "The Quiet Waters Community Center. But I meant it when I said my phone will be switched off. I'm even removing the battery. I don't want anyone tracking my location. When I'm back online, I'll call."

"Isn't that a little excessive?"

"Not after what happened today. I'll see you in a few weeks."

# CHAPTER 12

Dragon Head's Gulfstream began its early morning descent into Washington, DC. Aside from the pilot, copilot, and a flight attendant, the only passengers were Xin Li, Straw Sandal, and twelve *Shí bèi* fighters. The fighters, all male, did not look dangerous. In their twenties, they were dressed in T-shirts and jeans, and were playing games on their cell phones, or watching movies. A trained observer, however, could tell these young men were anything but young travelers. Their knuckles were calloused from countless pushups on their fists. The pads of skin on the outer edges of their palms were also calloused from untold hours of rigid hand chops into sacks of rice. Their arms were likewise lean and sinewy, in particular their forearms, which had been toughened and desensitized from years of sparring. All of them were extremely fit, with body fat percentages in the single digits, as evidenced by what they ate: protein and fat, with a few vegetables and small portions of rice.

Across the aisle from Straw Sandal, Xin Li was glaring at a photo of Talanov in his KGB uniform. The photo had been taken when he was in his late twenties. He had a firm jaw, like an actor, with dark hair and deep brown eyes. In the photo, he was wearing an ushanka, which was a Russian winter hat made of sable fur, with the ear flaps turned up and a gold-and-red Soviet star pinned to the front.

"You seem . . . angry," Straw Sandal remarked.

Xin Li tensed but said nothing.

"May I?" Straw Sandal asked.

Xin Li slapped the photo on top of an envelope of photos and handed them to Straw Sandal. She then got up and walked to the rear of the plane.

Straw Sandal watched her go. *What had aroused such anger?*

Xin Li had been looking at the photo of Talanov, and while they all knew the importance of their mission, there was something else going on with Xin Li that went beyond this assignment. Something about Talanov that evoked anger to the point of hatred. Did her father, Dragon Head, know what it was? Was that why he had been so adamant that Xin Li bring Talanov back unharmed and alive?

*What had happened between Xin Li and Talanov?*

Straw Sandal looked at Talanov's photo. He was handsome and strong, with a determined look that was indifferent and a little arrogant. She opened the envelope and removed the other photos. There were several more of Talanov, and all had been taken more recently. His hair was grayer at the temples, but still thick and dark, and he had a few wrinkles, although mostly surface lines, like he had been squinting into the sun. There was also a photo of Talanov's blonde Ukrainian girlfriend, Larisa Petrenko, from the hospital where she and Talanov had been visiting CIA station chief Bill Wilcox, who had been shot by the Russian mafia in Los Angeles. Straw Sandal remembered the occasion because she had taken the photos with her cell phone camera.

Her trip to Los Angeles at that time had been their first attempt to locate and apprehend Talanov, which she had almost managed to accomplish thanks to news reports about Talanov and Petrenko saving Wilcox's life during an operation to stop a human trafficking ring. The news reports described Talanov and Wilcox as being longtime friends, with Petrenko being one of the trafficking victims, which is no doubt how she and Talanov met. Details of a relationship between the two had been supplied by the helpful hospital staff, which would have made her job easy had Talanov and Petrenko not disappeared one night without a trace, after which Wilcox was removed to a secure location, so her opportunity vanished.

Using her cell phone, Straw Sandal retrieved a news article about the incident and scrolled down to a quote from Gustaves, who, on speaking of Talanov saving Wilcox's life, called him a hero and a good friend whose enduring service to the United States would never be forgotten. The article indicated an ongoing relationship among the three, which was further evidenced by her own photos of Gustaves and Talanov speaking cordially during the congresswoman's visit to see Wilcox in the hospital.

Laying aside her phone, Straw Sandal looked at a final photo from the envelope, which was of Talanov's old KGB mentor, Major Zakhar Babikov, who had a thick neck, square jaw, and drilling dark eyes. Records obtained from the Russian government showed Babikov to have been Talanov's instructor and mentor when Talanov began his military training, which included advanced lessons in Combat Sambo, which was a form of Russian martial arts that got straight to the point. No dancing around. No fancy moves. Just a terrifying assault with both speed and strength. Straw Sandal had once seen a seventh-degree black belt go up against a Spetsnaz commando and get flattened within the first minute. As to what had happened to Babikov after the collapse of the Soviet Union, she had no idea. He seemed to have vanished without a trace, which meant he was either one of the untold casualties of the Soviet collapse or had dropped off the grid like so many others had done.

Standing alone in the rear galley of the Gulfstream with a cup of coffee in her hand, Xin Li stared hard at Straw Sandal sorting through the photos. If the bitch weren't Dragon Head's daughter, she would have killed her months ago.

After finishing her coffee, Xin Li took out her cell phone and dialed. Half a world away, in a windowless room in the Zhongzhen Martial Arts Academy in Hong Kong, another cell phone vibrated.

The owner of the phone was a skinny twenty-nine-year-old Ukrainian hacker named Bogdan Kalashnik, or AK, as he was known in hacking circles because of his last name, Kalashnik, and its similarity to the iconic Russian assault rifle, the

Kalashnikov AK-47. Next to AK was a can of milk tea, which contained ginseng, chrysanthemum, guarana, and various herbs, the can advertised increased stamina and beneficial microelements.

Known for designing two worm viruses that crashed the systems of eight different European banks, AK had been lured to Hong Kong by Xin Li with an offer of unlimited wealth, which AK discovered to be a lie once he saw her antiquated equipment and dismal working conditions. Xin Li assured him the wealth was real, although not yet acquired, although within reach if he would help her acquire it.

When AK hesitated, Xin Li said with a pleasant smile, "Either that or I can shoot you."

After a nervous laugh, AK chose wisely, which was why he was very much alive sipping milk tea at his worktable in the darkened computer room, where he was surrounded by a series of monitors and routers. Harnesses of cables connected those routers and monitors to a series of processors crowded together on the floor, with other cables connecting those processors to a manifold on top of the worktable, which in turn was connected to AK's laptop. Beneath the worktable and across its top were dozens of tiny red and blue lights – LEDs, or light-emitting diodes – some of which were blinking while others were glowing steadily.

One monitor featured news coverage from around the world. Two others featured digital maps, one of which showed flight patterns over the Sea of Japan. Blinking triangles indicated aircraft and there were flight numbers beside each triangle. In the lower corner of the screen was a countdown clock, with green numbers ticking off seconds. The other monitor showed crisscrossing satellite orbits above the earth. The orbit paths were in four colors: red, green, yellow, and blue, with a legend in one corner indicating which colors belonged to which countries. The red paths were GPS and belonged to the United States. The green paths were Galileo and belonged to Europe. The yellow paths belonged to Russia and were marked Glonass. The blue paths belonged to China and were marked BeiDou.

The bulk of the satellites were Russian – more than thirteen hundred – followed by the United States, with just over six hundred and fifty. The European network, Galileo, and the Chinese network, BeiDou, had insignificant numbers. The altitude of the satellites in all four networks ranged from between a few hundred kilometers to as high as thirty-six thousand.

A fourth monitor showed a real-time satellite image of the aircraft carrier USS Ronald Reagan on maneuvers in the Sea of Japan, with a fifth monitor showing arrangements of fighter jets on the deck of the carrier. Sailors and pilots could be seen walking around. Even their shadows were visible.

AK did not hear his phone vibrating because he was wearing headphones. But he did see the screen light up, and after checking the Caller ID, slid the headphones down around his neck and quickly took the call.

"Sorry, I was busy," he explained.

"Have there been any changes?" asked Xin Li, speaking in Russian.

Wheeling his chair over to another laptop, AK entered a command on its keyboard. A monitor lit up with a record of internet activity on a particular IP address. "Normal activity, most of it encrypted," he replied, also in Russian, knowing he was to speak only Russian when the two of them talked so that no else in the academy could understand what they were saying.

"Which confirms she is there?" asked Xin Li.

"No question. Same starting time, same stopping time, like clockwork."

"And *Shāng Yī?*" asked Xin Li about a special program AK had designed.

"On schedule," AK replied, glancing at the live-feed image of the USS Ronald Reagan.

"Are you certain our signal cannot be traced?"

"I'm certain. I rerouted it using a series of electronic mirrors. They will never know what hit them."

Xin Li smiled and ended the call.

# CHAPTER 13

Over the years, Talanov had faced many opponents. He had faced them in the forests of central Europe and in cities like Berlin, Nairobi, Sydney, Algiers, Marbella, St. Petersburg, and London. He had even faced them in the remote mountains of northern China. But never had victory seemed as uncertain as it did right now.

Yesterday's flight from Washington to San Francisco was not to blame. The food in first class had been spectacular, as had the wine, and he had slept soundly until the flight attendant had gently awakened him for landing. Nor could he blame it on the fact that he and Zak had stayed up late last night talking. They hadn't. That's because Zak insisted he get some rest in preparation for today's contest.

Few of those observing the contest were on his side. Most were children and young adults between the ages of six and twenty-four. Some had been abused, others were runaways, and there were a number of young mothers, too – teenagers, mostly – plus several trafficking victims and dozens of neighborhood children who simply wanted a safe place to hang out, which the community center was known to be.

As a whole, the crowd was on the side of his opponent, a feisty French beauty in her thirties named Ginie Piat, who was coach of the Quiet Waters Community Center basketball team. Ginie was a full head shorter than the six-foot-one Talanov, but every bit as capable and competitive.

The Quiet Waters Community Center was a two-story brick building located uphill from Highway 101 as it cut through downtown San Francisco. Ginie had helped Zak revitalize the rundown center by raising funds to renovate the building. She then formed a basketball team, which she then volunteered to coach, after which she began teaching art classes and dance lessons. She even roped Talanov into teaching karate lessons whenever he was in town.

With the score tied 20-20, Ginie stood in center court in possession of the basketball, and when she began dribbling in place, the auditorium fell silent. "You do know there's a lot more at stake here than dinner," she said with a mischievous grin. Her black hair was tied back in a loose mess that was bound by a colorful scarf. Her green eyes danced with laughter. Like Talanov, she was dressed in baggy mesh shorts and a tank top. "I mean, how are you going to feel when you get your ass kicked by a girl?"

Talanov made a "bring it on" motion and Ginie tossed him the ball. With a smile, he tossed it back just as the kids began clapping and chanting, *"Go, Coach Ginie! Go, Coach Ginie!"* The kids had even learned to pronounce her name as Ginie had taught them, which sounded like Jeenie, not Jinnie.

"Go, Alex!" yelled eleven year-old Su Yin Cho. Su Yin had shoulder-length black hair and a beaming smile that lit up her face. She was dressed in a pink dance leotard.

Talanov gave Su Yin a thumbs up, then focused again on Ginie.

After dribbling several more times in place, Ginie faked right and drove left before cutting right again to drive diagonally toward the far right corner. With Talanov matching her step for step, Ginie paused, faked a baseline drive, then cut left to the top of the key for a fadeaway jump shot. The ball sailed in a clean arc toward the basket, hit the rim and bounced high in the air. Ginie went for the rebound but Talanov out-jumped her and sprinted down court for an easy layup.

A hush fell over the crowd like a wet blanket, except for Su Yin, who rocked her hips back and forth while pumping her fists up and down in the air.

Ginie walked over and gave Talanov a winded high-five. "Good game," she said.

"Backatcha," Talanov replied.

"You *were* lucky, though, you've got to admit. I mean, I matched you point for point, and would have won if my last shot would have hit."

Talanov smiled and shrugged.

"How about a rematch?" asked Ginie. "Double or nothing, winner takes all."

"Winner just took all. Dinner for two, you pay, restaurant of my choice."

"Then I say we eliminate any ambiguity."

"I won. Nothing ambiguous about that at all."

"Except you almost didn't win."

"Except almost doesn't count."

"Except I almost almost did."

"Almost almost? What does that even mean?"

"You're afraid of taking me on again, aren't you?" said Ginie, who began flapping her arms like a chicken. Many of the kids followed her lead. Others made clucking sounds.

When the clucking reached a crescendo, Talanov held up his hands. "All right, all right," he said. "Double or nothing. Shot for shot."

"Agreed," Ginie replied, tossing him the ball. "You won, so you go first."

Talanov dribbled casually to center court, turned, and shot. No calming breaths. No setup. No hesitation. Just a simple jump shot that was smooth and simple, and with a collective gasp, Ginie and the kids watched the spinning ball sail toward the basket.

*Swish.*

No rim. No bounce. All net.

Another deafening silence fell over the kids, except for Su Yin's clapping.

Talanov retrieved the ball and brought it to Ginie, who was staring soberly at the basket. "If you want to play hoops with the big guys," he said, allowing his sentence to dangle. "I mean, we *can* call this off, if you'd like. You know, to save you the embarrassment of losing again. Or is it not almost almost winning? What time were you picking me up?"

Seeing a momentary flash in Ginie's eyes, Talanov decided to stoke the fire.

"Why don't I give you a handicap?" he said. "Say, a few steps closer to the net? You know, like girls getting to do girl push-ups from their knees?"

Ginie snatched the ball from Talanov and waited until he backed away a few steps. Once he had, she dribbled in place several times, and with a calming breath, paused and focused on what seemed like an impossibly small target a hundred miles away. After adjusting the ball into a predominantly right-hand grasp, she brought the ball up over her head and launched it gracefully toward the hoop.

Talanov and the kids watched it spin noiselessly toward the basket.

*Swish.*

As one, the kids began clapping and cheering.

Pumping her fist, Ginie trotted down court, retrieved the ball and dribbled it back to center court, where Talanov was nodding with both incredulity and admiration. And with a sigh of resolve, he motioned for the ball.

"Sorry, my turn now to shoot first," Ginie said with a smile.

"But . . . I thought I got to go first."

"You were the *first* to get to go first. That's different from getting to go first every time."

A wrinkle of concern creased Talanov's brow.

With pursed lips, Ginie stared at the faraway hoop for a long moment, then walked to the basket and stood directly beneath it. After looking up, she took several steps toward the free throw line, where she laid down flat on her back, with her legs extended toward center court, her feet slightly spread.

"Wait a minute," objected Talanov. "You can't just lie down on the court like that."

"Says who?" Ginie replied. "In HORSE, anything goes."

"This is shot-for-shot basketball, not HORSE."

"Same thing."

"Says who?"

"Me. My town, my court, my rules."

With a grin of disbelief, Talanov shook his head.

Lying flat on her back while holding the basketball in both hands between her knees, Ginie craned her head back, and with stiffened arms, launched the ball. It sailed toward the goal in a high arc, where it bounced off the backboard and down through the hoop.

The kids began cheering and clapping.

"I don't *believe* this," said Talanov.

Ginie stood. "Hey, if you want to play hoops with the little guys . . ."

Talanov responded with a quizzical look.

"Grade school kids," answered Ginie. "These are the kinds of shots you've got to learn if you don't want to get whipped by a nine-year-old."

After retrieving the ball, Ginie tossed it to Talanov, who walked to the exact spot where Ginie had been, and after a steadying breath, lay down on the court, spread his legs, positioned the ball between his knees, then craned his neck and looked at the hoop. Sighting in on his target, he launched the ball, which sailed straight up in the air. No arc, no spin, dead weight going straight up and coming straight back down.

Seeing the ball plummeting straight for his face, Talanov rolled quickly aside to avoid getting hit just as the entire assembly of kids began jumping and cheering.

A grinning Ginie walked over and offered Talanov her hand. Talanov grabbed it and Ginie pulled him to his feet.

"Nice try, old man. I win," Ginie said with a grin.

"Another showdown. Winner take all."

"Are you kidding? I'm not that dumb."

By now, the kids were giving each other high-fives and mobbing Ginie with hugs. Standing beside Ginie, Talanov looked down at Su Yin, who had joined them. Her arms were folded in front of her and her tiny brow was furrowed.

"An admirable effort, Alex," she said, "but your exclusive

association with adults is what led to your unfortunate defeat. Even Jesus commanded His disciples to hang out with kids. Now you know why."

Talanov opened his mouth to reply but was absolutely stumped as to what to say.

"I have to go practice," Su Yin said. "But I do have some time later, after BMX practice, if you want me to teach you some better shots." She hugged Talanov around the waist and ran toward the stage, where several girls were practicing ballet routines.

"She's a very smart little girl," Ginie said.

"Did you hear what she just told me?" asked Talanov. He watched Su Yin jump up on stage and begin doing cartwheels. "She said, 'An admirable effort, Alex, but your exclusive association with adults is what led to your unfortunate defeat.' She's, what, eleven? She'll be a lawyer by the time she's thirteen."

Ginie laughed.

"She's a good little athlete, too," added Talanov. "Look at her up there doing cartwheels."

"You should see her on the BMX track. She gives her big brother, Kai, a run for his money, and Kai is good, believe me."

Talanov chuckled and shook his head while kids ran in circles around them, laughing and shouting and playing tag.

"Okay, everyone, gather around!" yelled Ginie, clapping her hands.

The kids all gathered around.

"You, too," Ginie said, motioning for several teenage mothers holding infants. Ginie waited until everyone was standing together before saying, "Okay, everybody, I want all of you to congratulate Alex here on a good game." When she began clapping, everyone joined her.

"What did you win, Coach?" asked one of the kids once the applause had died down.

"Alex will be cooking us dinner," Ginie announced. "And

that's *all* of us. Everyone here."

"All of us?" asked several kids.

"That's right."

The kids exploded in an eruption of cheering.

"Whoa, whoa, whoa," said Talanov, waving down the noise. "How did dinner for two in a restaurant become me cooking dinner for a gym full of kids?"

"Dinner for two in a restaurant is expensive," Ginie replied, "and since you lost, double or nothing, that means double what you were going to spend, which means I'm actually *saving* you money by having you cook, which is cheaper." To the kids: "Tomorrow at noon, everyone. It's Saturday. No school. *Free food.*" To Talanov: "By the way, these kids do not get many gourmet, home-cooked meals and will naturally want seconds, so be sure and factor that in."

Talanov laughed and shook his head.

"Okay, basketball team, start warming up!" Ginie shouted, clapping her hands to pump up the players. "Dance team, up on stage!"

Kids began running in various directions.

"Thank you for being such a good sport," Ginie said quietly. "You seriously made their day. And before you say it, yes, I did sucker you into that showdown, and, yes, I did sucker you with that last shot. Well, kind of, but not entirely, because it *was* a fair shot, which means I still own bragging rights, while you, my friend, get to cook dinner. No junk food, either. These kids get enough of that. I want a home-cooked, well-balanced meal."

"Does anyone ever say no to you?"

"A few people have tried," a grinning Ginie replied before dashing away.

Talanov watched Ginie vault up onto the stage, where Su Yin and several other girls were practicing in front of large mirrors.

"Alex, look!" shouted Su Yin.

Talanov watched her perform a double cartwheel and gave

her a double thumbs-up.

A basketball bounced toward him and Talanov kicked it up into his hand.

"Throw it to me!" several boys shouted, their hands up while dodging and scrambling around in zigzag patterns, trying to get open for a pass.

"Who's coming tomorrow for lunch?" asked Talanov.

The boys stopped running and raised their hands.

"Spaghetti sound good?" asked Talanov.

The boys all cheered.

"Vegetables sound good?" asked Talanov.

The boys all looked at one another but no one raised a hand.

"Okay, then, how about this?" asked Talanov, dribbling to center court. "If I make this shot, you eat whatever I cook. If I miss, I fix whatever you want."

"You mean, like, chocolate cake and ice cream? Or potato chips and pizza?"

"Whatever you want."

"What if you win but we don't like what you fix?"

"A deal is a deal," said Talanov.

"You won't make any weirdo stuff, will you? You know, like eyeballs or guts?"

"I'm a spaghetti kind of guy, so no eyeballs or guts. And that's a promise, and I keep my word. But, yes, there will be salad, which I expect you to eat."

"*If* you win," laughed one of the boys.

"If I win," agreed Talanov.

"And you're shooting from center court, right?"

"Right, no sneaky tricks, like the evil Coach Ginie pulled," said Talanov, glancing at Ginie, who was watching. "Center court. One shot."

The boys exchanged glances and finally nodded.

"I want a show of hands," said Talanov. "Nobody wimping out later."

The boys all raised their hands.

"Okay, let's do this," said Talanov, dribbling the basketball over to the tipoff ring, where he lifted the ball in one smooth motion and let it fly with a jump shot toward the hoop at the far end of the court. The auditorium fell silent while everyone watched the ball sail in a perfect arc through the hoop without touching the rim. "Vegetables it is," he said. "So I will see you boys tomorrow."

# CHAPTER 14

Evening had settled over Washington, DC, when Amber opened the office door and said, "Do you need me to get you anything before I leave?"

Gustaves looked up from a thick document. Behind her was a counter that ran the length of her paneled office. Bookshelves above, cabinets beneath, with a computer workstation built into the counter so that Gustaves could spin around and send emails whenever she wished. Not that she ever sent many emails because Amber was the one who handled her correspondence.

"I'm good, Amber, thanks," said Gustaves.

"By the way, I searched every database we're linked to but couldn't locate an address or phone number for the Quiet Waters Community Center. Either Colonel Talanov told you the wrong name by mistake or it's registered as something else."

Gustaves leaned back in her chair and frowned. "Did you check TRIP, IDENT, OPS-004 and the others?"

"All of them, using your secure access, but nothing came up for Zakhar Babikov or the Quiet Waters Community Center. So without additional information, I can't find out whether or not the property is listed as something else – like a corporation – or in someone else's name. I even called Mr. Wilcox to verify the spelling of Babikov's name. Incidentally, he said he was taking your advice about going on vacation."

"It wasn't really advice," Gustaves said with a smile. "It was quite a bit stronger than that."

Amber smiled.

"Did he tell you where he was going?"

"Disneyland, Magic Mountain, and the San Diego Zoo. He mentioned being a ten-year-old kid for the next two weeks.

Except when it came to the wine."

Gustaves laughed.

Amber stepped over and handed Gustaves a pink sticky note. "Everything I've told you is in your sensitive compartmentalized information folder. Your new password, updated per your request, is on that sticky note."

"Thank you, Amber."

"Good night, ma'am. Anything else?"

"That does it. Have a great weekend."

"You, too, ma'am."

Outside, the traffic was heavy along Independence Avenue, which was normal for a Friday night. Across the street, the Capitol was bathed in brilliant white light. With the sky clear and the temperature so pleasant, Amber opted to walk to the L'Enfant Metro station instead of hailing a cab. She was in no particular hurry – Friday was her Netflix night – so she relaxed her pace and strolled along the sidewalk with cars racing past in both directions.

Her search for the Quiet Waters Community Center had produced more questions than answers. That's because she could find no mention of it anywhere. Nothing in any public records, newspaper articles, or tagged photos, not that such a total absence was a serious concern, because business properties were often listed in the names of corporations or parent organizations. Still, there should have been some kind of a mention, especially if it was legitimately serving the community.

But there had been nothing. Nor was there anything on Babikov. But with what she had learned about Talanov and the KGB, that came as no surprise. Diane had already filled her in on Talanov's history as a spy for America during the Cold War, as well as his continuing service to the Intelligence Community. Still, Talanov seemed to regularly be in trouble with someone, so if Babikov had wanted to avoid similar trouble, he would have placed everything in someone else's name. At least that is what Mr. Wilcox had suggested when she had phoned to ask if he had any ideas where Babikov might be.

Walking along the sidewalk in the swirling eddies of automobile exhaust, Amber replayed her conversation with Mr. Wilcox, or Bill, as he insisted on her calling him. Amber smiled at how talkative he had become on the subject of Talanov, no doubt because he was about to leave on vacation and had started his partying early. After a lengthy, mostly comical, rant about Talanov's cavalier way of doing things, Bill confessed how much he admired those traits and Talanov's willingness to put his life on the line for other people.

To illustrate, Bill recalled the winter of nineteen eighty-five. By that time, Talanov, who was known to him only as November Echo, had been feeding the CIA a steady stream of intelligence on Soviet industrial and military operations, as well as KGB surveillance and sabotage activities in various countries, including the United States. In addition, he had also been furnishing the CIA with information on religious leaders and political dissidents who had been targeted for imprisonment or assassination. Hundreds had already been exiled to the gulags and coal mines. Others had simply disappeared. Entire families vanishing without a trace.

And Talanov was reporting it all.

It was indeed a dangerous tightrope Talanov was walking, because embedded sources in Washington had let Moscow know they had a leak, although no one knew who it was. The only names anyone knew were the leak's codename, November Echo, and the name of November Echo's contact, CIA station chief, Bill Wilcox.

Bill recounted how enormous the pressure became to reveal the name of his informant. The excuse: so that the information he was receiving could be authenticated. Bill said the accuracy of that information spoke for itself, and that the identity of the informant did not matter. Threats about the future of his career were made, but Bill did not back down. Others tried a more conciliatory approach, saying they did not wish to offend their Soviet counterparts. Bill did not back down to them, either, saying America should be more concerned about stopping Soviet atrocities than offending the perpetrators.

In fact, *I'm* the one who's offended, Bill recalled shouting at his boss. At the human rights abuses of those bastards. At the raping and pillaging of entire nations, which they've imprisoned behind an Iron Curtain and continue to bleed in order to support their failing socialist economy. And you're worried about *offending* them? Whose side are you on? If you want to fire me, go ahead, but I am not telling you the identity of the one man who's actually *doing* something to end their barbaric madness.

Amber remembered asking if anyone ever found out who November Echo was.

"Nope," Wilcox had answered, "but that's not to say they didn't try every dirty trick in the book. And I do mean dirty. It was the first time I realized how dirty – and deadly – Washington politics can be." He then continued his story about the winter of nineteen eighty-five.

The occasion was a European summit being held in a castle outside of Vienna. The setting was picture-book beautiful, with snow-covered Austrian peaks and a fairytale fortress jutting high above a thick forest. Wilcox described how he was attending the summit as the American Embassy's Third Viticultural Attaché, "which," he added, "was my cover as station chief for the CIA in London, which allowed me to pontificate about wine while discreetly courting the favor of potentially useful contacts."

"I've heard that's right up your alley . . . the pontificating part."

"Contrary to what you may have heard, young lady, I am not just a pretty face."

They both laughed.

"The castle was full of diplomats and dukes and countesses dripping with diamonds," Wilcox continued, "plus the usual collection of strutting cocks in uniforms festooned with medals. All very highbrow, including a harp being strummed by a woman in a magnificent translucent gown."

"What was the purpose of the summit?"

"To decide if and how to support pro-democracy efforts occurring behind the Iron Curtain. There was a lot of deliberation going on, with most West European nations wanting more discussion, and most East Europeans pleading for assistance. When you're starving and freezing, the last thing you need is more talk, so I was there to quietly goad our allies into action with offers of support. During the course of the evening, I somehow found myself cornered near a marble statue by a wine critic wanting to lecture me about the 'lolly water' we Americans called wine. He droned on and on until I was finally rescued by an elegant blonde. She begged the critic's forgiveness, saying an urgent matter with her ambassador required my attention. Feigning regret, I departed with the blonde, and once we were out of earshot, I quietly thanked her."

"Let me get this right. A gorgeous blonde asks you to follow her to an unspecified location in a castle for a meeting with an unnamed ambassador?"

"I know," confessed Wilcox, "and like a hog with a ring in its snout, I blindly followed."

"What happened next?"

"Linking her arm in mine, she led me into the kitchen, where a waiter was just filling a tray full of glasses with wine. The blonde asked for a glass and the waiter handed her one, which she handed to me before introducing me as an important expert on wine. Naturally, they waited expectantly for me to sample the wine, which I did – with great flair and technique, I might add – whereupon I nodded my approval, after which I was led out a servant's door into a hallway, which took us to another hallway, which brought us to a descending flight of steps. By this time, I was feeling dizzy, which the blonde credited to the thin mountain air. She then helped me down the stairs, and when we reached the bottom, this gorilla of a man stepped out of a doorway and grabbed me. My valiant fight to break free lasted all of three or four seconds before I passed out from whatever was in the wine, whereupon I was carried out the service door and tossed into the back of a van. I was then driven to an old warehouse in Vienna, which was a huge, dirty, empty place, with rows of high windows and rusty I-beams, where I awakened to see Talanov kneeling over me with a pistol in his hand. 'Wakey, wakey,' I remember him saying with that stupid grin of his. He used his pistol to point to five dead bodies on the floor. He then pointed to the gorilla, also dead from a single bullet hole in his head. 'What happened?' I remembered asking. 'Soviet agents,' Talanov replied, 'who were about to do some very nasty things to you, my friend.' And after helping me to my feet, he nodded to a stainless steel roller cart containing a wide variety of scalpels, forceps, hammers, pliers, and other torture tools and syringes."

"They were going to make you talk, weren't they?" Amber recalled asking. "To make you give up Talanov's identity."

"Whatever it took, and to this day we're still not certain who was behind it."

"Didn't Alex said they were Soviet agents?"

"He did, and they were, but the CIA has a dark side, and that dark side doesn't like anyone holding out on them. And I was."

"Why do you keep working for people like that?"

"Because the CIA has a good side, and the good that we do, makes the sacrifices worthwhile."

"They were going to kill you."

"All part of the job," Wilcox replied almost flippantly.

*All part of the job,* Amber thought with a snort while passing the cell-blockish Wilbur J. Cohen Federal Building. She had heard about the split personality of the CIA. Bill, however, was one of the good guys. If only there were more like him.

After crossing with the light at Fourth Street, Amber turned left, then angled southwest along Maryland Avenue, toward the L'Enfant Metro station at the corner of Seventh. She could always tell when she was getting close to the metro station by the line of food trucks parked out front. She knew a few of the vendors, especially the guy selling gyros wrapped in soft, homemade pita bread. Tonight, she would get hers with an extra squirt of garlicky tzatziki sauce and a double helping of onions. Hashtag, oh yeah.

After receiving her order, Amber slipped the takeaway container into her handbag and took the escalator down to the underground platform, where she boarded the Green Line train to its terminus in Maryland.

Fifteen minutes later, she was unlocking the door to her apartment.

Ten seconds after that, she was pinned helplessly on the floor with Xin Li's arm wrapped around her throat.

# CHAPTER 15

Most local residents knew the Hilltop Community Center as the Quiet Waters Community Center because of a faded Bible verse painted above the double front doors. The verse was from Psalm 23:2: *He leads me beside quiet waters.* Officially, however, the building was registered at City Hall as the Hilltop Community Center, having been built in 1910 and so named because it sat on top of a hill.

The hallmark of the center was its two bright blue front doors. No one could remember how many coats of thick enamel paint those heavy wooden doors had received over the years, but it was a lot. Some credited the hippie influence of Haight-Ashbury for the electric blue color. But photos predating the sixties showed the doors to have been bright blue as far back as the forties. Whatever the reason, the doors had made the community center a local landmark.

To one side of the imposing old brick building was a skatepark. A recent addition, it was used by neighborhood kids for skateboards, bicycles, and roller blades. The two-story eastern wall of the community center, which overlooked the skatepark, had been turned into a massive canvas for urban artists, who competed each year for cash prizes offered by sponsors. Tour buses had even begun stopping at the center so that visitors could take photos of the art.

A group of four boys raced up the street on their bicycles. It was lunchtime and they weren't about to miss out on the free food being offered today. After zipping around a police car parked in front of the center, they shoved their bikes into the rack, pulled open the bright blue doors, and almost plowed into Arcus Hill, a six-foot-four police officer, who was inside the door talking with Zak and his wife, Emily, a striking Chinese-American woman of forty-six. Emily's salt-and-pepper hair was tied up in a loose knot on top of her head, and she was pacing back and forth angrily. In avoiding a collision with Hill, the boys ran into one another and stumbled to one side, where they saw Su Yin's older brother, Kai, in the custody of Hill. Dressed in baggy jeans and a faded black hoodie, Kai had sinewy arms and a mop of shaggy black hair.

"Thanks, Arcus," said Zak, who was several inches shorter than Hill but had biceps twice the size.

Zak stuck out a beefy hand and Hill shook it.

"You got it, Zak," said Hill. "But I need to tell you that Kai is running out of second chances. I'm here for you, man, and you know that, because I was once a kid. But Kai has *got* to stop the breaking and entering. I know he's had it rough. But it needs to stop and it needs to stop now if you want him kept out of the system."

"I was only looking around," said Kai defensively.

"You *stole* their jewelry!" said Hill.

"And gave it back."

"And *then* picked my partner's pocket! You stole his phone!"

"And gave *it* back. I wasn't hurting anyone. I just wanted to see if I could do it."

"You're hurting *you*," Zak said gently. "All of this is hurting you. And *you* are the one I care about."

"Regardless," said Emily, jabbing a finger at Kai, "you do *not* get to steal other people's property. It's illegal. Do you get that? *Illegal.*"

"You help people sneak into America illegally. Isn't that breaking the law? Why the meltdown over this?"

Emily grabbed Kai by the arm and marched him into her office, which was located off the foyer. Hill flinched when Emily slammed the door, which rattled the window of her office, which overlooked the foyer. On the window was painted, in English and Chinese, the Law Offices of Emily Chang, and beneath this were additional details: Civil and Criminal Law, Legal Aid, Women's Rights, Immigration, and EIR, which stood for Entrepreneurs in Residence, which is a

Citizenship and Immigration Services program designed to help immigrant entrepreneurs start their own businesses.

"He's a good kid, Zak, and smart," said Hill. "But you've got to do something, okay?"

Zak nodded gravely and again shook Hill's hand just as the four boys entered the gym. Above the door into the gym was another sign that read 13:5.

Inside the gym, the boys dashed left across the basketball court and entered the community center's industrial kitchen, where Talanov had just picked up a large wooden spoon and twirled it in his hand, like a propeller. Surrounded by more than sixty kids ranging from seven to nineteen, plus twenty teenage mothers and their infants, Talanov was presiding over a pot of bubbling sauce. Beside the pot were two other pots. Above the stove, a stainless steel hood was sucking away steam.

"Look at him, showing off," whispered Ginie to nineteen-year-old Jingfei Cho, who was Su Yin's older sister. The two women were standing at a stainless steel table covered with fresh vegetables.

"Look at *him* showing off?" Jingfei replied. "You're as bad as he is, suckering him the way you did with that goofy basketball shot."

"Shut up, I am not," protested Ginie, elbowing Jingfei, who elbowed her back.

Talanov threw Jingfei and Ginie reprimanding glances before returning his attention to the array of eager young faces staring up at him.

"We arrive at the moment of truth," announced Talanov with dramatic flair. After twirling the spoon again, he removed the lid, gave the sauce a stir, then brought the spoon to his lips and savored the flavor as if it were fine wine.

"How is it?" Su Yin called out.

Talanov held up his hand – a signal to wait – then added pinches of freshly chopped basil, oregano, and thyme before grating in some fresh lemon zest, then a grind of black pepper, then an additional pinch of salt. He then grabbed a clean wooden spoon, stirred the sauce again, then once more brought it to his lips.

The kids held their breath and watched.

"Alex, how *is* it?" Su Yin called out again. "Tell us!"

"You tell me. Who wants a taste?"

The kids all raised their hands.

Talanov grabbed a ladle and theatrically filled a bowl with sauce. He then waved to Ginie and pointed at the utensils tray. "Spoons for my loyal subjects!"

"Seriously?" Ginie replied with a scolding glare.

Jingfei elbowed Ginie and nodded toward the utensils tray. "You heard the man."

Ginie growled while Jingfei gave four heads of romaine lettuce rapid whacks with a large knife.

"I give you *ragù à la sugo di pomodoro à la Talanov,*" Talanov called out while Ginie began distributing spoons to the kids just as Talanov slid the bowl of sauce onto the counter. "Orderly fashion, one taste, no double-dipping. Pay special attention to the exquisite notes of olive oil, garlic, and spices, all orchestrated in perfect harmony with the robust flavors of grass-fed beef, sausage, onions, and peppers."

"Why not just open a jar?" asked one of the boys.

"What's the fun in that?" asked Talanov in return. "Besides, if you and I don't show these girls how to cook, who will?"

The remark provoked an immediate outcry from the girls.

Inside Emily's office, Zak glanced toward the echoes of shouting coming from the kitchen.

"This behavior has got to stop!" Emily shouted at Kai, drawing Zak's attention.

"I didn't hurt anyone," mumbled Kai.

"But it's costing us, Kai," said Zak. "Money we just don't have."

"You mean it's costing *me,*" said Emily sharply. "I'm the one with the income, not you."

Zak flinched but maintained eye contact with Kai. "You

know we love you," he said, tussling Kai's hair affectionately, "but if you don't stop what you're doing, the courts will take you away."

Kai looked down at the floor and said nothing.

"Do you get how serious this is?" asked Zak.

Kai kept staring at the floor and said nothing.

"Is going to juvie what you want?"

"Maybe juvie is where he belongs," said Emily.

A tear rolled down Kai's cheek, but he kept staring at the floor and said nothing.

●

# CHAPTER 16

High above the State of Indiana, Wilcox recoiled from the glass of red wine he had just been served.

"You can thank NAFTA for that little surprise," remarked Stephanie, the forty-seven-year-old flight attendant. Dressed in a stylish navy blue slack suit and crisp white shirt, Stephanie was a slender brunette who had been working more than twenty years for the CIA. She had warm brown eyes that were twinkling with amusement at Wilcox's sour reaction.

Wilcox asked for the bottle and Stephanie handed it to him. "This dates back to the Bush administration," he exclaimed.

"And cellared just for you."

With a scowl, Wilcox handed the bottle back. Dressed in a Hawaiian shirt of bright pink and yellow frangipani blossoms, Wilcox's scowl made his bushy eyebrows protrude more than they normally did.

"By the way, nice B-29 you're wearing," Stephanie remarked about Wilcox's shirt collar. "If engines fail, we can all grab on and glide safely to the earth. Those colors will act like a beacon."

"I'll have you know, I had this and three identical shirts handcrafted for me by a tailor in Panama back in 1984."

"How very . . . practical."

"Real men are not afraid to wear pink."

"Of course, sir."

Wilcox scrutinized Stephanie suspiciously. "You're making fun of me, aren't you?"

"Never. Will there be anything else?"

"Yes, dammit! A glass of *Burgundy*. As in *France*."

"I'll file an immediate request."

"I'm the embassy's Third Viticultural Attaché, for crying out loud," proclaimed Wilcox, citing his well-known cover in the

American Embassy in London. "Do you know how many embarrassing situations I've saved us from? You would not believe the antifreeze our former ambassador tried serving the President of France, on not one but two occasions. And the Russians! I shudder to think what would have happened had I not intervened on *that* occasion. It would not be an exaggeration to say I've singlehandedly saved America from no fewer than six disasters."

Stephanie suppressed a smile but did not reply.

"Diplomacy – dare I say, world peace – can be won or lost with the wine."

"Of course, sir. Will there be anything else?"

Wilcox again eyed Stephanie suspiciously. "You *are* making fun of me."

Stephanie suppressed another smile, moving on to serve other passengers aboard the company Gulfstream.

Wilcox chuckled at the banter he had come to appreciate with Stephanie over the years. He watched her serve glasses of NAFTA wine to the poultry delegation of two men and three women seated near the rear of the plane. The women were seated together, laughing and chatting. The men, both military types with closely cropped hair, were busy at their laptops, hardly saying a word.

*Poultry delegates, my ass,* he thought of the men. He waved and caught Stephanie's attention and she returned to his seat.

"Something else?"

Wilcox nodded toward the two men. "Who are they?" he asked.

"A poultry delegation."

Wilcox raised a skeptical eyebrow.

"That's all I know," Stephanie replied.

"All you know, or all you're allowed to say?"

Stephanie smiled.

"Since when does the CIA handle poultry?" asked Wilcox.

"Perhaps Director Shaw would be the one to ask," Stephanie replied before heading toward the galley.

*Shaw. I should have known,* thought Wilcox. *Is he following someone . . . or hunting them?*

Wilcox saw his cell phone screen illuminate with a call from Gustaves. Picking it up, he touched the green "answer" button and put the phone to his ear. "Hello, Diane," he said.

Gustaves was standing in front of her desk in Washington with her phone on speaker. Angus Shaw was standing next to her, arms folded, his angular jaw clenched. Beside Shaw was his chief of staff, Adam Schiller, a bug-eyed man of thirty-five, whose coarse, well-oiled hair was brushed straight back. Behind the desk, a technician was working on Gustaves' computer. The technician's name was Álvaro and he looked more Irish than he did Hispanic, with curly brown hair that rose on one side, like he had slept wrong. He weighed just shy of three hundred pounds and grunted each time he moved. Right now he was working on his knees, which meant he grunted a lot.

"Álvaro, can you give us a minute?" Gustaves asked in Spanish.

"Of course, Madam Congresswoman," Álvaro replied, and with a grunt, he stood and left the office.

Once he was gone, Gustaves said, "Bill, I'm on speaker with Director Shaw and I'm calling with some very bad news. My assistant, Amber, was murdered last night by two Chinese women waiting inside her apartment. They jammed the alarm frequency, so the wi-fi signal wasn't able to alert our security team, although her security camera recorded what happened." She took a steadying breath, then continued, "After taking her captive, they forced her to log on to her laptop and navigate past our security protocols. One of the women then searched through my folders for information on Talanov before planting a virus in our system that crashed everything. One of the women then broke Amber's neck."

"Diane, I . . . who would . . . *why?*"

"We know who did it," said Shaw. "The *Chinese.* We also know why: to kill Diane."

"Sir, this doesn't make sense. My friend, Alice Ti, who's with the Hong Kong CIB—"

"She played you, Wilcox!" yelled Shaw. "The Chinese are behind this and Talanov is part of the conspiracy. He's finished, do you hear me? Finished!"

"Sir, I don't for a moment believe Alice played me. Or that Talanov is involved."

"If you are that blind, then maybe you should step down. Unless you're part of this conspiracy as well?"

Schiller responded with a smirk. He had never liked Wilcox and Wilcox had never liked him.

"Angus, I'll handle this," said Gustaves, nodding toward the door. "Take a break and calm down."

"I *will* get to the bottom of this, Diane, and you may not like what I find."

Shaw stormed out of the office with a grinning Schiller following after him.

Once they were gone, Gustaves said, "Bill, we're on very thin ice. Shaw wants Alex gone and I'm not sure I can stop it from happening."

"And you know as well as I do that Alex would never do anything to harm you or this country."

"I know, but all we have right now is a tangled mess of questions and two common denominators: China and Alex."

"Come on, Diane!"

"Look, I know Alex will say we can't assume this is all connected, but I don't see how we can ignore the facts any longer."

"Have we identified the two women who killed Amber?"

"No, but they're Chinese and we have them on video."

"Then I'd like to send Charlie the link to where that video file is located and have her place a copy in a dedicated cyberlocker so that Alice can have a look."

"After what Shaw just said? That is not a good idea."

"Alice won't be able to access our secure internet or intranet, or any of our SCI vaults. The cyberlocker will be totally outside of our system on an isolated provider, and the access link will be temporary. For viewing only, no downloads permitted, and Charlie will set it up. Please, let Alice have a look. Let her see if she can ID those women."

Gustaves exhaled slowly.

"I know Shaw thinks I was played," Wilcox added quickly. "Many people have tried through the years and I know when someone is trying. Alice is not one of those. Please, Diane, let Charlie set it up so that Alice can have a look."

Gustaves stared hard at the phone for a long moment. "All right, but like I said, we're on very thin ice."

"Not if it gets us an ID on those two women. If things go south, I'll take the fall."

"That kind of a fall would end your career."

"At this point, I would welcome it. With your permission, then?"

Another slow exhale from Gustaves, then, "I'll have Amber send Charlie—"

With a gasp, Gustaves stopped mid-sentence. Amber, of course, was dead.

"Diane, I am so sorry," Wilcox said softly.

"Thank you, Bill, but we don't have time to grieve. Right now, we have work to do." She walked around her desk and sat, then swiveled to face her computer. "I'll send Charlie the link myself."

"Thanks. I'll let her know," Wilcox replied, ending the call.

Sitting back in his seat on the Gulfstream, Wilcox thought about Amber. He couldn't believe the brutality of her murder. Diane, however, was right – there was work to do – and with that, he sent Charlie a text, then went to the galley for another glass of wine. At this point, even NAFTA wine sounded good.

After emailing Charlie the video link, Gustaves swiveled back around and thought about the horrific security footage that Charlie would soon be watching. Through the infrared eye of the camera, a recording had been made of two women breaking into Amber's apartment, then waiting until Amber arrived home. It recorded the taller of the two women smashing Amber in the face and then pinning her on the floor. Amber tried putting up a fight, but she was no match for the woman, who maneuvered her into a chokehold. The shorter woman then appeared with Amber's laptop and ordered Amber to log on. Amber refused. The shorter woman slapped Amber in the face, but Amber still refused. The two Chinese women then appeared to disagree on what to do next, which was settled when the tall woman tightened her arm around Amber's neck and cut off her ability to breathe. The camera showed Amber thrashing and kicking while the tall woman squeezed. The shorter woman finally intervened and the tall woman released Amber, who toppled to the side, gasping. The tall woman then yanked Amber up-right.

After an exchange of words with the tall woman, the shorter woman knelt before Amber and held out the laptop again. With blood running from her nose, Amber opened her laptop and logged on, and once she had navigated into the system, the shorter woman took the laptop, sat on the floor, and began working the keyboard. After a few seconds, she said something to the tall woman, who removed her arm from around Amber's neck.

At that point there was a glimmer of hope in Amber's eyes. Gustaves could see it, and everyone who had watched the footage had seen it. It was a moment when Amber thought she may get out of this alive. A moment when she took a sobbing breath.

Gustaves shuddered at what happened next.

Without warning, the tall woman grabbed Amber's head and wrenched it in a violent one-eighty twist. The sudden action shocked the shorter woman, who bolted forward, trying to stop the tall woman. But Amber was now dead, and after a long moment of restrained anger, the shorter woman continued working at the laptop while the tall woman dragged Amber's body out of sight. The shorter woman soon paused and read the laptop screen intently, then lifted a lanyard from around her neck. At the end of the lanyard was a USB drive, which she plugged into one of the laptop's ports, and after a few seconds, executed several commands before unplugging the flash drive just as the tall woman reappeared. The women exchanged more words, after which the shorter woman wiped the laptop clean of fingerprints and replaced it in Amber's briefcase. The two women then left the apartment.

Gustaves closed her eyes and fought back tears, then walked across the floor to her liquor cabinet, where she paused to wipe away a tear before opening the cabinet door.

While Gustaves was pouring herself a drink in Washington, Wilcox was finishing the last of his wine aboard the Gulfstream. With his empty glass in hand, he thought of Amber while absently looking out the window. He didn't really know her apart from her friendly smile whenever he visited Diane. Even so, her murder was personal. Amber had been part of the family.

Setting aside his glass, Wilcox picked up his phone and dialed Charlie. "Have you watched the footage yet?" he asked once Charlie had answered.

"Yes, and I wish that I hadn't, although I know I needed to see it. Amber was a friend. Not someone I knew all that well, but someone I really liked."

"Diane is taking it hard."

"I can see why. Do we know who those women are?"

"That's what I'm calling about," Wilcox replied. "How long would it take you to set up a dedicated cyberlocker? Secure and isolated, for Alice in Hong Kong to have a look at the footage. To see if she can ID the killers."

"Five minutes, tops."

"Text me when it's done."

After ending the call, Wilcox phoned Alice. It was early morning in Hong Kong and Alice was not polite when she answered the phone.

"Bill, you had better have a damn good reason for calling me at this hour."

"There's been a murder. I need your help."

Alice quickly switched on a lamp and sat up in bed. "Okay, I'm awake," she said.

Wilcox elaborated on Amber's murder, then told Alice he was setting up a secure cyberlocker, where security footage of the murder could be viewed. "I know this is a long shot," he said, "but if you can ID their faces, please let me know."

After expressing her deepest sympathies, Alice said she would happily assist.

"Thanks, I'll send you the link. Be warned, though, it's not pretty. In fact, it's downright brutal."

Within minutes of Wilcox ending his call with Alice, his phone chimed with a text message from Charlie. It contained the link and password to the cyberlocker. Wilcox replied with a quick text, then forwarded the link and password to Alice. He then sat back and allowed his mind to drift back to happier times, when he and Alice first met in Italy during the summer of 2003. They were both visiting the Tuscan village of Montalcino when he ran into her coming out of a restaurant with a glass of wine. The village was famous for its *Brunello di Montalcino* – an earthy Sangiovese – which was the main reason Wilcox was there, after having visited Talanov in the nearby city of Florence in order to hand him the latest of several cash payments for services rendered as a spy. The encounter not only knocked Alice down onto the cobblestones, but drenched her with the wine she was set to enjoy at an outdoor table. A new shirt and a whole bottle of *Brunello di Montalcino* later, Wilcox convinced Alice to spend the afternoon with him.

They were an unlikely couple, with careers they could not talk about, but ultimately did, at least superficially over big plates of ossobuco, then ice cream while strolling among Montalcino's ancient walls and narrow streets. He smiled at the memory of Alice swearing at him in Chinese when he tried wiping off the wine.

Wilcox refocused when his phone chimed and he saw that it

was an email from Alice. The email read, simply, *"Bill, I hope this helps. Regards, Alice xx*

Attached to the email were a number of attachments, the first being Alice's summary of the infrared security footage taken in Amber's apartment, which showed a greenish image that had been lifted from the footage. Wilcox stared at the faces of the two women shown in the image. He then read Alice's notes, which identified the shorter of the two women as Chin Chi Ho, aka Straw Sandal, who was the daughter of a Hong Kong crime lord named Dexter Moran, aka Dragon Head.

Of Irish ancestry, Moran had been born in Hong Kong when it was a British colony, with his father, Arlo, controlling much of Macau's gambling industry until he was killed by Chao Lin's father, Kun Lin, after a rigged card game in which Kun Lin won the title to Arlo's casino. A fight ensued, which Arlo started and lost. When the courts failed to obtain a guilty verdict against Kun Lin for cheating and killing Arlo, Dexter moved quickly to do what the courts would not, and within weeks, had quietly executed Kun Lin, which in turn made him a regional hero, with Dexter soon becoming the leader of his own secret society, the *Shí bèi*, which was created for the purpose of protecting Hong Kong neighborhoods from corruption.

But Moran was still a *gwai lo* – a white-skinned foreigner – which Kun Lin's son, Chao, continued to exploit in an ongoing rivalry. So Moran cemented his presence on the island by marrying the daughter of a prominent Chinese industrialist. Together they had one daughter, Chin Chi Ho, known now as Straw Sandal, who works as Dragon Head's second-in-charge.

"Aside from his criminal and gambling enterprises, Moran actually does a lot of good," Alice's notes went on to say. "He feeds the poor, provides people with jobs, protection, and stability, with crime in the neighborhoods he controls almost nonexistent."

"Except for the crimes he commits," Wilcox muttered to

himself, and with a swipe of his finger, he brought an image of Dragon Head onto the screen.

Moran's Irish ancestry was obvious because of his stocky physique and white skin, especially on his bald cranium, tattooed as it was, as were his shoulders and arms. It was a move no doubt calculated to make him look less *gwai lo* and more fearsome, with body art the color of storm clouds.

Another swipe showed Moran in the company of more than a dozen *Shí bèi* fighters. Moran was in a tank top that showed off his muscular arms. The fighters, all lean and young, were in loose black karate "gi" pants and T-shirts. A footnote from Alice explained the term *Shí bèi*, which means "ten tens," which Alice said was a reference not only to the level of pain a fighter must endure, but be able to inflict as well.

The next swipe brought an image of two women onto his screen. They were standing together in front of the heavy wooden doors of the Zhongzhen Martial Arts Academy, which doubled as Dragon Head's residence. The taller of the two was identified as Dragon Head's lover, Xin Li. The shorter of the two was identified as Straw Sandal. Body language indicated hostility between the two women.

*Division in the ranks,* thought Wilcox. *Looks promising.*

Another swipe brought an enlargement of Xin Li onto his screen. She was leaving a highrise building in Hong Kong and was looking to her left, her expression hard, her lips pinched, like she was angry. She had coal-black hair, cut short to her neck, and was a full head taller than the two Chinese men with her, one of whom was Dragon Head himself, along with an unnamed bodyguard.

Wilcox swiped his screen again and looked at the next photo. It was an enlargement of a passport photo of Straw Sandal. She had none of her father's features save flawless white skin and rosy cheeks. Other images showed Dragon Head conversing with each of the women individually in various locations, plus more photos of him conversing with both women together. A final photo showed Xin Li and Dragon Head dining in a restaurant. Also at the table was Straw Sandal, who was glaring at Xin Li, who was glaring back at her. In total, the pictures established an undeniable link between Dragon Head and the women who murdered Amber.

Sitting back, Wilcox thought about what he had just read and seen, and with a troubled frown, he forwarded Alice's email to Gustaves and Charlie, then sent a text to Alice, thanking her for her help. He then went to the bathroom to splash water in his face.

Returning to his seat several minutes later, he saw the poultry delegates, specifically the women, still chatting and laughing. The two men were still focused on their laptops, although one of them did look up and make eye contact. When Wilcox nodded, the man did not respond.

Once in his seat, Wilcox picked up his phone and dialed Charlie, who was staring intently at the photos on her screen. In her left ear was a soft plastic bud, which was connected by an air tube to a tiny inline microphone, which was wired to her cell phone several feet away.

"What have you found?" Wilcox asked.

"First, the good news," said Charlie. "I ran the women's names through the usual databases and got hits. As we speak, they're on board a commercial flight to San Francisco."

Wilcox sat forward. "San Francisco? That's where—"

"—Talanov is, yes, I know, which brings me to the bad news. We can't reach him because his phone is switched off. And we don't know where he is."

"So the women who killed Amber weren't after Diane?"

"Nope. They're after Alex."

"Do we know why?"

"Not yet."

"And the virus they planted?"

"My guess at this point: a distraction, to keep us chasing our tails while the women went after Alex. Shaw of course thinks the Chinese government is involved, but I disagree. Dragon Head? Yes. Beijing? No way."

"Are you sure the virus was nothing more than a distraction?"

"I'm working to confirm that, because there's some code that I haven't been able to dissect and analyze yet, but as it looks to me now, the virus doesn't have much of a function except as an oil slick."

"Translation, please?" asked Wilcox just as Anshika Kumar, one of Charlie's analyst colleagues, touched Charlie on the shoulder.

"Coffee?" Anshika asked.

"You know I don't drink that awful stuff they serve in the cafeteria," Charlie replied. "I only go for — "

" — the freshly ground organic, shade-grown, fair-trade, single-plantation Central American espresso beans, yes, I know. I was asking if I could have one."

Anshika nodded toward the espresso machine nestled in a cubicle beside Charlie's copy machine.

Charlie grinned. "Help yourself. The old man's out of town."

"I heard that!" shouted Wilcox over the phone.

Anshika covered her mouth and laughed, then tiptoed toward the espresso machine, as if Wilcox might hear her footsteps.

"You were saying?" asked Wilcox irritably.

"That's right, my oil slick," said Charlie, speaking into her phone again. "As you know, oil spills are a mess to clean up. Just the other night, for instance, I dropped a bottle of olive oil on the floor. It took me forever to clean up, and I went through a ton of paper towels, and because it made such a mess, I forgot about my casserole in the oven, which meant I ended up torching the thing. I mean, I still ate it - well, some of it, anyway - and it wasn't all that bad, even though the top was kind of charred and the inside was kind of burned, but not entirely. But that's beside the point. My point is, if I hadn't made such a mess by dropping that bottle of olive oil — "

"You're going to have to stop with the olive oil analogy and spell this out for me."

"Don't you ever cook?"

"*No,* I don't cook," snapped Wilcox, "and you know that. Now, what are you talking about?"

"Don't be so grouchy. Jeez. What do you have, low blood sugar? I've said this before, sir, but I'll say it again: you really should go keto."

"*Charlie!*"

"Okay, *okay.* The virus is, well, a virus, and as such, is alarming, although it doesn't appear to have the DNA necessary to penetrate very deep or do much damage apart from making a huge mess for us to clean up. But in doing so – in cleaning up that mess – we're being distracted from their actual intention, which is locating Alex."

"Then Alex was right," said Wilcox. "The assassination attempt on Diane and the search for him by someone in China are completely unrelated."

"Correct, even though they tried locating his whereabouts by including searches on you and Diane, which confirms a connection among you three."

"Which is why they targeted Amber –"

" – to access Diane's SCI files –"

" – figuring she would know where Alex was."

"Which of course she did," said Charlie, completing the thread. "I called Diane to let her know that I'd located the two women, and she called Shaw, who's ordered a grab team to apprehend them once their plane lands."

"Good work, Charlie, but I still think we should order protection for Alex."

"We don't know where he is, remember? How can we order protection if we don't know where he is?"

"Those two women seem to know."

"We don't know that for sure."

"Then why are they on a flight to San Francisco?"

Charlie did not reply.

"I'm rerouting my flight," said Wilcox. "Those women seem

to know where he is, and that means Alex has been compromised."

"Can you reroute a flight like that? I thought you were just hitching a vacation ride."

"As of now I'm back on the clock, which means I've got seniority."

"And the grab team?"

"They may succeed, and I hope they do, but in case they don't..."

"What do you need me to do?"

"Get me an address for Talanov by the time I land. You've got an hour."

# CHAPTER 17

Forty minutes later, Wilcox's phone vibrated and Wilcox answered it on the second ring. "Tell me you found him," he said.

"Yes and no," Charlie replied, entering a command that brought a series of receipts to her screen. "His phone is still switched off, and untraceable, but there are several credit card purchases in and around the Mission District, The Castro, and Bernal Heights, so we know he's in that part of the city. But there's no discernible pattern or cloister of purchases that would allow us to pinpoint a location in proximity to any specific community center. And no hotel, either, meaning he's obviously staying with Babikov. Unfortunately, everything we're getting is after the fact, meaning nothing yet in real time."

"How about his call history? Can you identify Babikov's number from that list? Maybe trace it to a location?"

"One number stands out – Babikov's, no doubt – but it's a burner – i.e., a cash purchase from a kiosk – and the caller has been careful not to phone or text Talanov from a single location. Cell tower use is all over the map."

"Where is it now?"

"No signal. No idea."

"Did Alex rent a car? Can we track it with GPS?"

"Nope," answered Charlie. "Someone no doubt picked him up."

"What about the Quiet Waters Community Center?"

"Are you sure that's the name of the place? I can't find any record of it anywhere."

"That's what Alex said it was."

"Sorry, Boss, but there's no record of any community center by that name."

"Then run a search on every community center, charitable organization, sports facility, youth club, gym, and halfway house in the city, especially those that are privately owned, including schools that have closed and been sold, old warehouses, and commercial buildings."

"On it."

"Do the same with Babikov, too. Get me the address of every variant spelling you can find."

"Already tried," answered Charlie. "There are a few Babikovs, or close variations, in other parts of California, but none in San Francisco."

"How about a marriage license, driver's license, or Social Security Number?"

"Nothing. There's no Zakhar Babikov in any databank."

"Relatives? A sister? A wife?"

"Sorry, Boss, I tried finding someone – anyone – but there are no primary or secondary listings anywhere. I've never encountered anyone without a digital footprint of some kind."

"Then how the hell does Talanov keep in touch with him?"

"Apart from that burner cell, I'm guessing they communicate via email, or snail-mail to a PO box in someone else's name. As far as email goes, owners of anonymous addresses take time to identify, especially if they're pseudonymously registered, and since I could find no San Francisco IP address in any of Talanov's emails – which, yes, I was able to hack – I'm guessing Alex is using an anonymous account himself."

Wilcox swore under his breath. "Keep looking," he said just as a series of beeps occurred on the line. Checking his screen, Wilcox saw an incoming call was being patched through from Gustaves. "Gotta go," he said. "Let me know the minute you find him."

"You got it."

After ending the call with Charlie, Wilcox took the call from Gustaves, which was a looped-in conference call from FBI task force commander Skip Shields, who was phoning from Terminal 2 of the San Francisco International Airport.

The airport itself was originally one hundred and fifty acres of cow pasture on the western shore of San Francisco Bay. Today, there are no cows within sight. Only asphalt and concrete and the never-ending blast of jet engines.

According to Shields, the flight from Washington, DC had landed and the aircraft was taxiing toward the arrival gate, where Shields and his team were waiting. Passengers in the arrival area had been cleared and the area cordoned off.

The takedown would be quick, Shields went on to explain. Agents would flood the air-craft and remove the two women. A passenger manifest had confirmed their targets to be in seats 34A and 34B, with Chin Chi Ho by the window and Xin Li on the aisle.

As planned, the plane pulled up to the gate and eight men in black uniforms streamed onto the aircraft and took the women into custody, with Shields furnishing a real-time report from his position near the cockpit door. Once the women were off the plane, Shields led the group along the jetway, then out a side door and down a private stairway to the tarmac, where two black SUVs were waiting. There he directed his men to put Xin Li in the lead vehicle and Chin Chi Ho in the other, both with their hands zip-tied behind them.

"Mission accomplished," Shields said into his phone moments later. "Xin Li and Chin Chi Ho are in custody, in separate vehicles, unable to communicate."

"Was there any trouble?" asked Gustaves.

"No, ma'am. Went like clockwork."

"Neither one put up a fight?"

"We didn't give them a chance."

"And you confirmed their identities?" asked Shaw, who was standing beside Gustaves.

"Yes, sir, as far as we could."

"What do you mean, as far as you could?"

"The faces of the two women matched the photos we were carrying, which in turn matched their names on the passenger manifest."

"But?"

"Neither woman was carrying ID. We searched their clothing and handbags, but came up empty."

"How can that be? IDs are required to purchase tickets. The airline verified their identities using Chinese passports, with surveillance cameras confirming that. Other cameras recorded them showing their passports and boarding passes to officials when they passed through airport security."

"All I can tell you is what we found," answered Shields, "which was nothing."

"And you searched them thoroughly?"

"Not a strip search, of course, but as thoroughly as we could."

"My people will take care of that. Let me know when you arrive at the interrogation site."

"Yes, sir."

At the same moment Shields and his team were leaving San Francisco International Airport, a Gulfstream was parking in front of a corporate hangar at the southern end of Oakland International Airport. On board the Gulfstream were Xin Li and Straw Sandal, plus the twelve *Shí bèi* fighters.

Their diversionary plan had been simple. Allow surveillance cameras in Washington to capture them purchasing tickets for San Francisco. Allow surveillance cameras to capture them passing through airport security. Allow surveillance cameras to capture them boarding the aircraft.

Except the two women boarding the aircraft were not Xin Li and Straw Sandal. They were imposters.

What the cameras did not capture was an identity switch inside the women's bathroom near the gate, where Xin Li and Straw Sandal exchanged clothing and wigs with two Chinese women waiting there for them. Ten minutes later, after makeup adjustments, the imposters boarded the San Francisco-bound aircraft looking like Xin Li and Straw Sandal. As predicted, Federal agents took the two imposters into custody when the aircraft landed.

Xin Li's phone chimed as she was leaving the Gulfstream. It was a text from AK in Hong Kong, who, like Charlie, had been trying to locate an address for the Quiet Waters Community Center. Unlike Charlie, AK had been monitoring Talanov's internet and cell phone usage for more than three months, as ordered by Xin Li, who wanted a backup plan in case she was not able to extract the needed information from Wu Chee Ming. As expected, Talanov was taking precautions to not reveal any identifying information between him and Babikov, including use of their names or where they were located. However, AK's search also involved generic internet and cell phone usage involving specific combinations of keywords in both Russian and English, such as Colonel, Major, Andrea, Spetsnaz, Russia, Wilcox, and Gustaves, and their frequency of usage, along with several KGB-specific codewords that only a former KGB agent would know. The result was a San Francisco IP address in the Hilltop Community Center.

With a cold smile, Xin Li led Straw Sandal and the *Shí bèi* fighters toward a pair of brown Suburbans parked near the hangar. Before long, they would arrive at the Hilltop Community Center. Before long, Talanov would be hers.

*Before long, she would have her revenge.*

# CHAPTER 18

Talanov, Ginie, and Su Yin were the only people left in the kitchen. The big meal was over and the kids were gone, although their excited shouts could be heard in the gym. Talanov was rinsing the last of the stockpots when a lanky Hispanic teenager named Manuel appeared in the doorway dressed in basketball gear.

"Hey, Mr. Talanov," said the boy.

"Hey, Manny, what's up?"

"After practice, a few of us will be hanging around for a game of HORSE. We thought maybe you'd want to join in. You know, maybe bet a few bucks on the side?"

Talanov feigned a steely glare and Manny grinned.

"Is that a yes?" asked Manny.

"It's a yes, but if I win, you're doing dishes around here for a year."

Manny ran back into the gym. "He's in!" he shouted to resounding cheers from the other kids.

Talanov looked over at Ginie with an exaggerated glare. "This is your fault, you know," he said. "You and that sucker shot of yours."

While Ginie laughed, Su Yin finished putting the utensils away in a drawer and came over to position herself directly in front of Talanov. She was still in her pink leotard and her hair was pulled back in a ponytail. "There's nothing ignominious in losing, Alex, especially when you gave it your best. Besides, if you'd won, Ginie would have done the cooking and she's nowhere *near* as good as you."

"Hey!" protested Ginie, flicking water at Su Yin.

Su Yin giggled, gave Talanov a hug, then turned and ran from the kitchen.

"She certainly adores you," said Ginie.

"What eleven year-old kid uses words like ignominious?"

"The three of them – Jingfei, Kai, and Su Yin – were home-schooled by their parents, who were eccentric geniuses, according to Jingfei."

"Is that why you run a homeschool program here at the center?"

"It's what started it," Ginie replied, "which has now grown into a charter school for more than twenty kids, with Jingfei and several parents lending a hand. We get to tailor our courses to what kids actually need, with greater one-on-one, and courses that include life skills as well as the basics."

"What happened to Jingfei's parents?" asked Talanov.

"Car crash. Jingfei doesn't think it was an accident, but the police report said differently. So the case was closed and so-cial workers were brought in to find the kids a foster home. When that didn't work out, there was talk about splitting them up. So the kids took off and have been on their own ever since. Jingfei and Kai were pretty angry when they arrived here at the community center. At God, the police, adults, the whole system. Which explains why Kai keeps getting in trouble, although Jingfei, who went through her own rough patch, seems to have stabilized. I'm not sure what caused her to straighten out, but she did."

"And Su Yin?"

"She's always been the sunny little moral compass of the three. And she certainly has taken to you."

"My cheering section of one," said Talanov with a chuckle.

"The kids all love you, Alex. I mean, sure, they love me more. Who wouldn't?"

Talanov laughed.

"So, if you ever get tired of that boring life of yours down in La La land, move up here. We could use another basketball coach."

"For what, comic relief while you keep suckering me with more of those crazy shots?"

"Sounds good to me," replied Ginie.

With a laugh, Talanov finished rinsing a stockpot and placed it upside down on a rack. With a grin, Ginie picked up the pot and began drying it.

"Besides," added Ginie, "how else am I going to keep feeding all of these kids?"

Talanov laughed again and dried his hands on a towel.

"Seriously, you were great," said Ginie. "So many of these kids have never had an adult male in their lives. Especially one who's such a good sport."

"It was fun being . . . normal."

"Alex, you are anything but normal."

"Yeah, well, I've never had much of a normal life, so when you finally get a taste of it, you really don't want it to stop. Has Zak told you much about us?"

"He said you were in the military together, and that you're working now as a consultant in Washington. That's about all I know."

"Zak gave you the sanitized version. The unadulterated version includes us being in the KGB, which was the Soviet Union's secret police, which means enemies from those days sometimes come calling to try to even a score. And others get caught in the crossfire."

"It can't be as bad as that."

Talanov continued to absently dry his hands while images of his wife's death slashed through his mind. Then the death of Larisa's friend, Jade, who had been a trafficking victim like Larisa. He could still see Jade's blood flooding the floor after she had been shot by the Russian mob.

Then another image, this one of a window exploding into a thousand pieces when Wilcox was gunned down in a hotel room.

"Alex, are you all right?" asked Ginie.

Talanov refocused and smiled. "I'm good. Are we done?"

Ginie laid aside the stockpot and looked up at Talanov with her dishtowel still in hand. "Okay, so maybe Zak did tell me a little more than I let on. He said your wife was killed."

"She wasn't just killed, Ginie, she was assassinated, and died in my arms. So did someone named Jade, as well as a good friend of mine named Bill, who almost did, except Larisa and I got him to a hospital and saved his life."

"Who's Larisa?"

Talanov looked away and thought about what to say. Was sending Larisa away the biggest mistake of his life? Or had it indeed saved her life, even if no one but he appreciated that fact?

"Alex?"

Talanov looked back at Ginie. "Point is, I'm the common denominator in everything that's happened. I'm the reason people get shot. I'm the reason people die. That's why I find it easier and safer to withdraw."

"That's a lousy way to live."

"I know, which is why I started driving up to see Zak. He says I need to start living again. That I can't keep living in fear of what *might* happen."

"Sounds like good advice."

"Maybe. But Zak's not the one who keeps getting people killed."

"Then why do you keep driving up to see him?"

Talanov frowned and again looked away.

"Is it because you want to believe him, and that down deep you know he's right?"

Talanov shrugged.

"But that it's taking a little more time to adjust than you thought it would?"

Talanov shrugged.

"Are those shrugs a yes?" asked Ginie, elbowing Talanov playfully.

"They're maybes," Talanov replied.

"Then, how about we practice those maybes?"

Talanov responded with a quizzical look.

"Pizza, tonight, with Zak and Emily. My treat."

Talanov shuffled uneasily.

"Don't tell me you don't eat pizza?"

"Of course I do. Who doesn't?"

"If it's an issue of wheat, they offer gluten-free as well as genuine organic sourdough. Awesome flavor. Perfect crust."

"It's not that, it's just . . . you know."

"Let's see, now, what was it Zak said again?" Ginie asked, rubbing her chin thoughtfully, as if struggling to recall what Zak had said about Talanov needing to start living again.

Talanov rolled his eyes.

"Look around you," said Ginie. "You've been playing basketball in a community center, which is about as public as it can get. You just cooked a huge meal for sixty neighborhood kids, who have been talking about you all over the place. Has anything bad happened as a result? No. You've been teaching martial arts, too, and going to the store, and doing all kinds of things. Don't you see? You *are* living again. You're taking Zak's advice."

Talanov was still unsure and his face showed it.

"We're talking pizza in a cafe down the hill," said Ginie. "A local joint. Now, hurry up and wipe down the kitchen while I make a reservation." She laid down her dishtowel, picked up a dishrag and tossed it Talanov's way.

"How come I have to wipe everything down?" asked Talanov, catching the rag.

"Because you lost the bet."

"You can be a real smart ass, you know that?"

"My middle name," Ginie replied.

# CHAPTER 19

Ten minutes later, Talanov and Ginie left the kitchen, crossed the basketball court and pushed through the double doors into the foyer. To their right was a large window that looked into an office. Behind a front counter were four desks, two of which were occupied by counselors Amina and Ramona. Their heads were down and their eyes were focused on their computer screens. Ramona had spiked black hair and metal studs in her nose, and her arms were covered with tattoos. Amina had auburn hair matted into dreadlocks, and was dressed in a tie-dyed T-shirt. Both girls were in their early twenties. Both were former prostitutes and former drug addicts who had made successful new starts in life.

Ginie rapped on the window and the girls smiled and waved.

Across the foyer was Emily's office, which was really an office within an office, with a small, windowed office built into one corner of a larger office. The inner office was where Emily had her desk. The outer office was like a waiting room, with a front counter, sofa, two chairs, a tall plant, and a wall of books.

The door into Emily's inner office was closed, but through the windows Talanov could see Zak and Emily on each side of Kai, who was staring at the floor, his shoulders slumped, his hands in the pockets of his baggy jeans. Zak was on one side of Kai, his hand on Kai's shoulder, talking earnestly, while Emily, angry and exasperated, kept throwing up her hands while lecturing Kai from the other side.

"What's happening in there?" whispered Talanov.

"Kai keeps getting in trouble, but the cops all know Zak, so when they catch Kai, they bring him here rather than throwing him in lockup. So Zak pays the damages – or Emily does, as she constantly reminds everyone – after which she and Zak lecture Kai."

"How's that working out?"

"Take a wild guess. Personally, I'd let Kai sit inside a jail cell for a few days before having him assigned to a work detail somewhere. Once his actions start costing him, he'll figure things out."

Sitting huddled on the sofa, Jingfei looked up from her phone and saw Ginie and Talanov. She hurried out of the office and ran over to them. "Can we talk for a minute?" she asked.

"Sure," answered Ginie.

"I'll head back into the gym," said Talanov.

Jingfei grabbed him by the arm. "Actually, it's your help I need."

"Mine? Okay, what's up?"

"You've got to talk to Zak," Jingfei said. "They've been in there for, like, two hours, and Zak needs to lighten up."

"What do you mean?"

"He needs to quit telling Kai the courts are going to take us kids away."

"Is that true? Is there a danger of that happening?"

"I suppose."

"You suppose?"

"Okay, yes, there is," Jingfei conceded. "But you don't understand."

"Understand what? What is it that Kai keeps doing?"

"Break-ins, shoplifting, stealing stuff. Kai's really good at stealing stuff, and he almost never gets caught, until lately, and now it's become this big issue."

"Seems like an easy fix. Kai stops doing what he's doing. Zak then stops the lecturing. Everybody wins."

"It's not that simple."

"Why not?"

"Because Kai won't stop, and before you ask why, it's because Kai thinks the courts are going to take us away, so why quit, because Zak keeps saying they're going to take us away, which to Kai is the same as Zak saying he's going to *let* the courts take us away, which means Zak is deserting us in spite of all that I-will-never-desert-you bullshit of his."

Talanov responded with a look of bewilderment at Jingfei's rambling sentence.

"I don't understand," Talanov said.

Taking Talanov by the arm, Jingfei turned him around and pointed at the 13:5 sign above the doors into the gym. "See that sign up there?"

"Yeah."

"It's a reference to a Bible verse – Hebrews 13:5 – which says, I will never desert you. So when Zak tells Kai the courts are going to take us away, he's saying that sign up there is a lie because Zak's the same as *letting* the courts take us away, which makes Kai want to keep breaking into places and stealing stuff because he wants the courts to hurry up and take us away since it's going to happen anyway, so why not get it over with now rather than later, before he starts liking it here, which he doesn't want to do because it would be too painful to start liking it here and then get sent away, you know what I mean?"

*That is absolutely the longest sentence I think I've ever heard,* Talanov wanted to say. But he didn't. Instead, he said, "I don't know much about the Bible, but I do know Zak, and if Zak says he'll never desert you, then he won't."

"Look, I'm not saying Zak's a bad guy – okay? – or that Kai doesn't need to stop what he's doing. And I know Zak is, like, trying to let Kai know how serious this is, and that there are consequences for his actions, but he's *got* to quit telling Kai about the courts taking us away. Talk to Zak. You know him better than anyone. Maybe he'll listen to you."

"Are you saying this is Zak's fault?"

"Yes!"

"Seriously?"

"Okay, no, maybe not entirely, or maybe not at all, but if Zak wants Kai to stop, then he's got to stop first, and that's just the way it is, like it or not, and you're the only one who can make him stop."

Talanov opened his mouth to reply but Jingfei cut him off.

"*Please!* I already told you how long Zak and Emily have been in there with Kai, which is, like, for two hours. Would you listen to anyone yelling at you for that long?"

Talanov remembered being yelled out for hours on end when he was sixteen and in the military, where he was made to stand in line with other recruits while drill sergeants at their training camp in Siberia took turns marching back and forth in front of them, yelling insults and dousing them with freezing water. The only way he made it through those sessions was by thinking of a warm beach somewhere, which was precisely what Kai was doing right now: tuning out.

"You know I'm right, don't you?" said Jingfei. "I mean, look at them. Emily and Zak don't even listen to one another, and believe me, I've heard them yelling and fighting, so how can they expect Kai to listen when they don't listen? Kai didn't even get to eat with us, so I brought him some food because they wouldn't let him leave, and he's still in there, getting hammered. You've got to do something!"

Talanov opened his mouth to reply but Jingfei cut him off again.

"I'm right, aren't I, Ginie? Go ahead and tell him. Tell Alex to do something. Tell him to talk to Zak."

With a grin, Ginie made a sweeping motion with her hand toward the office for Talanov. It was a gesture that said, "Over to you."

Talanov responded with a, "Gee, thanks a lot," scowl before returning his attention to Jingfei. "What kinds of things do Zak and Emily fight about?"

"Money, mostly, and political crap. Emily thinks socialism is great, and, well, you can imagine what Zak thinks about that."

"Yeah, that the only people who think it's great are those

who have never lived under it."

"Word for word. I mean, Emily keeps giving away all kinds of freebies to strangers, but splits a seam when Zak helps Kai. She's, like, this super hypocrite, and Zak needs to grow a pair and stand up to her. But he's first got to quit saying the kind of stuff he's been saying. Otherwise, we get sent away. So, *please*, talk to Zak."

Before Talanov could reply, a cry of panic erupted from the office.

"No, no, no, no, *no!*" Amina began shouting. Her attention was on her computer and she was hurriedly entering commands. She then jumped up and began grabbing her hair, not knowing what to do.

"Talk to him!" Jingfei said a final time before running into the office, where she eased Amina aside and slipped into her chair.

"What happened?" asked Jingfei.

"Everything just . . . froze. Some government office – or so I thought – sent a notice of some money we supposedly owed. They said an invoice was attached . . . that this was their final notice before turning it over for collection."

"Don't worry," said Jingfei, entering a flurry of commands.

"I'm really sorry," said Amina.

"Seriously, it's okay. They're sneaky, the assholes who send out this kind of shit."

"Wow, I've never heard you swear like that."

"Yeah, I know. I just get so . . . angry at people who do this kind of thing."

"Gee, I never would have guessed."

Jingfei laughed and kept working the keyboard.

"How do you know what to do?" asked Amina.

"My dad was, like, this king of the computer nerds and he homeschooled me in everything he knew."

"Dude, that is so cool that you were homeschooled by your dad."

"Not so cool that somebody killed him."

By now, Talanov and Ginie were standing behind Jingfei, watching her work the keyboard like a seasoned professional.

"You were homeschooled by your dad?" asked Talanov.

"Dad and Mom, both," answered Jingfei. "Mom taught us to cook and sew and haggle with fishermen down at the wharves. She was the practical one. She even taught us how to change a car tire. Dad loved video games, computers, and how the internet was being used to monitor the masses. My dad was a white hat who could hack any system in the world."

"You said he was killed. What happened?"

"We were living in New Jersey, in this small town due west of New York, when they were killed in a car crash in rural Pennsylvania. The cops said it was an accident but I don't think it was. Anyway, me and Kai and Su Yin were placed in the system and got shuffled around a lot. Nobody wanted three Asian kids, especially ones as old as me and Kai, so when the social workers began talking about splitting us up, we took off and ended up here."

"Are the cops, like, looking for you now?" asked Amina.

"Zak pulled some strings, so we're okay."

"Well, I'm glad you're here," said Amina.

"Me, too," responded Jingfei, bridging three keys with her fingers, tapping Enter, then entering another command, then using another bridge command before tapping Enter a final time. "Done," she said, leaning back.

"I'm, like, so impressed," said Amina, "but I have no idea what you did."

"I first had to find the rootkit, then locate and remove the executable file."

Jingfei looked up at Amina and knew by her blank stare that she had not understood a single word.

"Never mind," Jingfei said, giving Amina back her chair. "It's gone. You're good."

The door to Emily's office slammed and everyone looked to see Kai storm across the foyer and into the gym.

"Kai, wait!" shouted Jingfei, running after him.

After Jingfei pulled open the double doors and entered the gym, Talanov looked across the foyer at Emily lecturing Zak in her office. She was waving her arms angrily while Zak listened patiently, his muscular arms folded in front of him.

"Maybe we should cancel our pizza," suggested Ginie.

"From the looks of it," said Talanov, "I think pizza is just what we need."

# CHAPTER 20

Talanov knew he was not much of a diplomat, so he simply walked into Emily's office and told Zak and Emily to go upstairs and get ready, that they were all going out for pizza. After a variety of excuses and protests, which Talanov refused to entertain, Zak and Emily grudgingly went upstairs to shower and change clothes.

An hour later, they returned. Emily, who was focused on her phone, was dressed in a long maroon cardigan over an ill-fitting floral dress. With her graying hair pinned back in a loose bun, she looked more hippie than lawyer. Zak was wearing ironed cargo jeans and a black-and-white striped shirt that made him look like a football referee.

Talanov and Ginie were standing near the front door with Jingfei when Zak and Emily approached. Talanov was wearing jeans and a bulky sweater. Ginie was wearing a blue denim vest over a lightweight summer dress. The dress was emerald green and her black hair was hanging loose across her shoulders. Jingfei was in her usual black tights and a white cotton work shirt, with the tails tied in a knot near one hip.

Over the echoes of a basketball game being played in the gym, Emily looked up from her phone when she heard Kai laughing with Amina in the front office. They were pointing at something on Amina's monitor while Su Yin flicked a feather duster across the keyboards at other desks.

"What is he doing?" Emily demanded. She pointed at Kai with her phone.

"Taking a break," Jingfei replied.

Emily then noticed the canister vacuum on the floor in her office. "My office door is open!"

"And I will make sure it gets locked once Kai is finished."

"I want that floor spotless by the time we get back."

A text message chimed and Emily looked back at her phone.

Jingfei took a calming breath and with a smile looked at Zak. "I brought the van around," she said, tossing Zak the keys before noticing his referee shirt had been tucked into his cargos, which had been carefully ironed with a crease down the front. "Ironed cargoes? Seriously? No way am I letting you walk out the door looking like that." With a growl of disgust, she pulled out his shirttail and smoothed out the wrinkles.

When Jingfei was finished, Zak began rocking his hips back and forth while pumping his fists up and down in the air.

Jingfei grabbed Zak by the arm and physically stopped him. "What are you *doing?*"

"The happy dance," Zak replied. "Su Yin taught me. 'Cause we are going out for pizza and I am looking *good.*"

"Do not *ever* do that again. Anywhere. Ever. Are we clear?"

Zak laughed and kissed Jingfei on the forehead.

"Get out of here," Jingfei said, pushing Zak toward the door.

Zak motioned for Emily, who stopped abruptly when her cell phone chimed again. "Something's come up," she said, reading a text message on her screen. "One of my undocumented clients is worried about losing her benefits. I need to hang back and take care of this."

"She'll be fine," Jingfei said, snatching the phone from Emily's hand.

"Hey!" cried Emily. She reached for her phone but Jingfei blocked her.

"When was the last time you went out with your husband?" Jingfei asked.

Emily tried grabbing her phone again but Jingfei blocked her again.

"Jingfei! Give me my phone," demanded Emily.

"No," Jingfei replied.

"Jingfei, it's all right," said Zak.

"No, Zak, it's not all right. You guys never go out. You're always stressed. Some things are more important than work."

"That's because someone around here needs to keep making money," snapped Emily. "Now, *give me my phone.*"

"Not going to happen," answered Jingfei. "You're going out for pizza with your husband and you're going to enjoy it."

"You are the child here, Jingfei, and you will do what I tell you."

"Actually, I'm nineteen and legally an adult, so you can be mad at me all you want because I am not giving you this phone. That's because you don't know when to switch it off and pay attention to the one person who matters more than all of your stupid clients."

"Jingfei!" said Zak. "That's enough."

"It's true, Zak. She'll spend fourteen hours a day helping welfare recipients – i.e., total strangers – but won't take an hour away from her beloved phone to go out and eat pizza with her husband." To Emily: "It's a stupid phone, Emily. You'll survive. So will your clients."

"My phone has sensitive information on it – private information – so I am not about to go out and leave it with a teenager in an unsecured location."

"All right, then, give me your keys."

"What? Why?"

"Your keys. So I can lock it up."

"*Give me my phone.*"

"No."

"Jingfei!"

Jingfei folded her arms and stood firm. "I am not surrendering this phone, so you might as well hand me your keys so that I can lock it up safely in your desk."

The two women glared at one another for nearly a full minute, with neither one backing down until Emily finally slapped her keys into Jingfei's outstretched hand and Jingfei took them into Emily's inner office, unlocked her desk drawer, slipped the phone inside the drawer, locked it again, then brought the keys back to Emily.

"Safe and sound," said Jingfei with a smile.

"I will deal with you later," hissed Emily, storming past Zak and out the front door.

Avoiding eye contact with the others, Zak silently followed.

"He looks tired, and beaten," observed Ginie.

"He is," Talanov replied.

"We'll be at the Sour Dough Pizza Parlor," announced Ginie.

"Dude, I *love* that place!" Ramona called out from behind her desk in the front office. "Doggy bag. Don't forget!"

"Have you ever known me to walk out of there with a doggy bag?"

Ramona laughed.

"See you in a couple of hours," said Ginie, nodding for Talanov to follow as she, too, pushed open the heavy, blue front door and stepped out into the night.

The Sour Dough Pizza Parlor was not that far from the community center, although there was no easy way to get there because streets in this part of town twisted, turned, and zigzagged all over the place. Not only that, the location of the restaurant was beyond the crisscrossing lanes of Interstate 280 and Highway 101.

Sandwiched between a corner grocery store and an office supply, the Sour Dough Pizza Parlor had an awning that looked the Italian flag, with wide stripes of red, white, and green. In the window was a neon sign that lit up the night with its name.

Zak parked across the street in a lot that was already full of cars. Squeezing his van into a no-parking zone, he switched off the engine and everyone climbed out. The evening was cool and the establishment was full of chatting couples.

"That awning has the same national colors as Ingushetia," Talanov said while they were crossing the street.

"Ingu-what?" asked Ginie.

"Ingushetia."

"You're making that up."

"Geography, for two hundred," proclaimed Talanov. "And the answer is: what is the name of Russia's tiniest republic, which lies north of Georgia, between the Caspian and Black Seas?"

"Do *not* tell me you watched Jeopardy in Russia."

"At KGB headquarters," said Talanov. "At first, recordings had to be smuggled in, since TV shows from our corrupt, capitalist enemy were forbidden. I convinced them to relax the ban by arguing how Jeopardy was actually a good source of American trivia, which would be extremely useful for a spy. Among the agents and guards, we'd have contests to see who was smartest. I was grand champion, of course."

"Unbelievable," said Ginie with a shake of her head.

"Don't encourage him," said Zak, pulling open the front door.

Inside, Ginie bypassed a line of waiting people and approached the front counter, where a voluptuous Italian hostess had a phone wedged between her shoulder and ear. Without interrupting her conversation, the hostess signaled them to the back of a line. Ginie looked into the restaurant and caught the eye of a thin man with dark curly hair, who hurried toward them when he recognized Ginie.

"Ginie, how lovely to see you!" the thin man gushed. He kissed her on each cheek, then snapped his fingers for some menus, which the hostess handed to him.

"Everyone, this is Marcelo, the owner," said Ginie, presenting Marcelo to the others. "He makes the best sourdough pizza in all of California."

Marcelo beamed proudly and bowed.

"What's the difference between sourdough and normal?" asked Talanov. "What makes this one so great?"

Ginie leaned toward Marcelo. "As you can tell, dear Alex is a sourdough pizza virgin."

"A *virgin?*" asked Marcelo with a nod, his eyebrows arched with delight.

"That's right. His first sourdough pizza ever."

"Then you have brought him to the right place," Marcelo replied. "Come, your table is waiting." He led them through the crowded restaurant toward a circular booth in the far corner of the restaurant.

"Your bathrooms are where?" Talanov asked Marcelo before reaching the table.

"Front counter, turn right, down the hall."

Talanov thanked Marcelo and made his way back to the front counter just as the hostess laid the receiver crossways on the cradle and updated her reservation seating chart.

"Keeps it from ringing when we already have a waiting line two hours long," the hostess explained. "How can I help?"

Talanov handed the hostess his American Express card. "The people I'm with are going to insist on paying for our meal. I'd like you to make sure that doesn't happen. Run a tab using my card. No one at my table sees a check." He took out a fifty-dollar bill and slipped it to the hostess. "For the extra trouble."

"No trouble at all," the hostess replied with a flirtatious smile. She stuffed the cash into her bra, then processed Talanov's card and handed it back. "Anything else, you let me know."

With a polite smile, Talanov accepted his card, thanked her, then turned toward the bathroom at the same moment two brown Suburbans took the exit ramp off the 101. They were following a GPS map on a small screen on the dashboard. Their destination: the Hilltop Community Center.

# CHAPTER 21

The CIA Gulfstream parked in front of the Asia Pacific Global Enterprises hangar, which the CIA owned and used as their San Francisco port of entry. The hangar was a large rectangular metal shed with an office at one end. Above the door was a lighted sign that made it look like a legitimate business. In truth it was anything but that, with domestic and international secrets shuttled in and out of the hangar every single day, three hundred and sixty-five days a year.

Wilcox peered out the window of the Gulfstream into the darkness. For a man who spent most of his career operating in the shadows, he had never felt comfortable living that way. It was simply a requirement for the career he had chosen.

That choice had been a costly one. Three ex-wives and a drinking problem – according to some people, anyway – not that he agreed, although, admittedly, it was not something he could entirely deny.

Then there was Danny, his estranged son for over a decade until Talanov brought them back together again. In fact, apart from Talanov and Gustaves, he had no friends. How pathetic was that? And yet, strangely, he knew his work with the CIA had accounted for something, even if his accomplishments were small in the grand scheme of world politics. Simply put: he had chosen this job because it was the right thing to do, just as Danny had joined the Marines because it was the right thing to do.

Maybe he had done something right, after all, in spite of everything his ex-wives had said about him, not that he could entirely deny those ugly truths, either.

When the engines began to whine down, Wilcox retrieved his carry-on case and wheeled it toward the front of the craft. Close behind were the poultry delegates, who were grumbling about having had their flight rerouted to San Francisco.

"See you next trip," Wilcox told Stephanie, who was standing by the door.

"Can't wait," Stephanie replied.

When Wilcox narrowed his eyes, Stephanie playfully shoved him out the door.

At the bottom of the stairs, Wilcox angled across the tarmac toward a nondescript gray sedan, where a young man was holding a placard with Wilcox's name on it. Sporting a trendy haircut and dressed in a tailored blue suit, he looked fresh out of an Ivy League school. Twenty feet away was a minibus toward which everyone else was walking.

Wilcox approached the young man. "I'm Wilcox," he said.

"And I'm Bradford," the young man replied. "I'll be your driver tonight."

"Is that your first name or your last?"

"First. My last name is Tambling-Humphreys."

"Of course it is. Well, Bradford, you're off the hook. I won't be needing a driver."

"But I was given specific instructions."

"And I'm canceling those instructions. Give me your keys."

"I need to call this in."

"If you don't hand me your keys, as in right now, you're in for a big career change. Are we clear?"

Bradford reluctantly handed Wilcox the keys.

"Smart lad," said Wilcox, pushing a button on the fob that opened the trunk, where he placed his carry-on suitcase.

"Can I at least grab a ride back to the rental agency?" Bradford asked, watching Wilcox slide behind the wheel.

"Hitch a ride on the minibus," Wilcox replied, inserting the ignition key and starting the engine just as his cell phone vibrated with a call from Charlie. He touched the answer button, put the phone on speaker, then shifted into gear and squealed away. "What did you find?" he asked.

"I've got some good news, some bad news, and some really bad news. Which do you want to hear first?"

"Charlie, I'm not in the mood."

"All right, let's start with the good news," Charlie said, looking at one of her monitors, which showed a photo of the Quiet Waters Community Center. The photo had been enlarged to show the bright blue double doors with Psalm 23:2 painted above the door. Charlie explained how the community center, which is actually the Hilltop Community Center, was known informally as Quiet Waters. "A quick call to the local police station confirmed that fact," she added. "Ownership is in the name of Emily Chang, attorney-at-law, whose office is located there."

"No wonder we couldn't find it," said Wilcox. "It's owned by a third party. Text me the address. I'm on my way."

"You may want to hold off on that."

"What for?"

"Because Talanov isn't there. Credit card activity shows him to be at a restaurant called the Sour Dough Pizza Parlor. I am texting the address . . . now."

Wilcox's phone chimed receipt of the text.

"Now for the bad news," Charlie continued. "The two Asian women we took into custody at San Francisco International Airport were imposters."

Wilcox cursed, then said, "Call Talanov. He needs to be warned."

"His phone is switched off. Babikov's, too."

"How about Emily Chang?"

"Her phone keeps going to voicemail."

"Then call the restaurant."

"Sorry, Boss, but that's the really bad news. I've tried more than a dozen times but their phone is constantly busy."

Wilcox cursed again.

"What do you want me to do?" asked Charlie.

"Call San Francisco PD. Have them send a squad car to the center, then follow up with photos of the two women and say they're armed and dangerous. I'll head to the restaurant."

"Want me to send a squad car to the restaurant?"

"No. I don't want sirens and I don't want anyone broadcasting Talanov's location."

"You got it. Anything else?"

"Yeah. Pray we're not too late."

# CHAPTER 22

"See you tomorrow," said Jingfei to the last of the basketball players leaving the community center. It was a healthy mix of about sixty-percent boys and forty-percent girls, about half of whom were Chinese. A few remained out front, talking and laughing, but most headed away in different directions carrying their gym bags.

Having already locked the front gate of the skatepark, Jingfei pulled closed the heavy blue doors and made sure they were locked. When she did, she didn't notice the pair of brown Suburbans driving past.

Jingfei paused in front of Emily's open office door to watch Kai vacuuming the floor of the inner office. The vacuum was a canister that Kai was wearing like a backpack, with a long hose that extended to a nozzle that Kai was using to get into the corners. In the outer office, Su Yin was dusting the leaves of a cornstalk plant. The plant was actually taller than Su Yin, who had to stand on her tiptoes in order to reach the highest leaves.

When Jingfei entered the office, Kai saw her make a slicing motion across her throat and Kai switched off the canister.

"Talk to me," Jingfei said. "Are you okay? What they put you through was crap."

Kai shrugged.

Jingfei walked around Emily's desk and gave Kai a hug. "I love you, little brother. I mean, you're an annoying little brat, but I love you with waterfalls of kisses."

Waterfalls of kisses was a reference to what their mother used to say when she smothered them with kisses before bed, which Kai used to fend off, even though he eagerly waited for them each night. In the years since, Jingfei kept the tradition alive by smooching and hugging Kai and Su Yin to cheer them up.

When Jingfei advanced toward Kai with puckered lips and making kissing noises, Kai ducked away with a cry of disapproval. But Jingfei caught him and they hugged each other.

"Why do you fuss over Zak so much?" asked Kai, sitting on the edge of Emily's desk.

"Same reason I fuss over you. Because he needs someone to fuss over him, and he doesn't get much from Emily, who's too busy to notice the dumb stuff he does to try and get her attention."

"Like tucking in his shirt?"

"And ironing his cargoes. One he does for attention, the other because he's clueless. So I fuss over him, which is something families do."

"Except Zak isn't our family," said Kai.

"Yes, he is. Not like a blood relative or anything like that, but being a family is a lot more than DNA. It's a bond you make and keep, no matter what."

"Until he kicks us out."

"Zak would never do that," said Su Yin, joining them.

"Maybe not you," said Kai. "But look at how him and Emily keep yelling at me. I'm the one they want to get rid of."

"That is so not true," said Jingfei. "I know Zak isn't handling things the way he ought to, and that he doesn't stand up to Emily, but you got to remember something: Zak never had a dad. I mean, he did, but not one that he knew. All he knew were his drill instructors, who trained him to be this commando badass. He had no parents to learn from, and here he is, trying to be one, because he wants to be one for us, even though he doesn't know how."

"How do you know all of that?"

"Because I talk to him, Kai, and I listen, and I spend time with him. You could, too, if you'd quit getting in trouble. Zak's trying really hard, but you don't make it easy. Does he need to quit hammering you with that threat about the courts taking us away? Yes, and I've talked to Alex about it, and Alex says he'll talk to Zak."

Kai snorted and shook his head.

"He will!" insisted Jingfei.

"Yeah, right."

"He said he would, Kai. Come on!"

"Even if he does, what good will it do?"

"You need to give him a chance."

"Don't you get it?" yelled Kai. "The courts are going to take us away."

The shout drew the attention of Ramona and Amina, who were working in the lighted office across the darkened foyer. They both looked up from their keyboards, then went back to work.

"Zak will not let that happen," Jingfei said, taking Kai by the hands.

"You can't promise that," Kai replied, jerking away. "Zak's married to Emily, and not even a commando badass can stand up to her."

"Well, I can, and I won't let it happen. Now, hurry up and finish while I shut off the lights in the gym. We can then go practice some jumps."

"How about we watch a movie?"

"Boring. So, come on and finish up so we can go outside."

"She just doesn't get it," said Kai once Jingfei had disappeared into the gym.

"Get what?" asked Su Yin.

"I know Jing believes Zak won't ditch us, but Zak is for sure going to ditch us, and there's nothing we can do."

"But Zak promised he would never—"

"I know you want to believe him," said Kai, butting in, "but that stupid sign of his out there is bullshit."

"It is not!"

"Yes, it *is*, Su Yin. Zak won't stand up to Emily because they've got no money, and Emily blames me because I've become, like, this huge problem. So she yells at Zak, and Zak won't stand up to her – or can't – because she makes all the money."

"How do you know they've got no money?"

Kai unstrapped the canister, let it slide to the floor, then grabbed two paperclips off the counter and bent them open. After making sure Ramona and Amina weren't watching from across the foyer, he walked over to Emily's desk, where he knelt down in front of the drawer and inserted the paper-clips into the lock.

"What are you doing?" Su Yin whispered.

"A while back, Jingfei installed some spyware on Emily's phone," said Kai, twisting and maneuvering the paperclips until the lock clicked.

"Why?" asked Su Yin, kneeling beside Kai and watching him remove Emily's phone from the drawer.

"Doesn't matter, listen to this," said Kai, activating the phone, then navigating to the cloud, then navigating to a folder that contained audio files. He clicked the start button and they both listened to a recorded conversation between Emily and Zak, with Emily saying the community center was out of money and that her income was unable to absorb the added cost of three kids.

"Especially a problem like Kai," said Emily. "Juvie is where he belongs."

"Juvie is not the answer."

"He's not responding to anything else. He doesn't want to be here, Zak, and, frankly, I don't want him here, either. I've reached my limit. I'm done."

"Some wounds take time to heal, and those kids have been through a lot."

"It's been two years! How much time does he need? Look, I was happy to step in as a foster parent for a while, but this isn't working out. Do you hear the way Jingfei talks back to me? Never mind the money we've spent on Su Yin for all of her activities. This has to stop."

"Jingfei became the head of a family when she was barely a

teenager. As for the money we've spent on Su Yin, we haven't spent a dime. Her dance leotards were donated. Same with their bicycles and skateboards. They were rattletraps that I fixed up. Any costs were next to nothing."

"Regardless, it's my money you've been spending."

"I'll talk to Kai."

"The time for talking is over. We can't solve an unsolvable problem, and that's exactly what Kai is. I've already called a friend of mine down at the Juvenile Justice Center."

"They're our kids, Em," said Zak. "You don't toss out your kids when the going gets tough."

"They're *not* our kids and you need to get that through your head."

"I will not kick them out."

"Yes, you will. I've supported this fantasy of yours long enough. Don't forget, you came to this country illegally."

"Why would you bring that up?"

"To let you know how serious I am."

"And so you threaten me with, what, deportation? I have American citizenship!"

"In the name of Zachary Pyne, not Zakhar Babikov."

"And you know why I did that. I used British documents created for me so that I could come here legally . . . to get away from my old life . . . to make a new start."

"Those British documents were fake, and if the State Department finds out, they'll deport you. Because, like it or not, you're a former Soviet commando."

"You were fine with that when we met. We agreed that I would I buy the building, which cost me everything, and you would set up your practice here, while I took care of the daily operations."

"Which was fine until you brought those kids into our lives. I am tired of it, Zak, and I will not keep having my life turned upside down. Once Alex is gone, they are, too."

Kai shut down the application and returned Emily's phone to the desk drawer.

Tears welled up in Su Yin's eyes. "Zak said he would never desert us."

"Zak doesn't have a choice. They're kicking us out, Su Yin, and we need to get out of here before that happens."

# CHAPTER 23

"Wait a minute," said Talanov, holding up a hand to halt the conversation that had been going on around the table. "God spoke to you on TV? You mean, like, a voice? Are you sure you hadn't been drinking?"

Zak laughed. "No voice. I was watching this interview with a man who was on the upper deck of a passenger ferry when he saw a young boy fall into the water. So the man jumped in after him, and he wasn't even the boy's father. He was just this guy. No lifebuoy, no lifejacket, no nothing. He just jumped in. The danger, of course, was that the panic-stricken boy would grab him around the neck and both of them would drown. So the man swam over and stuck out his arm, which the boy grabbed, and while treading water, the man kept the boy afloat so that he could cough out the water he had swallowed, then calm down, then allow the man to talk him through what to do."

"How did this speak to you?" asked Ginie, taking a sip of her wine over the backdrop of laughter and conversation.

"After it was over and the boy was safe," Zak continued, leaning forward with his elbows on the table, "a reporter asked the man why he did it. And the man said, 'That's what love is all about; you make sacrifices for people.' The reporter, of course, reminded the man that he had never met the boy or his family, so how could he love someone he didn't know. And the man replied, 'Because that's what love is all about.' At that moment, I realized how many times God had jumped overboard to save me. And when I asked why, I heard him say, 'Because that's what love is all about.'"

Zak paused and shook his head.

"Trouble is, the guy I used to be was not a man of peace."

"Sometimes, that's just the kind of person God needs," said

Ginie. "Evil triumphs when good men do nothing."

The remark made Zak lean back with a thoughtful frown.

"Okay, my friends, one sourdough supreme," announced Marcelo, placing a large pizza in the center of the table. It was two feet in diameter, with a thick golden crust and toppings of red and green peppers, chorizo, goat and pecorino cheeses, roasted almonds, and chives. On top of this was a mix of fresh basil, oregano, and thyme, and on top of this was a generous drizzle of orange-flavored balsamic vinegar and garlic-infused olive oil.

"Looks good and smells terrific," said Talanov, scrutinizing the pizza. "But I've seen good-looking pizzas before. What makes this one so different?"

Ginie picked up a slice and jammed it in Talanov's mouth, forcing him to take a bite.

Talanov's startled expression suddenly brightened. "Thith ith *good*," he said, his words garbled because of food filling his mouth.

Ginie laughed. "And now you know."

While Talanov and the others were enjoying their pizza, Jingfei was pushing open the rear door of the community center and stepping out into the alley, which had once been paved, although years of neglect had taken its toll in the form of deep ruts, potholes, and broken chunks of concrete.

Retrieving her bike from a small shed attached to the rear of the community center, Jingfei walked it over to the skatepark, which adjoined the center and was surrounded by a high chain-link fence. Floodlights normally lit the area, but they had long since been shot out.

Built three years ago with grant money obtained from the city and state by Ginie, the skatepark was twice the size of a tennis court. Unlike a tennis court, however, which was flat, the skatepark was a three-dimensional obstacle course, with elevated platforms, ramps, walls, rails, steps, and two large depressions, or "bowls." One was called the "Small Bowl." It was the size of a two-car garage. Next to it was the "Big

Bowl," which was twice as large, but with a series of jumps in the middle.

Jingfei opened the squeaky gate and entered the skatepark just as Kai shot past on his bike. When Jingfei jumped back with a yelp, Kai let out a howling laugh.

In the dim light from a streetlamp half a block away, Jingfei watched the darkened silhouette of her brother racing along the top of a wide concrete wall. "Showoff!" she yelled just as Kai sailed off the end of the wall for several seconds of air time before landing on the angled side of the Small Bowl, where he picked up speed on the downhill, then across the bottom, then up the other side, where he pumped his legs and jumped his bike up onto an elevated concrete platform, where he hit his brakes and skidded to a stop.

"I can teach you that, if you want," Kai called out. "Unless of course you're scared."

"Jerk," muttered Jingfei while walking her bike around the perimeter. "Where's Su Yin?"

"Out here," Su Yin said from the bottom of the Big Bowl, where the shadows were deep.

Jingfei walked out to where Su Yin was lying on a sloping wall beside her bike, her hands folded behind her head, looking up at the sky. Jingfei laid her bike down and joined Su Yin on the concrete.

"What are you doing?" asked Jingfei.

"Remember when Zak used to come out here with us and tell us about the stars? He doesn't do that anymore."

"I remember when he took us out to that dirt track and you were doing three-sixties off those tabletops."

A long moment of silence passed while the wind turned suddenly cool.

"Is Zak really going to send us away?" Su Yin finally asked.

Jingfei sat up. "What? *No.*"

"Kai said he was."

"And Kai is wrong."

"But I heard Emily say it. From the spyware you put on her

phone."

"You *are* a jerk!" Jingfei shouted to Kai, who was still on top of the wall catching his breath. To Su Yin: "Not everything sounds like what you think it does."

"Emily said Kai's a problem that can't be solved. That he belongs in juvie. That she wants us gone."

"Yeah, well, sometimes Kai *is* a problem, just like I was, remember? But I came out of it and so will he. So don't worry. We're not going anywhere."

Jingfei reached over and pulled Su Yin close just as Kai tipped his front wheel off the edge of the platform, bounded down the angled ramp and sped out to his sisters, where he plopped down beside them.

"I told you not to tell her about Emily," Jingfei said, punching Kai on the arm.

"She needed to know," Kai replied.

"We are *not* getting kicked out, so quit scaring her like that."

Kai snorted and looked out toward the street, where a car drove past.

"Why did you do it?" asked Su Yin. "Why did you put spyware on Emily's phone?"

"It doesn't matter," Jingfei replied.

"Yes, it does," Kai called out. "Jing installed it because she heard Emily yelling at Zak about them not having any money and how I was to blame, so she put spyware on Emily's phone so that she could hack into their bank account and see for herself."

"What did you find out?" asked Su Yin.

"It doesn't matter," Jingfei said again.

"Yes, it does," answered Su Yin. "Quit treating me like I'm a kid."

"You're eleven. You *are* a kid."

"Kai thinks I'm old enough. He said I needed to know."

"Kai has a big mouth."

"Come on, Jing," said Kai. "She's smarter than either me or you were when we were eleven."

After an exasperated growl, Jingfei said, "Okay, yes, Zak and Emily are having some money problems, but not as bad as Emily says."

"What do you mean?"

"Ginie's applied for a lot of grant money – and got it – over a hundred thousand dollars – so the center's got plenty of operating funds, and Zak is great about getting donations like food and clothing. And he works his *butt* off making sure stuff gets done around the place."

"Then why is Emily making such a big deal about them not having any money?" asked Kai. "And why does she keep saying this is all my fault?"

"Because a lot of it *is* your fault, and Zak doesn't want to use the center's operating funds for the damages you've caused. Plus, Emily considers her income to be hers, not theirs. She even tried taking Zak's name off the bank account, which I know about because of the spyware, although the bank wouldn't let her do it because it was a joint account."

"So this really *is* my fault," said Kai.

"No, it's not," said Jingfei, "at least not all of it. I mean, I was a handful, too, when we first got here, which you probably don't remember. I argued with Zak all the time, I threw tantrums, I was hanging around with that gang of kids down the hill. We even broke into some stores and stole some stuff."

"You did all of that?"

"I tried to keep it from you, because, you know, I was supposed to be the responsible one, but I was just so . . . angry. But, yeah, I did all of that, and if I hadn't changed, I'd be in juvie by now."

"What made you change?" asked Su Yin.

"When I saw how much Zak was spending on Kai and how he was bending over backward to keep him out of trouble – I mean, even the cops were helping out because Zak kept pleading with them – I kind of woke up one day and realized he wasn't like all the other foster parents we'd had, that maybe I needed to quit making life so hard on him."

"Why didn't you tell me any of this?" asked Kai.

"I was embarrassed, and you kind of looked up to me, so I didn't want to admit any of the stuff I'd done. I didn't want you to think less of me, I guess."

Sitting together in the darkness of the skatepark, in the bottom of the largest bowl, the three kids felt the cool evening winds blowing through their hair. Su Yin snuggled close and laid her head in Jingfei's lap. Kai drew his legs up to his chest and leaned against Jingfei's shoulder.

"I don't think less of you," said Kai at last, looking up at the darkened face of his sister, "but do you think less of me? I mean, I've caused more trouble than you ever did."

"Of course I don't. All of us mess up, and when you've messed up a lot, like I have, and when you wake up one day and see yourself for who you really are, it makes you more compassionate with those who are still messing up. That's why Zak won't let anything happen. I don't know much about his past or what he did, but I think he messed up a lot, which is why he's sticking by us."

"But you heard what Emily said."

Jingfei gently brought Kai's head back to her shoulder and began gently tickling Kai's neck, like she had always done for Kai and Su Yin when they were sleeping under a bridge, or in a barn, or on rescue mission cots. Three kids who had no one but themselves.

"Yeah, I know what Emily said," answered Jingfei. "But I also know what Zak said, that he would never desert us. I also know what Alex said about Zak – that he would never desert us – and that's what I choose to believe. I believe Zak's love is stronger than Emily's anger."

"So 13:5 is true?" asked Su Yin said quietly.

"Yes, it is," Jingfei replied as the nighttime winds picked up and the kids all snuggled closer.

# CHAPTER 24

Keeping to the deeper shadows of a wooden fence bordering the alley, Xin Li, Straw Sandal, and the twelve *Shí bèi* fighters moved silently along in a single file to the rear door of the community center. Their feet barely made a sound, and what sounds they made were drowned out by the wind.

Xin Li approached the heavy metal door and tried the handle. It was unlocked. Pulling it open, she led the way inside.

The group moved diagonally across the darkened basketball court. Ahead, slivers of light were visible beneath the double doors leading into the foyer.

Busy at their computers, Ramona and Amina did not hear anything until Xin Li and six of the *Shí bèi* fighters rushed into the office. Ramona jumped out of her chair but Xin Li backhanded her with her pistol. Ramona flew back and hit the floor hard on her back.

Xin Li barked a command and two of the fighters picked Ramona up and placed her in a chair.

"If you're looking for money, we don't have any," Ramona replied after glancing up at the sound of running footsteps vibrating above. *Someone was searching upstairs.*

With her pistol in one hand, Xin Li stared hard at Ramona while more footsteps echoed in the foyer and still others echoed from the stairwell off the foyer. Within a minute, Straw Sandal and the other fighters entered the office.

"No one is upstairs," Straw Sandal said in Chinese.

Xin Li nodded thoughtfully.

"What do you want?" asked Ramona.

"Where is he?" Xin Li demanded.

"I told you, we have no money."

"Where *is* he?"

"Where is who?"

"Talanov. Do not lie. We know he is here."

"No one is here but us."

Xin Li aimed her pistol at Ramona's head. "I will ask you one more time."

"They went out," blurted Amina.

"When will he return?"

"We don't know."

With pursed lips, Xin Li thought for a moment, then nodded to one of the *Shí bèi* fighters, who grabbed Ramona by the head and broke her neck with a violent twist. Amina screamed as Ramona's body toppled to the floor. Xin Li then smashed Amina in the face with her pistol, knocking her out of her chair. When Amina hit the floor, Xin Li straddled her waist and pointed her pistol directly at her head.

"Where is Talanov?" demanded Xin Li.

Outside, the kids had already leaned their bikes against the back wall of the community center and entered the gym by the heavy metal door.

"Can we order some pizza?" whispered Su Yin while crossing the darkened basketball court. They were walking quietly, hardly making a sound.

"Let's see what's in the kitchen," Jingfei whispered back.

"They don't ever have pizza in the kitchen."

"Yeah, but there's other good stuff."

"Why are we whispering?" asked Kai.

"Because it's, like, creepy and dark. You always whisper when it's creepy and dark."

They were about to enter the kitchen when the sound of a scream halted them.

"What was *that?*" whispered Kai.

With Jingfei in the lead, they ran on their tiptoes to the double doors leading into the foyer, and after taking a steadying breath, cracked open one of the doors.

What they saw made each of them gasp.

Visible on the floor of the office was the body of Ramona. Her neck had been broken and her body was lying crooked and bent, her face angled upward, her eyes open and vacant. The sight was both grotesque and mesmerizing, and all they could do was watch, frozen with shock, their mouths agape, a column of three faces, one above the other, staring through a narrow crack at the unfolding scene.

Beside her, on the floor, was Amina, who was sobbing and quivering. Standing over her was a tall woman with a pistol.

"Where is Talanov?" the tall woman demanded again. She placed the barrel of her pistol against Amina's knee. "If you lie, I will shoot you in the leg, then the other leg, then your arms, until you tell me."

Amina stifled her sobs and began telling the tall woman about the Sour Dough Pizza Parlor.

"They're trying to find Alex!" whispered Jingfei. "We've got to warn him."

"What about Amina?" whispered Kai. "We've got to call the police!"

"With what? Our phones are up in our rooms and those stairs make all kinds of noise."

They peeked back through the crack in the doors again and saw Amina sobbing again. They were deep sobs, the kind that shook her entire body.

"Stop crying!" Xin Li shouted. "Where is this Sour Dough Pizza Parlor?"

But Amina continued to cry.

Xin Li paced back and forth several times, clearly frustrated, but stopped when she saw a display board covered with photos. Her eyes scanned the collection, although her attention fell on several photos of Zak and the three kids. She pulled off one of the photos and motioned for the *Shí bèi* fighters to put Amina back in her chair. Once Amina had been seated, Xin Li showed her the photo.

"Who are these children with Babikov?" she demanded.

Amina kept sobbing and did not reply.

Xin Li backhanded Amina again. Blood flew from her nose and she almost fell out of her chair again.

Two of the *Shí bèi* fighters caught her and placed her back in the chair.

"Are these Babikov's children?" demanded Xin Li.

"N-no," Amina sobbed.

"Who are they?"

"Three kids who l-live here now."

"Why are there so many photos of them with Babikov?"

Amina did not answer.

"Where are they now?" asked Xin Li.

Amina did not answer.

Xin Li backhanded Amina again.

"I don't know," Amina cried.

"Do they live upstairs?"

"Yes."

"Then I will ask you again. Where are they now?"

"I don't know."

Xin Li backhanded Amina again. Her face was now covered with blood.

"I *don't know,*" Amina sobbed. "Hit me all you want, but I don't know where they are. For all I know, they're with Zak and—"

Amina gasped and stopped mid-sentence.

Xin Li grabbed her by the chin. "With Zak and whom?" she demanded. With her gun in hand, she bent toward Amina, their eyes now inches apart. "Is Babikov with Talanov?"

Kai pulled Jingfei and Su Yin away from the door and allowed it to ease closed. "They're going to kill her if we don't do something."

"Yeah, but what?" asked Jingfei. "We've got no phones."

"What about Emily's?" asked Kai. "It's in her office, inside her desk."

"No *way,*" whispered Jingfei emphatically.

"We've *got* to," said Kai. "It'll take me, like, a minute to crawl in there and get it, then crawl out again."

"What if they see you, or hear you?"

"They won't. Wait for me in one of the locker rooms. I'll join you as soon as I can."

"Kai, no!"

"We've got to."

"I am *not* leaving you here alone."

"And if I have to make a run for it, they'll catch us for sure if you're hanging around here, by these doors. Now, go! We're wasting time."

The kids all hugged, and after Jingfei and Su Yin had run quietly across the basketball court, Kai slowly pulled open one of the double doors and crawled across the darkened foyer to Emily's outer office door, where he paused to make sure no one had seen him, which they hadn't. They were focused on Amina, who was crying again.

Reaching for the knob, Kai gave it a twist. The door swung inward. When it did, it squeaked lightly on its hinges.

Crawling quickly inside, Kai closed the door but left it ajar.

In front of Kai now was a long counter. It stretched halfway across the room from the wall on his left. Crouching while he ran, Kai rounded the counter, located the trashcan in a recessed area beneath the counter. He felt inside the trashcan and fished out the two straightened paperclips he had used earlier.

A scream from the office made him freeze.

Kai peeked up over the top of the front counter. Through the windows, he could see a fresh cut on Amina's forehead. Blood was streaming down her face and her head bobbed back and forth.

"I do not want to hurt you," Xin Li shouted. "I want Talanov, that is all. But if you do not tell me where he is, I *will* find Babikov and I *will* find these children and I *will* kill them one by one. And you will have to live with that for the rest of your miserable life. Is that what you want?"

Amina continued to sob.

Kai crept into the inner office and over to the front of Emily's desk, where he again picked the lock on the drawer where Emily's phone was located. Sliding open the drawer, he retrieved the phone and stuck it in his pocket. He then shut the drawer and crept out of the inner office only to drop to his knees when he saw a darkened silhouette approaching the outer office door.

A surge of panic swept over Kai. Someone had heard the outer office door squeak and was coming to investigate. Which meant his only choice now was to hide, but where? The space beneath Emily's desk was a logical choice, although it would be the first place the killer would look. He then remembered the recess located midway beneath the front counter. It, too, would be searched, but probably not before the killer had first checked beneath Emily's desk, which just might give him enough time to make a run for it.

Still on his knees, Kai crawled over to the recess, removed the trashcan, then backed into the recess just as the outer office door squeaked open. Thankfully, the entire office was dark and there were pockets of deep shadows from the furniture.

*Sorry about calling your 13:5 sign up there bullshit, God, but please don't let him turn on the light.*

Kai could feel his heart pounding while he waited in the darkened hole. His legs and lower back were beginning to burn from being hunched over at such a sharp angle. His chin was pressed against his knees.

The silhouette appeared to Kai's right, where it paused, then moved silently toward the inner office door, which appeared like a tall black rectangle into an even blacker void. The silhouette entered the void. Emily's desk stood in the center of the room, so it would take a few seconds for the killer to round the desk in order to inspect the space beneath it.

Kai eased himself out of the recess and crept toward the end of the counter.

Emily's desk lamp suddenly came on.

Kai instinctively looked toward the light just as the killer looked at him.

Springing to his feet, Kai bolted around the end of the counter just as the killer shouted something in Chinese. Running out into the foyer, Kai saw everyone look his way.

Xin Li grabbed Amina by the head and broke her neck just as Kai burst through the double doors and sprinted across the basketball court. At the far corner of the court was the corridor that led to the rear door of the community center.

"Run, Jing, run!" shouted Kai.

With the sound of footsteps echoing toward her, Jingfei shoved open the heavy metal fire door for Su Yin and Kai. Once Kai was outside, she pushed it closed again.

"The bicycles!" shouted Kai, bracing his shoulder against the door.

Jingfei and Su Yin hopped on their bikes while Kai grabbed a brick and wedged it like a doorstop against the bottom of the door. After stomping on the brick to jam it in place, he jumped on his bike and raced to catch up with his sisters, who were pedaling along the darkened alley as fast as they could.

Behind him, Kai could hear the pounding of shoulders on metal. Several seconds later, the brick gave way and *Shí bèi* fighters poured into the alley. Several seconds after that, Su Yin hit a pothole that sent her cartwheeling over her handlebars.

# CHAPTER 25

When Su Yin landed on her back, the bicycle landed on top of her. Jingfei heard a scream and looked back just as Kai skidded to a stop beside Su Yin.

"Give me your hand!" he shouted.

Su Yin reached out from beneath the wreckage and Kai pulled her up onto his handlebars. "Hang on," he said as he began pedaling furiously. To Jingfei: "I've got her! *Go!*"

At the end of the alley, they turned right and raced toward the lighted corner a block away, where a T-junction required traffic to go left or right. But there was also a narrow alleyway trucks that continued straight ahead. It was used primarily by trash trucks.

"Which way?" shouted Jingfei as they approached the corner.

Before Kai could answer, a brown SUV screeched to a stop in front of them. Jingfei veered left around the vehicle and Kai veered right, and in the light of an overhead streetlamp, Kai saw a Chinese woman pound angrily on the steering wheel.

Kai shot into the alley, followed by Jingfei, who was bent over now, pumping hard. Suddenly, from behind came the sound of squealing tires as the SUV reversed, then fishtailed into the alley.

The SUV's high beams soon bathed them in brilliant light, its engine straining as it careered along the alley knocking trash cans into garage doors and fences.

"Follow me!" Kai shouted, turning right onto a sidewalk that was bordered by high wooden fences. At first, the sidewalk was level, although it soon became a flight of concrete steps that descended between two rows of houses built on a hillside overlooking San Francisco bay.

"Hang on," Kai told Su Yin, who was bouncing back and

forth, trying to keep her balance, her feet dangling out in front of her like a two-pronged fork.

The SUV skidded to a stop in the alley behind them. Doors opened and a woman began shrieking orders in Chinese. The replies were brief. A cacophony of shouts. Then came the slap of footsteps.

"I can't hold on," cried Su Yin.

"Lean against me," Kai shouted, hunching forward to brace his shoulder against his sister's back.

They reached the bottom of the steps, bounced over the curb and began pedaling downhill toward the corner, where a feeder street ran parallel with an elevated freeway that ran perpendicular to the street they were on. The roar of traffic could be heard on the freeway and cars could be seen flowing past.

At the corner, Kai swung right onto the feeder street, then left onto a sidewalk that cut beneath the freeway. Massive pylons supported the freeway like a gigantic bridge. When Kai emerged on the other side, he glanced back.

The *Shí bèi* fighters were gaining.

Ahead was an old pickup truck. It was white with a faded red quarter panel. The truck hadn't been driven in months. That's because it had no battery. Kai knew this because he had stolen the battery. He also knew there was a driveway in front of the truck that led to a small block of apartments, where there was a sidewalk that connected to an alley, which connected to a street that would take them all the way downhill to the Sour Dough Pizza Parlor.

"This way!" Kai shouted, whipping into the driveway.

Jingfei overshot the turn but looped back and followed Kai. When she did, she glanced to her right.

The *Shí bèi* fighters were almost upon her.

# CHAPTER 26

Sitting beside a donut shop in the shadows of some overhanging trees, Xin Li could see the pizza parlor from where she was parked. She was close enough to see who came and went, yet far enough away not to be noticed. It was imperative she not be noticed until those wretched kids were in custody. Their relationship to Babikov was unclear but that did not matter. The photos showed them to have some kind of a close relationship and that was all that mattered. That meant Babikov – and Talanov, by extension – would care what happened to them.

She knew the kids were headed this way. Of all the places they could have fled, they chose the restaurant, obviously because Talanov and Babikov were there. Straw Sandal and the *Shí bèi* fighters were in pursuit, and may well have captured them by now, although she was not counting on it. The *Shí bèi* fighters were young and strong, but the kids were on bicycles and knew the streets. This is why she had chosen to wait at their destination, just as she had waited for Wu Chee Ming at his. This time, however, she would not fail. This time, she would accomplish her mission.

The front door of the restaurant opened and Talanov stepped out onto the sidewalk. He was laughing and the pretty dark-haired woman accompanying him was laughing, too.

Xin Li placed her hand on the pistol beside her just as Dragon Head's words echoed through her mind. *Alive, do you understand?* She resented the order because Talanov deserved to die. But Dragon Head was right. They needed him alive. Talanov *would* die, but not tonight. Tonight was about taking a hostage.

Half a mile away, Jingfei glanced behind her again and saw the killers were gaining. They were just seconds behind her now. She wondered how anyone could run this long and hard, then remembered how Native American Indian warriors used to capture horses by running them down. Horses were faster in the short run, but the warriors could outdistance them, never letting up until the horses collapsed from exhaustion.

*Well, you will not capture me!*

Jingfei stood up out of her seat and began pumping faster. Her heart was pounding and she was gulping air, and her thighs were aching and burning. But she couldn't quit, not now, and certainly not this close to the restaurant. She looked over at her brother. She couldn't see his face because the street was so dark, but she could hear him groaning and straining.

In the distance was the lighted intersection where the pizza parlor was located. It was around the corner to the left, and at this speed, they would need to first swing wide to the right in order to make the turn. Thankfully, the intersection was a four-way stop, and traffic tonight was light, so the risk of getting hit was minimal.

Twenty yards from the intersection, Jingfei and Kai swung right in preparation for the turn, looking left, anticipating the turn.

Suddenly, Straw Sandal's SUV raced around the corner and sped toward them before doing a skidding quarter turn and coming to a stop in front of them. Kai attempted to swerve around it but lost his balance and fell, sending Su Yin tumbling across the pavement. Jingfei broadsided the vehicle, where she bounced off the driver's door and fell.

Straw Sandal and four *Shí bèi* fighters jumped out just as the other fighters arrived on foot. Like attacking ants, they swarmed over the kids and began dragging them toward the SUV. Su Yin was scuffed and crying, while Jingfei and Kai were shouting and kicking.

"Get them into the vehicle!" Straw Sandal barked in Chinese over a clap of metallic thunder. Except it was not thunder. It was footsteps on the hood of her SUV. Straw Sandal and the fighters looked up to see two shadows descending upon them.

Landing on their feet, Talanov and Zak began hurling fighters away like ragdolls. Some skidded across the pavement. Others landed on their stomachs. Most hit the concrete and rolled up onto their feet.

"To the restaurant! Find Ginie!" shouted Talanov. "Tell her to call the police!"

Grabbing Su Yin by the hands, Jingfei and Kai looked one way then the other, not knowing which way to run. Talanov and Zak were in front of them like a wall, but the *Shí bèi* fighters were racing back and forth in front of that wall, like wolves circling for the kill.

"This way," Jingfei said, opening a door of the SUV and crawling across the back seat.

Straw Sandal yelled a command that sent the *Shí bèi* fighters forward in a massive attack. The flurry of fists and feet was dizzying. But Talanov and Zak responded with reflexes and counterattacks that were equally dizzying.

A leaping front kick by Zak caught one fighter in the chin. The fighter staggered backward and toppled to the pavement.

But the numbers were overwhelming and weariness began to set in. Talanov and Zak were strong and experienced, but they were also decades older than the *Shí bèi* fighters, who trained daily and whose stamina and ability was almost beyond description.

With Talanov and Zak occupied by the *Shí bèi* fighters, Straw Sandal did an acrobatic leap over the hood of her SUV just as the kids emerged out the other door. In the distance, she could see a crowd of spectators at the intersection. Crowds meant witnesses and protection.

And that she could not allow.

A leaping chop dropped Jingfei, allowing Straw Sandal to yank Su Yin away from Kai. Kai flew forward to protect Su Yin, but Straw Sandal landed a pair of stunning blows that dropped him where he stood. Grabbing Su Yin around the waist, Straw Sandal rounded the rear of the SUV and began running back up the darkened street.

Zak heard Su Yin screaming. "Go after her!" he shouted over the yips and yelps of fighters.

Talanov sprang forward with a series of punches that allowed him to burst through the line. Two fighters gave chase but Talanov dropped them with backfists.

Straw Sandal glanced back and saw Talanov closing in. Knowing she could not outrun him, she dropped Su Yin and leaped at Talanov with a flying combination of punches and kicks. Talanov sidestepped Straw Sandal's barrage to deliver a roundhouse kick to the back of her head. Straw Sandal flailed briefly before landing face down on the street, where she lay groaning.

Talanov ran over and lifted Su Yin to her feet. "Run!" he said. "Find Ginie."

Ginie had just finished helping Jingfei and Kai to the curb when she saw Su Yin running toward her.

"There she is!" shouted Ginie. She ran to Su Yin and scooped her up. "Are you all right?"

With a quivering lip, Su Yin nodded and began to cry.

Ginie brought Su Yin's face to her shoulder and carried her toward the corner, where Jingfei was bent over, vomiting, and Kai was bleeding from his nose.

Suddenly, blinding headlights came roaring toward them and Ginie froze at the sound of skidding tires. The vehicle stopped a few feet away from where Ginie was standing. The driver's door swung open and Xin Li got out, a pistol in one hand, a cell phone in the other.

Xin Li walked to the front of the SUV, looked at Ginie, then fired into the crowd of onlookers. Single shots. Dead aim. Flesh wounds for the sole purpose of creating panic.

With screaming people running in all directions, Xin Li approached Ginie and backhanded her with the pistol. The blow sent Ginie sprawling to the asphalt, where she lay bleeding and dazed.

Grabbing Su Yin around the waist, Xin Li put the phone to her ear. "I've got her," she said in Chinese. "Get everyone back to the plane and ready for takeoff. I'll meet you there. Once we're in international waters, we'll be safe all the way to Hong Kong."

Turning toward the screams, Talanov did not hear Straw Sandal's cry for the others to get back to the plane. He was focused on the brown Suburban parked in the intersection. That meant he almost didn't see the roundhouse kick coming straight for his head.

Almost.

And with a last-second pivot, Talanov ducked beneath the arc of the kick, grabbed Straw Sandal by the ankle, and with a full-circle spin, slammed her against the side of a parked car. After denting the car door with her head, Straw Sandal slid to the pavement.

Talanov knelt and checked for a pulse.

*Alive, but unconscious,* he thought, staring down at Straw Sandal's ghostly white skin.

The sudden screech of tires pierced the night and Talanov stood and looked toward the corner.

The brown Suburban was gone.

# CHAPTER 27

The remaining fighters fled. Two were unconscious and had to be carried away, but within minutes, they had melted away into the night.

"Who *were* those guys?" asked a winded Zak.

"No idea," Talanov replied, looking toward the sound of screams coming from the corner.

"That sounds like Jingfei," said Zak, looking toward the noise.

"Go," said Talanov. "I'll bring our prisoner. Find me some duct tape, if you can."

"You got it," said Zak. He rounded the front of Straw Sandal's SUV and ran to the corner, where Jingfei was crying uncontrollably. Nearby, Ginie's bloody face was being tended by Emily, while Kai was seated on the curb, staring absently down at the pavement. On the sidewalk in front of the corner grocery store were three wounded people. They were being given first aid by Marcelo and his waiters. Spectators were standing around them in small groups, taking pictures and whispering.

Jingfei saw Zak and ran over to him.

"We've got to get her back!" cried Jingfei, whose face was red and streaked with tears.

"Get who back?" asked Zak. "What happened?"

"Su Yin! Some woman took her!"

Jingfei buried her face against Zak's shoulder and began crying again.

Zak blinked several times. Su Yin was gone? Who would do this? Why?

After a quick glance toward Talanov, with imposed calm Zak gently pulled away from Jingfei and tenderly wiped her face with his thumbs. "I need you to tell me what happened," he said. "Everything you can remember."

But Jingfei couldn't speak. All she could do was bury her face against his shoulder again.

"The woman who took Su Yin was at the community center," said Kai, standing. "She was leading the guys who chased us."

"They came to the center? You saw them?"

"Yeah, in the front office. The tall woman who kidnapped Su Yin is the one who killed Amina. I saw her do it, but I didn't see who killed Ramona. She was dead by the time we got there."

Zak's mouth fell open and he could not speak. All he could do was stare open-mouthed at Kai. *Ramona and Amina were dead?*

"They were all Chinese and they wanted to know where Alex was," Kai continued, speaking calmly, without emotion, almost mechanically. "But Amina wouldn't tell them. So the tall woman smashed her in the face with her pistol. It looked like she had been hitting Amina a lot, because her face was already bloody. I knew we had to do something, like call the police, so I crawled into Emily's office and got her phone. But they saw me, so the tall woman killed Amina and then they started chasing us." Kai paused and looked down at the pavement. "Amina would be alive if I hadn't done that."

"Kai, this isn't your fault," said Zak.

"Yes, it is. I'm the reason for all of this trouble. I'm, like, this problem that can't be fixed."

"Kai, you're *not* a problem."

"Yes, I am! Emily said so. I heard her. I heard her say she wanted to send me to juvie because you've got no money. Look at how you two fight. So go ahead and ditch me, Zak. I know you're going to, anyway. But, *please*, get Su Yin back. Don't punish her. Punish me. I'm the one they saw. I'm the reason they chased us. I'm the reason they took Su Yin."

Emily touched Kai on the arm. "Kai, that's not what I meant."

"Leave me alone!" shouted Kai, knocking her hand away and scooting closer to Zak.

With sirens growing closer, Zak wrapped an arm around Kai and drew him close while Jingfei continued to sob. He could tell they both felt responsible. Jingfei, the oldest, felt as if she had failed to protect Su Yin. Kai, a broken boy already carrying an unbearable burden of guilt, felt as though he were the main cause of the tragedy.

Looking left, Zak saw Talanov dragging an unconscious body toward them. Looking right, he saw Ginie sitting on the curb, her face a smear of dried blood. Filling the street around them was a churning mass of people.

Several horn blasts sounded as an ambulance arrived. Close behind were two police cars. Their flashing lights made Zak squint. The ambulance pushed slowly through the crowd and parked near the wounded victims, who were still on the sidewalk being attended by Marcelo and his staff. Paramedics jumped out with emergency kits, while police officers piled out of the squad cars and gathered around their sergeant, Arcus Hill, who began issuing orders. Two officers began herding the spectators away from the victims. Others began directing traffic that had backed up for several blocks. The final two officers began cordoning off the area with yellow tape.

Hill saw Zak and hurried over. "What happened here, Zak?" he asked.

After motioning for Hill to wait, Zak gathered Jingfei and Kai in front of him. "This is not going to be easy, because we're all upset, but I need you to tell Officer Hill what happened. Tell him everything you can remember. Do you think you can do that?"

Kai nodded while Jingfei shrugged. Zak motioned for Hill to join them, and while Kai told Hill what happened, Zak walked over to Marcelo and asked for a roll of duct tape.

"One of my waiters will bring it to you," answered Marcelo.

Zak thanked Marcelo and headed for Talanov just as a nondescript gray sedan parked across the street. Wilcox was the driver and he had just shown his identification to one of the uniformed officers, who allowed him to park on the sidewalk in front of a dry cleaning shop.

Wilcox sat in his car for a moment and watched the activity. Paramedics were tending the injured and there were several, by the looks of it. Behind him, two more police cars arrived and parked at various angles. Their red and blue lights lit up the night.

After climbing out of his car, Wilcox spotted Talanov, who had stopped in the middle of the street to catch his breath. The body of a woman was on the pavement beside him, face down.

Talanov gave a start when he saw a Hawaiian shirt hurrying toward him. "Bill?" he asked with surprise. "What are you doing here? I thought you were on vacation."

Wilcox knelt beside the body and adjusted her head so that he could see her face. "My God, it's her," he said.

"Do you know this woman?" asked Talanov.

Wilcox stood. "We need to talk."

"And I asked if you knew this woman."

"And I said we needed to talk. But not here. Someplace private."

Zak arrived with a roll of duct tape and tossed it to Talanov, who glared briefly at Wilcox before kneeling beside Straw Sandal and using the tape to secure her knees.

Wilcox turned to Zak. "I didn't know you were in our country, Major Babikov," he said while Talanov ripped off a strip of tape and placed it across Straw Sandal's mouth.

Zak did not reply.

"How'd you get in without anyone noticing? Without setting off alarm bells in Washington?"

Zak shrugged and did not reply.

Both men watched Talanov pull Straw Sandal's arms behind her and began securing them with tape.

"What the *hell* do you think you're doing?" Hill called out, running toward them.

After a quick glance at Hill, Talanov finished taping Straw Sandal's wrists with crisscrossing loops.

Hill paused when an announcement crackled over his intercom. "Your one-eighty-seven is confirmed at the Hilltop Community Center. Two bodies. Necks broken. Coroner's on the way."

Talanov stood and stared questioningly at Hill, who turned away to speak quietly into the microphone strapped to his epaulet.

"What bodies?" asked Talanov.

After a steadying breath, Zak said, "Ramona and Amina have been murdered."

"*What?*"

"By the same woman who kidnapped Su Yin," said Zak.

Talanov stared dumbfounded at Zak.

"And she's one of them," said Kai, who had now joined them. He looked down at Straw Sandal, who was beginning to protest with muffled cries, then at Talanov. "They killed Ramona and Amina because they wanted to know where you were. But Amina wouldn't tell them. So they killed her. Who are they, Alex? What did they want to find you? Why did they kidnap Su Yin?"

"Untape that woman," said Hill.

"No!" cried Kai. "She needs to tell us where Su Yin is. And why they killed Ramona and Amina."

"Don't worry, I'll make her talk," said Talanov, pulling Straw Sandal to her feet.

"Not going to happen," said Hill.

"She knows where Su Yin is!" said Kai.

"Stay out of this, son," said Hill. "That woman is coming with me."

"Not until she gives me some answers," said Talanov, "which we will never get if she goes with you."

"I *said* — "

"If I may?" said Wilcox, stepping forward.

"And you are?" asked Hill.

Wilcox opened his identification wallet and held it up. "Wilcox, CIA."

Hill glanced briefly at the ID, then back at Wilcox, unimpressed. "In case you didn't know, the CIA has no jurisdiction on United States soil, and since this is a murder investigation *on United States soil,* I suggest you stay out of this."

"It's a matter of national security."

The remark made Hill laugh. "Some big shot from the CIA – in a pink and yellow Hawaiian shirt, no less – conveniently shows up to a murder investigation of two social workers, claiming it's a matter of national security. Do you seriously expect me to believe that?" To Talanov: "Untape that woman. Don't make me tell you again."

"Officer Hill, let Alex question her," said Ginie. "Her partner kidnapped Su Yin and is taking her back to their plane."

"What plane?"

"I don't know. They were speaking Chinese, and while I speak a little, I'm not fluent, but I think I heard the woman tell someone on the phone to get back to the plane, that she would meet them there. She also mentioned Hong Kong, so I think that's where they're headed."

"You speak a little Chinese and you *think* that's where they're headed? In other words, you really don't know."

"Which is why I need to question this woman," said Talanov. "Before they get away."

"Like I said, not going to happen," said Hill.

"Come on, Arcus, help us out," said Zak. "They're leaving the country. You've got to call this in and ground all private jets with flight plans to Hong Kong."

"You know I can't do that, Zak. Not even Ginie knows what she heard."

"But I do," said Jingfei. "I speak fluent Chinese and I heard the same thing Ginie heard. The kidnapper said to get everyone back to the plane and be ready for takeoff, that once they were in international waters, they would be safe all the way to

Hong Kong."

"And our people will investigate that."

"When? Tomorrow? Next week?"

"You need to stay out of this, Jingfei."

"Well, I don't," said Wilcox while working the screen of his phone. When finished, he tapped Enter. "There, done. All Chinese flight plans will be looked into immediately."

"You had no right to do that!" exclaimed Hill.

"And yet I just did," answered Wilcox with a smile.

Hill jabbed a finger at Wilcox. "Any further interference and I will be filing an official complaint." To Talanov: "Last time: *untape that woman,* or I'm arresting you for obstruction."

Motioning for Talanov to remain where he was, Wilcox began working his phone again.

"What are you doing?" asked Hill.

"Don't worry. This won't take long."

"Look, I get it," said Hill. "You want to get even for what your victim did. Maybe rough her up a bit."

"We're the victims here, Arcus, not her," said Zak.

"But you got caught, and your friend here, Mr. Big Shot CIA, steps in to pull a fast one with the local LEOs." He glanced at Wilcox. "Isn't that what you call us, the local LEOs? Well, this time it it's not going to work. Now, for the last time, untape that woman before I lock all of you up."

"Don't let the Hawaiian shirt throw you," replied Wilcox, not taking his eyes off his phone, "which, by the way, I was planning on wearing to Disneyland until I ended up here. But you are right about one thing: the CIA does not normally conduct operations on United States soil. And, yes, there have been instances where Federal agents have overstepped their boundaries. Question is: am I doing that now? Am I trying to pull a fast one, as you put it so eloquently?" He tapped the screen of his phone, which sent the text message he had been composing. He then folded his arms, and, with a contented smile, adjusted his posture to a more comfortable position.

Hill was not sure how to respond, so he and Wilcox just

stared at one another for a long moment, Wilcox with his unnerving smile and Hill with a look of growing uncertainty.

Approximately fifteen seconds later, the sharp trill of a phone broke that silence. When Hill realized it was his phone, he fished it from his pocket and took the call. "This is Hill," he said, pausing briefly to listen. "Yes, sir, he's right here and he claims to be—"

Whoever was on the other end of the call cut Hill off, forcing him to listen.

"Yes, sir," tried Hill, "but—"

Hill got interrupted again and was forced to listen.

"Sir, I—" Hill tried again.

But there's another interruption, this one more scathing than the others, causing Hill to swallow hard.

"Of course, sir, I understand," Hill said meekly. Clicking off, he lowered his phone. "My apologies, Mr. Wilcox. I'm to render any assistance you may require."

"If I need some, I'll let you know," Wilcox replied.

After glancing awkwardly at Zak and the kids, Hill walked away. Once he was gone, Talanov stepped over to confront Wilcox face-to-face.

"What the *hell* is going on here, Bill?"

"You're welcome, by the way."

Talanov responded with an impatient glare.

"Like I said, we need to talk," said Wilcox. "But not here. Someplace private."

"You knew about this, didn't you? You know who this woman is and that they're after me. That's the reason you're here, isn't it? *You knew.*"

"Like I said—"

"How could you let this happen? How could you not have given me some kind of a warning?"

"And how, exactly, should I have done that?" Wilcox fired back. "Your phone is off. Oh, and let's not forget this important little fact: there *is no* Quiet Waters Community Center, not in any database, anyway, and there is no Babikov listed, either, *anywhere*. So please explain to me exactly how I should have gotten hold of you."

"And yet, here you are. What a coincidence."

"Yes, no thanks to you."

"How did they find me, Bill? Never mind how you found me. How did *they* find me? No one knew I was here except you and Diane."

Wilcox glanced uneasily at everyone staring back at him. To his right were Jingfei and Kai. Their clothes were torn and dirty. Emily and Ginie were standing next to them. Ginie had a black eye and an aluminum splint on her nose. Wilcox's eyes then fell on Zak, who appeared to be waiting with growing impatience, his fingers forming and unforming fists. A not-so-subtle warning, like a cat flicking its tail.

"Let's take a walk," said Wilcox, looking back at Talanov.

"We don't have time," replied Talanov. He yanked Straw Sandal in front of Wilcox, forcing him to look at her. "Who is she, Bill? How did she find me, and why? I know you know something because you recognized her when you got here."

"Not now," responded Wilcox.

"Yes, now!" shouted Talanov angrily. "She and her gang murdered two girls! They *kidnapped* Su Yin. So quit stalling and talk to me. *What do these people want?*"

# CHAPTER 28

Xin Li parked her brown Suburban in a residential neighborhood across the bay. Two driveways away was another brown Suburban. She had to assume someone at the restaurant had snapped a picture when she sped away. That picture would soon find its way to the police, who would use traffic cameras to identify and apprehend her. Switching plates with a similar vehicle would give her breathing room for the next few hours.

After making the switch, she slid back into the driver's seat. Su Yin was where she had left her, sitting huddled on the floor, her face between her knees, sobbing quietly. Xin Li asked Su Yin what her name was. Su Yin did not reply. Xin Li asked again but Su Yin kept sobbing.

"Tell me or you will never see your family again," Xin Li said.

After several more sobs, Su Yin told her.

"Look at me," commanded Xin Li.

When Su Yin did, Xin Li snapped her picture, composed a text message, then tapped Send.

Seven thousand miles to the west, AK's cell phone chimed. When he heard the chime, he read Xin Li's instructions concerning the image.

Connecting his cell phone to one of his processors, AK went to work on the photo. Seconds later, his cell phone rang.

"Did you get my text message?" Xin Li asked in Russian once AK had answered. Shifting the Suburban into gear after switching license plates, Xin Li began driving again.

"Yes, and Dragon Head is going to freak out when he hears about his daughter."

"Leave Dragon Head to me. How long to work your magic?"

"Sixty seconds," AK replied while embedding a virus in the image that would activate once someone opened the image.

"Has Talanov come back online?"

AK wheeled over to another monitor that showed Talanov's number to still be inactive. "Not yet," he replied, wheeling back to the first monitor, where he continued working for another thirty seconds. "Okay, it's done," he said.

"Good. Send Talanov a text message. Tell him to wait for my call. Attach the girl's photo as proof of life and let me know when he opens it."

AK entered Talanov's number, typed Xin Li's message, attached the photo, then tapped Send. "Done," he said. "The moment he opens it, I'll know."

"Let me know when that happens."

"What about *Shāng Yī*? We are running out of time."

"How long have we got?"

AK wheeled over to another monitor, where a maze of dotted lines indicated commercial flight paths over the Pacific Ocean. In the center of the maze was a red circle.

Adjusting his glasses, AK highlighted the red circle portion of the map and clicked the zoom function, which enlarged the map to reveal the USS Ronald Reagan carrier group. AK studied the various orange triangles blinking near the red circle. Each triangle represented a commercial aircraft, although there were none above the red circle because they had been diverted around the carrier group's airspace. But there were several just outside the perimeter and all were moving in various directions. Near each triangle were some fluctuating numbers that indicated speed, altitude, wind direction, and other statistics.

AK zoomed in on the carrier itself and kept enlarging the image until the deck of the majestic warship became clearly visible. The image was in real time and AK watched a fighter jet move into position. Several other fighter jets were already in the air, as indicated by moving green triangles out over the ocean.

"Our window opens in seventeen minutes," AK said.

"And lasts for how long?" asked Xin Li.

"Forty minutes."

Xin Li turned a corner and sped along a darkened street that edged the back side of the airport. The beams of her headlights illuminated a series of parking lots along each side of the street. Then came an ugly building, then more parking lots, then more buildings. Some buildings were metal sheds. Others were concrete, painted gray, with rows of high windows. All of them were built for utility. None of them were built for aesthetics.

"Are you sure about this?" AK asked, still speaking Russian. "If we carry through with *Shāng Yī*, the Americans will come after us with everything they've got. So will the Chinese."

"If what you promised is true, then no one will know who we are, where we are, or how we did it."

"What I told you is true, and we may get away with this once, maybe twice. But if you want me to create a permanent veil that no one can penetrate, then I need better software and better equipment. I need those unlimited resources."

"And you will get them," Xin Li replied to the vibrating rumble of a commercial airliner taking off in the distance. "Which is where Talanov comes in."

"What do you need me to do?" AK asked just as Xin Li approached a boom gate.

"Hang on a minute," Xin Li replied, stopping at the boom and looking toward a lighted hut, where a security guard was watching a small TV. The guard was wearing a blue uniform and a security company baseball cap.

Carrying an electronic tablet, the guard stopped in front of the vehicle, shown a flashlight on the license plate, compared it to a number on his tablet, then approached the driver's side window.

"If you cry out or make any protest," Xin Li told Su Yin, "I will shoot the guard and you will be responsible for his death. Do you understand?"

Su Yin nodded just as Xin Li rolled down her window. "Good evening, officer," she said with a smile. "I am sorry to be so late. I'm with the Hong Kong law enforcement delegation and I just got out of a meeting."

"No problem," the officer replied. "The others are already here. How did everything go?"

"Your police chief loves to talk. Especially after a bourbon. Or was it three?"

The guard laughed, then noticed a pair of eyes peering up at him from the darkened floorboard. "Who's that?" he asked with a look of concern.

"My daughter," answered Xin Li, "who is throwing an absolute tantrum because I would not buy her another Happy Meal."

The guard laughed again. "I got the same problem with my kids. Have a good flight." Returning to his hut, he raised the boom and waved her through.

After closing the window, Xin Li steered the Suburban past several hangars to where Dragon Head's Gulfstream was parked on a darkened patch of tarmac. After parking the Suburban near a lighted office, she switched off the ignition and put her phone back to her ear.

"I'm at the Gulfstream now," she said, still speaking in Russian, "so here's what I need you to do. Text Dragon Head and tell him we're on our way, although Straw Sandal will not be with us. Tell him she's been captured."

"No way is Dragon Head going to let you leave without his daughter."

"He has to. Let me talk to him."

"Whatever you say," AK replied, working his phone. In less than a minute, he heard the bounding of footsteps. "Putting the phone on speaker," he said, laying his cell phone on the worktable.

Seconds later, Dragon Head stormed into the room. "Where is my daughter?" he yelled.

"Straw Sandal is safe," Xin Li's voice replied in English from the phone, which was the only common language that Xin Li, Dragon Head, and AK spoke, with AK speaking Russian and English, and Dragon Head speaking Chinese and English, and Xin Li speaking all three.

AK discreetly wheeled aside so that Dragon Head could position himself over the phone, his muscular arms braced on the table.

"How could you allow this to happen?" Dragon Head demanded.

"Talanov and Babikov are responsible. When I went to apprehend the hostage, they took her."

"Who's Babikov?"

"Talanov's closest friend. They were both in the KGB."

"The KGB? Two men – two *old* men – defeated Straw Sandal and a dozen of my fighters?" yelled Dragon Head. He kicked a chair and sent it spinning across the floor. "Go back and get her! Kill anyone who gets in your way. Kill Talanov, if you have to."

"As much as I would love to do that, you and I both know we cannot, at least not yet."

"He has my daughter!"

"And he will not harm her. In fact, one of our demands will be that he bring her to us in Hong Kong."

"What makes you think he will do that?" replied Dragon Head with a skeptical squint.

"Because the hostage I took, an eleven-year-old girl, is important to Babikov, which means Talanov will do what we tell him so that no harm comes to the girl. But I must leave now, before the authorities ground all private aircraft with Chinese ownership."

"So you were seen?"

"Yes, but not identified. But as I said, we must leave now."

While talking, Xin Li climbed out of the Suburban and motioned for Su Yin, who hesitated, then crawled across the seat and climbed out of the Suburban. Xin Li took her by the arm and led her up the staircase into the Gulfstream, where one of the *Shí bèi* fighters took her to a seat.

"How will you communicate our demands?" Dragon Head asked.

"By phone, when we're in the air."

"And if the Americans trace your call, identify us, and have Hong Kong authorities waiting when you arrive?"

"AK will make sure that doesn't happen. I will route the call through him."

"Can you do that?" Dragon Head asked, looking at AK.

"Of course," AK replied in English. "I encrypt call and route through servers in Shenzhen, Kunming, Chengdu, Nunjing, Qingdao, and Beijing. Maybe more, I do not know. No one can trace point of origin, or who we are."

Dragon Head assessed what he had just heard. Finally, he looked back at the phone. "As you wish," he said. "But if *any harm* comes to my daughter . . ."

"It won't. She will be fine."

And with that, Dragon Head glared briefly at AK before marching out of the room.

With a kick of his foot, AK wheeled himself back over to the phone. "It's me again," he said in Russian just as Xin Li saw a security vehicle driving toward the Gulfstream with amber lights flashing on top.

"Hang on a minute," Xin Li said. Tucking her pistol out of sight near the small of her back, she watched the security vehicle stop near the bottom of the staircase. Saw the guard switch off the engine and get out with an electronic tablet in his hand.

"Are the lights necessary?" asked Xin Li. "My daughter is asleep."

"Oh, yeah, sorry," the guard replied, leaning in the window and switching them off. Rounding the front of the vehicle, he checked his tablet again. "Your flight plan says Hong Kong, so I'm to make a quick check of everyone's ID."

"We are an official delegation."

"I know and I'm sorry," said the guard, "but orders are

orders. Once I verify your IDs, I click approved and off you go."

With a smile, Xin Li walked down the staircase and approached the officer. "Of course. Where do I sign?"

"No need to sign anywhere. I just need to see —"

The guard never finished his sentence because Xin Li chopped the guard in the neck, dragged him to his car, shoved him inside, and shot him twice in the head.

Walking back to where the guard had dropped his tablet, Xin Li picked it up, touched the Approved button, tossed it inside the car and closed the door. In less than a minute, she was back inside the Gulfstream with the staircase being retracted.

Looking into the cockpit, Xin Li said, "Wheels up in five." She then put her phone back to her ear while making her way along the aisle to her seat. "I'm back," she said, glancing at Su Yin, who was watching her with frightened eyes from her seat near the rear of the plane.

"Everything okay?" AK asked. "You took a while."

"Nothing I couldn't handle. How long until we initiate *Shāng Yī*?"

"A matter of minutes," AK replied just as a ping sounded from his monitor and a red dot began flashing along the right-hand margin of the screen.

"What was that?" asked Xin Li, hearing the sound.

"It's Talanov. He switched on his phone."

# CHAPTER 29

Back in the parking lot of the pizza parlor, Talanov's phone had been chiming repeatedly with text messages and emails since he switched it on. With Straw Sandal in hand, Talanov led her toward Zak's van, which was parked in the far corner of the lot in a no-parking zone. It was after midnight and the area was still swarming with gawkers attracted by the flashing lights. Another ambulance was now on the scene, which further lit up the area with strobes of red and blue. Several news vans had just arrived and their crews were setting up.

Another chime indicated another text message but Talanov did not bother looking. He would get to all of them later. Right now, all that mattered was getting Straw Sandal into Zak's van before a reporter saw him leading a duct-taped woman across the parking lot.

Wilcox caught up with Talanov. "For the umpteenth time, we need to talk."

"Oh, we'll talk, all right," said Talanov, sticking his cell phone in his hip pocket, "because you've got some explaining to do. But now is not the time. Right now, I need you to find us a place to regroup. Someplace close but not too close, like a freeway motel. As soon as you find one, text me the address and room number. And please don't start with the I-don't-work-for-you bullshit. We've been attacked, Bill. Murders were committed. Su Yin was kidnapped. I need your help."

Wilcox nodded and headed for his car while Talanov escorted Straw Sandal to the van, where Zak was waiting beside the rear door.

"Get in," said Talanov when Zak opened the door.

Straw Sandal balked when she saw the utility space. A spare tire was mounted to one side. A dirty rubber mat lined the floor.

"Fine, the hard way it is," said Talanov, picking up Straw Sandal and stuffing her into the vehicle. When she started kicking and twisting, Talanov flipped her over, wound more tape around her ankles, then pulled her feet up behind her and connected them with a length of tape to her wrists. He then reinforced the connection several more times. "Don't go anywhere," he said, slamming the door just as several more chimes sounded from his hip pocket.

Taking out his phone, Talanov saw a series of missed calls. Many of the numbers he recognized. Many he did not. There were also a number of text messages from Wilcox and Gustaves.

He then saw a text message that read, "The girl is alive. Wait for my call." Talanov clicked the link and an image appeared on his screen. It was of Su Yin and she was curled up in what looked like the floorboard of a car. Her eyes were red from crying and she was staring up into the camera.

Talanov went rigid with rage.

"What's wrong?" asked Zak, seeing Talanov staring angrily at his phone.

Before Talanov could answer, his phone rang. He checked the Caller ID and saw it was from an unidentified number. Swiping the answer button, he put the phone to his ear.

"I see you received the photo," Xin Li said.

"Who is this?" demanded Talanov.

"Not important. What *is* important is that you do exactly what I tell you."

"If you so much as touch that girl . . ."

"Save it, Colonel. You have something that I want. I have something that you want. Do what you're told and no one gets hurt."

"What exactly do you want?" asked Talanov, his brow furrowed in thought while trying to determine whether or not he recognized the voice. There was something familiar about it. The accent, perhaps? It was almost American, but not quite, much like his own American accent, which he had learned years ago during his KGB training at Balashikha. This person spoke in a similar manner.

"For you to bring Straw Sandal with you to Hong Kong. If you fail to do so, Su Yin will die. If you fail to arrive within two days, or if you involve the authorities, Su Yin will die. If Straw Sandal is harmed in any way, Su Yin will die. Two days, Colonel."

"And then? What happens then?"

But the line had already gone dead.

# CHAPTER 30

Several minutes later, Talanov huddled everyone in the shadow of the van, away from the activity and lights. "Su Yin is alive," he announced, showing everyone the image. "The bad news: I have no idea who has her, where she is, or what it is they want." He then told the group what he had been told, that if he delivered Straw Sandal to Hong Kong, no one would get hurt.

"And you believe her?" asked Zak.

"We don't have a choice," answered Talanov, "so for now, we'll do what they say. I got us into this mess, so I will get her back, whatever it takes."

"For the record, this isn't your fault," said Zak.

"Yes, it is," said Talanov. "None of this would have happened if it weren't for me."

"Then you might as well blame me for welcoming these kids into my life. If I'd sent them away, none of this would have happened. Or if I hadn't hired Amina and Ramona, then they'd both be alive. This is not your fault."

"I beg to differ," said Emily. "I say this *is* his fault. And I want the record to show that."

"You want *what* record to show that?" asked Zak.

"The legal record. And I know a judge who will accommodate me on that. A judge who will make sure this never happens again."

"Come on, Em. Don't start."

"You said your old life was behind you, Zak, but you never really closed that door. And you let Alex drag you back in. And for what? To help him work through his grief? Well, we are done with that. Look at the grief he has caused. His wife is dead. Ramona and Amina are dead. How many more people have to die? We have enough grief in our lives without taking on his, and I, for one, am tired of sacrificing *my* life and *my* work for some misguided loyalty. We would all be better off if you would—"

"Shut up!" yelled Jingfei, stepping up to confront Emily when she saw Talanov take a step back, as if punched in the stomach.

"I beg your pardon?"

"I said, shut up! No one asked for your opinion, anyway, and I, for one, am tired of listening to it. At least Zak and Alex are trying to do something. But you? You're threatening to take them to court. You don't care about Su Yin any more than you care about me and Kai. We're your big source of grief, anyway, right? Well, you know what? I don't care about you, either. All I care about is finding Su Yin. So don't *ever* threaten Zak or Alex again."

"Or *what?*" demanded Emily.

"You don't want to know."

"That's enough," said Zak, easing Jingfei back.

"She needs to stay out of this," yelled Jingfei while jabbing a finger at Emily. "All she does is complain and make threats."

"Are you going to let her talk to me like that?" demanded Emily.

"Jingfei was harsh, but right," said Zak. "You need to quit making threats and casting blame where it doesn't belong." He glanced over at Talanov and saw him staring down at the pavement, visibly shaken. Making eye contact with Jingfei, he gave a quick nod in Talanov's direction. Jingfei understood and stepped over to give Talanov a hug.

"This *isn't* your fault," she said.

"Emily is right," admitted Talanov. "My wife is dead, which never would have happened if I hadn't—"

"—you did not pull the trigger," said Zak, cutting in.

"But I'm the one who—"

"—no buts, Alex! We don't have time for self-pity. Now, what do we do next? How do we stop these people?"

With flashing lights still bathing the area in red and blue,

Talanov saw everyone looking at him, and after a steadying breath, he said, "The first thing we do is get out of here. Then we question our prisoner and make her tell us who they are, why they did this, and what it is they want. Once we know that, we'll figure out a way to beat them at their own game. That's how we find Su Yin. That's how we bring her back."

"Are you really going to take Straw Sandal to Hong Kong?" asked Jingfei. "What makes you think she won't kill you the first chance she gets?"

"Because for some reason, they want me to bring Straw Sandal with me to Hong Kong. Not just send her back, but bring her with me. That means they want something from me. I don't what it is, but for now, we play along."

"What if they, like, torture Su Yin?" asked Kai.

"It serves no purpose," answered Talanov. "Right now, everything is simple and clean, and we all want to keep it that way."

"Promise you'll get her back," said Kai with tears in his eyes. "*Please*, Alex. She's my kid sister, and she's, like, smart and funny, and she trusted me to take care of her, and I didn't. Promise you'll bring her back."

"I wish I could promise you that," Talanov said gently. "But you know I can't. But I do promise I will go to the ends of the earth trying. Whatever it takes, Kai, whatever the cost, I will do everything in my power to bring Su Yin safely home."

Kai nodded just as Talanov's phone chimed. Talanov saw that it was a text message from Wilcox with directions to a motel, which was half an hour to the south. Zak said he knew the place, and after everyone had piled into the van, within minutes they were headed south on the 101. Zak was behind the wheel and Talanov was in the passenger seat. Emily and Ginie were in the seat behind, with Jingfei and Kai in the bench seat behind them. Straw Sandal was still on the floorboard of the utility space, kicking and protesting with muffled growls.

Talanov looked back at Ginie and asked her to describe the

kidnapper. Ginie replied that she was Chinese, female, and tall – maybe six feet – with shoulder-length black hair that was seasoned with gray. Ginie estimated her to be forty to fifty years old.

"She was gorgeous," said Ginie, "but cold and ruthless in the way she shot all those people. I think she had a scar on her face. Hardly visible, like it was from a long time ago."

The van fell silent again while Talanov stared thoughtfully off into the darkness. There were barren hills on the right and San Francisco Bay on the left. In the far distance, across the water, was a necklace of lights hugging the other shore.

"Can we ever go back to the center?" asked Kai.

"Not until this is over," answered Talanov.

"How long do you think that will that be?"

"A week. A few months. Hard to tell."

"But all of my stuff is there."

"What about my practice, and my clients," asked Emily. "I can't just leave people hanging."

Rotating in his seat, Talanov looked at the four sets of eyes staring back at him. "Is any of this worth your life?" He scanned their faces over the hum of the tires. "There is no going back," he said. "Not for clients, for stuff, or anything else, at least not now. You need to disappear while I figure out a way to rescue Su Yin. If we succeed, we live. If we don't . . ."

Talanov did not finish his sentence. He simply let his grave expression finish it for him.

And everyone understood.

From this point on, they were on their own.

# CHAPTER 31

The sky at thirty-two thousand feet is almost always blue, and for Captain David Baker, the sight of endless blue was one of the enduring joys of being a pilot. With nearly forty years under his belt with the airline, Baker, who was known for his infectious laugh, had flown more miles than any person could count. Without question, some aspects of the job had lost their romantic appeal. But not the sight of endless blue. Endless blue reminded him of endless possibilities.

After checking his coordinates, Baker brought the intercom to his mouth. "Good morning from the flight deck, everyone. I hope you've had a pleasant flight. This is Captain Baker and we'll soon be commencing our descent into Shanghai." Baker went on to tell people what the weather was like in Shanghai, how much time remained for duty-free shopping, and how much he had enjoyed serving them on this flight. He then wished them a pleasant week.

A knock sounded on the cockpit door just as Baker clicked off. Easing himself out of his seat, he peered through the peephole and saw Terry, the lead flight attendant, holding a coffee pot on a tray. The coffee pot was chrome-plated and steam wafted from its mouth. Beside it were some porcelain cups. Baker smiled. Terry knew he loved drinking coffee from china, not plastic. After unlocking the door, Baker greeted the fifty-three-year-old blonde with whom he had worked for more than two decades.

"One pot of double-roast Italian espresso," announced Terry, entering the cockpit and pouring Baker a cup. "Coffee, Nick?" she then asked Baker's copilot, Nick Blair.

"No, thanks. Bladder trouble."

"Did I *really* need to know that?" asked Terry with a grin.

Blair laughed and Terry left.

After locking the cockpit door, Baker returned to his seat to check his gauges as the big airliner began its computerized auto-descent. As captain of the aircraft, he was still tasked with the monitoring of everything, but experience with manual controls was less important these days than an ability to understand computers.

Sipping his coffee, Baker panned the dashboard and took note of their global positioning, angle of descent, altitude, speed, temperature, moisture, and wind speed. His mind quickly analyzed the readings. Everything was as it should be.

Beneath them now was a layer of cumulus clouds that stretched as far as the eye could see. Dense and white, the clouds were lumbering south, like an immense migration. Baker smiled at his childhood memories of lying out in the back yard, staring up at the clouds. Those carefree days were what led him to become a pilot. Faraway lands. Endless blue. The sky is the limit.

After finishing his coffee, Baker went to the first class galley for a refill, and by the time he returned, the giant airliner had entered the cloud layer. Gray on all sides, like fog, with zero visibility except for intermittent bursts of light where the clouds parted and stabs of sunlight beamed through.

"How we looking?" asked Baker, sliding into his seat.

"Wake me when we get there," quipped Blair as the airliner continued its descent.

Over the drone of jet engines, Baker drank more coffee while again checking his dashboard. As usual, his mind analyzed the readings. As usual, everything looked normal. That all changed when the airliner broke through the clouds and Baker saw an F/A-18E Super Hornet coming straight toward them like a guided missile.

Dropping his coffee, Baker yanked back on the stick, which overrode the automated controls just as the fighter pilot reacted by shoving his stick forward. The Super Hornet thundered beneath the airliner so closely it caused oxygen masks to fall from their overhead compartments throughout the plane. Coffee and food slid off trays. Passengers screamed while being slammed back in their seats from the force of the airliner surging upward.

Baker heard the cries and crashes but didn't care. All he cared about was getting his bird away from that fighter jet.

"Where did *he* come from?" shouted Blair. "He wasn't on radar. He wasn't *anywhere!*"

Baker had no answer. His instruments had said the coast was clear all the way to Shanghai. Nothing had shown on any screen. Air traffic control had issued no warning. What the hell had gone wrong?

With Terry's fists pounding on the cockpit door and Blair on the phone demanding answers from air traffic control, Baker took the airliner back up through the clouds. Only then could he begin trying to figure out what had had happened.

Seeing patches of blue above, Baker eased up on the stick and felt the gravitational force of their climb begin to recede. He wondered how many passengers were wearing their coffee and eggs. He looked down and saw a large wet spot in his crotch where he had spilled his coffee. The sight of it made him laugh. At least he was alive *to* laugh.

The cloud cover soon gave way to endless blue and Baker breathed a sigh of relief.

He then saw a slow-moving shadow out the top of his cockpit window. Leaning forward, he looked up.

His eyes widened.

His mouth fell open.

Another airliner was descending on top of them.

# CHAPTER 32

The jumbo airliner above them had just begun its descent. Originating out of Los Angeles, it, too, was destined for Shanghai. Unlike Baker, however, the captain of the other airliner was blithely unaware of what had just happened below. He couldn't see a thing other than blue sky ahead and thick clouds below. His instruments showed no aircraft within miles.

"Hang on!" Baker yelled, jamming the control stick forward to send his plane into a downward dive.

A downward dive for an airliner is not as easy as it sounds, especially when the airliner is already in an upward trajectory. Unlike fighter jets, which have instant maneuverability, jumbo jets respond like aircraft carriers, and Baker's airliner was no exception. In the main cabin, overhead bins flew open. Luggage spilled out. Flight attendants and passengers were falling in the aisles. Children began to cry.

The two giant airliners tobogganed downward into the cloud layer, one above the other, inching nearer each other with each passing second. Baker looked at his gauges, wishing there was something he could do. But his engines were already straining with everything they had.

Baker was about to say his final prayer when a realization hit him. *By God, that's it. We need less speed, not more.*

Praying this would work, Baker eased back on their speed, and the whine of the giant engines decreased as they slowed their thrust, allowing the other airliner to rumble past. When it did, Baker dipped the nose of his aircraft out of its jet blast and banked away to the south.

Once they were safely away from the other jumbo, Baker felt his blood pressure return to normal. *How could this have happened?* He turned the question over in his mind as they leveled off. Three aircraft – two commercial airliners and a fighter jet – in near-collisions over the Pacific.

*Without any warning from Air Traffic Control.*

Baker switched channels and listened to the chatter. From the sound of things, no one else had experienced anything remotely similar. Not only that, nothing alarming was being discussed. Just normal conversations between various pilots and air traffic control. That meant no radar or satellite had observed the incident. The absence of any chatter meant the other jumbo pilot had no idea about what had just happened. The fighter pilot of course would be using one of his military channels to communicate with ground control, not that he expected the military to admit to anything. For now, at least, everything appeared normal.

Except that it was not normal. It was not normal at all.

*How the hell could this have happened?*

"Dave, are you going to get that?" Blair asked for the third time.

Baker replied with a blank stare, then refocused when he realized the intercom was ringing off the hook. Fists were still pounding on the cockpit door.

"They need assurance," said Blair. "An explanation."

Baker glanced toward the cockpit door, then pushed a button and brought the phone to his mouth. When Terry answered, Baker said he would make an announcement in a moment, and without waiting for a reply, clicked off and sat back with the phone still in his hand, thinking about what to say.

In truth, there was not a lot he could say, mainly because he was clueless himself about what had actually occurred. Obviously, he could not tell passengers they had narrowly escaped two mid-air collisions. *Reassurance, not information,* he told himself. *That's what they need to hear.*

Baker brought the phone to his mouth again and said, "Ladies and gentlemen, this is your captain," he began before telling everyone how they had experienced technical difficulties but that everything was now under control. He then clicked off.

Blair gave a start. "That's it? That's all you're going to say?"

"That's all they need to hear."

"We were nearly killed!"

"But we weren't," said Baker, "and the fact that we came close is not something we're going to be telling people right now."

"People need to know what happened."

"*We* don't know what happened, and I'm not about to start fueling the fires of speculation. Here, take the controls."

"Why? What are you doing?"

Baker switched radio frequencies and again put the phone to his mouth. "Finding out what the hell *did* happen. But if I'm right – and I hope to God I'm not – I'm guessing none of our people know."

"Someone has to know."

"Not necessarily."

"Meaning what, exactly?"

"That our GPS network has been hacked. Someone wanted us to crash."

# CHAPTER 33

The locked door was opened for Diane Gustaves and she was admitted into the security council meeting, where a whole alphabet soup of Federal officials, including the president, DNI Shaw, and several of the joint chiefs, were watching a bank of television monitors. The pilot of the F/A-18E was on one of the screens, his flight helmet in hand. He was speaking to a reporter against the thunder of jets from the deck of the USS Ronald Reagan. Gustaves listened to him describe the near-miss and how his instruments had shown nothing coming toward him.

*Hooray for embedded reporters,* Gustaves thought with a shake of her head.

She turned her attention to the next monitor, where a Chinese official was being interviewed, then to the next monitor, where a senior airline executive was speaking. On other monitors were more officials and experts. On others, the talking heads were having a field day with analyses and opinions. One expert was blaming climate change.

Glancing around, Shaw saw Gustaves and threaded his way over to where she was standing.

"This is on you!" he hissed. "A dead secretary, *two* near-misses over the Pacific, a computer virus infecting half of Washington. The common denominator to all of this mayhem: Talanov! And who's responsible for bringing him aboard? You and Wilcox and that phony hearing of yours. I know what a Cold War hero you say he was. In my book, he was nothing more than a disgruntled Commie wanting to cash in big, which we were happy to accommodate because we needed information. So we used him until the Soviet empire came crashing down. But instead of kicking him to the curb, you and Wilcox open the gates of the city, and in he comes, like the Trojan Horse that he is. And now *this.*"

Shaw drew to within inches of Gustaves' face.

"You will pay for this, Madam Congresswoman," he vowed, "and so will Talanov. Now, get him back here so that I can lock his sorry ass behind bars until we determine *exactly* what part he played."

And with a parting sneer, Shaw made his way back to the front of the room, where he joined the circle of advisors surrounding the president.

A few people glanced discreetly at Gustaves. She smiled awkwardly, glanced at her watch, and left the room.

Out in the corridor, Gustaves made her way to the women's bathroom, where she leaned over the sink and stared at herself in the mirror, knowing she would forever bear the guilt of what had happened to Amber. She also knew this was not the time for grief. Right now, she had work to do.

With a quick glance to make sure no one else was in the bathroom, Gustaves took out her cell phone and dialed a private number that was routed through an encrypted bandwidth in the CIA's Advanced Extremely High Frequency network, which utilized a constellation of satellites operated by the United States Air Force. The call was answered on the first ring by Charlie, who was still at her desk at Langley. She had been watching the live feed of news reports being broadcast from the deck of the USS Ronald Reagan.

"Charlie, this is Diane," Gustaves said.

"Yes, Madam Congresswoman?" answered Charlie, sitting forward and muting the news.

"I take it you've heard?"

"Yes, ma'am."

"There's a reason I'm calling you on a secure line. This conversation stays between us."

"Of course, ma'am."

"The virus. Tell me what happened."

"I've walked the cat backward and confirmed their point of entry to be Amber's laptop. What I didn't realize until a few minutes ago was that they planted what I call an onion virus – one with many layers – with the center being where the real danger lies, like a bore worm, with the outer layers keeping us occupied long enough for the bore worm to do its work, which in this instance was entry into and control of our GPS network by way of classified access in your name, which spoofed us into thinking our planes were on course when in fact they weren't."

"Forgive me, Charlie, but I'm exhausted. Can you translate that into something I can understand?"

"Of course, ma'am. As you know, navigation these days – both civilian and military – depends on electronic signals broadcast via our global positioning satellites, which we call GPS. The hackers, whoever they are, took control of our GPS signal by way of Amber's laptop, where they were able to redirect those planes toward one another without any of the pilots realizing it."

"So they weren't just looking for Talanov?"

"They want him, no question, although we don't yet know why. But they specifically targeted you because they also wanted access to our GPS network, which is what Amber's laptop provided."

"But Amber did not have access."

"No, ma'am, but yours did, and she had access to yours via our secure intranet. She had obviously saved your passwords and access codes on her laptop, and once inside our system, they fed in false coordinates for the selected aircraft while invisibly steering them toward one another. That's why no one picked it up. All instruments – on board the aircraft and on the ground – kept receiving the false coordinates, while a separate signal – a cloaked signal – took over their steering. Quick thinking on the parts of the fighter pilot and one of the commercial pilots kept this from becoming a catastrophe."

"Do we know yet who was behind this?"

"The signal appears to have originated in Beijing, although I detected ghost trails back through several other servers in several other cities, so at this point, I'm not really sure."

"Is the Chinese government behind this?" asked Gustaves.

"Someone wants it to look that way."

"But you don't agree?"

"No, ma'am, I don't."

"Why is that?"

"A number of keyword intercepts enabled my software to have recorded a partial conversation between an unidentified male in Hong Kong and an unidentified female in San Francisco. That recording makes me think Dragon Head is behind this. Terms and phrases were used, such as the USS Ronald Reagan, Babikov, electronic mirrors, Shenzhen, Kunming, Chengdu, Nunjing, Qingdao, Beijing, and Straw Sandal, plus something called *Shāng Yī* – which translates to Entropy One – plus the repeated use of Talanov's name."

"Talanov's name was part of that communication thread? You're sure about that?"

"Yes, ma'am. He and *Shāng Yī* were the two main subjects of conversation, along with several references to Straw Sandal. Factored together with everything we know, this unmistakably links Dragon Head with both the USS Ronald Reagan and Talanov. What the connection is, I'm not yet sure."

"This definitely ups the ante on questioning Talanov. Has Bill managed to locate him yet?"

"Yes, ma'am, but there's a problem. Some kind of an attack by Dragon Head's people."

"What happened? Was anyone hurt?"

"Bill didn't elaborate. He said he would fill me in later, although he did confirm that one of the women who murdered Amber had been taken prisoner."

"This changes everything," said Gustaves. "We need to question Talanov and that woman. In fact . . . hang on a minute." Putting Charlie on hold, Gustaves dialed Wilcox, but after two rings, the call went to voicemail. Gustaves left Wilcox an urgent message for him to bring Talanov and his female prisoner back to DC for questioning, saying this was

Alpha Priority. After ending the call, Gustaves reconnected with Charlie and said, "I tried reaching Bill but the call went to voicemail."

"Want me to keep trying?"

"I left him a message to bring Talanov and his prisoner back to DC for questioning. In the meantime, we'll keep giving Bill whatever help he requires, by whatever means."

"Of course, ma'am, but when you say, by whatever means, what exactly are you referring to?"

"Are you willing to bend some rules?" asked Gustaves. "Full disclosure: it could land us in a shit-storm of trouble."

"Great sales pitch. Count me in. What do you need me to do?"

"Set up shop away from the office. What we'll need from you – and by 'we' I mean Bill and I – are results – i.e., information – by whatever means are required to obtain that information. You will be housed in an offsite facility, away from prying eyes."

"I assume you mean Shaw, and, no, I'm not asking you to confirm that. What I would like to know is whether this offsite facility will be properly wired and equipped."

"It already is," said Gustaves, "including a secure line through an encrypted bandwidth so that we can talk freely. Let me know if there's anything else."

"Does an espresso machine count?"

Gustaves smiled. "I'll have one delivered. With a supply of organic, shade-grown, fair-trade, single-plantation Central American espresso beans."

"Madam Congresswoman, you never cease to amaze me."

"I feel the same about you."

"Thank you, ma'am."

"From this point on, it's total secrecy. Our eyes only. Yours, mine, and Bill's."

"Of course, ma'am."

"Alex is already on very thin ice with Shaw, so we need to control what happens next – i.e., the questioning – and I cannot emphasize that enough. There's a connection between Talanov, Dragon Head, and that virus, and we need to find out what it is."

"Do you think Dragon Head will strike again?"

"I think he's just getting started."

# CHAPTER 34

On their way to the motel room, Zak stopped by several ATMs, where Talanov withdrew his limit in cash from each of the machines. Zak was careful to park in blind spots away from the surveillance cameras, and after Talanov was finished, continued south for another twenty minutes before turning east on the 92.

Following the map on Talanov's phone, they took an exit ramp, turned right, then wound their way past some industrial parks and apartment complexes to the motel, where Zak parked in another darkened blind spot, next to an office building that shared the same parking lot. Unlike the motel, which was a relic of the eighties, the office building was sleek and white and triangular-shaped, like a stealth bomber, with seven rows of what looked like dark slits for windows. There were a few other vehicles parked around the building, but for the most part, the lot was dark and empty.

Once Zak switched off the engine, Talanov outlined what was going to happen. He would take Straw Sandal to Hong Kong and negotiate the release of Su Yin. Everyone else would remain with Zak.

"The first order of business," said Talanov, "is making sure you're all safe. And that means disappearing completely."

"How did they find us?" asked Jingfei. "I mean, we know they were looking for you, but how did they know where to look?"

"That's what I intend to find out."

Talanov handed his money to Zak and told him to use it for whatever was needed.

"It should last a few weeks," said Talanov, "and if you need more, I'll get it to you."

Zak nodded and pocketed the money.

"What do you mean, disappear?" asked Kai.

"Someplace remote. Where nobody knows who you are."

"You mean, like, out in the woods?"

"One of our donors owns a cabin in Twain Harte," said Zak, "which is a charming mountain village east of here."

"From now on, you purchase everything with cash," said Talanov. "No credit cards, no bank cards, no phone calls to clients or friends. Nothing that can be traced. Keep to yourselves and stay inside. You're not there to make friends. You're there to disappear until this is over."

"How long will that take?" asked Kai.

"A week, maybe two. Hopefully, not longer."

Talanov looked out the window and saw Wilcox standing in a dark spot near the motel office. His face was not visible although his silhouette was unmistakable.

"Okay," said Talanov, "let's go inside."

"Can we sit here for a minute?" asked Kai.

Talanov looked over his shoulder and saw Kai huddled in the corner, arms crossed like he was cold, his hands tucked out of sight.

"Sure," said Talanov with an understanding smile.

Talanov knew why Kai wanted to linger. The familiarity of Zak's old van made him feel safe. His home, the community center, was now a murder scene. His sister had been kidnapped. His whole world was being threatened. Except this old van, and not just because it was Zak's van, but because the people he loved were all here, too, except for Su Yin, with her absence only heightening the importance of being anchored in the one remaining place he felt safe.

"May I see that picture again?" asked Jingfei, leaning forward between Ginie and Emily. "The one the kidnapper sent of Su Yin?"

Talanov handed his phone to Jingfei, who opened the image and scrutinized the photo.

"Something wrong?" Talanov asked, reading Jingfei's troubled expression.

"This image came as an attachment to a text message, right?" asked Jingfei, returning the phone.

"Yeah," said Talanov just as Wilcox rapped hard on Talanov's window, scaring everyone.

Seeing it was Wilcox, Talanov rolled down his window and said, "Quit creeping around like that."

"How long are you going to keep sitting out here?"

"We're coming in now."

After rolling up his window, Talanov opened his door and stepped out just as Ginie opened the side door and did the same. After everyone had gathered together, Talanov asked Wilcox for the key card, which he handed to Zak. "Go on ahead," he said. "Bill and I need to talk."

"And our guest?" asked Zak over the muffled cries of Straw Sandal kicking against the rear door of the van.

"I'll bring her inside when I come. She still sounds a little upset."

Zak took Talanov by the arm and led him a few steps away. "I need a favor," he said.

"Of course," said Talanov. "What is it?"

"I need to know you'll take care of these kids if something happens to me."

"Nothing is going to happen. That's why you're taking them to the mountains."

"Promise me, Alex."

"Nothing is going to happen."

"We do not know what lies ahead, or to what lengths these people will go. I need to know my kids will have someone to look after them. A parent."

"They already do."

"Promise me. I need to know my kids will be taken care of."

Talanov led Zak a few more steps away. "And Emily? What about her?" he asked quietly.

"The bond of love is not there. You know that as well as I do, and if something happens to me, Emily will send them away. Don't get me wrong. Emily is not a bad person. But she *will* send them away if something happens to me. If that happens, I need to know they will have someone who will love and care for them, no matter what. Someone who will never desert them."

"Like I said, that someone is you."

Zak clasped Talanov on the shoulder. It was a firm clasp that communicated emphasis. "I need to know you will be there for them."

Even in the darkness of the parking lot, Talanov could see the intensity in Zak's eyes. "With pleasure, my friend."

Zak gave Talanov a brief embrace before returning to the others and leading them toward the motel.

"I'll be there in a minute," Ginie told Zak before running back to where Talanov was standing. "I just want to say, don't worry about things at my end. Zak will be watching over us and I will be watching over him. I know it must sound stupid for me to be saying something like that . . ."

"Not at all," said Talanov. "You've always had his back, and with so much else going on, he needs someone watching his back."

After hugging Talanov and kissing him on the cheek, Ginie ran and caught up with the others, who were waiting for her in front of the motel room door.

"Is there something going on between you two?" asked Wilcox.

"I think you know better than that."

"Does she know about Larisa?"

"I think it's time we talked," said Talanov, leading Wilcox to the shaded side of the van, where they could hear Straw Sandal still kicking against the door. "Okay, Bill, what gives? Who am I dealing with here? Why am I involved in whatever this is?"

"Your prisoner's name is Chin Cho Ho," answered Wilcox, "although she goes by the name Straw Sandal. She's from Hong Kong and is the daughter of a crime boss named Dexter Moran, also known as Dragon Head."

Wilcox then gave Talanov a summary of Moran's history and rise to power.

"So Dragon Head's not Chinese?"

"Nope, he's Irish," said Wilcox, "although he was born on the island back when it was a British colony."

"And you know his daughter how?"

"She and another Chinese woman murdered Diane's secretary, then used her laptop to hack Diane's server in order to find out where you were. The murder was caught on camera and a friend of mine in the Hong Kong CIB confirmed her identity."

"Wait a minute," said Talanov. "Moran's people flew all the way to Washington, killed Diane's secretary, then hacked her server in order to find me? For God's sake, why?"

"We don't know. They're Chinese, so we think it's all related to the assassination attempt on Diane."

"Come on, Bill, we've been through that already. Unless of course Turquoise Girl has confirmed something that I don't know about. Is that the case? Has she provided you with a name? Has she given you anything solid?"

"No, and she isn't saying much, either, not that she knows much, anyway."

"Then you need to shake things up," said Talanov. "You need to cut her loose and tell the media your main suspect is being released on a technicality, but that investigators will be taking her into custody again once the correct paperwork has been filed."

"We can't do that! Whoever hired her will hunt her down."

"Exactly. And your people will be waiting. Only then will you know who's behind this, and I'm betting it won't be Dragon Head."

"How can you be so sure?"

"The pieces don't fit. For one thing, Dragon Head wants me, not Diane. He has no motive to kill her."

"Which we can determine by questioning Straw Sandal. That's why we need you both in DC."

"I'm sorry, but I can't."

"What do you mean, you can't?"

"Su Yin's kidnapper has ordered me to bring Straw Sandal to Hong Kong. If I don't, Su Yin will die."

"We need you in DC. It's a matter of national security."

Talanov remembered Wilcox bluffing the policeman back at the pizza parlor with that excuse. "No disrespect, Bill," said Talanov, "but how is this an issue of national security?"

Wilcox knew the details were classified, but he also knew Talanov was the focal point of Amber's murder, or at least one of the focal points, and if they wished to find out why, they needed his cooperation. Yes, Talanov could be put into an interrogation room and grilled as a hostile witness. Angus Shaw would certainly be in favor of that. He and Gustaves, on the other hand, favored a friendlier approach, and that meant looping Talanov into what had actually occurred.

Inviting Talanov to walk with him, Wilcox spoke on the condition of absolutely confidentiality, and once Talanov agreed, proceeded to bring him up to speed with what Gustaves had told him, namely, that Chinese hackers had penetrated their GPS network and fed in false coordinates that almost caused a mid-air collision over the Pacific. And while the reactionaries in Washington were blaming the Chinese government, he and Gustaves knew Dragon Head was to blame.

"That's why I've been ordered to bring you and Straw Sandal back to DC," Wilcox said, pausing beside a neatly groomed tree. "Look, I'm sorry about the little girl, but we need to find out why Dragon Head went to such lengths to find you, and how you relate to the hacking of our GPS. That's why this is an issue of national security. You're at the epicenter of something huge, and we have in our possession the daughter of the man responsible. We can't let this go to waste."

"Go to waste? If I don't deliver Straw Sandal to Hong Kong, Dragon Head will kill Su Yin. That's her name, Bill, Su Yin.

She's not just some nameless little girl. Zak loves her as if she were his own flesh and blood. And I'm now her godfather now, so I feel the same."

"I understand your predicament," said Wilcox, "but you've got to understand mine, and what takes priority. What I can do, though, is phone my friend in the Hong Kong CIB and have her look into it. Maybe she can help."

"*Maybe* she can help? That's not good enough. We're talking about an eleven-year-old girl who's been caught up in something she doesn't understand, and sure as hell doesn't deserve. Her life is on the line because of me, so if you think I'm going to hand her future over to someone who can *possibly* help, you've got another think coming."

"It's all I can do right now."

Talanov started to lecture Wilcox about bureaucratic bullshit, but decided instead to walk away before he said something he would later regret. Yes, he was angry – furious, in fact – but Wilcox was a friend and a good friend at that.

He understood the tough spot Wilcox was in. Gustaves, too. A catastrophe had almost occurred and Diane's congressional opponents would be scheming ways to exploit this for political gain, with top dogs like Shaw barking orders to subservients like Wilcox. The orders would be hastily issued and geared to make the top dogs look authoritative and in charge.

Unfortunately, those orders would not be practical or beneficial. They would only make matters worse, because the top dogs had already decided who was guilty, and in their one-eyed efforts to prove that, would ignore the trails of actual evidence, which these days did not seem to matter. To people like Shaw, destruction of political opponents was more important than anything else.

"Will you please stop?" Wilcox called out while trying to keep up with Talanov's long strides.

Talanov paused beside another of the groomed trees that dotted the parking lot. When Wilcox caught up, he suddenly noticed the Hawaiian shirt and plaid shorts that Wilcox was wearing.

"Do you know how ridiculous you look?" asked Talanov.

"I was on my way to Disneyland," snarled Wilcox, "but rerouted my plane so that I could come and get you. So quit giving me a hard time."

Talanov laughed, then grew serious. "You have your orders, Bill. I get that. But do you really think questioning Straw Sandal in DC is going to help us find out why Dragon Head wants me in Hong Kong?"

"Actually, yes, I do. In DC, we control the narrative. Right now, the narrative is controlling you."

"And that right there is their blind spot. A blind spot we can exploit. But we can only do that in Hong Kong."

"And I can't let you do that."

"You have to," said Talanov. "If we do this your way, Su Yin dies."

"I don't think you understand how serious this is. They *hacked* our GPS. If a midair collision had occurred, up to a thousand people would have died. National security is not some abstract term. Lives are at stake here, Alex. Potentially, millions of lives if this continues."

"I understand that. But you need to think this through. Flying us to DC will not give you the answers you need. If Dragon Head is behind the hacking, and if you really want to stop him, then the only place to do that is in Hong Kong. DC is a waste of time. We need to do this my way."

"And I'm telling you that's not going to happen. My people are going to question Straw Sandal . . . in DC."

"How long will that take? Days? Weeks? Months? How reliable will she be? What if she decides to stall so that Dragon Head can hack your GPS again? Who's controlling the narrative then?"

Wilcox did not reply.

"There are times you stay on the highway, Bill, and times you go off-road. That's because the highway doesn't always go where you need to go. Sometimes, the only way to reach your destination is on a path that doesn't exist. Except we do have a path, and that path is me, and Hong Kong is where I'm going."

# CHAPTER 35

Inside the motel room, Ginie was finishing her shower while Jingfei and Kai were on one of the queen-sized beds, arguing over the remote. Emily was in the other bed, reading the motel Bible. She was propped against the headboard, pillows stuffed behind her, the Bible in her lap. She was trying to concentrate but found it hard with all the noise. At regular intervals, she would throw the kids sharp glances, but they were too busy to notice, or didn't care. Leaning against the credenza, his arms folded in front of him, Zak was lost in thought.

Jingfei soon abandoned the fight and jumped up off the bed. "When are we going to do something?" she complained, pacing back and forth.

Motioning for Jingfei and Kai to follow, Zak stepped outside and, once the kids had joined him, closed the door and said, "We'll get her back. Alex will get her back."

"No way can you promise that," Kai replied.

"Technically, no, I can't. But I've known Alex since he was a skinny cadet of sixteen. I'm also the person who trained him. So in many ways I know his ability better than he does. Which is why I can assure you, he'll get her back."

"But you don't know that, right?"

With a rueful smile, Zak watched a young couple enter their room three doors down. "Like you and Alex," he said, looking back at the kids, "my parents were killed when I was young. In my case, I was two. Having no family, I grew up in the military with a bunch of other recruits. But when I turned seventeen, I met Annika."

Zak paused and smiled at the memory.

"Annika had hair the color of maple syrup," he continued, "thick and long, to her waist, and eyes so blue they made the sky looked pale. She was sixteen and smart as a whip. Funny, too. Anyway, we fell in love and she soon got pregnant, which was the happiest day of our lives. Nine months later, our little girl, Yana, was born. I was so happy to be a father. About three months later, I was sent away to Siberia for maneuvers, and while I was gone, Annika and Yana were taken to the hospital for a round of required vaccinations. Four days later, they were dead. Faulty vaccines, I was told."

"My *God*," Jingfei exclaimed, covering her mouth with her hand. "Zak, I never knew."

"Years later, Alex found out the KGB had stepped in to make sure I didn't have any 'distractions,' as they called them, or divided loyalties, or potential weaknesses that a foreign agent could exploit."

"You mean, they killed them?"

Zak nodded. "It took Alex two years to track down the agents who murdered my Annika and Yana, but he did, and he made them pay."

"You mean, like . . ."

"Yes," said Zak. "And while that's probably the worst example for me to use right now, let me assure you, Alex *will* get Su Yin back. You need to hang on to that."

Jingfei and Kai both nodded.

"Do you still think about them?" asked Kai.

"Every day," Zak replied. "Annika was the love of my life."

"So, why'd you marry Emily?" asked Jingfei, then flinching. "Sorry, that's none of my business."

"It's okay," said Zak. "Emily has a good heart, and we both shared this burning desire to change the world. Her way of doing it is through the legal system. Everything a battle. My way is through the community center. Everything personal and chaotic. Emily wasn't prepared for that."

"Do you think you can work things out?"

"I made a commitment and I'll honor it."

"What if she doesn't honor hers?"

"All you need to remember is," said Zak, wrapping a burly arm around each of the kids, "I will honor my commitment to you. No one is taking you away."

Jingfei gave Zak a hug.

"Although I am curious," added Zak, "about how you were able to listen in on that original telephone conversation between Emily and me."

Jingfei and Kai shuffled uneasily.

Zak waited and did not speak.

Finally, Jingfei said, "I put some spyware on Emily's phone that recorded your conversation and uploaded it automatically to the cloud."

"Why on earth would you do that?"

"Because Emily was always complaining how you had no money. So I put some spyware on her phone that allowed me to access your bank account and see how much money you really had. It also recorded her conversations."

Rubbing his chin, Zak nodded thoughtfully. "When did you install it?" he asked.

"Nine months ago, maybe, I guess. That's when I learned how much you were spending on Kai, and how you were always bailing him out and paying for stuff he stole. I knew then you were the real deal."

Zak chuckled. "Then that explains it."

"Explains what?"

Zak recounted the change that he noticed in Jingfei's attitude nine months ago. Prior to that time, she had been defensive and sour. After that time, she began volunteering in the kitchen, doing odd jobs, helping in the office.

"You also began to smile," said Zak.

"I smiled before then."

"Really?" asked Zak, amused.

"Okay, so maybe not a lot. But I smiled, though, didn't I, Kai? Go on, tell him I did."

Kai grinned and shrugged.

"I did!" insisted Jingfei.

Kai grinned and shrugged again.

"Jerk," grumbled Jingfei, punching Kai on the arm.

"Hey, after what you three went through, I don't blame you for not smiling a lot," said Zak, recalling the night he met the kids.

They had been sent to him by "Dutch," the seventy-something-year-old Chinese owner of Little Sami Sun's convenience store down the hill. Little Sami Sun's was a neighborhood icon, with neon signs advertising an ATM, check cashing, beer, lotto, and fresh coffee, plus windows full of decals featuring ice cream, soft drinks, dim sum, phone cards, hamburgers, French fries, and, of course, his famous wonton tacos, which were spicy meat-filled dumplings made with tortillas instead of rice paper.

"How did he get that name" asked Jingfei. "A man from China named Dutch?"

Zak laughed and said he remembered asking Dutch the same question. "And do you know what he told me? He said, 'You remember me good, yes? Not many Chinamen named Dutch.'"

"So, he just . . . made it up?"

Zak laughed again, then told Dutch's version of how the kids had entered his store about ten o'clock one stormy night. "He said you were ragged and soaked and shivering, so it was obvious you weren't there to buy anything, which he could tell by the way you lingered in front of the fast food section. So he called you over to the front counter—"

"—and gave us free corndogs and fries!" said Kai. "Dutch was a really cool guy, even though he was, like, really old."

"Those corndogs tasted *so* good," added Jingfei. "And while we, like, wolfed them down and drank that weirdo Chinese canned drink, he phoned a taxi."

"And told the driver to bring you to me," Zak said, completing the story.

"He said you were a good friend who served free food to anyone who came through his doors."

"And eat you did," said Zak, recounting how Jingfei and Kai devoured four helpings of leftover meatloaf while Su Yin chatted happily about storm clouds and how they were formed.

"And you asked, 'Where did a young girl like you learn about equatorial evaporation and cumulonimbus cloud formations?' And with her hands on her hips, Su Yin said—"

"—'I'm nine years old,' as if that should be reason enough."

Everyone laughed at the memory and stood in silence until the sound of voices drew their attention toward three silhouettes moving toward them across the parking lot. And while it was too dark to see their faces, their physiques were unmistakable. Talanov was the tall one, Wilcox the wide one, with Straw Sandal the petite one in between.

Jingfei looked back at Zak. "So, are you, like, mad at me about the spyware?"

"How can I be mad about something that's caused so much good?"

"What do you mean?"

"For one thing, it let you know we weren't lying. For another, it let you know how much you mean to me, and that I will always be there for you."

"What about Emily? Not to rub it in or anything, but she pays all the bills and definitely wants us out. She said so herself, and that she's already called some friend of hers down at the Juvenile Justice Center."

"13:5, remember?"

"No disrespect, Zak, but Emily's word seems to carry a lot more clout than God's. I mean, yeah, I know God will never desert us, and I know you don't *want* to, but we can still get the boot if Emily gets her way."

"And I'm trying my best to be the peacemaker and not doing a very good job. I guess that's because I've never been much of a peacemaker before, and I'm not sure how to do it. Back in the day, if someone caused us trouble, I'd break them in half. Problem solved. Then God came along and began teaching me a new way . . . a kinder way."

"Kind doesn't mean wishy-washy," said Jingfei. "No

woman wants a pajama boy. I mean, you don't need to be a Neanderthal, either, but don't be afraid to be a man. Women want men to be men."

Zak drew back and squinted hard at Jingfei. "Since when do you know about men? Do we need to, you know, have *the talk?*"

Jingfei slugged Zak on the arm. *"Ew,* no, shut up!"

Zak grabbed both kids in a bear hug and laughed.

Seeing Talanov and the others approach, Kai looked up at Zak and said, "Can Alex really get Su Yin back? I mean, he has to go to China, but does he even speak Chinese? How will he get into the country?"

Zak stiffened slightly – hopefully not enough for the kids to notice – because he wondered the same things, too.

But now was not the time to introduce doubts. Now was the time for reassurance.

"Don't worry, he'll figure it out," Zak replied.

He just hoped the kids believed him.

# CHAPTER 36

"Shaw will *never* agree to this," Wilcox was saying when he and Talanov joined Zak and the kids outside the motel room. Straw Sandal's legs were free although her hands were still taped behind her. The cool evening winds had picked up and were rustling the leaves of some nearby trees.

"Don't ask for his permission," Talanov replied.

"And exactly how am I supposed to get away with something like that?"

"Get away with what?" asked Zak.

"Alex wants me to steal the company jet and fly him to Hong Kong," said Wilcox, throwing up his hands and turning away, then spinning back around again. "There is no way that I can do that. I can't just steal a jet."

"Why not?" asked Kai. "You're from the CIA. You can do whatever you want."

Wilcox growled and shook his head.

"Good point, Kai," agreed Talanov. "Bill *can* do whatever he wants."

"That is bullshit and you know it," Wilcox fired back.

"You told me they made the Gulfstream available to you," said Talanov. "So they can hardly accuse you of stealing something they gave to you in the first place."

"They *loaned* me the Gulfstream for the express purpose of flying you and Straw Sandal to DC, which, in case you'd forgotten, is east of here. Hong Kong is west. I doubt me saying, 'Oops, I got turned around,' will get me very far, except maybe to Leavenworth for twenty years."

"You're the spy king, figure it out. Now, come on, let's head inside. We have a lot to discuss."

Muttering and fuming, Wilcox followed Talanov and Straw Sandal into the motel room. Jingfei and Kai were next, followed by Zak, who made a quick scan of the parking lot before entering the room and closing the door.

Ginie and Emily stood when the group entered. They had been sitting on one of the beds, watching a news report about the near-misses over the Pacific. Streaming along the bottom of the screen was a ticker tape report about the community center murders, the kidnapping, and the shootings at the Sour Dough Pizza Parlor.

Talanov introduced the women to Wilcox before making Straw Sandal sit in a stuffed chair by the window. He then switched off the television and turned to face the group.

The first order of business was filling the group in on what he knew, namely, that he had been targeted by a Chinese crime lord named Dragon Head, who was responsible not only for the murders of Amina and Ramona, but also the kidnapping of Su Yin. No, he did not know why he had been targeted, although he would find out when he got to Hong Kong, which was where he was taking the woman seated in the corner of the room, who would be exchanged for Su Yin.

"I'm going with you," said Ginie.

"Out of the question," said Talanov.

"Look, I understand why you want us tucked safely away in the mountains," Ginie replied. "You can't be worried about our safety while trying to navigate the challenges you'll encounter. I can help. I speak the language."

Talanov again refused, saying, "Bill has a friend in the Hong Kong CIB. She'll help me. He's known her for years."

"What's the CIB?"

"Their Criminal Intelligence Bureau. It's like our FBI."

"Is this friend planning to accompany you everywhere you go? Do you know and trust this person? As a law enforcement official, will she go along with whatever it is you're planning to do, which I doubt will be totally by the book?"

Ginie paused to let her words sink in.

"Alex, *think*," she continued. "If you need speed and stealth – and I'm guessing not everything you're planning will *not* be by the book – then you'll need someone to help who is not part of the system. Someone you trust. Someone who can translate what's being said around you."

"Ginie's right," said Jingfei, "except I'm the one who should go. I speak the language fluently and Su Yin is my sister."

"The fact that Su Yin is your sister is precisely why you shouldn't be going," countered Ginie. "You're too emotionally involved."

"Ginie, you don't speak the language, not fluently, anyway. I mean, yes, you speak a little, but nowhere nearly as good as me."

"And you'll be arguing with Alex every step of the way. I know you, Jing. You throw some of the worst tantrums I've ever seen, especially when you don't get your way."

"And you're injured," Jingfei fired back. "You look like a zombie with that splint on your nose. Everywhere you go, people will stare."

"Enough, both of you," said Talanov. "Neither one of you is going. Bill and I can handle this ourselves."

"Really?" asked Jingfei, stationing herself in front of Talanov and confronting him eye to eye. "I heard you and Spy Bill over there arguing outside, and let's just say he's not exactly in favor of your harebrained scheme."

"Spy Bill?" asked Wilcox with a raised eyebrow.

"In fact," Jingfei continued without missing a beat, "Spy Bill said helping you could land him in Leavenworth. So you'll excuse me if I'm not exactly brimming with confidence about you two handling this on your own."

"We'll manage," Talanov replied.

"You'll manage? Did you not hear what Spy Bill said? He's been *ordered* to fly you back to DC. It wasn't a suggestion. It was an order!"

"What's with the Spy Bill stuff?" asked Wilcox irritably.

But Jingfei didn't let up.

"But let's say Spy Bill is willing to throw his career down the tubes and help you out. How do you think the suits in DC are going to respond when they find out Spy Bill has stolen the company jet and flown it to China in the middle of a national security crisis . . . *with China?* Do you think they'll be sympathetic and understanding? Will they say, 'Aw, that's okay, Bill, we understand. You needed to help out a friend.' But let's say by some miracle that Spy Bill gets away with it. What do you plan to do when you get there? Ginie is right. You don't speak the language, and Spy Bill's cop friend may not be the look-the-other-way kind of friend you need her to be."

"Are you finished yet?" asked Talanov.

"You need help!" cried Jingfei.

"Maybe so, but it's not going to come from you," stated Talanov. He worked the screen of his phone, found the image of Su Yin, and held it up for Jingfei to see. "They have your sister. Do you get that? Your *sister*. I can't negotiate her release with an emotional teenager tagging along. It's why doctors don't allow family members in the operating room. They can't handle it. They freak out. They get in the way."

Jingfei snatched Talanov's phone and showed him the same image of Su Yin. "Do you have any idea what this is?"

Talanov reached for his phone but Jingfei batted his hand away.

"Believe me, it's not what you think," she said while working the screen. "Photos are usually shown as part of the message. But not this one. It came as a link to an attachment – a seven-megabyte attachment – when photos are normally no more than two. Do you know what that means?"

Jingfei glanced up when Talanov exhaled impatiently.

"Precisely. You haven't got a clue," she said, working the phone some more, then showing Talanov the screen again, which was filled with computer code.

"I have no idea what I'm looking at," said Talanov, his frustration growing.

"It's a code that activated your camera," said Jingfei, working the screen again, then holding it up again for Talanov to see. "Any idea what *this* is?" When she spoke, the screen showed an oscillating graph of her voice.

Talanov glanced uneasily at Wilcox.

"It's spyware, you moron, installed as an executable virus that *you* activated when you opened Su Yin's photo. That means they've been watching everything, hearing everything, recording everything. They're tracking your every move!" Jingfei threw the phone on the floor and stomped on it. "You're a *dinosaur*," she shouted while Talanov watched her smashing his phone into pieces. "You'll get us killed. Get *Su Yin* killed. You. Need. Help!"

Talanov stared down at his phone lying in fragments on the carpet. If Jingfei was right, he did need help, because he didn't know the first thing about hacking, spyware, and viruses.

But he was not about to accept help from a hotheaded kid who had just destroyed his phone. Jingfei was smart, no doubt about that, and she had just proved it, and he knew he could use her help.

But she had also just proved what a liability she could be. Cool heads, not hot ones, were what he needed, which meant he would have to figure out another way to compensate for his technological ignorance.

Bending down, Talanov began picking up the shards of plastic and electronic components. He tried fitting them together, knowing it was a futile attempt, and with a sigh of resignation, walked over and dropped them into the trashcan.

"Well?" Jingfei asked.

"You're going to the mountains," declared Talanov.

Jingfei glared at Talanov, then ran over to Zak and grabbed him by the hands. "Talk to him," she pleaded. "Tell him to let me go. Su Yin's life is on the line. He'll get her killed!"

Zak looked over at Talanov, who shook his head, and with a heavy sigh, he looked back at Jingfei, his eyes saying what his mouth could not.

"I hate you, hate *both* of you!" Jingfei shouted, storming out of the room.

"Jingfei!" Zak shouted to the sound of the slamming door.

He started to go after her but Ginie gestured for him to stay, saying that she would go. Motioning for Emily to come with her, the two women hurried after Jingfei.

Standing near the door into the bathroom, Kai watched Ginie and Emily leave. Watched Zak close his eyes in anguish. Watched Talanov rub his forehead anxiously. Watched Wilcox staring up at the ceiling with a hopeless look on his face. He then looked over at Straw Sandal, who was sitting in her chair with a smirk on her face.

"Seems pretty simple to me," said Kai, drawing everyone's attention. "I mean, I know I'm just a kid, but why does it have to be either/or? Alex wants Bill to fly him to Hong Kong. Bill says he can't because he's been ordered back to DC. But if that happens, Su Yin gets killed. And neither one of you wants to give in." He paused to make eye contact with each of the men. "So, why can't you do both?" he asked, looking at Wilcox. "Why can't you fly Alex to Hong Kong, help him get my sister back, then fly him to DC? I mean, sure, you might get yelled at, but isn't saving a life worth getting yelled at?"

"It's not that simple," said Wilcox.

"Kai's right, why not do both?" said Talanov. "Like one of those round-the-world tickets."

"Because *she* gets off in Hong Kong," enunciated Wilcox while nodding toward Straw Sandal, "and we lose our ability to question her. We need to find out what she knows, as in why they wanted to find you, and why they tried killing Diane."

"You're still assuming the two are connected."

"They have to be. Aside from you as the common denominator, what other common denominator do we have? China. Specifically, Dragon Head."

"And I'm telling you that may not be the case. It may be but it may not be, and if you assume Dragon Head is the one who tried to kill Diane, you're blinding yourself to the possibility that someone else is behind it."

"All the more reason to question Straw Sandal," countered

Wilcox. "To find out what she knows."

"Why not question her on our way to Hong Kong? You've interrogated prisoners before. Do it on the airplane. You know the drill."

"The drill, as you call it, cannot take place in a comfy seat aboard the company jet. It can only take place in a concrete cell in Cuba, where Straw Sandal knows she will never see daylight again unless she cooperates."

"And Su Yin? Will she ever see daylight again? Will she see her family again? I seem to remember you convincing me to join Diane's committee because it was the right thing to do. Well, this is the right thing to do. Like you yourself said, national security is not just some abstract term. It's about people. People like Su Yin Cho. We have to do this, Bill. We have to go to Hong Kong. You know it and I know it. It's the right thing to do."

# CHAPTER 37

"If we do this," said Wilcox, "and I cannot believe I'm actually entertaining that possibility, my career is finished . . . in the sewer."

"Not if we succeed."

"Which is a mighty big if."

"There are huge risks either way. The question is, which choice carries the greatest opportunity for success? DC isn't that choice. On the surface, it may appear to be the best option, and for you personally, it probably is. You'll be obeying your orders. But if you truly want to stop Dragon Head, Hong Kong is where we need to go. Shaw will get angry and make threats, but in the end, it will all go quietly away because we will have delivered. We will have averted a national security crisis *and* saved a little girl's life. They may even give you one of those stars on the wall."

Wilcox snorted and shook his head.

"Please," pleaded Kai, his desperate eyes on Wilcox.

"Come on, Bill, let's do this," said Talanov.

Wilcox looked like he was physically chewing on something sour until, finally, he growled with resignation. Talanov grinned and clasped Wilcox on the shoulder just as a knock sounded on the door. Zak went to the door and looked through the peephole. When Jingfei cocked her head and made a face into the peephole, Zak chuckled and opened the door.

Jingfei entered with Ginie and Emily.

"Are you guys okay?" asked Zak.

"We had a good talk," replied Emily. "We worked a lot of things out."

Jingfei approached Talanov and shuffled awkwardly in front of him. "I know I can be a handful," she confessed, "but it's only because I know I can help. But you won't let me, and that frustrates me because I'm good at the stuff you need. I talked it over with Emily, and she said it was okay with her if I went along. But she said I could go only if you and Zak agreed, and that I had to promise to do what I'm told, that you were the boss. So I'm asking you to please let me go."

"I can help, too," said Kai. "I can do stuff Jing can't."

"Kai, don't mess this up!" shouted Jingfei.

"He needs my help, too," argued Kai. "Sure, you're good at the tech stuff, but I know the streets, and if Alex and Spy Bill have to split up, I can go with one of them and you can go with the other. I speak Chinese, too. Maybe not as good as you, but good enough to keep them out of trouble."

"I can handle this on my own."

"No, you can't. They're old white guys, Jing. They'll stand out like a pair of marshmallows."

Talanov sat Jingfei and Kai on the edge of the bed and knelt in front of them. "I've never been called a marshmallow before," he began.

"No offense," said Kai, "but it's true. You'll stand out. Big time. Me and Jing won't. We're Chinese, which means we can get stuff done without attracting attention. If someone's talking behind your back, or if they're lying to your face, we'll be there to tell you the truth."

"I agree," said Talanov, "and of the surface, your reasoning makes sense. But if you come with us, I would be worried about something happening to you."

"And if something happens to you?" Jingfei asked. "What then?"

"Bill will be there. So will his friend, Alice."

"And if something happens when Alice or Bill isn't around?"

"We'll figure it out," said Talanov.

"You'll figure it out?" exclaimed Jingfei, jumping to her feet.

Talanov stood. "I need you to quit fighting me on this. You've seen what these people can do."

"I've seen how easy it was for them to put a virus on your phone. Will you be able to see the next trap they set? You may trust Alice, but I don't, and it's my sister's life we're talking about. You need to let us come with you."

"What happens if they kidnap you?" Talanov asked in return. "They kidnapped Su Yin, and right now, Su Yin is their only leverage, and Straw Sandal is ours. Right now, we have a chance. But if they kidnap one or both of you, everything changes. Please, go with Zak to the mountains."

Jingfei and Kai looked angrily away.

"Please," said Talanov again. "I'd like to leave with your blessing."

Finally, grudgingly, Jingfei and Kai both nodded.

With an understanding smile, Talanov encircled them with a hug. "You're Zak's kids, and that means you're my kids, too."

"Do you mean that?" asked Jingfei, looking up at him.

"Absolutely."

"Then you need to let us go with you. Su Yin is my sister, and she's a minor, and if you run into legal trouble, I can intercede because I'm her family and I'm legally an adult. Come on, you know I'm right."

Talanov laughed. "You just don't quit, do you? However, if I do run into any legal problems, I promise to phone Zak, and he and Emily will involve you to help solve whatever problems I may encounter."

"Promise to call if you have any questions? I can still help, even if it's over the phone. Translation. Legal stuff. Tech stuff. Anything Spy Bill and his team of trained monkeys can't handle, which I'm guessing will be a lot."

Wilcox growled and rolled his eyes.

"Absolutely," replied Talanov with a smile.

"Don't forget, the people you're up against are expert hackers, so do *not* open any attachments, and if you're ever unsure about anything, *call*. I'm available twenty-four-seven."

Talanov nodded. "Okay, it's time to go."

"Where do you leave from?" asked Jingfei.

"San Francisco airport. The Jonsair hangar."

Wilcox cleared his throat.

"Oh, come on, Bill, it's not like it's a huge secret or anything."

Wilcox responded with a reprimanding glare.

"Okay, so maybe it is," Talanov conceded, "but these guys need a point of contact in case of an emergency."

"In an emergency, they should call Charlie."

"Who's Charlie?" asked Jingfei.

Wilcox took a card from his wallet and handed it to Jingfei. "My assistant. If there's a problem, call her. She'll take care of it. So do not – and I repeat, do *not* – make contact with anyone at the hangar. That facility is strictly off limits."

"You got it," said Jingfei, pocketing the card. "I promise not to tell anyone you're operating undercover and illegally out of the Jonsair hangar."

Wilcox forced a clenched-teeth smile that showed his patience was wearing thin. Jingfei grinned and punched Wilcox playfully on the arm.

Talanov turned to Wilcox and said, "I'll need your cell phone."

"Why?"

"For Zak. Mine got broken, remember?" Talanov threw Jingfei a quick grin and Jingfei grinned back.

"My phone is a satellite cell."

"Which is why he needs it," said Talanov. "There's no coverage where he's going."

"It's an *encrypted* cell," replied Wilcox, enunciating carefully to communicate his implication.

"It's your work phone, yeah, I get it. Functional anywhere in the world. Which is exactly what Zak needs. Now, let me have your phone."

"And if I need to call Charlie or Diane? Or any of several dozen other people that I know? What if they need to call me?"

"We'll buy you a new phone when we get to Hong Kong.

You can text everyone your number once we know what that number is."

"And if I need to discuss classified material?"

"Easy," said Talanov. "Don't."

"It's not that simple!"

"Yes, it is. You're supposed to be on vacation."

"Which was cancelled, thanks to you."

"Point is, DC was prepared to function without you for two weeks, anyway, so it's not like we're inconveniencing anyone."

"You're inconveniencing me!" cried Wilcox.

"Yeah, well, you don't count."

"Vacation or not, I'm supposed to always be reachable."

"You will be."

"My directory's in my phone. Numbers that are private."

"I can transfer your directory," offered Jingfei. "Once you get it, text me your new number and I'll take care of the rest."

"My directory is password protected."

"Easy. Tell me your password."

"And give you access to sensitive information? Absolutely not."

"I promise not to look."

Wilcox glared at Jingfei.

"Delete the important things," said Talanov. "It's backed up on one of your encrypted clouds, anyway, so it's not like you're going to lose it."

"What happens if someone needs to reach me before we get to Hong Kong? What if I need to call Charlie? What if the phone we buy in Hong Kong is locked into a different network? What if it can be hacked by the Chinese? What if it's already been programmed for eavesdropping? The last thing I want is the Chinese government listening in on official calls. This is too risky. I can't take the chance."

"I've got a phone," said Kai. He dug Emily's phone out of his pocket and held it out.

"Hey! How did you get that?" exclaimed Emily. "My desk

drawer was *locked!*" She reached for her phone but Jingfei blocked her.

"We needed it," Jingfei said.

"How did you get into my desk?" demanded Emily.

"Easy," answered Jingfei. "After Ramona was killed, we wanted to call the police, so Kai crawled in and picked the lock."

"Well, it's mine. I want it back."

"Sorry, that's not going to happen."

Taking the phone from Kai, Jingfei stepped around Emily and handed it to Talanov, who smiled his thanks before handing it to Wilcox.

"There you go," said Talanov. "Unlimited text and talk." To Emily: "We'll return it when this is over."

"I am *not* surrendering my satellite cell," said Wilcox, handing it back.

"We're wasting time," said Talanov, replacing the phone in Wilcox's hand. "And Zak needs yours. Now hurry up and do your password thing. We have to go."

Wilcox glared hard at Talanov before grudgingly turning his back and entering a lengthy password, then navigating to his directory of primary contacts. And after a slow, deliberate exhale, he handed his phone to Jingfei, who tried accepting it but Wilcox would not let go.

"I promised I wouldn't look, and I meant it," Jingfei said. "I know I give you a hard time, but I would never do anything to violate your trust. Please, this is really important."

Wilcox reluctantly let go and Jingfei began working the screen. "That is certainly a colorful shirt," she remarked.

"What's wrong with my shirt?" Wilcox snarled.

"Simply making casual conversation to put you in a happy mood," Jingfei said with a grin while still working the screen.

Wilcox growled and threw Talanov a look of irritation.

Talanov tried not to smile but couldn't help it.

"Emily, what's your number?" Jingfei asked. Emily told her and Jingfei entered the number into Wilcox's phone, and after working the screen some more, Emily's phone chimed. "Okay, you're set to go," she said, looking at Wilcox. "Your directory has been installed. Obviously, Emily's phone can't utilize your encrypted bandwidth because it contains no encryption software, so keep the spy talk to a minimum. Don't forget to let your contacts know you're on a downgraded device, too. If you want, I can send them all a text message in a fraction of the time it would take you."

"I think I can manage," grumbled Wilcox.

"Do not open any attachments, either," Jingfei cautioned, "unless you know what you're doing. Remember, your prisoner over there knows exactly how clueless you and Alex are in that department, never mind that neither of you can read a street sign or will have the slightest idea about what's going on or what to do if you get lost, because you don't understand the language."

"I wish I could say I'm going to miss you," Wilcox replied.

"Oh, you'll miss me, all right, but by then it will be too late."

"And on that note, I think we'll leave," said Zak, ushering Jingfei and Kai toward the door, then motioning for Ginie and Emily.

"I'll walk you out," said Talanov. He paused to whisper in Wilcox's ear, then followed the others outside.

With Wilcox remaining in the room to guard Straw Sandal, Talanov accompanied Zak and the others to the van, where the two men embraced while Emily climbed into the front seat, with Jingfei and Ginie in the seat behind, and Kai in the rear seat by himself.

"*Kak odin,*" said Zak, repeating their "as one" motto.

"*Kak odin,*" Talanov replied.

"By the way," said Zak, clasping Talanov on the shoulder. "There's a wonderful parable in the gospel of Luke, where Yeshua, Jesus, asks this question: 'Which among you, upon learning you've lost one of your sheep, does not leave the ninety-nine and go find the one that was lost?'" He paused to smile, then said, "Like David, we take on the lion or the bear.

We go to the ends of the earth . . . to the pits of hell itself."
With a broad grin, he squeezed Talanov on the shoulder.
"That is you, Alex. You say you don't know much about God,
but you have more of God in you than you realize. You are
fighting for the one who needs help."

"Like you did for me in Afghanistan."

"It's what we do."

And with a final embrace, Zak climbed into his van and
drove away.

Inside the motel room, Wilcox positioned himself by the
door and sent a text message to Charlie. Seconds later, the
phone in his hand rang.

"You're using an unsecured phone?" asked Charlie.

"Long story, but, yes. You got my text?"

"I did, but I want to be sure I understand you correctly. You
want me to make it look as though Talanov and Chin Chi Ho
are on a commercial flight tonight to Hong Kong?"

"That's right," Wilcox replied.

"And I'm to do whatever it takes to make them appear to be
on that flight?"

"Correct."

"Even if they're not?"

"Correct."

"So, when you say, whatever it takes, do you mean, literally,
whatever it takes?"

"Correct."

"Care to elaborate?"

Wilcox did not reply.

"Are you keeping your end of the conversation vague because someone is seated nearby?"

"You got it."

"Whatever it takes, then," said Charlie. "What about you?
Are you heading back tonight?"

Wilcox did not reply.

"A flight plan's already been filed that shows you heading
back soon," said Charlie, reading the Gulfstream's flight plan.

"Arriving late tonight or early tomorrow morning, whatever you like calling it. Is that still correct?"

Wilcox did not reply.

"Are you heading back at all?" asked Charlie.

Wilcox did not reply.

"And if anyone asks where you are and what you're doing?"

Wilcox did not reply

Charlie smiled. "You got it, Boss."

At the far end of the parking lot, near the stealth bomber building, a blue sedan was parked in the shadows. Inside the sedan were the two men from the poultry delegation, now dressed in black fatigues and sweatshirts. The driver went by the call sign Alpha and he had a cell phone to his ear. His partner, Bravo, was holding an electronic tablet that showed a digital street map of the area. When Babikov's van drove away, a blinking dot on the map began to move.

"Yes, sir, we have them in sight," said Alpha into his phone.

"Are they together?" asked Angus Shaw from the sidewalk in front of his Colonial mansion in rural Virginia. In the darkness surrounding Shaw were four armed security guards.

"They were," Alpha said, "but they've parted company. Babikov, his wife, and three others, including a couple of kids, have just driven away, leaving Talanov, Wilcox, and Straw Sandal at the motel. The GPS on Wilcox's phone shows his phone to be on the move, but Wilcox isn't with it."

"Wilcox must have given his phone to Babikov, which means Babikov is heading into a region with poor cell coverage, i.e., someplace remote."

"What do you want us to do?"

"Wilcox has already filed a flight plan for DC, which means he'll soon be headed this way."

"Want us to keep him in sight? Make sure he and Talanov get on the Gulfstream?"

Shaw paced the sidewalk in the darkness. A few fireflies were drifting among the trees. "My concern is why Wilcox would give his cell phone to Babikov. Is it possible you've been made and that this is a diversion?"

"No, sir, no way," replied Alpha.

Leaving the sidewalk, Shaw began strolling among the maple trees dotting his spacious lawn. A perimeter of security guards went with him. "Then the only reason Talanov would be sending Babikov and the others away would be for them to go to ground somewhere." Shaw thought about that some more. "Which means Talanov considers Babikov and the others to be his point of vulnerability." Shaw thought about that some more. "Have you got your equipment packs?"

"Of course, sir," Alpha replied.

"Good, then stay with Babikov. You've got them on GPS, so remain well out of sight. If we need leverage with Talanov, I want you in place."

# CHAPTER 38

After leaving the parking lot, Zak turned onto Metro Center Boulevard, heading east. Designed by the same people who designed the office park near the motel, Metro Center Boulevard was verdant with shrubs and trees.

In a little over a minute, they came to the light at Foster City Boulevard. It was a major intersection with six lanes of cross traffic. Even at this late hour, traffic was steady. Through the intersection ahead was a brightly lit service station. Next to the service station was an IHOP.

"Can we get something to eat?" asked Kai.

"How about in a couple of hours?" Zak replied. "I'd like to get through the hills."

"You're filling up with gas, though, right? There's an IHOP right next door. IHOP equals food, equals I'll be back before you know it. You get the gas and I'll get the burgers, and fries, and milkshakes, too. And maybe some of those batter-fried apple pies."

"I'd hardly call that food."

"Come on, Zak, *please?* We need comfort food to take our minds off everything we've been through. That's why they call it comfort food. To give comfort. Ginie needs some, too. She got whacked in the face pretty hard."

Zak eyed Ginie in the rearview mirror and she smiled and shrugged.

"They have been through a lot," said Emily. "And we really do need gas."

"All right, I know when I'm licked," laughed Zak. "Burgers and fries it is."

Jingfei and Kai cheered just as the light changed to green. Zak accelerated through the intersection and pulled into the lighted service station, where he steered right and stopped beside the pump nearest the street. Two other cars followed him into the service station. The first, a small red sedan, stopped beside the pump farthest from Zak. The second, a blue sedan, drove past the pumps and parked in a space beside the minimart.

After switching off the ignition, Zak took out his wallet and handed Jingfei a hundred dollar bill, which was some of the money Talanov had given him.

"Double meat, double cheese, extra bacon," said Zak. "Do *not* forget the bacon."

"How come you're giving her the money?" asked Kai.

"Because I'm the responsible one," answered Jingfei.

"Yeah, right," grumbled Kai.

"Large or small on the fries?" asked Jingfei.

"Do you seriously need to ask?" asked Zak in return.

By now, Kai had climbed over the back of the seat and settled in between Jingfei and Ginie. The girls protested the invasion because he had to spread out in their laps in order to reposition himself up into a sitting position.

"You're like a slithering *python,*" Jingfei cried. She elbowed Kai, slid open the door and jumped out.

"I'm going, too," said Kai. "No way am I trusting you to order for me." He piled out of the van and rubbed his hands together excitedly. "Okay, who wants what?"

While the others began discussing food, Zak headed toward the minimart to prepay for a fill-up.

"Zak, wait!" Jingfei called out, running over and giving him a hug.

"What's that for?" asked Zak.

"I just want you to know that I love you. Me and Kai both."

"Thanks. I love you too."

"No matter what?" asked Jingfei. "You'll love us, no matter what?"

"Of course," said Zak. "What's going on?" He leaned back and looked down at Jingfei with a smile of concern.

"I know we've made life hard for you."

"I love your kind of hard," said Zak, "and no one is taking you away, if that's what you're thinking."

"It's not that."

"Then what?"

"I just want to make sure you'll love us, no matter what."

"Of course I will. What's this about?"

"Nothing," said Jingfei. She hugged Zak again, then ran back to the van, where she and Ginie hugged.

Zak watched Jingfei curiously for a moment, then turned toward the minimart with a chuckle. *She is definitely a handful,* he thought.

On his way across the pavement, Zak instinctively looked at the two vehicles that had followed him into the service station. The driver of the small red sedan was a pizza delivery boy who looked to be sixteen. He had already activated the pump with a credit card and was filling up. His car had a lighted pizza sign on top. The blue sedan was parked in a darkened space off to his right, and from what he could tell, there were two men inside, although neither had gotten out yet.

Pulling open the minimart door, Zak knew he was probably overdoing it with the precautions. *No one knew where they were, or who they were,* he thought, stepping up to the counter and handing the attendant some cash. The attendant punched some buttons, activated the pump, and told Zak to come back for his change.

Walking back to his van, Zak saw Emily hug Ginie. By now, Jingfei and Kai were gone, to the IHOP, no doubt, and when he approached the van, Emily and Ginie stepped away from one another and wiped their eyes.

"Everything okay?" asked Zak.

Ginie nodded and said she was going inside to use the bathroom.

Zak watched Ginie disappear inside the minimart, and with a troubled frown, lifted the nozzle and began filling the tank. "What's going on?" he asked, looking over at Emily.

"She's taking things pretty hard," Emily replied. "Looking into the eyes of that crazy woman. Seeing her shoot those people. Seeing Su Yin get kidnapped. Getting smashed in the face. I think she feels responsible. She and Jingfei were talking and hugging."

"Did you hear what they said?"

Emily shook her head. "They went off by themselves."

"Is there anything I can do?"

"You're her rock, Zak, her father figure, the man who can weather any storm. Keep being that man."

"And you? How are you doing?"

Emily chuckled. "I am such a mess. Getting offended all the time. Making demands that are totally unreasonable."

"Don't be so hard on yourself. We've all been through a lot."

"Yeah, well, Jingfei and Ginie let me know in no uncertain terms what a bitch I've been. And they were right. I got so caught up in . . . myself."

Zak opened his arm and Emily slid into his embrace.

"Jingfei puzzles me, though," said Emily, stepping away when the nozzle clicked off. "Do you think she's been acting weird?"

"Weird, how?" asked Zak, topping off the tank.

"Weird in that she was hugging me and saying how much she loved me, then telling me to remember that, no matter what."

"She said the same thing to me."

"Jingfei has never expressed feelings to me that way. What do you think's going on?"

"I think she's realizing how quickly life can change. What happened to Su Yin hit all of us pretty hard. I know those kids had it tough, traveling cross-country like they did, and Jingfei has always been the one in control. The mama bear of the three. But this has rendered her powerless and ignited emotions she didn't know she had."

"No wonder she pestered Alex so much to go with him. She wanted to be doing something. And if I'm being honest, I actually think she would have been an asset for what Alex is trying to do."

"To tell you the truth, so do I," agreed Zak. "But I know where Alex is coming from. He'd worry about their safety, and that worry would split his focus."

Zak replaced the nozzle just as Ginie returned to the van. "Are you okay?" he asked.

Ginie nodded and climbed into the van.

"Make sure she's all right while I grab my change," said Zak.

Emily nodded and climbed into the van while Zak headed toward the minimart. On his way across the pavement, he looked again at the pizza delivery kid. He wondered if the kid ever ate vegetables. He thought briefly about the hearty stews he'd eaten most of his life. Lots of meat. Lots of gravy. Lots of vegetables. The Soviet military may not have been the most affectionate place on earth, but they sure knew how to cook.

Pulling open the glass door, Zak went inside, and after receiving his change, came back out.

Back at the van, Zak retrieved a long-handled squeegee out of a bucket of water and washed the windshield. He then wiped off the streaks using some paper towels, and after repeating the process for all of the windows, replaced the squeegee in the bucket.

When finished, Zak looked toward the blue sedan. The occupants were still inside. With a wrinkle of concern, Zak pulled open his car door and slid behind the wheel.

"How long does it take to get burgers?" he asked.

"You gave them a hundred dollars," said Emily. "They're going to buy everything they see."

"I told them to bring me some change."

"Good luck with that."

Firing up the engine, Zak shifted into gear and accelerated away from the pump. Two minutes later, he was pulling into a parking space in front of the IHOP restaurant. The large windows facing them showed the restaurant to be full of families, couples, groups, and singles, in booths and at tables, eating, drinking, talking, and working their phones.

"Want me to go in and check?" asked Emily.

"Let's all go in," said Zak. "Hit the bathrooms and get some coffee."

The decor inside the restaurant was friendly and bright and rich with the smells of fast food and coffee. Waitresses hurried about, some with plates stacked up their arms.

"I don't see them," Emily said.

"Check the women's bathroom while I check the men's. Ginie, check the floor. See if they've found a table."

Thirty seconds later, Zak emerged from the men's bathroom to see Emily and Ginie waiting for him. Neither woman needed to speak for Zak to know what was wrong. He could see it in their eyes.

*Jingfei and Kai were gone.*

# CHAPTER 39

Wilcox slowed his sedan for the turn into an unmarked gate at the southernmost corner of the airfield. News had already reached him about the murder of a guard at the Oakland airport and how a Gulfstream owned by a Hong Kong corporation had taken off.

*Dragon Head,* Wilcox thought.

After rolling down his window, Wilcox showed the armed guard his CIA identification. After inspecting the badge with his flashlight, the guard turned his halogen beam on Talanov, who was seated beside Wilcox, then Straw Sandal, who was in the backseat with her hands duct-taped behind her.

"Who are those two?" asked the guard.

"That's classified," replied Wilcox, taking back his ID.

The guard glared at Wilcox, then ambled back to his hut and raised the barrier.

Wilcox accelerated across a row of retracted steel spikes and along a painted lane toward the Jonsair hangar, which was a large flat shed with huge sliding doors. An oval neon sign was mounted beside the office door. The perimeter of the sign was white and the lettering inside it was blue.

Sitting in the darkness in front of the hangar, with its stairs folded open, was a modified Gulfstream G650ER. It had a flight range of nearly 14,000 kilometers, or roughly 8650 miles, with a cruising altitude of up to 51,000 feet. Manufactured by General Dynamics, the Gulfstream was a sleek twin-engine jet aircraft that was just under one hundred feet long. The aircraft's wingspan was two inches shy of its length, with turned-up wingtips and eight small oval windows along each side of the fuselage.

"You leave your Gulfstream unguarded?" asked Talanov.

"It's a sterile area," answered Wilcox.

Wilcox parked near the front door of the office, and when he did, the door swung open and three people emerged. The first was an armed guard. He was a big guy in a uniform with a nine-millimeter pistol strapped to his waist. The second was pilot Mark Nutt, who was a seasoned veteran of more than twenty years. Mark was dressed in a short-sleeved white shirt. The third was Stephanie, who was dressed in another of her stylish navy-blue slack suits.

After greeting everyone, Wilcox tossed his car keys to the guard and led the way up the stairs into the aircraft. Talanov and Straw Sandal followed, with Stephanie and Mark bringing up the rear. Once inside, Stephanie activated a switch that folded up the stairs and closed the door.

Talanov led Straw Sandal to a seat, where he cut the tape off her wrists, then used a plastic zip-tie to secure one of her ankles to a security ring anchored to the floor. "Can't have you getting lost," he said, taking a seat across the aisle.

Mark was accelerating the Gulfstream away from the hangar when Wilcox stepped into the cockpit. In the distance, a big Boeing was thundering its way up into the sky.

"Strap in up here, if you want," Mark said, gesturing Wilcox to the copilot's seat. "We've got a beautiful flight ahead. Clear sky all the way to DC."

"Are we carrying a full load of fuel?" asked Wilcox over the hushed whine of the Gulfstream's two Rolls-Royce jet engines.

"Per your orders," Mark replied.

"Good. We'll be needing it."

"Why, are we taking the scenic route?" asked Mark while checking his gauges. He flipped several switches while the radio crackled with call signs and flight numbers.

"You might say that. I'm rerouting our flight to Hong Kong."

Marked laughed. "You crack me up." When Wilcox did not reply, Mark looked over his shoulder to see Wilcox staring back at him. "You're not joking," he said.

"And I need you to not file an amended flight plan," added Wilcox, "at least not right away. Delay it as long as you can."

"Bill, I . . . there's no way."

"You have to. I'll take the heat."

"So you're saying there will be heat?"

"Mark, I need you to do this."

"Bill, I can't. We'll both end up in prison. We're stealing the company jet!"

"You'll be fine. I promise."

"With respect, I need more than a promise. I need to know the nature of this trip and who authorized it."

"That's classified."

"And that's bullshit, and you know it. Look, you and I have known each other a long time, and I have never known you to do something this crazy. Tell me what's going on. You're asking me to disobey a direct order by the DNI to bring you back to DC."

"I can't."

"Can't or won't?" asked Mark.

"Plausible deniability, old friend. The less you know, the better. You can say that I gave you no choice, that I ordered you to comply under the guise of national security. At the end of the day, I'll be the one they string up."

"And I'll be the one who didn't call this in or try and stop you."

"If there were any other way, I'd jump on it in a heartbeat. But there isn't. We have to do this."

"If we do, you're finished, you know that, don't you?"

"I know," said Wilcox. "But this isn't about me or what it will cost me if we do. It's what it will cost others if I don't."

With a melancholy smile, Wilcox clasped Mark on the shoulder and went back to his seat.

"You okay?" asked Talanov when Wilcox sat across from him in one of the plush leather seats.

"Oddly, yes," answered Wilcox. "So before I come to my senses and realize what we're doing, I'm going to catch a few winks."

Nestling back and closing his eyes, Wilcox fell asleep quickly while the Gulfstream climbed to a cruising altitude of fifty thousand feet. Once they had leveled off over the Pacific, Stephanie appeared with a silver tray. On it were two glasses of wine and a paper cup of water. Wilcox opened his eyes just as Stephanie handed Straw Sandal the paper cup of water. She then offered Talanov and Wilcox the wine.

"Compliments of Congresswoman Gustaves," explained Stephanie to Wilcox's wary scowl. "Some La Tâche for La Tâche, is what she said I should to tell you."

Wilcox handed one of the glasses to Talanov. "Enjoy the moment," he remarked, extending his glass toward Talanov in a toast. "Gustaves will not be in such a generous mood once she finds out what we've done. Shaw, either, who will want my head on Stephanie's silver tray once he—"

Wilcox was interrupted by the vibrating of his phone on the console beside his seat. After checking the Caller ID, Wilcox set his wineglass on the console and put a finger to his lips. A signal for Talanov to remain quiet.

After swiping the answer button, Wilcox put the phone on speaker. "Director Shaw," he said. "What a pleasant—"

"What the *hell* do you think you're doing?" yelled Shaw, who was pacing back and forth in front of his desk. Behind the desk was a wall of bookshelves. On another wall were dozens of photos of Shaw with famous people. "Did you think I wouldn't find out?"

"I had to. Talanov escaped."

"He did *what?*"

"Got away. He jumped on a commercial flight with Dragon Head's daughter, Straw Sandal, and is headed to Hong Kong because Dragon Head kidnapped a little girl and ordered Talanov to return his daughter to him or the little girl dies."

"I don't care about some random kid! I want Talanov in custody!"

"Sir, the only way I can do that is to go after him. To get there first and be waiting when he lands."

"How you could let this happen?"

"He's Talanov, what can I say? I'll call you when I know more."

Wilcox hurriedly clicked off and slumped back in his seat. Dots of perspiration had already formed on his forehead.

When Shaw heard the dial tone, he threw his phone against the wall. And with a loud curse, he grabbed another cell phone out of a desk drawer and dialed Adam Schiller. When Schiller answered, he said, "I need you to find out if Talanov's on a flight to Hong Kong."

"Of course, sir," Schiller replied.

"What's the status on Saya Lee?" asked Shaw.

"She's being released on a technicality."

"Good. You know what to do."

On board the Gulfstream, Talanov looked at Wilcox with amused disbelief. "He's Talanov, what can I say?"

Loosening his tie, Wilcox finished his wine, motioned for a refill, then nodded for Talanov to join him at the rear of the plane. Talanov knew what that meant. Wilcox wanted to talk without Straw Sandal overhearing them. Once they were seated at the rear of the plane, Wilcox waited until Stephanie had served his second glass of wine before asking Talanov whether or not he thought they could pull this off. Before Talanov could answer, Wilcox said, "Personally, I don't like the odds. We have the element of surprise – for now – but that won't last for long."

"What about your friend with the CIB?"

"Alice will get us into the country through the diplomatic gate, but we *are* holding a Chinese citizen hostage, and not even Alice can overlook that. We'll need to cut Straw Sandal loose before we enter the airport, which means we lose our leverage."

"Maybe not," said Talanov.

"What other leverage do we have?"

"The fact that Dragon Head kidnapped Su Yin."

"I don't understand."

"Why go to all of that trouble?"

"I still don't understand."

"This was all about finding me," explained Talanov. "Not about killing me, but finding me. In other words, he wants something. What he wants, we don't yet know, but it leads me to think we still have leverage, because for whatever reason, Dragon Head needs me in Hong Kong. That means we'll still have bargaining power, with or without Straw Sandal."

"Maybe," said Wilcox, "but we'll still be on our own, and we don't speak the language, and we *are* dinosaurs when it comes to technology. Alice will give us some help, but she is still in the CIB, and I can't expect her to violate the law for an unsanctioned operation like this. What we're attempting is a long shot at best."

"When a long shot is your only shot, you take it."

"And that is one of the corniest lines I've ever heard."

"What other choice do we have?"

Wilcox thought for a moment, then chuckled and raised his glass. "Then here's to long shots," he said, "and a prayer that we're not the ones in the crosshairs."

# CHAPTER 40

After dinner, the cabin lights were dimmed and Wilcox reclined his seat and went to sleep. Talanov, however, was unable to sleep. His mind was focused on Su Yin and how she reminded him of his first love . . . a girl whose name he never knew. The occasion occurred when he was a boy of twelve, when he had been sent to the ancient martial arts monastery of *Lóngshù*, in the mountains of northern China. His instructors, the *dăoshī,* had chosen the girl for a carefully calculated act of betrayal designed to harden young Alex into the warrior he was chosen to become.

The *dăoshī* accomplished this by assigning the girl to be his sparring partner. However, the use of names was forbidden at *Lóngshù* – even speaking to one another was forbidden – which was why Alex never knew her name, nor did she know his.

The attraction between them happened slowly. Disarmingly modest and shy, the girl was much more accomplished in martial arts than Alex. Time and again he would attack, and time and again she would effortlessly flip or punch him to the mat. So he would try harder, and fall harder, again and again. Ultimately, the girl became the reason he never resented being defeated by a woman, and she was likewise the reason he never gratuitously handed victory to a woman. If a woman wanted it, she had to earn it. No double standard. No going easy.

During their sparring matches, the girl came to admire his unconquerable spirit. He remembered seeing it in her eyes. Remembered feeling it in the punches she would pull. Punches that would still knock him to the mat but without the force she could have used. He recalled seeing her watch him practice *katas* among the peach trees, in the soft green grass, with cool mountain breezes rustling the leaves. He recalled the morning he found a peach hidden in the cleft of the tree where he practiced.

A gift from the girl whose name he never knew.

He could still taste the sweetness of that piece of fruit, and for years afterward, would lie awake at night thinking of her and how the *dǎoshī* had forcibly sent her away. Her cries for help when she was being taken still haunted him, and he wondered now, at forty-seven thousand feet, if the agony of that loss was fueling his resolve to rescue Su Yin.

Then there was Noya, the teenage girl whose family had been executed years ago in Spain by his KGB partner, Sofia, who then turned her hatred on him, and would have killed him had he not killed her first. Noya had been deliberately infected by Sofia with an engineered strain of anthrax, and later died, or so he thought until months later when the Americans got word to him that she had survived.

Talanov jerked awake, not realizing he had dozed off until a thump from somewhere in the plane awakened him. He glanced at Wilcox, who was still asleep, then at Straw Sandal three rows ahead. She, too, looked to be asleep. He then glanced toward the front of the plane and saw Stephanie at work behind the curtain.

After a yawn and a stretch, Talanov raised the window shade and looked out at the Milky Way. *The original fairy lights,* he thought with a smile, and after another yawn, he pulled down the shade.

He then heard another thump, this one from the rear of the plane, and after stepping quietly into the aisle, made his way to the rear galley. The cabin lights were off, although a night-light enabled him to see the area was deserted. To his left were some luggage compartments. To his right was a small kitchen. Ahead was a small bathroom. He checked the bathroom and found it empty.

Habituation, or training the subconscious to determine which sounds were normal and which were not, especially when asleep, was a skill he had learned during his military training. Normal sounds triggered no alarm and required no response. Abnormal sounds *did* trigger alarms. The trick was learning which sounds were normal and which were not.

Talanov listened for several more minutes but heard nothing. But as he turned to leave, he heard a scuffing sound.

Stepping back into the galley, Talanov looked closely and saw that one of the luggage compartment latches had been rigged with a piece of folded paper that kept it from locking. Alarm bells sounded in his brain and he knew why. The staircase of the Gulfstream had been open upon their arrival at the hangar. *A sterile area,* Wilcox had replied when he voiced his concern about no guard having been on duty outside.

Talanov looked around but there were no potential weapons of any kind. Standing opposite the hinges, Talanov readied himself to pull open the door and deliver a front kick to whoever was inside. Surprise would be his weapon.

But when he yanked open the door, he jerked back when he saw Jingfei and Kai staring out at him.

"What are . . . how did you . . . ?" stammered Talanov.

"We are not about to let our sister get killed because of your incompetence," Jingfei snapped.

Talanov stepped back while she and Kai unfolded themselves from the cramped compartment just as a yawning Wilcox appeared in the doorway.

"What are you looking at?" hissed Jingfei. She pushed past Wilcox and stormed up the aisle toward the front galley.

Wilcox watched her go, then looked at Talanov with obvious bewilderment.

"Man, those compartments are tight," said Kai, rolling his shoulders.

"Does Zak know where you are?" asked Talanov.

"He probably does by now. Ginie was in on it from the start. I mean, we knew we had to tell someone, but we couldn't tell Zak or Emily, who would never let us do something like this, so we told Ginie but swore her to secrecy."

"So you ditched him?" asked Talanov. "And ran off without him knowing it?"

Kai nodded sheepishly, then said, "You said we couldn't come, but we knew you needed our help, so when Zak stopped to fill up at the Valero, we asked him for some money so that we could go next door to the IHOP and get something to eat. We used the money for a taxi instead."

"How did you beat us to the hangar and get on board without being seen?"

"Ginie called us a cab when she went to the bathroom, and the plane was, like, totally unguarded when we got to the hangar."

After a quick glare at Wilcox, Talanov shook his head.

"Please don't get mad, okay? Su Yin's our little sister, and those ninja guys are, like, super bad news, and there's, like, a million of them, and they know a whole lot more about phone viruses than you do. Besides, you really can't get mad, because aren't you and Spy Bill doing the same thing by, you know, like, stealing this jet?"

Talanov wanted to say something, he really did. He wanted to lecture Kai about their foolhardy, irresponsible actions. Except Kai was right: he did need their help, and he *was* doing the same thing. So how could he be mad at these younger versions of himself, when in truth he was glad they were here?

"Can I get something to drink?" asked Kai. He looked toward the front galley, where Jingfei was gulping down a bottle of orange juice. When Stephanie held one up for Kai to see, his eyes lit up, but he hesitated and looked up at Talanov, as if waiting for permission.

Talanov nodded in the direction of the galley.

Kai grinned and gave Talanov a hug. "You are a total badass superhero. You, too, Spy Bill," he added, giving Wilcox a hug. "Cool plane, by the way."

Talanov and Wilcox watched Kai hurry up the aisle toward the front galley.

"How can two kids be so lovable and so infuriating at the same time?" asked Wilcox. "And what is with the Spy Bill stuff?"

"What I want to know, is why didn't Zak call to tell us what happened?" asked Talanov with a worried frown.

"Probably because we don't have cell service out here over the Pacific, so there is no way he could have gotten through. Even if he'd tried phoning Charlie, his call would have gone to voicemail."

Talanov watched Stephanie take out a tray of sandwiches and begin unwrapping them to eager smiles from the kids. "Those two are certainly a handful," he said.

"Which we don't need," agreed Wilcox. "Good thing we're sending them home."

Talanov did not reply.

Wilcox noticed the lack of response and turned to face Talanov. "I know that look," he said, reading Talanov's thoughtful frown. "You're thinking of letting them stay."

Talanov did not reply.

"Do you know how much danger you'll be putting them in? They're kids, Alex. Minors. You *have* to send them back."

Talanov rubbed the bridge of his nose.

From her seat midway up the aisle, Straw Sandal quietly smiled.

# CHAPTER 41

In the windowless computer room of the Zhongzhen Martial Arts Academy, Chao looked over AK's shoulder at the monitor, which showed a digital map of an open section of the Pacific Ocean. No coastlines or islands were visible to give a perspective on where that section of ocean might be. The only indicators were some numerical coordinates along one side of the screen. Also visible were two small, blinking orange triangles with flight numbers beside them.

"What are we looking at?" asked Chao in English.

"Two commercial aircraft, bound for Hong Kong," AK replied.

"American?"

"This one," said AK, pointing at one of the triangles. "Other one Chinese."

"Probability of success?" asked Xin Li in Russian.

"Ninety-four percent," responded AK in Russian. "Our first attempt, *Shāng Yī*, did not accomplish what was desired, thanks to quick reflexes by two of the pilots, although it did enable me to adjust our algorithms for our second penetration, *Shāng Èr*. We now control not only the Americans' GPS network, but also the speed, altitude, and direction of any aircraft using it. We can now bring one aircraft down upon another, without either detecting the other, quite literally as if this were a video game that I alone control."

Chao looked quizzically at Xin Li, who translated what AK had told her.

"Why the names, *Shāng Yī* and *Shāng Èr*?" asked Chao.

Xin Li replied, "Entropy One and Entropy Two, as the terms translate, indicate our ability to send the Americans' GPS into a state of entropy, or uselessness . . . chaos."

"The extortion value of such a program is incalculable," said

Chao. "As will be the price on your heads. Are you certain your signal can't be traced?"

"I am certain," Xin Li replied. "Beijing and Washington will blame each other."

"Incredible. I'm impressed."

"How impressed?" asked Xin Li, locking eyes with Chao.

"Enough to give you what you want."

Xin Li smiled. With Chao's backing, she would soon be the new Dragon Head. Moran's empire would be hers.

"Execution has begun," AK announced, drawing their attention while he worked three keyboards simultaneously.

High above the Pacific Ocean twelve hundred miles to the east, two airliners pushed westward through the nighttime sky. With no visible points of reference apart from the stars, and with modern navigation dependent solely on satellite technology, coordinates and speed were all but impossible to gauge. Hence, neither of the pilots detected any change in their direction. That's because their instruments indicated everything to be normal.

"*Chao?*" a voice called out.

Chao turned to see Dragon Head enter the room with several of his *Shí bèi* fighters.

"Very impressive," Chao remarked with a nod toward the monitors.

"Get him out of here," commanded Dragon Head.

The *Shí bèi* fighters surrounded Chao and muscled him from the room.

"You will regret this!" Chao shouted angrily while being manhandled across the gym floor and out the front door.

Dragon Head knelt beside AK and rested his elbow on the edge of AK's worktable. The pistol was still in his hand. "You allowed Chao to witness *Shāng Èr?*"

"Do not blame him," Xin Li said. "I was the one who invited Chao to witness our achievement."

Dragon Head stood and moved to within inches of Xin Li's face. She was several inches taller than he, but his muscular presence dominated the room. "Why would you do such a thing?"

"Because of the predicament we are in."

"A predicament that is set to change if what you told me is true."

"It is true," Xin Li replied. "We have the girl. Talanov will give us what we want."

"Then why involve Chao?"

"Because he is a powerful man. Better to have him as an ally than an enemy."

"He *is* the enemy."

"But an enemy you can own. An enemy you can use."

Dragon Head turned to AK. "Will *Shāng Èr* be a success? Your first attempt was a failure."

AK entered an unimportant command on one of his keyboards and thought about what to say. The fact that Dragon Head failed to appreciate the lessons learned from *Shāng Yī* was irrelevant right now. No one had ever managed to do what he, Bogdan Kalashnik, had done, and yet Dragon Head called it a failure. What an idiot. It was, of course, a thought he dared not utter. Instead, he pointed to the monitor, where the blinking orange triangles grew closer.

"Last forty-eight hours have been to me very useful," AK explained in clumsy English.

"Meaning what, exactly?" asked Dragon Head.

Speaking in fluent Russian, which Xin Li translated, AK talked of newly developed algorithms, packet sniffers, hash encryptions and rootkits, adding that his unheralded zero-day attack was the first of its kind ever. He then used information being displayed on other monitors to illustrate technical points, adding sidebar explanations about the electronic dance taking place between his software and the GPS network of the United States.

"My virus keeps mutating and attacking with increased speed," AK continued. "That's because I've factored their response codes into my next generation of attack codes, which allows us to be proactive while they can only react. That is because they do not know who we are or where we are, nor can they trace our signal in order to penetrate our defenses with a virus of their own."

Dragon Head glared briefly at Xin Li, who could tell he did not understand a word of what AK had said.

"Continue," Dragon Head said, looking back at AK.

Tapping the screen with the blinking triangles, AK said in English, "With *Shāng Yī*, which was first generation, we had seventy-six percent success chance. With *Shāng Èr*, which is second generation, we have now ninety-four percent."

"Why not one-hundred percent?"

"Impossible with outdated equipment that I use."

"If you need a new laptop, buy one."

AK thought for a moment, gathering his vocabulary to express himself in English. "It not just matter of buying new hardware, but constructing *new* hardware to handle software, which I am all the time creating, with codes that, how do you say, *transmutatsiya* . . .

He looked back at Xin Li, who said, "Transmute . . . evolve."

"Yes, transmute codes, that contain own intelligence that react in instant to American defense and strike back."

He paused and looked back at Xin Li, asking if he could speak again in Russian so that he could better explain himself.

Xin Li smiled and nodded.

Speaking in Russian, AK continued, with Xin Li translating into Chinese.

"Thus far, thanks to cloaking techniques I've managed to create, I've caught the Americans off guard by striking quickly and then vanishing. This will only work a few times before they respond with countermeasures that close those windows permanently and backtrack our signal. Without advanced capabilities and speeds, I cannot guarantee how much longer we will maintain our advantage."

"Which is why I brought in Chao," added Xin Li, looking at Dragon Head. "He has money. He can help us construct the new hardware that we need."

"I do not want Chao involved," Dragon Head replied. "Talanov will give us what we need."

"And if something goes wrong?"

"Then you had better make sure that it doesn't. How soon before we know whether *Shāng Èr* is a success?"

AK worked his keyboard against a hum of electronic activity, and almost immediately, rows of numbers began scrolling down one side of his screen. The information let AK know the exact positions of each aircraft, their speeds, angles, altitudes, and other fluctuating factors. "Minutes," he replied, wishing he could watch what was about to occur. If only there were a giant camera up in the sky.

There were, of course, many cameras in the sky. They were called satellites. Hacking those satellites, however, would require algorithms of infinite complexity, not to mention military-grade enhancement software that was beyond the capacity of his hardware. He just hoped Xin Li's trap for Talanov proved successful.

As for *Shāng Èr,* hacking the Americans' GPS network a second time was another example of his own brilliance, in spite of Dragon Head's antiquated equipment. One plane would collide with the other. In his mind, he could see a massive fireball lighting up the sky for hundreds of miles. Satellites would record it. Ships on the ocean would see it, as would other aircraft. The elegance would be spectacular.

China and America would be dumbfounded and, by design, would each blame the other, although factions in the American government would no doubt blame the Russians, especially with the discovery of Talanov's presence. Their incompetence would be comical, and no one would know what happened, or how, or by whom. Even Dragon Head, for all his fearsome power, bowed before such skill. Even Xin Li, who was more terrifying than Dragon Head, bowed before such skill. Neither of them knew what he knew. More importantly, neither of them could duplicate what he knew.

AK smiled to himself. *My survival – my prosperity – is assured.*
He looked again at the blinking triangles on his screen.
An instant later, both of them vanished.

# CHAPTER 42

Stephanie had just served Wilcox a breakfast frittata when Mark signaled Wilcox to the cockpit for an emergency call from Gustaves. The fact that Gustaves had chosen to contact him on a secure line meant she knew what he had done, which meant the proverbial shit was about to hit the fan. The call, however, was not what Wilcox was expecting.

"Two hours ago," Gustaves said gravely, "there was a mid-air collision over the Pacific. Not a near-miss, like last time, but an actual collision, with over a thousand people killed."

"Was it Dragon Head?" Wilcox asked.

"It was the same signal echo and the same origin of Shenzhen," said Gustaves, "so our experts, including Charlie, are saying yes." Her phone was on speaker and her eyes were fixed on the large flat screen television in the bookshelf across the room. She had been flipping from channel to channel, witnessing the faces of grieving family members collapsing into the arms of friends.

Having seen enough, she switched off the TV and turned her attention to her phone, which was laying on her desk.

"Beijing is blaming us," she continued, "because the signal was made to look as if it originated at the NSA's SIGINT Operations Center in Oahu."

"Are you serious? The Hawaii Cryptologic Center?"

"We detected the Shenzhen origin, but China hasn't – or can't – make that determination yet because their tracking and analysis programs are not as sophisticated as ours. But that's not all. The hackers made the signal appear to have been relayed by way of the CIA's ground control facility at Pine Gap, Australia."

"How on earth did they manage that?"

"We don't know, but it makes us look guilty as hell, since

Australia is arguably our closest ally and since FORNSAT and COMSAT interceptions are one of Pine Gap's major functions. For whatever reason – obfuscation, is my guess – Dragon Head wants to pit China against America, which of course keeps the spotlight off him. I know it wasn't us, but we can't prove that to Beijing without some kind of proof that Dragon Head was responsible, which we can't do."

"Are you certain the hackers were Chinese?"

"Like I said, we traced the echo to Shenzhen, although Charlie thinks Dragon Head is behind it."

"Isn't Dragon Head in Hong Kong?"

"Yes, he is. But a good friend of mine at the NSA let Charlie take a look at his data on the hacking-stream, what little they were able to grab, and Charlie found several highly specific code sequences in both the hacking signal and the virus that Straw Sandal planted in our system. Charlie likened it to the same fingerprints found at two different crime scenes, with the presence of those fingerprints proving the same perpetrator committed both crimes."

"Dragon Head."

"Exactly. And since Dragon Head controls Hong Kong and most of Kowloon, Charlie's take – and I tend to agree – is that Dragon Head is behind this but is masquerading his signal to make it look like someone in Beijing is disguising the signal to look like it originated in Shenzhen. That keeps China and America squabbling with one another, which diverts attention away from what he's doing."

"How can we find out for sure?"

"That's where you and Alex come in. We need eyes on the ground – eyes I can trust – which means this insane scheme of yours may well be our best shot."

"So I'm not headed to Leavenworth for taking the scenic route back to DC?"

"That's a creative way of describing it. I won't kid you, Bill. When I first heard that you'd hijacked a company jet, I wanted to wring your neck. You disobeyed a direct order by

Shaw to bring Talanov and Straw Sandal to DC. That woman, or her accomplice, killed my secretary, so, yes, I wanted to question her – hard – but your little stunt ruined my opportunity. So let's just say if this latest collision hadn't occurred, you probably would be on your way to Leavenworth. Shaw still wants your head on a stick, because you embarrassed him, although he knows, like the rest of us, what the intel says, and right now you're our best bet of stopping Dragon Head before he brings down more planes."

"What do you need me to do?"

"Stop him, simple as that. If you do, you'll still get your hand slapped, but in the end, all will be forgiven. If, however, you don't . . ."

"I presume this stays off the books?"

"That's putting it mildly. No one here can officially sanction what you've done and are doing. In fact, Shaw's already creating a paper trail of official charges. He's an expert in C-Y-A. However, these charges will never see the light of day unless you're identified or caught. If you are, then I hope you like orange, because you'll be wearing it for a very long time. Plus, if Dragon Head brings down any more planes, Shaw will pin the blame on you. You've got one shot, so make it count. Stopping Dragon Head is your number one priority."

"And Alex, what about him? His number one priority is rescuing Su Yin."

"And I admire that, really, I do. But we have a national security crisis on our hands, so I need Alex to set aside his personal agenda."

"And I've tried to convince him of that, believe me. But he regards his mandate to be more important. He's willing to help, but not at the expense of Su Yin."

"This isn't a request, Bill. It's an order. Put Talanov on the phone. I'll tell him myself."

"And how, exactly, do you plan to enforce such an order? With threats? I've already tried reasoning with him, but this is beyond reason. This is personal."

"He can't go around pulling stunts like this. Right now, Shaw considers him to be a loose cannon and I tend to agree."

Wilcox started to rebut that argument, then paused and took a breath. "Why do you think I risked my career on this?" he finally asked. "I commandeered the company jet. I'm flying Alex and our witness to Hong Kong instead of DC. Why do you think I did that?"

Gustaves did not reply.

"Because I believe his way is the right way," Wilcox said, answering his own question. "Because I believe we can accomplish both goals without sacrificing either."

"Do you seriously think he can pull it off?"

"For some reason, Dragon Head wants Talanov in Hong Kong. So badly, in fact, that he used his own jet to fly a team to DC, hack into your system, kill Amber, then fly that same team to San Francisco, kill again, then kidnap a little girl. Why? We don't know the answer to that yet. The one thing we do know is this: Dragon Head wants Talanov alive and he wants him in Hong Kong."

"Maybe Dragon Head was trying to kill Talanov, and when the attempt failed and his daughter was captured, his people kidnapped the girl in order to lure Talanov into a trap."

"Assassinations are usually performed by individuals working alone, not by a team of more than a dozen men and women. This feels like an attempt to capture him. But let's assume you're right, that Dragon Head's purpose was to kill Talanov, but because he failed, his new purpose is to lure Talanov and Straw Sandal to Hong Kong in order to kill Talanov and rescue Straw Sandal. What do we lose by proceeding as planned? Nothing. In fact, we stand to win big if Talanov turns the tables. Don't forget, Dragon Head has ordered Talanov to bring Straw Sandal to Hong Kong. That means a time and place will be established for some kind of a trade, even if the whole arrangement is nothing but a set-up. In other words, we have an opportunity to turn the tables. Which means, if we allow Talanov to proceed – and if we assist him – we stand a good chance of not only saving the life of a little girl, but identifying Dragon Head's location, pinpointing his vulnerability, and using it to bring him down."

"You're starting to sound like Talanov."

"I'll take that as a compliment," said Wilcox, "although I'm not sure it was meant that way."

"This had better work, is all I can say."

"And you know there are no guarantees. However, I really do believe this is our best shot."

"All right, then, how can I help?"

"I'll need technical support from Charlie," answered Wilcox, "and someone to keep Shaw off our backs."

"The former's been taken care of. Charlie has temporarily been reassigned to me, where she'll be working in a facility operated by Naval Intelligence. She'll give you whatever you need. The latter, I'm afraid, is a problem. You did, after all, steal one of Shaw's jets, and, officially, you still work for him."

"How do I get around that?"

"Be creative. You'll figure it out."

"What, exactly, does that mean?"

"Be creative. You'll figure it out."

# CHAPTER 43

"How about I give this to you?" Stephanie asked Kai about the frittata she had cooked for Wilcox. "Bill's being long-winded again on the phone. Otherwise, I'll have to pitch it, and I hate to see food go to waste."

"What is it?" asked Kai. "And what's that green stuff?"

"Kale," answered Stephanie, who was pouring more coffee for Talanov, who was seated across the aisle. "Along with sausage, cheese, mushrooms, tomatoes, green peppers, and eggs."

With a scowl, Kai wrinkled his nose.

"Unless you'd prefer something less daring, like oatmeal or Cream of Wheat? Something without all of those awful vegetables?"

"Is that your attempt at reverse psychology?" asked Kai.

Stephanie smiled.

Kai scowled and looked away.

"By the way, my frittata was spectacular," said Talanov. "The cheese, was it *Provolone valpadana?*"

"*Piccante,*" Stephanie replied.

"The sharp notes, I should have known," Talanov said, kissing the tips of his fingers and tossing them away, like the petals of a flower bursting open.

"You two are sick," muttered Kai.

Stephanie smiled and turned to go.

"Okay, I'll take it," said Kai.

Stephanie looked back. "Are you sure? Vegetables are, like, good for you, right?"

Kai replied with an exaggerated smile, and after Stephanie had placed the frittata in front of him, he asked Stephanie if she had any ketchup.

Stephanie responded with a reprimanding glare.

Kai grinned and said, "Ketchup is a vegetable and vegetables are, like, good for you, right?"

Stephanie laughed just as Kai sliced off a section of frittata and stuffed it in his mouth.

Once Stephanie was gone, Talanov picked up his coffee and moved across the aisle to sit with Jingfei and Kai.

"Don't even bother," said Jingfei, who was curled up in her seat.

"With what?"

"Convincing us how it's for our own good that you're sending us back, or that we're too young and inexperienced, or that we'll be in danger if you let us stay."

"How would you reply?" asked Talanov.

"I'd say the positives outweigh the negatives. But that doesn't really matter, now, does it, because you've come over to tell us Spy Bill's plane will touch down to refuel, then take off again – with us on it – and there's nothing we can do, because we don't have passports, which means we can't get into the country, which means Su Yin doesn't stand a scintilla of a chance because you're such a dinosaur, and a pigheaded one at that, because you won't listen to anybody who tries to tell you differently, especially me, because, after all, I'm just a dumb kid – right? – so who cares what I think?"

Talanov was poised to take another sip of coffee but stopped with the mug in front of his mouth to listen with both admiration and disbelief at another of Jingfei's rambling sentences. "How do you do that?" he asked. "Long sentences are, like, an art form with you."

"Gee, I'm sorry. Do long sentences and big words confuse your dinosaur brain?"

Jingfei's frustration was understandable. She was capable of helping and she wanted to help, and she knew he needed her help, which of course he did. And by most accounts, allowing her to stay made sense. Except allowing her to stay put her within Dragon Head's reach. Plus, by now Zak had to be worried sick. After all, Zak had already lost Amina and Ramona – brutally – so there was no way he would allow —

Wilcox tapped Talanov on the shoulder and handed him a slip of paper. Talanov asked what it was. Wilcox told him it was a printed email from Zak, which had been sent from Zak's new satellite cell to Charlie, who had forwarded it to the Gulfstream using a secure channel, which Stephanie then printed in the Gulfstream's communications bay.

Talanov looked at the note, which read, *Afghanistan, Colonel. They're you.*

"I take it you know what that means?" asked Wilcox, sitting on the armrest of Talanov's seat.

Talanov chuckled and looked out the window.

Not able to stand the suspense, Jingfei snatched the note from Talanov's hand and held it so that she and Kai could read what it said.

"What happened in Afghanistan?" asked Kai.

There was a long pause before Talanov answered. "You've heard of the Viet Nam conflict?" he asked.

Kai nodded while Jingfei just stared at Talanov with her arms folded across her chest defensively.

"Well, Russia had its own Viet Nam conflict," Talanov continued, "and it was our invasion of Afghanistan. Zak was there with Spetsgruppa A, which were elite units of our special forces. Zak's unit was about a hundred miles south of Kabul, near the border with Pakistan, near a small town called Khost, which is located up in the mountains. One night, on a reconnaissance mission, they were attacked by *Mujahideen* guerillas, and during that skirmish, Zak was captured. They took him to a remote location and began torturing him for information on our troop movements. I was in Moscow when I heard Zak had been captured, so I asked for some time off to organize a rescue. Zak was as tough as they came, but I knew he couldn't hold out forever. No one can. My request was refused because I was overseeing KGB activities in Europe, and my superiors thought my job there was far more important than any single individual. So I went anyway, by hopping aboard a military transport to Afghanistan, where I met up with a few of Zak's team members. That night, we captured one of the guerillas and made him tell us where Zak was being held, which was in a network of concrete bunkers inside a mountain. But when we got there, all we found were a bunch of dead bodies."

"What happened?" asked Jingfei, unfolding her arms and leaning forward. "Where was Zak?"

"Gone. We could tell he'd been tied up because we found pieces of bloody rope, which he'd cut loose from his hands using the rusty edges of his chair. Obviously, he got the jump on his guards and killed them, then used their AKs to shoot the others before grabbing the rest of their weapons and escaping up into the mountains."

"What did you do?" asked Kai, now on the edge of his seat.

"In what proved to be the ultimate irony, our group became trapped in that same bunker by the *Mujahideen,* who pinned us down with heavy gunfire. Bullets were flying everywhere. Chunks of concrete were spitting down on us and we had nowhere to run, and our ammo began to run low."

"What happened?" asked Kai.

Talanov picked up his empty mug and waved at Stephanie. "Anyone for coffee?"

Jingfei grabbed the mug away from him. "Quit being a jerk and tell us what happened."

Talanov chuckled and said, "Guess who came to our rescue?"

"Zak!" exclaimed Kai, scooting even closer.

Talanov nodded. "You know how he's built, like a bear, and even after being tortured and beaten, he was able to escape with a ton of weapons and ammo. He knew they'd come after him, so he was not about to let them take him without a fight. Little did he know he'd need those guns to rescue the men who'd come to rescue him. Anyway, there we were, on the verge of being overrun, when suddenly the shooting stopped and there was a lot of yelling and shouting. When I looked out, I saw heads exploding like watermelons. I knew right away it was Zak, especially when the guerillas began shooting up into the mountains and running for cover. So while Zak rained fire and brimstone down on our enemy, we made it out of that bunker."

"Did you get in trouble for going after Zak?"

Talanov nodded. "I had disobeyed a direct order, so I was threatened with demotion, disciplinary action, termination, even prison."

"They wanted to send you to prison?"

"They called my actions criminal, reckless, irresponsible, and pigheaded. Can you believe it? One of my superiors actually called me pigheaded. He used that exact word. Personally, I've always found pigs to be highly intelligent creatures."

Jingfei saw the gleam in Talanov's eye and kicked him on the shin.

"So they let me off with a stern reprimand because Zak defended my actions. 'Kak odin,' he told them . . . as one. Which is how we lived then and how we live now. I have his back and he has mine."

"Zak's note, then, what does it mean?" asked Kai.

"He was reminding me of my own actions."

"So . . . it's okay with Zak if we stay?" asked Jingfei with growing excitement.

"That depends," answered Talanov.

"On what?"

"On you. Because Zak was also reminding me – reminding us – about the chain of command."

"Because he addressed you as Colonel?" asked Kai.

Talanov nodded. "Don't get me wrong. There are times we buck the chain of command in order to save lives. You did it, I did it, and Bill is doing it right now. Even so, these are genuinely rare occasions, and we should never abandon the chain of command."

"In other words," said Jingfei, "you're still the boss and we have to do what you say, even if you're a dinosaur and don't know what the hell you're doing?"

Talanov smiled patiently and said, "When we were heading up into the mountains to rescue Zak, that didn't mean we were all doing our own thing. We worked together as a team. I was the ranking officer, so I had the final word. But the other men on my team were more experienced than I at desert warfare, so I consulted with them constantly about what to do. The same holds true here. You know things that I don't, and I will always consult with you. Yes, I'm a dinosaur, but I am still the ranking officer, and what I say goes. If you can live with that arrangement, then you can stay. If not, I'm sending you back. It's up to you."

After glancing at one another for a long moment, Jingfei and Kai both nodded.

"Are you sure?" asked Talanov. "Because if you commit to this, I can't have you storming off on your own. We have to work together."

"I'm sure," responded Kai.

Jingfei scowled and folded her arms.

"Come on, Jing," said Kai. "You know I can't do this without you. Tell him you'll play by the rules."

"What if he keeps making dumb decisions?"

"He said he'd consult with us."

"I don't know if I can trust him."

"And he may not want to trust you. Isn't it time we start?"

Jingfei looked away for a long moment, then grudgingly nodded.

"All right, then, we have a deal," said Talanov. *"Kak odin.* As one."

# CHAPTER 44

Zak looked across at Emily, who had fallen asleep to the hum of the tires, curled up in her seat, her head against the window, her mouth open slightly. Ginie was asleep in the back seat, also curled up in her seat, also with her head against the window, also with her mouth open slightly.

Ginie had been ashamed at having kept silent about the kids' scheme. In truth, he was glad she had, because he would not have allowed them to go. In retrospect, however, he admired how Jingfei and Kai had executed their escape. Two teenage kids outwitting three seasoned professionals. If only he could have seen Talanov's face when he discovered them aboard the Gulfstream. Mr. and Mrs. Cho had done something very right with their kids.

Zak pushed a button on Wilcox's satellite cell phone and the screen lit up with a map showing their GPS position. They had taken the 580 east through the barren hills of the Diablo Range, then merged onto the 205, which took them through Tracy and onto I-5, heading north. There was not a lot to see out here – groves, farmlands, emptiness, and pollution – so traversing it at night was actually a good thing. The rhythm of the highway through the endless darkness was comforting, and reminded him of the many times he had flown night missions to various parts of the world. The drone of the aircraft engines. Endless darkness in all directions. Pinpoints of light far below. There was nothing like it, although it was almost as exhilarating to be driving the open road at night, with a window cracked open and a mug of hot coffee in his hand. Speaking of which . . .

In the distance Zak saw the illuminated sign of a truck stop. Truck stops meant coffee, as well as fuel, as well as hot food, bathrooms, and a chance to stretch their legs before the long drive east through the citrus groves of the central valley. There would be no truck stops along those lonely stretches of highway. It was now or never.

Ginie and Emily opened their eyes when Zak turned into the twenty-four-hour truck stop, which was illuminated like a football field. In the center of the massive facility was a restaurant and souvenir shop. Extending in each direction were long rows of fuel pumps beneath towering flat awnings. Beyond the lights, in a darkened rest zone, were rows of big rigs parked side by side, their engines idling while their drivers caught a few hours of sleep.

After refueling in one of the bays, Zak drove to the other end of the parking lot and pulled into an empty space in a row of parked cars, He had chosen the spot because it, too, was dark, like the rest zone for the big rigs, but much nearer the restaurant.

"Must be good. The place is packed," Zak remarked, switching off the engine. He looked toward the restaurant, where a wall of large windows revealed a full house of hungry people leaning into whatever it was they were eating. Others were chatting and laughing. A few were hunched over their phones while waitresses crisscrossed the floor carrying plates of food stacked up their forearms. It was just like the IHOP, only larger.

"How much farther to the cabin?" asked Ginie.

"We're halfway there," Zak replied, opening his door. "Come on, let's go inside."

"Zak, wait," said Emily.

Zak paused and looked over at his wife.

"Jingfei was right," she said. "I was paying more attention to my clients than I was to you, and I got so mad at her for saying that. Thing is, down deep, I knew she was right. Plus, if I'm being honest, I was jealous of the way she always fusses over you."

"Why? There is nothing inappropriate going on. She treats me like her clueless dad."

"I know. It's just that . . . we never had children because I knew it would interfere with my professional ambitions, even though I knew it was a longing of yours. But you were willing to make that sacrifice for me, and never once did you complain or express resentment. Then Jingfei, Kai, and Su Yin show up, and I saw how your eyes lit up, and how they lit up around you, even though they were a lot of trouble . . . and a lot of work."

"Tell me something in life that isn't."

"Point is, I should be the one fussing over you. But I'm not that kind of person. I don't like doing that, Zak."

"And that's okay. But Jingfei does, and it's become a game we play. It's what makes families . . . families."

"But we're not a family."

"Yes, we are. Like Ginie is part of our family."

Emily looked away and did not reply.

"So, where does that leave us?" asked Zak. "The threat you made is not something that's easily forgotten."

"What threat?" asked Ginie.

"Emily threatened to have me deported unless I kicked out the kids."

"She did *what?*" asked Ginie, looking with disbelief at Zak, then at Emily. "Did you do that, Emily? Did you threaten to have Zak deported unless he kicked out the kids?"

"I was angry, okay? I said things I shouldn't have said."

"Uh, yeah. But is that how you really feel?"

"I don't know how I feel!"

"Well, maybe you should figure that out instead of threatening your husband," said Ginie with disgust. She slid open the side door of the van and got out. "I'm going inside."

"Why did you have to tell her that?" said Emily once Ginie was gone.

"I think the larger issue is why you felt the need to threaten me in the first place," Zak replied. "I'm a package deal, Em. I come with kids and, yes, they're a handful. You need to decide what it is you want the most. Now, come on, let's settle down and go inside and get something to eat. We still have a long way to go."

Zak and Emily locked their doors and walked inside under the watchful eyes of Alpha and Bravo. They had watched Zak fill up, then managed to discreetly find a parking space near Zak's van once he had parked. Bravo was in the passenger seat of the blue sedan with a GPS tracking device that showed a blinking dot on the screen. The blinking dot represented the GPS signal on Wilcox's satellite phone, which was in Zak's hand.

Alpha's cell phone buzzed and he answered the call.

"Where is he?" asked Angus Shaw.

"Truck stop near Stockton," replied Alpha, switching the phone to speaker.

"What are they doing?"

"Having something to eat. We saw them just walk in."

"I told you to stay out of sight."

"They didn't see us. Do you know yet where Babikov is headed?"

"We're not sure," answered Shaw. "Probably to the mountains."

"And Talanov?"

"On board a commercial flight to Hong Kong with Dragon Head's daughter."

"Has this been confirmed?" asked Alpha.

"Adam's working on that now —" Shaw began, then stopping mid-sentence when his phone chimed. "Just confirmed," Shaw said, reading Schiller's text.

"What exactly is Wilcox planning to do when he lands?"

"He plans to arrive before Talanov."

"And then? He can hardly take Talanov into custody."

"If Talanov won't listen to reason, that's where you come in."

"Meaning what?" asked Alpha.

"That if we need to force Talanov's cooperation, Babikov and the women will be our leverage."

"What I don't understand," said Bravo, "is why Dragon Head wants Talanov in Hong Kong in the first place. A Chinese crime lord going to all of this trouble for a former KGB colonel? To me, that doesn't make sense."

"Talanov is at the center of everything that's going on," answered Shaw. "Exactly how, I don't yet know, nor do I know what his connection with Dragon Head is. Whatever the reason, I intend to find out, which is why I want him in custody. One way or another, I'll make him talk."

"And if he doesn't? Or if Wilcox doesn't come through?"

"Like I say, that's where you come in."

"Does this include extreme measures?" asked Alpha, keeping a casual eye on the blinking dot on the screen of their GPS tracking device. The map had been enlarged to show the overall shape of the restaurant. The blinking dot was on top of a table in the center of the floor.

"Is that a problem?" asked Shaw.

"No, sir. I am merely clarifying the rules of . . . *holy shit!*"

"What's wrong?" asked Shaw.

Alpha and Bravo threw open their car doors and jumped out. "The tracking dot. It's disappeared."

# CHAPTER 45

Zak was out of breath from running around the darkened perimeter of the parking lot. He was not sure who the two occupants of the blue sedan were, but he remembered the same or a similar vehicle pulling into a parking space at the Valero station. Two occupants had been in that vehicle and there were two occupants in this one. Was it a coincidence? Possibly, but probably not. Regardless, it was enough of an irregularity to catch his attention.

After filling his tank and washing the van's windshield, Zak drove to the opposite side of the restaurant, out of sight of the sedan, where he paused in a no-parking zone, engine idling, and got out to inspect a tire. He took his time feeling the tread, then got down on all fours and peered along the under-carriage. It was a ruse, of course, because if indeed he was being followed, the occupants of the sedan would not allow him to remain out of sight for long.

And he was right. While down on his knees, he saw the blue sedan drive slowly around the end of the restaurant and continue to the end of the aisle, as if looking for a parking spot. With his suspicions confirmed, Zak stood and slid behind the wheel again, and after shifting into gear, drove to a parking space on the perimeter of the lot. And sure enough, before long, the blue sedan pulled into a parking space in the next row.

His concern was how they had found him, because he had taken every precaution necessary to make sure no one had been following. How then had these *cheykas* managed to pin-point his location?

In asking himself that question, Zak realized he had not used the term *cheyka* in years, which was a slang term he and his men had used to describe enemy assassins.

The term originated from the word *ishcheyka,* which meant beagle. The reason: beagles were used as hunting dogs in Russia because they possessed the personality and stamina to track down and kill their prey. And these *cheykas* were definitely on the hunt.

The question, however, still remained: how had these *cheykas* managed to pinpoint his location? What "scent" had they been following?

The possibility of a tracking device having been planted on his van was unlikely but certainly possible. His guess: these *cheykas* were following Wilcox's cell phone using its GPS signal. Which eliminated Dragon Head's people because they did not know his number. That left only one possibility.

These *cheykas* were CIA.

Another question then emerged: were they after Wilcox or did they know about the switch in phones? If the latter, it meant he and the women were targets. However, at this point, there was no way to tell without additional information.

After being seated at their table, Zak handed the phone to Ginie and told her to wait five minutes before removing the battery. Emily was to stay with her and they were to not to move until the five-minute mark, at which time they were to casually get up and leave by way of the kitchen door. Once outside, they were to make their way quickly to the front corner of the restaurant, where they were to hide until he, Zak, waved them to the van.

In the darkness outside, Zak moved into a crouching position behind the blue sedan, where he watched one of the *cheykas* run into the restaurant with his hand near the small of his back. *No question what's located there,* he thought, knowing it was a gun. *Thank God the kids are with Alex.* Turning his eyes onto the second *cheyka,* who was standing beside the driver's door of the sedan, Zak knew he had, at most, ninety seconds before the first *cheyka* figured things out. Thankfully, the second *cheyka's* attention was focused on the restaurant, where the establishment's large windows afforded a cinematic view of everything going on inside.

Moving quietly into position behind the second *cheyka*, Zak could see the silhouette of a pistol in his hand. He was holding it close to his thigh so as not to be obvious. It had a silencer on its barrel, which extended its overall length to roughly a foot.

A car engine started off to the left and Bravo glanced in that direction. Concealed in the shadows, Zak did not move until Bravo looked back toward the restaurant. When he did, Zak sprang forward and delivered a hand-chop to the back of his neck.

Bravo went limp but Zak caught him beneath the armpits and dragged him out of sight, so that when the first *cheyka* returned to the car, he would not know where his partner had gone, which would give them additional time.

With a sharp whistle, Zak signaled Ginie and Emily, and the two women sprinted to the van while Zak used Bravo's pistol to fire single shots into the front tires of the blue sedan. Small explosions of hissing air saw the vehicle sag down onto its rims.

Running to the van, Zak jumped behind the wheel, fired up the engine and squealed away. He knew he would have no more than a five-minute lead before the two *cheykas* came after him.

What he did with those five minutes would spell the difference between life and death.

# CHAPTER 46

Gazing contentedly out the window at the shimmering ocean below, Talanov was about to finish his second mug of morning coffee when he saw Wilcox emerge from the cockpit with an ashen face.

Nodding for Talanov to follow, Wilcox walked to the rear galley of the Gulfstream, and once Talanov had joined him, pulled the curtain across the opening.

"What is it?" asked Talanov.

"Another call from Diane," Wilcox replied in a low voice, "who just sent me this." He worked the screen of Emily's phone and followed an email link to a video report about the midair collision over the Pacific. The footage showed debris floating on the ocean and rescue vessels looking for survivors. Shown next were clips of witnesses from other flights describing the giant flash they had seen in the sky. Photos were then shown of the crew, especially the pilots. The footage then showed wailing family members in the arms of friends. Embedded reporters on board ships were then shown against a backdrop of rescue helicopters taking off. Then came a medley of experts pontificating about what had happened. Many used technical terms and a variety of diagrams and illustrations, followed by government experts, both American and Chinese, all of whom were blaming the other side. Then came images of protests in front of the Chinese embassy, as well as candlelight vigils across America. When the video report ended, Talanov and Wilcox stood together in stunned silence, staring at one another, unable to speak.

"Naturally, Shaw's blaming Diane and me," Wilcox finally said, "not directly but by innuendo, alluding to our friendship with you, a former Russian spy, which the media is lapping up because they love blaming everything on the Russians."

"Why is Shaw going after you and Diane instead of the people who did it?"

"It's the way things are done in DC. Surely you know that by now?"

"I'm serious, Bill."

"Unfortunately, so am I. Simply put, Shaw wants Gustaves gone from politics. She is, after all, his political opponent and a major pain in the ass as far as he's concerned. As for me, it's because I didn't bring you and Straw Sandal back to DC. In other words, I defied him. Diane is keeping him at bay for now, but she told me in no uncertain terms what our priority is, and it's not rescuing Su Yin. It's stopping Dragon Head."

"Which we will do."

"Not with those kids around," said Wilcox, pausing to peek around the curtain to make sure the kids were still seated. "If one of them gets hurt or killed, of if Dragon Head manages to capture one of them, it most definitely *will* be on my head. We have to send them back."

"Bill, we need those kids. Jingfei speaks the language and she can handle technical issues. Things we're clueless about."

"They're kids, Alex. As in *children.*"

"Jingfei is nineteen. An adult. Su Yin is, what, eleven?"

"Your point?"

"Su Yin is a minor, and since neither one of us is Su Yin's guardian, things could get messy with Chinese officials unless there's an adult family member on hand."

"And I must reiterate our position: we are not here to rescue Su Yin."

"And I will reiterate my position: the hell I'm not."

"Come on, Alex. These planes going down have changed everything. More than a thousand people were killed."

"Look, I know we're here to stop Dragon Head. And I will help you do that. But I will not leave Su Yin behind. If Gustaves or Shaw doesn't like it, tell them to sue me when we get back. Until then, we do this my way."

"Dammit, Alex! Those kids put everything at risk."

"I'm not saying we keep them with us every moment. We'll house them somewhere else. Out of Dragon Head's reach."

"Neither kid has a passport," Wilcox replied. "Entry into Hong Kong will be impossible."

"Call Alice. Explain the situation."

"Don't you get it?" said Wilcox, his voice rising. "I'm not even supposed to be in Hong Kong. Alice is already doing me a huge favor by allowing me in through the diplomatic gate. Same with you. She's circumventing protocol in order to help us as much as she can. She wants the hacking stopped, too. But allowing those kids into the country? It's not going to happen. We have to send them back."

"I knew it!" exclaimed Jingfei, yanking back the curtain and stepping up to confront Talanov and Wilcox. "I knew you were back here planning a way to ditch us. I hate you. Hate you *both!*"

She turned and stormed back up the aisle.

Wilcox groaned and closed his eyes.

"Find a way, Bill," said Talanov. "Find a way to get them some passports and do it now."

More than two thousand miles to the east, Alpha ran past his blue sedan looking for Bravo, who was nowhere to be seen. He knew Bravo would not have moved from his post unless someone had jumped him. Cursing silently, he ran between the rows of vehicles until he found Bravo lying between two parked cars. Kneeling down, he slapped Bravo awake and helped him to his feet.

"My gun. Where is it?" asked Bravo.

"Babikov must have taken it."

The two men ran to the sedan, and Alpha was just opening the driver's door when he noticed the flat tire. With a curse, he slammed the door, then saw a silver SUV pulling into a nearby parking space. Fitted with a reinforced bull bar and halogen spotlights for off-road use, it was big and shiny and looked as if it had been driven right off the showroom floor. It was a hot night and the windows were down and Alpha could see the faces of an adult couple, two kids, and a dog. The rear compartment was packed with coolers, tents, sleeping bags and backpacks. A young family on its way to the mountains.

"Grab our equipment packs," he told Bravo, and with his pistol in hand, he ran over to the SUV, pulled open the driver's door and ordered everyone out. The father tried protesting but Alpha flashed his pistol in the father's face. "Out, *now!*" he yelled. "Before you really piss me off."

The family climbed out with their dog and ran inside while Alpha and Bravo jumped in. Seconds later, they were speeding out of the parking lot.

While Alpha raced east along the same highway Zak had taken, Bravo called a real-time satellite image of the area onto his cell phone screen. He entered several commands that enhanced the image and showed their GPS position on a digital map in the form of a blinking green dot. Other vehicles on the roads were shown as yellow dashes of light because the geosynchronous satellite was picking up the glow of their headlights.

"I've got seven possibles heading east," said Bravo, "which is the direction Babikov was headed. Four on the main highway and three on secondary roads."

"Let's go with the secondary roads," said Alpha. "Can you enhance the image to determine vehicle shapes?"

Bravo worked the zoom function, which enhanced the satellite image to show the silhouetted shape of the first vehicle, which was a pickup truck bouncing along a dirt track among the groves. The image appeared jerky because of enhancement and reception speed limitations of their device.

"Looks like a farm worker. Strike one," Bravo said, zooming in on another pair of dots. They belonged to a larger vehicle – an SUV – on a paved, single-lane highway. "Nope," he said, zooming in on the third pair of headlights. "There," he said, pointing at the headlights, which were turning onto another paved road. "Boxy shape. An older van. Looks like our man."

Alpha punched the accelerator just as his cell phone rang.

Bravo picked up Alpha's phone and checked the Caller ID. "It's from Shaw," he said.

"Put it on speaker," said Alpha.

Bravo did.

"What's the status on Babikov?" asked Shaw.

Alpha said, "He knows we're onto him and gave us the slip in a truck stop parking lot."

"I told you to stay out of sight!" shouted Shaw. "If you lose him—"

"We won't, sir," Alpha cut in. "We're tracking seven possibles via satellite, which we've narrowed to a single probable."

Shaw fumed for a long moment, then said, "Margin of error?"

"Ten percent or less."

"Stay on course but don't rule out the others until you've confirmed him to be your target. Error is something we cannot afford."

# CHAPTER 47

The sun was high in the sky when the Gulfstream parked on a yellow line at the airport's diplomatic gate. Alice was waiting on the tarmac when the stairs folded out of the Gulfstream and touched down on the pavement.

Standing at the base of the stairs with her arms folded across her chest, Alice was dressed in a tailored black business suit and black heels. Her long black hair had been pulled back in a ponytail that nearly hung to her waist.

"You're wearing your hair longer," Wilcox remarked after descending the stairs. Striding toward her, he extended his arms to give her a hug.

Alice batted his arms away. "Do not try charming your way out of this, Bill! Your president is accusing us of hacking your GPS."

Wilcox started to respond but Alice cuts him off.

"Obviously, what happened is horrible. A thousand people were killed. But we are not responsible. Does anyone listen? No! Can anyone present the *slightest* shred of evidence that we were involved? No! Your president is threatening reprisals and many congressional leaders are echoing his thoughts. An international crisis between our nations is occurring and you decide to just drop in for an unsanctioned visit?"

Wilcox again started to respond but Alice cuts him off.

"Oh, but that's not all, is it?" she continues. "You also want me to slip you and Colonel Talanov and two children into the country . . . off the books! I could *strangle* you right now!"

Wilcox held up his hands in a pacifying gesture just as Talanov and the others joined them. Avoiding the heat of Alice's glare, Wilcox introduced Alice as his longtime friend and colleague.

"I demand you arrest these men," Straw Sandal said, taking

refuge behind Alice. "I was on vacation in America when they abducted me as their prisoner. You must arrest them!"

Alice worked the screen of her phone and showed Straw Sandal the surveillance footage from Amber's apartment. "Did your vacation include murdering a woman?" she asked pointedly.

Straw Sandal looked away with a hardened glare.

"Unless and until this footage is corroborated with additional evidence," Alice warned Straw Sandal in Chinese, "it is not enough to convict you in a Hong Kong court of law. But that can easily change, especially if you or your father's people harm any of these guests. Are we clear?"

Straw Sandal glared at Alice but did not reply.

"Are we *clear?*" repeated Alice emphatically.

Straw Sandal grudgingly replied with a nod.

"Shall we?" Alice said, ushering the group toward a glass door being held open by two armed guards.

Wilcox fell in step beside Alice. "Remember the great time we had in Italy?" he asked brightly.

"Don't!" Alice hissed, holding up a hand, then gesturing everyone through the door.

Once inside, Talanov, Straw Sandal, and the kids were directed through a security scanner. While they stepped through one at a time under the scrutiny of guards, Alice pulled Wilcox aside.

"How dare you bring a Chinese citizen into this country as a prisoner, then have the *audacity* to ask that I admit you and Colonel Talanov and two children without passports, which of course you somehow managed to solve by pulling a hat off of a rabbit and getting Charlie – whoever that is – to email digital passports to my private number, asking if I could arrange visas for all of you until permanent documents could be couriered to my office."

"It's rabbit out of a hat," said Wilcox, "and it's a reference to –"

"*I don't care* what it references!" said Alice in a harsh whisper. "You are not even supposed to be here. In fact, some of our sources in Washington claim you actually *stole* that airplane outside. Is that true?"

Wilcox opened his mouth to reply but Alice held up a hand. "Never mind, I don't want to know."

"Call it a goodwill visit," said Wilcox with a smile.

"The only reason we are allowing this – never mind your official title as an embassy wine attaché, which we both know is nothing but a ruse, is because I have known you for so many years."

"And what good years they've been," added Wilcox.

"Shut up, Bill. Good years or not, my superiors consider you to be a friend – one of the few we trust in your CIA – which of course we cannot admit publicly because you *are* CIA. But it is not just you that we are allowing into the country, is it? You are asking us to allow a former KGB colonel to come in with you. And not just any colonel, but one who is a notorious American spy. And if that isn't enough, he also consults for the CIA. And if *that* isn't enough, he is also wanted for questioning by your Director of National Intelligence. Is this true?"

"Uh . . . not entirely."

Alice threw up her hands and stormed to the window and back. "Not entirely? What does that even mean? That it's forty percent true? Seventy percent? Ninety percent? The only reason we are considering this insane request is because Diane Gustaves phoned me to personally plead your case, explaining how you were here with her blessing to help us identify and capture the monstrous hacker responsible for that airline collision. She concurs with your belief that Dragon Head is behind it, although Beijing disagrees. They believe the signal originated out of Hawaii by way of Australia."

"We've traced the signal to Shenzhen," said Wilcox.

"Which precludes Dragon Head from being involved. He never ventures beyond the confines of Hong Kong and Kowloon."

"Which would be the perfect cover were he able to mask the

signal to make it look like it originated out of Shenzhen, or Hawaii, or wherever. Dragon Head's behind this, Alice. You saw the evidence I sent. You identified the photos. You saw the video."

"A video is hardly proof. Videos can be staged by anyone with a camera and some actors."

"True, if that were all, but taken in concert with other evidence, it paints a picture we can't ignore."

"What kind of other evidence?" asked Alice.

"The same electronic fingerprints on both the virus that was planted in Diane's computer system by Straw Sandal, as well as in the GPS hacking signal. Those fingerprints link Dragon Head with the hacking."

"As in functional code sequences? Is that what you mean?"

Wilcox responded with a blank stare.

"Never mind. You say he kidnapped a young girl. Why would he do something like that?"

"Dragon Head wants Talanov in Hong Kong."

"Why"

"That we do not know."

"So the girl is his way of forcing Talanov to come here?" asked Alice.

"Yes, and her name is Su Yin."

"Who is this girl to Talanov?"

"Su Yin and her siblings, the ones over there who came with us, are the foster children of Talanov's best friend."

"So, Su Yin is kidnapped, but in the process, Straw Sandal is captured?"

"Yes, which is why the higher-ups in my government are so upset with me right now. They ordered me to bring Talanov and Straw Sandal to DC for questioning. Dragon Head, presumably, ordered Talanov to bring Straw Sandal with him to Hong Kong."

"Presumably?"

"We're assuming it was Dragon Head, because the kidnapper, Xin Li, who works for him, communicated the demands by threatening to kill Su Yin unless we complied."

"I can't say that I disagree with your superiors," said Alice. "although you didn't hear that from me. From your point of view, Straw Sandal should have been taken to Washington for questioning. You cannot give in to criminal extortion, and you of all people should know that. Besides, with an issue like this, precedence must be given to the protection of many lives over the saving of one."

"Alex thinks he can do both."

"Both?"

"He thinks he can rescue Su Yin *and* stop Dragon Head from bringing down any more planes."

"How does he plan to do that?" asked Alice.

"Dragon Head needs something from Alex. We don't know what it is, but we know it's important. Otherwise, Dragon Head would not have resorted to such extreme measures to get him here."

"As in kidnapping a little girl?"

"Yes. Dragon Head is holding Su Yin as leverage to force Talanov's cooperation. But we've got Straw Sandal, which keeps Dragon Head from harming Su Yin."

"Like a bargaining chip?"

"Yes!"

"Allow me to reverse the situation," said Alice. "Would you allow me to bring a United States citizen into America as a hostage, then allow me to retain that hostage as a bargaining chip while conducting my own private investigation of some-one I claimed had committed a crime?"

"Come on, Alice . . ."

"Would you?"

Wilcox scowled and looked away.

"Do you see the position you have placed me in? I can allow you certain liberties, so long as you do not violate our laws, but I cannot allow you to retain Straw Sandal. She is a Chinese citizen. Nor do I have any warrants that have been issued in America against her or her father, which would justify further investigation on our part against your claims."

"Alice, please! The moment Straw Sandal goes free, we lose our leverage."

"And I am sorry about that, Bill, really, I am."

"Can't you at least bring her father in for questioning? Or get a warrant and search his premises?"

"Not without some kind of evidence that he is guilty."

"He's holding a young girl hostage! Find her. She's your evidence."

Alice gave Wilcox a you-should-know-better-than-that look. "We have rules of investigation here in Hong Kong just as you do in the States," she said. "I can't just kick in his door and hope to find something."

"We have security footage of his lover murdering a congressional secretary. His daughter was in that footage, and we have witnesses who *saw* Xin Li kidnap Su Yin. They're right over there. Su Yin's brother and sister."

"And I am telling you the law does not permit me to conduct investigations against our citizens based on claims made in America."

Wilcox bit his lip in frustration.

"I realize this is a noble attempt to save a young girl's life – which I admire, really, I do – which Colonel Talanov no doubt initiated by convincing you to fly him here on a Gulfstream you probably *did* steal. I am sorry, Bill, but officially, my hands are tied."

"That is bureaucratic bullshit and you know it. A little girl has been kidnapped and your main priority seems to be protecting Dragon Head's rights and the rights of his daughter. What about Su Yin's rights? What about the escalating tensions between our two nations because a hacker is operating here, in your own back yard, and making it look like you did it? Help me out, Alice. Unofficially is fine, but please don't leave us floundering. We need your help."

"I will do what I can," said Alice. "If someone has seen the girl in Dragon Head's custody, then we can take further measures. But like I said, we cannot just kick down his door and hope to find her. As for Straw Sandal, officially, she is to go free."

"Officially? What exactly do you mean?"

Alice glanced at her watch. "I must get back to the office."

Wilcox scrutinized Alice's eyes in an effort to interpret what she had just said and not said.

"Please don't ask for clarification," Alice said in response to his scrutiny over the sound of an airport announcement. "If you do, I will say what I do not want to say and you will definitely not like my answer." And with a polite hand gesture, she ushered Wilcox through the security scanner.

No one spoke while they walked along the lighted concourse, which was like a huge tunnel, with an arching roof that made the structure look like a gigantic fuselage, with geometric ceiling panels and a gray terrazzo floor polished to the sheen of a mirror. Arrival and departure gates were interspersed with boutique shops and flower beds bursting with color. Lighted panels on walls advertized famous brands.

Moments later, the group stepped through some glass doors and out into the bright sunshine, which was filtered through the reinforced glass of a massive overhead canopy.

"Since your passports have not yet arrived," said Alice, "I can take you to a hotel that will allow you to check in without them."

"Accommodation has been arranged," Straw Sandal said.

The remark drew everyone's attention to Straw Sandal, whose eyes were fixed on Talanov, as if warning him to comply.

Talanov assessed Straw Sandal for a moment, then looked at Wilcox and nodded.

"Then I guess we're set," said Wilcox with a smile.

"Are you sure about this?" asked Alice. Her eyes were now laden with warning.

After a quick glance at Talanov, Wilcox nodded.

"As you wish," Alice replied. "Call me once you are settled

and let me know where you are."

"I will," answered Wilcox. He gave Alice a kiss on the cheek just as an unmarked sedan stopped in front of them.

Wilcox stepped over to the car and opened the door for Alice.

"Be careful, Bill," said Alice in a low voice before getting into the back seat. "If your suspicions are correct and Dragon Head has already killed over a thousand people in a midair collision, he won't think twice about killing you."

# CHAPTER 48

Zak looked in his rearview mirror and saw a pair of head-lights in the distance behind them.

"They've found us, haven't they?" asked Ginie, noticing Zak eyeing the mirror and looking back to see the headlights.

"Hard to say," Zak replied, turning right onto a smaller highway. "Bill's phone is still disabled, so if they are follow-ing us, they couldn't have found us that way."

"Then how?" asked Ginie, glancing out at the vast groves of citrus trees flanking each side of the highway.

The highway they were on had a broad ribbon of gently graded gravel. Beyond the shoulder, the groves stretched off into an impenetrable darkness.

"Aircraft or satellite imagery," answered Zak, "and for them to have found us this quickly, I'm guessing the latter, which means they're with the government."

"Why would the government be chasing us?" asked Emily.

"I'm not sure. So far, they've only been tailing us."

"But you don't know why?"

"No, I don't," said Zak, his eyes on the mirror, where he noticed the headlights turn the corner in the distance behind them. "They must have been watching us at the motel, and after we parted company with Alex and Bill, they stayed with us. The question is, why? They obviously know who we are – that we're not Wilcox – and, yet, after we ditched them at the truck stop by removing the SIM card from Bill's phone, they located us again. Why go to all of that trouble? We're of no value to anyone, unless . . ."

"Unless what?" asked Ginie.

"Unless they need leverage with Alex. We're to them what Su Yin is to Dragon Head, and Alex is caught in the middle. My God, that's it. They're keeping us on a leash in case they need leverage with Alex. Which means the government is very interested in whatever Alex is attempting to do in Hong Kong."

"What are we going to do?" asked Emily.

Zak glanced at the dense groves bordering the highway. Just ahead was another highway that branched off to the left.

"We're going to lose them," Zak replied.

Less than a mile behind, Alpha had the accelerator pressed to the floor of the SUV.

"They just turned left onto another highway," said Bravo, his eyes on the jerky, real-time image of a van on the digital map illuminating the screen of his phone.

"How far ahead?"

"Half a mile."

"Where does that highway lead?"

"Through more groves."

Seconds later, the SUV's headlights illuminated an intersection of pavement branching off to the left. Alpha touched the brakes and accelerated around the corner. The SUV rocked to the right before leveling itself again.

Alpha handed his pistol to Bravo. "When we get up behind them, I'll swing left like I'm going to pass. When I do, shoot their rear tire."

Bravo popped the magazine out of Alpha's pistol. It was fully loaded. After jamming the magazine back into the handle, he slid the metal lever and cocked the weapon. "Old habits," he remarked when he saw Alpha grinning in the dim wash of the dashboard lights.

Traveling nearly one hundred miles an hour, the SUV quickly caught up to Zak's old van. When Bravo rolled down his window, a blast of night air filled the cab.

Alpha pulled out into the other lane as if he were going to pass. When he did, Bravo readied his pistol.

In his outside mirror, Zak saw the SUV swing wide to his left. "Hang on!" he said, hitting the brakes. When he did, the SUV shot past them just as Zak hit the gas and cranked the steering wheel to the left, causing the van to clip the rear bumper of the SUV. The jolt sent the SUV spinning across the highway and down onto the shoulder, out of control.

Zak continued off the highway into grove of citrus trees. Branches slapped and scraped the van as Zak sped along an aisle. A short distance into the thicket, Zak slowed to a crawl, switched off his lights, then turned into another aisle.

Hearing a moan in the back seat, Zak looked around to see Ginie with her hand to her head. "Are you all right?" he asked.

"I smashed my head against the window. I think I feel something sticky."

"Let me get a little deeper into the trees and I'll stop and have a look. Emily, are you okay?"

"I banged my head, too, but I'm all right."

Back on the shoulder of the highway, Alpha hit the brakes and brought the SUV to a stop in a cloud of dust, where he angrily pounded the steering wheel just as his cell phone began to ring. Alpha told Bravo to answer it while he did a squealing U-turn and sped across the highway into the citrus grove after Zak.

"Why me?" asked Bravo, seeing the call was from Shaw.

"Because I'm driving and we can't lose Babikov."

Bravo took a steadying breath and answered the call.

"What the hell just happened?" yelled Shaw. He was looking at a satellite map of the citrus groves while operators in the communications center worked furiously to enhance the area in an effort to locate Babikov.

"He rammed us off the road," Bravo replied.

"How could you be so careless!"

"Don't worry, sir, we'll find him."

"How do you plan to do that when *we* can't even see him?"

"He's obviously turned off his headlights," said Bravo, "which means he'll have to creep along in the darkness, which means, sooner or later, he'll run out of grove, or come to an irrigation canal, or have to turn his headlights back on. When he does, we'll have him. Right now, he's driving blind. He can't keep doing that forever."

By now, Zak's eyes had adjusted to the night, but because there was no ambient light, the surrounding forest was a dense, pitch-black montage of shadows and silhouettes.

With branches scraping the outside of the van, Zak steered the vehicle slowly into another aisle. He was not even sure which way they were heading because he had lost his sense of direction, and there was no time now to stop and navigate by the stars, not that he could see much of the sky, anyway, because the grove was so thick and dark. His focus now was putting as much distance between him and the *cheykas* as possible. The good news: the grove was vast and there were miles and miles of arrow-straight aisles. The bad news: the *cheykas* had satellites on their side, and because he could see no other headlights poking through the trees, that meant there was no way to tell where they were.

Zak slowed and turned again. His strategy was to keep zigzagging in an unpredictable pattern toward the far corner of the grove. Thankfully, the aisles were straight and the sound of branches scraping the sides of the van kept him more or less in the center of the aisle.

If he remembered correctly from previous trips, the highways bordering this section of groves formed a perimeter in the shape of a trapezoid, with an angled top, where the highway cut diagonally to the southeast. Farther south was another highway that cut due west. It formed the bottom of the trapezoid, with smaller roads crisscrossing the interior of the tract. He needed to reach one of those smaller roads, which would take him to one of the highways, which would take him back to the interstate, where they could disappear in the flow of traffic. Twain Harte would have to come later.

Zak turned again and almost immediately branches began scraping heavily on the right-hand side of the vehicle. So he adjusted his steering to the left, then straightened it when the scraping subsided.

"How are you feeling?" asked Zak, glancing over his shoulder at Ginie.

"My head really hurts," she replied. "I think I need to lie down."

"Not until I look at you first."

Zak took his foot off the accelerator and allowed the van to coast to a stop in an intersection of aisles. With the engine idling, he switched on the interior light and rotated in his seat.

Ginie's forehead was bloody.

With his attention on Ginie, Zak did not hear the roar of tires and snapping of branches until a blinding burst of headlights lit up the interior of the van seconds before the SUV broadsided them with a deafening crash.

Zak heard Ginie and Emily scream. Heard groaning metal as the van flipped onto its side. Felt his head smash the steering wheel as the smell of gasoline filled his nostrils.

An instant later, everything went black.

# CHAPTER 49

The red and white taxi stopped in front of a highrise hotel. No one had talked during the ride from the Hong Kong airport, especially the driver, who kept glancing uneasily in the rearview mirror at Straw Sandal, who was wedged between Talanov and Wilcox. In the front seat beside the driver were Jingfei and Kai.

Talanov climbed out, then motioned for Straw Sandal to get out while Wilcox tried paying the driver. The driver refused with hand gestures that said he did not want any money. Wilcox insisted but the driver was adamant. He kept motioning for Wilcox to close the door, and with a shrug, Wilcox complied, and the driver squealed away.

Straw Sandal led the way through a rotating glass door into the lobby of the hotel, which was cold and impersonal in its attempt to achieve opulence. The interior walls were huge panels of polished stone. The white floor was ceramic tile. A sitting area to one side featured a collection of stuffed chairs and sofas. A tall plant in a pot was the only sign of life.

With her footsteps echoing off the floor, Straw Sandal approached the front counter. The attending clerk was a young Chinese woman in a cream-colored suit. She had short black hair, alabaster skin, and bright red lips.

The young woman blanched when she looked up to see Straw Sandal glaring at her. The young woman picked up her phone and called the manager. Within seconds, the manager appeared. Thin and delicate, he was dressed in a smart black suit.

"Welcome, honored one," the manager said, bowing.

"These people need a room," Straw Sandal replied.

The manager snapped his fingers and the clerk fetched two key cards and ran them through a scanner. Once the key cards had been programmed to one of the hotel's luxury suites, the clerk handed them to the manager, who handed them to Straw Sandal, who turned away before the manager could say how pleased he was to serve such esteemed guests.

The group followed Straw Sandal to the elevator, where two couples were waiting. When the couples saw Straw Sandal, they left quickly. Seconds later, the doors dinged opened and Straw Sandal stepped inside just as Talanov's cell phone vibrated.

Talanov checked the Caller ID but saw the number had been blocked. After a moment of hesitation, he touched the green answer button and put the phone to his ear.

"Commercial jet, my ass," a voice growled.

Talanov turned away from the others and lowered his voice. "I'm trying to save a girl's life."

"Not my concern. My concern is stopping these attacks by China against the United States. So, before I decide whether or not to charge you with treason, I'm ordering you to get back on my plane and bring that prisoner of yours back to the DC for questioning."

"Sir, if you'll let me explain."

"Get back on my plane!"

"Bringing Straw Sandal to DC was a waste of time. The only way of stopping those attacks is here, in Hong Kong."

"What part of 'Get back on my plane' don't you understand?"

"And I'm telling you the only way to end this is by letting me proceed."

Shaw worked the keyboard on his cell phone.

An instant later, the phone in Talanov's hand chimed with a text message. Talanov looked at the text message, which read, OPEN THE FILE, COLONEL. Talanov hesitated, then heard Shaw repeat the message to him verbally.

"Open the file, Colonel," said Shaw. "You're going to want to see this."

Even though Talanov did not have the phone to his ear, he

could still hear Shaw's voice. And so could everyone else.

Although wary because of the spyware incident back in San Francisco, Talanov opened the attachment, which was a video file. He clicked Play and saw Zak, Ginie, and Emily kneeling on the barren ground in a dense citrus grove. Their hands had been zip tied behind their backs. Zak's forehead was cut and his face was black-and-blue. Ginie's face was covered with blood that had dried in crusty rivulets. Emily's hair was tangled and she was silently crying. With soft music playing in the elevator, Talanov watched each of them look up into the camera.

Talanov heard a man's voice order them to stand, after which Zak and the women struggled to their feet. The camera then followed them to the rear door of an SUV, which a man in a ski mask opened. The camera showed the man emptying the utility space of camping gear. The man then shoved Zak, Ginie, and Emily inside the utility space, one on top of the other. It then showed the door being slammed, and the man in the ski mask disappeared.

"So allow me to make myself clear," Shaw said. "If you don't stop what you're doing right now and get back on my plane, and I mean you, Wilcox, and that Chinese bitch, then I will put bullets in the heads of Babikov and those women and send you the pictures."

And with that, the line went dead.

When the elevator doors opened seconds later, Talanov stood rigidly in place while everyone else stepped out of the elevator, where they gathered in a group, unsure what to do.

Straw Sandal waited until Talanov looked at her before nodding for him to follow.

Talanov stepped out of the elevator and followed the others along the carpeted corridor to a numbered door, where Straw Sandal inserted the key card in a slot above the handle. With a heavy click, the door unlocked and Straw Sandal pushed it open.

Wilcox and the kids entered and looked around. To one side

was a couch and two stuffed chairs. At the other end of the room was a boutique kitchen and well-stocked mini-bar.

When Talanov approached the doorway, Straw Sandal offered him the keycard and said, "We will call you with instructions."

But instead of accepting the key card, Talanov shoved Straw Sandal into the room and closed the door. Straw Sandal jumped into a fighting position, feet apart, fists ready, teeth clenched.

Wilcox scooped the kids to safety just as Talanov strode calmly forward. Behind Straw Sandal was a large sliding glass door that led onto a balcony that overlooked the Hong Kong skyline.

"For now, I'm giving the instructions," Talanov said, rolling up his sleeves. "One way or another, you're going to tell me where your father is. Then you're going to take me to see him." He shook his arms, as if preparing for a fight.

"You are not giving the orders," Straw Sandal replied.

"I think I just did, but if you prefer to fight it out again like you tried in San Francisco, I'm fine with that."

Straw Sandal glared angrily at Talanov.

"So far, the CIB has stayed out of this," Talanov remarked. "But if you do something stupid, like attacking a visitor in a hotel room, they'll have enough reason to launch an investigation into you and your father, and who knows what they'll find, as in a kidnapped little girl. Up to you. What's it going to be?"

Straw Sandal's eyes flashed but she did not reply.

"Call Alice," said Talanov, glancing at Wilcox. "Tell her we've been attacked. Be sure and mention the attack was initiated by Dragon Head's daughter."

Wilcox started to dial.

"Stop!" Straw Sandal said.

Talanov narrowed his eyes. The seconds stretched.

"The Zhongzhen Martial Arts Academy," Straw Sandal finally said.

"Call him. Tell him we're coming over."

Straw Sandal continued to glare defiantly at Talanov, who picked up the cordless phone and tossed it to Straw Sandal, who continued glaring at Talanov before grudgingly dialing a number. Once the connection was made, she stepped out onto the balcony.

"Keep an eye on her while I talk to Bill in the hall," Talanov told Jingfei quietly. "I'll leave the door ajar. Any problem, give a shout."

Jingfei agreed, and Talanov nodded for Wilcox to join him in the hallway.

While Straw Sandal conversed on the balcony, Jingfei made a "watch her" gesture to Kai and hurried across the carpet to the slightly open door, where she cocked and ear and listened.

Out in the corridor, Talanov paced back and forth several times before showing Wilcox the video clip he had just been sent.

Wilcox watched the video, then leaned back against the wall. "I knew Shaw would be furious," he said, "but *this?* I can't believe he would sink that low."

"I can't believe it, either," said Talanov, "but you heard what Shaw said. He's demanding we leave immediately or he says he'll kill Zak and the women."

Without listening to anything more, Jingfei ran back to the couch and plopped down beside Kai, where she drew her knees up and sat in a ball, arms folded tightly across her shins, lips pinched, eyes staring angrily at the floor.

"What's wrong?" whispered Kai.

"Talanov and Wilcox, they're leaving!"

"What do you mean, they're leaving?"

"Talanov played some kind of a video clip for Wilcox, then said they were leaving. I *knew* this was going to happen."

Outside in the corridor, Wilcox slumped back against the wall. "I thought I could buy us some time by telling Shaw you got away. Everything we did. It was all for nothing."

"Maybe not," Talanov replied.

Half a world away, in Tyson's Corner, Virginia, Shaw was pacing the floor in front of his desk, talking to Alpha on a scrambler phone.

"Take Babikov and the others to the termination site," he said. "I'll text you the coordinates."

"Termination for how many?" asked Alpha, inspecting the SUV to make sure it was drivable. The bull bar was bent and the spotlights had been demolished, but otherwise it had suffered little damage.

"All of them," Shaw replied. "No loose ends. But not until I give the order. We first need Talanov to comply, but after he does, they're all yours."

"Copy that. We'll need a clean-up crew for the van. Babikov tried losing us in an orange grove and I had to ram him. The van's on its side, so we'll need a flatbed. I left a tracking beacon inside the cab."

"I'll send a crew. Let me know when you've arrived at the site."

Shaw clicked off, then dialed another number. Ten seconds later, the phone was answered by Special Agent "Delta," who was on board the USS Ronald Reagan.

Delta and Special Agent "Zulu," their gray T-shirts stained with sweat, had just finished a workout in the gym, which was a rectangular room of exercise equipment, weights, mirrors, mats, and treadmills. The decor was like everywhere else on the carrier: pipes, conduits, girders, and boilerplate steel, all painted gray. Both agents were Chinese-Americans, and both were in their thirties. Delta spoke fluent Cantonese and Zulu spoke fluent Mandarin. Both were five-feet, eleven inches tall.

"Delta here," the agent said.

"We've got a problem," said Shaw. "How soon can you deploy?"

# CHAPTER 50

When Talanov reentered the hotel room with Wilcox he could tell something was wrong. Kai had a scowl on his face and Jingfei refused to look at him. Why they were acting that way, he didn't know. Nor did he have the time to placate their emotional whims.

"He's waiting," announced Straw Sandal. She had been waiting by the slider. Sunlight was reflecting off a neighboring highrise and filling the room with light.

Talanov gave Wilcox a nod and Wilcox told the kids to come with him. Without a word, Jingfei and Kai got up and followed Wilcox out the door and to the far end of the corridor, where Wilcox pushed open a heavy metal door.

"Stairs? You've got to be kidding," complained Jingfei when Wilcox led the way into a shaft of unpainted concrete and switchback steps.

"We're taking the back way out," said Wilcox.

"We're on the nineteenth floor!"

"Don't worry, it's all downhill."

"Why don't we take the elevator?" asked Kai. "This is, like, way beyond stupid."

"I want to make certain that nobody sees us."

"Seriously? A big white guy in a pink and yellow Hawaiian shirt? Everybody's going to see us."

Wilcox rubbed the bridge of his nose. *Why did I let Talanov rope me into babysitting these two?*

The kids descended the stairs two at a time and were soon out of sight, although their feet could be heard slapping the concrete.

"Wait for me at the bottom," Wilcox called out.

Seven minutes later, a winded Wilcox reached the ground floor, where the kids were leaning against the concrete wall near the back door. Jingfei and Kai had been conversing quietly, but when they saw Wilcox, they quit talking and stepped away from each other.

Pausing to catch his breath, Wilcox eyed them suspiciously.

"Where to?" asked Jingfei with an impatient sigh.

"How about we get something to eat?"

Jingfei threw Wilcox a sarcastic look. "You make us walk down nineteen flights of stairs because you didn't want anybody to see us, then say we're going to a restaurant to get something to eat? Kai was right. This is way beyond stupid."

Wilcox maintained a pleasant smile. "Chinese sound good to you?"

"Gee, that's imaginative," Jingfei replied. She pushed open the fire door and stepped outside.

With his patient smile still fixed in place, albeit with effort, Wilcox followed Jingfei and Kai out onto a wide pedestrian walkway between more of Hong Kong's ubiquitous office towers. It was certainly not as crowded as the bustling sidewalk in front of the hotel, but neither was it the quiet walkway he had hoped. There were hundreds of people streaming past them in both directions, men and women, mostly young, focused on their electronic devices, texting, talking, keeping to themselves, no one paying them the slightest bit of attention.

"Okay, Spy Bill, which way so that no one sees those neon colors of yours?"

*God help the man who marries her,* Wilcox thought.

He looked in both directions. To the left was a quiet business district. Office buildings and office workers, all Asian. The kind of place where a big white guy in a Hawaiian shirt *would* be noticed. To the right, at the end of the block, was a more touristy section of Hong Kong. In that direction, he could see colorful banners, gaudy neon signs, and swarms of people. The kind of place they would not be noticed.

"This way," he said.

Kai looked over at Jingfei. "Does he have any idea where he's going?"

"Take a big fat wild guess."

Jingfei and Kai followed Wilcox into the pedestrian chaos at the end of the block.

"Stay close," Wilcox said, dashing with the kids across the street to a currency exchange. Beside the thick glass window of the kiosk was a framed menu of exchange rates for various currencies.

Taking out his wallet, Wilcox exchanged all of the cash he was carrying. It totaled just shy of four hundred dollars, which would be enough to keep them functioning until Charlie wired him some more. After receiving back a small stack of colorful Hong Kong dollars, Wilcox led the way to a small electronics shop, where he purchased a prepaid cell phone. The phone was packaged in sturdy, clear plastic. Stepping outside, he motioned the kids to follow him past a long line of customers ordering fast food from a counter. Displayed in windows flanking the counter were racks of smoked ducks hanging by their legs.

Ahead was a flashing sign of Chinese symbols that Wilcox did not understand. Below the symbols, however, was an English word he did understand: *restaurant*.

With the kids in tow, he entered the establishment.

The decor inside was like a shrine to the Great Wall of China. Covering one wall was a mural of the wall as it followed the elevations and contours of the land. Elsewhere were collections of photos and paintings, including images of Genghis Khan and Kublai Khan, with illustrations depicting Mongol invasions. Chair rails and door trims were decorated with Chinese dragons, knots, and lotus flowers.

Wilcox and the kids were shown to a booth.

"Okay, boss, what's the plan?" asked Jingfei.

"I text Alex my new number and tell him we're safe."

"And then?"

"We eat."

A waitress appeared. She was slender and traditionally attired in a body-hugging dress with a stand-up collar. The dress was yellow with red trim, which accented her long black hair tied up in a loose bun. Her dark eyes were warm and friendly. She bowed politely and handed out menus.

"Do you serve coffee?" asked Wilcox.

"Tea," the waitress replied softly.

"Tea will be fine," said Wilcox, holding up three fingers, meaning one cup for each of them. The waitress bowed politely and disappeared.

"Can't we get something else?" asked Kai with a sour frown.

"Tea soothes the savage soul," Wilcox replied, glancing at Jingfei, who replied with an exaggerated smile.

"So does beer," Kai replied.

Wilcox picked up the menu and opened it. Everything was written in Cantonese. "What looks good?" he asked, looking at Jingfei.

"Number sixteen," Jingfei replied.

"What is it?"

"Trust me."

"What are you getting?"

"Number twenty-two."

"How come you're not getting sixteen?"

"Because I don't like rat tail soup."

Wilcox responded with a deadpan stare that showed he was not amused.

"I'm *kidding*," Jingfei said. She rotated in her seat and looked around for the women's bathroom. It was located opposite the men's bathroom in a small corridor toward the rear of the restaurant. "Back in a jif," she said, sliding out of the booth.

"What sounds good to you?" Wilcox asked while continuing to tear open his cell phone packaging.

"Tacos," Kai replied.

Wilcox paused. "We're in China and you want Mexican?"

Kai grinned and thumbed toward the men's room. "I gotta go pee," he said, scooting out of the booth. "Go ahead and order. But *not* sixteen."

With a chuckle, Wilcox finished unwrapping his new cell

phone, switched it on, followed the start-up prompts, then sent a text. He then placed a call to a memorized number. The phone rang several times before it went to voicemail. "Mark, it's me," said Wilcox. "Call me back on this number." He then clicked off. Ten seconds later, his cell phone rang.

"New number?" asked Mark.

"Long story. Have you heard? Shaw's ordered us back home. In no uncertain terms."

"He called and told me the same thing . . . in no uncertain terms."

"What did you say?"

"That we'd take off as soon you got here. I presume that's why you're calling me now, to tell me you're on your way?"

"Officially, yes. On my way."

"And unofficially? Do I need to be worried about what you're going to say next?"

"Are you willing to go out on a limb?"

"Is Talanov the name of that limb?"

Wilcox did not reply.

"Am I to presume this limb extends out over a bottomless, fiery abyss from which there is no survival and no return should it break, which it most probably will?"

Wilcox did not reply.

"I tell you, in all my years as a pilot . . . of all the people I have carried to every far-flung corner of the world . . . never have I been so pissed off with anyone as I am now."

"Mark . . . I," Wilcox stammered, shocked Mark's reaction. "I never meant—"

"No, Bill, *no,* not you!" Mark cut in quickly. "*Shaw.* The man is a total douche. You're, uh, not recording this, are you?"

Wilcox laughed. "No, I'm not."

"Then what do you need me to do?"

# CHAPTER 51

Two blocks away and nineteen floors up, Talanov heard his cell phone chime with a text message that confirmed Wilcox had a purchased a new phone and that he and the kids were safe. "Okay, let's go," he said, walking to the door and opening it. He waited for Straw Sandal to exit the room, and when she did, she stiffened instinctively.

Talanov smiled at her reaction, then followed her along the carpeted hallway to the elevator. Less than two minutes later, the elevator doors opened on the ground floor and Straw Sandal led the way across the lobby toward the front door. Seeing them, the manager and all clerks stopped talking and watched. Hotel guests in the lobby likewise stopped talking and watched.

Seated in the far corner of the lobby, three men appeared to be reading newspapers. Dressed in black T-shirts and slacks, they were seated together with the newspapers held high in front of their faces, not that Talanov would remember their faces from his previous encounter with them in San Francisco. Dragon Head, however, was taking no chances. He had underestimated Talanov before and it would not happen again.

Once Talanov and Straw Sandal had left the hotel, two of the *Shí bèi* fighters rode the elevator upstairs to check Talanov's room. If anyone was there, they were to be taken hostage. The other *Shí bèi* fighter followed Talanov and Straw Sandal, where he would report their movements to Dragon Head.

In an alley two blocks away, Jingfei and Kai ran out the back door of the restaurant. Wilcox had been talking on his new cell phone and did not see them slip into the kitchen.

The kitchen had been abuzz with activity, so no one stopped to look at two kids passing through. After dashing out the back door, Jingfei and Kai paused in the alley. It was narrow and littered with trash. Dumpsters stood beside rows of back doors, and the air was humid with the sweet odor of rotting garbage.

An old kitchen worker with a wrinkled face was hosing debris into the center of the alley, where the dirty water trickled into a central channel that drained into a grate.

Jingfei and Kai ran up to the worker.

"Where is the Zhongzhen Martial Arts Academy," Jingfei asked in Cantonese.

The old man pointed to the corner and to the right.

Jingfei thanked the man and ran with Kai to the corner, where they turned right and hurried along the busy sidewalk as fast as they could walk, one behind the other, threading their way around and between people like speeding cars on a freeway. They passed a variety of small shops and fast food outlets separated by narrow walkways between the buildings. The flow of pedestrians was like a moving obstacle course made more difficult by jutting racks of trinkets, postcards, jewelry, shoes, magazines, neckties, and souvenirs.

"There he is . . . there's Talanov," Jingfei said, pointing.

"I see him," Kai replied.

Jingfei and Kai bypassed several pedestrians and fell in step several feet behind Talanov and Straw Sandal, heads angled downward, in case one of them looked back. By all appearances, they were simply two more Chinese faces in a river of Chinese faces. No one knew who they were or what they were doing.

Except someone *did* know.

Four feet behind Jingfei and Kai, the *Shí bèi* fighter from the hotel took out his cell phone and flipped through the images taken by Xin Li in San Francisco. He had been following Straw Sandal when two kids rushed past him, slowed abruptly, then said a name he recognized.

*Talanov.*

He compared the images on his phone with the faces of the girl and boy as they looked back and forth at each other while talking, which made it easy for him to make a positive identification. With a smile, he touched a speed dial button, and within seconds, Xin Li had answered. The *Shí bèi* fighter relayed his news and Xin Li told him what to do. The *Shí bèi* fighter ended the call and slipped his phone back in his pocket. He then grabbed several silk scarves off a stand and fell in step behind the kids, who did not notice him because of the surrounding crush of pedestrians. Everyone was jostling slowly along. A river of humanity.

They passed more racks and more stands and more narrow walkways between the buildings. They passed noodle bars and clumps of people waiting for steaming dumplings.

Opening his wallet, the *Shí bèi* fighter took out some cash. At the next narrow walkway, he touched Jingfei and Kai on the shoulder and said, "You drop," and with a smile, held out the money.

The kids instinctively stopped to look at the man, then the money, then the man again, who smiled and politely scooped the kids to one side, out of the bustling pedestrian traffic.

"You drop," the fighter said again, offering them the money.

It was a natural reaction to look at the money in the man's hand again, and neither Jingfei nor Kai would remember what happened next because it happened so quickly. All they would remember was the blur of being shoved into a narrow walkway and being stunned with immobilizing neck chops that dropped them to the concrete.

# CHAPTER 52

While Jingfei groaned on the pavement, the *Shí bèi* fighter used one of the scarves to gag Kai's mouth. He then rolled Kai onto his stomach and used another scarf to secure his wrists behind his back. He then dragged Kai twenty feet into the darkness of the narrow walkway before returning to focus on Jingfei, who was attempting to sit up. The *Shí bèi* fighter shoved her back down and shook his finger. A warning to lie still and keep silent. Producing a third scarf, he used it to gag Jingfei's mouth.

*Do something,* Jingfei thought. But she was too immobilized with fear. She felt herself being rolled onto her stomach. Felt a knee brace her face-down on the dirty pavement. Felt her hands being pulled behind her.

*If only we had stayed in the restaurant,* Jingfei thought as fear rose in her throat like bile. Wilcox was a dinosaur, to be sure, yet in spite of that, she trusted him as much as she trusted Zak. He was genuine, like the grandfather she always wished she'd had.

Jingfei felt the bite of the silk scarf around her wrists. Heard Kai's muffled groans in the distance. *Oh, God,* she thought.

Suddenly, Jingfei heard an expulsion of air. An instant later, she felt the attacker collapse on her back, where he remained, heavy and motionless, like a sandbag. She craned her head and saw the man's face. His cheek was mashed against the pavement beside hers and she could feel the heat of his sour breath. He was alive but unconscious.

*What was going on?* Jingfei wanted to move out from under him but could not. She was trapped.

Seconds later, she felt the weight of the man being lifted off her. She then saw the man being dragged by another man deeper into the walkway. Craning her neck, she saw the second man kneel down, untie Kai, and help him to his feet. She then saw the man come back and kneel beside her. Felt him gently untie her hands, then the scarf from around her mouth.

"Are you all right?" Wilcox asked.

Jingfei scrambled to her knees and hugged Wilcox tightly.

"It's okay. You're okay," Wilcox said, patting her reassuringly on the back.

"We were following Alex and Straw Sandal," Jingfei said as tears began streaming down her cheek. "We figured they'd lead us to Su Yin. To where she was being held."

"But that other guy must have been following us," added Kai, kneeling beside them.

"Don't worry, we'll get her back," Wilcox replied. He used his hand to dry Jingfei's tears. "Which we can't do if you don't start trusting us."

"How can you when you're leaving?"

"What are you talking about?"

"I heard you out in the hall. Alex said you've been ordered to leave."

"What else did you hear?"

"You're leaving! What else is there to hear?"

"We're not leaving, at least not yet."

"Bullshit! I *heard* Alex say you were leaving!"

"Okay, yes, I admit he said that," said Wilcox, "but there's more to the story than—"

"*See?* I *knew* it! You're abandoning Su Yin!"

"We are not abandoning Su Yin," Wilcox replied patiently, "and if you'll just allow me to—"

"I *heard* you!" Jingfei blurted out. "Well, me and Kai are *not* abandoning Su Yin, no matter what you do. You're nothing but a sycophant who blindly obeys bureaucratic—"

"It's Zak," said Wilcox, interrupting. "He's been captured, along with Emily and Ginie. The kidnappers are threatening to kill them."

Jingfei could not speak. All she could do is stare open-mouthed at Wilcox in the trash-littered confines of the narrow walkway.

Wilcox described what he and Talanov had seen on the video, which had been sent to them by Angus Shaw, who was behind the kidnapping. He described Zak, Ginie, and Emily, on their knees with their hands zip-tied behind them, their faces bloodied and bruised. He went on to repeat Shaw's threat to kill them if Talanov didn't bring Straw Sandal back to DC for questioning. Wilcox then said that he was glad Jingfei and Kai had stowed away on board the Gulfstream, because if they hadn't, they, too, would have been captured.

"So when I say we are not abandoning Su Yin, I mean it," concluded Wilcox, "which may well get Zak and the others killed if we don't play this right, which Alex thinks we can do."

"How? By doing something stupid, as in going with Straw Sandal to the Zhongzhen Martial Arts Academy alone, which we saw him do, no doubt thinking – or not thinking, as dinosaurs are famous for doing – that he can rescue Su Yin without anyone's help, even though he needs ours because he doesn't speak the language but is too pigheaded to admit it, meaning it will be easy for that bitch to double-cross him, which she *will* do, which means he'll get himself beat up or captured, which eliminates any chance of anyone rescuing Su Yin – or saving Zak – which means everyone loses."

Wilcox squinted with concentration while trying to follow another of Jingfei's rambling sentences. "Don't underestimate Alex," was all he could say. "For now, let's stick with the plan."

"What plan?"

Wilcox bit his lip.

"You don't have a plan, do you?"

"We're working on one."

"Working on one? Come on, Bill. No way can Alex do this on his own. He's walking into a trap."

"And he is willing to take that risk in order to find out

what's going on."

"He needs help! Needs *my* help, and Kai's."

"And he will involve you at the right time. It's why he insisted I let you stay and not ship you back to the States."

"So . . . Alex wants us here? He actually said that?"

"Yes. But you can't go running off like this. If they capture you, which they nearly did, Alex loses, which means Su Yin loses and they win. We need you – Alex needs you – so I am begging you to let this play out. Let Alex find out what Dragon Head wants. Once we know, then we can figure out what to do."

"And if they decide to take him prisoner?"

"They need him to do something for them, so taking him prisoner is unlikely."

"But it's possible, right?"

"Yes, it's possible, but you getting caught would have made things worse. If Alex doesn't come back within a reasonable period of time, we go to plan B. For now, though, we stick with plan A."

"You don't have a plan B."

"All the more reason to stick with plan A."

Offering Jingfei and Kai his hands, Wilcox pulled both kids to their feet.

"Can we, like, get something to eat?" asked Kai. "We ran out of the restaurant before we could order."

And Wilcox could not help but laugh.

# CHAPTER 53

Five blocks away Straw Sandal led Talanov into a neighborhood where tourists seldom ventured. There were no gleaming skyscrapers in this part of the city. Only rows of small shops lining the narrow streets, with roller doors that went up each morning and back down again each night. Above each shop were five to fifteen stories of small apartments dotted with tiny balconies with tiny windows and hundreds of tiny air conditioners mounted on rusty metal frames.

Turning a corner, Talanov saw a two-story building on the other side of the street. The building was a converted warehouse, with a flat roof, walls of brick, and two rows of windows running the length of the building. There was a large sign above a heavy wooden door, with yellow Chinese characters outlined in red. Beneath this was an English translation that read, *Zhongzhen Martial Arts Academy*. On each side of the door were elaborately carved beams with Chinese symbols representing the academy's twelve fighting virtues.

Loitering in front of the academy were half a dozen *Shí bèi* fighters. When they saw Talanov and Straw Sandal coming toward them, one fighter ran inside while the rest strode aggressively to meet them. Straw Sandal peeled away when the group arrived, leaving Talanov alone in their midst.

The fighters formed a circle around Talanov and Talanov eyed them. He recognized several from the attack at the pizza parlor in San Francisco. Many still had scabs on their faces.

"I'm here to see Dragon Head," said Talanov.

No one moved, and Talanov could also see they were looking to even the score. Perhaps that's why they had been waiting outside in the first place. Dragon Head was allowing them the opportunity to restore honor to themselves and the academy. Plus, Dragon Head wouldn't mind them softening him up before their meeting. To let him know who was boss.

Talanov stood a head taller than any of the fighters, who were all thin and wiry. Talanov also had a longer arm reach, which was great in hand-to-hand combat.

But there were five of them and only one of him, and like a pack of hyenas surrounding a lion, the pack would wear down the lion until the lion could fight no more.

*Best I not let that happen,* Talanov thought.

The fighter to his left looked to be the oldest, in his late twenties, perhaps, with a ponytail tied up in a knot. Talanov guessed him to the group leader by the way the others kept glancing at him while he, in turn, kept glancing at Straw Sandal, as if waiting for her command.

Talanov smiled at the ponytail guy. It was not a friendly smile but one of mockery, a smirk.

"Somebody lose a fight?" Talanov asked, touching his face in the same places where ponytail guy had scabs. He knew ponytail guy didn't speak English by the way he looked at Straw Sandal, and sure enough, as predicted, Straw Sandal translated his remark.

The ponytail guy reacted as Talanov thought he would. His eyes flashed with anger. His nostrils flared. His hands formed fists and he took a breath and held it in preparation for a strike. So Talanov took ponytail guy out with a leaping front kick to his jaw. The kick snapped the ponytail guy's head back and dropped him where he stood.

*Four against one.*

Talanov then hammered an elbow into the jaw of the man directly to the left of ponytail guy. It was not enough to drop him because the young fighter avoided its full impact by ducking to the side, but Talanov followed it with a spinning second elbow that did connect. The blow sent a spray of saliva from the man's mouth before his legs went rubbery and he collapsed.

*Three against one.*

Talanov was now outside the group. Before, he had been

surrounded. Now he had room to move. He could hear Straw Sandal shrieking orders, but with his focus on the remaining fighters, he didn't have time to look at her face, which by the sound of her voice was rabid with fury.

The other three fighters flew at him in a phalanx of leaping front kicks. The advantage of a leaping front kick is that if it doesn't connect, it allows the fighter to land on his feet, well-balanced and prepared for additional kicks or punches. Another advantage is its height. A leaping front kick can strike an opponent in the throat or face, and its snapping power is like a hammer. The one disadvantage is its brief air-borne moment, when its forward direction cannot be changed until the attacker's feet are again on the ground.

Milliseconds after the attackers sprang into the air, Talanov spun to his right and drove a leaping roundhouse kick into the back of the nearest attacker's head. By the time the other two came down on their feet, the nearest attacker was face-down on the pavement.

*Two against one.*

The remaining pair of fighters turned to face Talanov. But not before Talanov had shoved the nearest fighter into the other one with a two-handed pop to the chest. Caught off balance in their turns, the first fighter toppled backward into the second fighter and both of them fell. The first fighter used his momentum to do a back roll off the other fighter. That left the second fighter exposed for the instant needed for Talanov to crack a fist across his jaw.

*One against one.*

Talanov and the remaining fighter circled one another, looking for an opening. The *Shí bèi* fighter kept dancing, feinting, and darting with his upper body in an effort to throw Talanov off balance. He then tried a gymnastic move that looked like a horizontal cartwheel, hoping to knock Talanov's feet out from under him.

It failed.

Talanov hopped back, then leaped forward with a front kick

into the fighter's head just as he was coming out of the cartwheel.

*Game over.*

Straw Sandal looked at the collection of groaning bodies in the street. By now, spectators were observing them from the sidewalk and in upstairs windows. With a glare at the spectators, Straw Sandal turned and marched into the academy.

Talanov slowly followed.

The fact that he had just defeated another group of Dragon Head's fighters would hopefully earn him some respect. More likely, it would inflame Dragon Head's resolve to repay this additional insult. Dragon Head wouldn't kill him, that much he knew, nor would they kill Su Yin. Dragon Head needed them both alive, at least for now. But he would definitely want to break him, to establish dominance, to instill fear and force compliance.

*This is going to hurt.*

Inside the wooden front door of the academy was a small lobby. On the far side of the lobby, which was illuminated by soft light, was a doorway that led into a corridor that made a sharp turn to the right. On the wall to his left was a framed drawing of some Chinese symbols. Also on the parchment was an ink drawing of an old man of indeterminate age. He had wispy white hair, fearsome eyes and crinkled skin, with each line around the eyes seeming to represent decades of wisdom. Below the framed parchment was a fountain. It stood waist high and made a peaceful sound as water tumbled gently into a small pool hewn from stone.

Talanov paused to focus his senses. He could hear grunts and chatter in the next room. He could smell the perspiration and hear the scuffing of bare feet and the pops and slaps of boxing gloves and fists.

*Time to get this over with.*

He entered the corridor and followed it to the right, where it opened onto the wooden floor of the gym, which was a large rectangular room, with rows of windows near the ceiling and what looked to be a kick-boxing ring in the center. Two fighters with padded fighting gloves were in the ring. Beyond the elevated platform were more fighters using exercise equipment, balance beams, and weights. Much of the floor was covered with mats. People of all ages – men, women, boys, girls – were practicing individual routines. To his right were several long tables stacked with food parcels, where lines of old men and women were being served by half a dozen fighters in tank tops.

When Talanov entered the gym, all activity stopped. He paused and scanned the faces looking back at him, then proceeded toward Straw Sandal, who was waiting by the corner of the kickboxing ring. When he drew near, Straw Sandal uttered a sharp cry. Seconds later, he was set upon by more than twenty fighters, who pinned him face-down on the floor.

"No one make fools of us," Straw Sandal said.

"You don't need me for that," Talanov replied.

Straw Sandal kicked Talanov in the ribs. Pain exploded through his body and made him want to curl up in a ball. But he had been immobilized on the floor and could not move. Seconds later, he heard the approach of footsteps. They were long, authoritative strides that stopped near his head. The entire gym was still in silence. Straw Sandal said something to whomever was standing over him, but because it was in Chinese, he did not know what she said.

A long moment of silence passed.

"I demand to see Dragon Head," Talanov finally said.

"You are in no position to be making demands," replied the voice of a woman.

Talanov tried craning his neck to see who was speaking but could not move. He recognized the voice but knew it was not Straw Sandal. He had heard it before, but where?

Suddenly, it dawned on him. He had heard it on the phone in San Francisco. It was the same woman who had texted him the images of Su Yin. The same woman who had planted spyware on his phone.

And yet there was something else familiar about the voice. Had he met this woman before? If so, where?

Talanov tried looking up again but the hands clamping his head in place would not allow it. Finally, the woman spoke again – a sharp command in Chinese – and his head was released. When he looked up, he saw the face of a woman he was certain had killed. Xin Li was her Chinese name although Talanov knew her by her Russian name, Sofia Dubinina, and she was his former partner in the KGB.

And Talanov could only peer up at her with an open-mouthed stare.

"Nothing to say?" Sofia asked, screwing a silencer on the pistol she was holding. "No clever remarks? No witty retorts?"

"But you're . . . *dead*. I killed you!" stammered Talanov.

"Apparently not," Sofia replied, "although you will soon regret that fact."

And with a cold smile of satisfaction, Sofia cocked her pistol and aimed.

# CHAPTER 54

A lifetime can pass before a person's own eyes in less than a second. Decades of failures, successes, frustrations, hopes, dreams, pleasures, romances, and regrets . . . everything.

One night in particular stood out among Talanov's memories. It had been a turning point in his life, almost as much as the murder of his wife, and he had thought about this night many times since it occurred in 1985, when he and Sofia had been traveling together along the Mediterranean coast of Spain. Their purpose had been to track down a defecting scientist carrying vials of weaponized anthrax.

Talanov had openly defied Moscow on this assignment. They wanted him to sneak quietly into Spain, apprehend the doctor and his family, then sneak them on board a Soviet freighter for the ride back home. Talanov did not want to do that because inverse logic told him that sneaking into Spain quietly was a bad idea, even though it made sense on the surface. The reason: the CIA, which was assisting the doctor with his defection, would be expecting the KGB to attempt a covert rescue, and they would be prepared. An opposite strategy must therefore be adopted.

Which is exactly what he did. With Sofia on his arm, he chose the limelight in lieu of the shadows, which translated into a flamboyant two weeks of partying in the fast lane that included a Ferrari, tuxedos, elegant gowns, dancing, casinos, and fancy hotels. Talanov's aim: to have every eye following their every step. It was a classic misdirect.

The ruse worked as he calculated it would. What he did not realize, however – what he did not see coming because he, too, like the CIA, was looking in the wrong direction – was Sofia's betrayal. She had plans of her own.

Those plans included orders to kill him. Those plans included stealing the anthrax for herself, which she would then sell to the highest bidder. But instead of carrying out those orders, she offered to share the wealth. Why? Because she had fallen in love with him, or, more accurately, with the idea of someone like him. And when he rejected that love, she decided to kill him after all.

Talanov could still see her hanging in the open door of the car, gun in hand while they raced through the streets of Marbella that warm summer night. Still see the hatred in her eyes. Still hear her screaming at him because of the defecting doctor's teenage daughter, Noya, whose life he was trying to save after her men had deliberately infected her with a genetically engineered form of anthrax. Sofia could not understand why Talanov was risking his life to save the girl after she, Sofia, had offered him the world. He could still see her raising her gun to kill him. Could still see the shocked look in her eyes when he managed to shoot her first. Could still see her falling from the car, and, in his rearview mirror, see her bouncing and flipping before skidding under a truck. No one could have survived being shot at point blank range. No one could have survived such a fall from a speeding car.

And yet she had.

And here she was, standing over him with a pistol aimed straight at his head.

Talanov closed his eyes.

"Release him!" a voice shouted in English.

The *Shí bèi* fighters immediately stepped away and Talanov looked up to see a muscular white man entering the gym with more *Shí bèi* fighters accompanying him. It was Dragon Head, wearing a tank top that showcased his tattooed shoulders and arms.

Sofia stormed over to confront Dragon Head while Talanov climbed slowly to his feet. "I have waited *years* for this moment," she cried.

Dragon Head stopped in front of Talanov and looked back and forth between him and Sofia.

"Look at me! At what he *did!*" Sofia screamed, yanking open her shirt to show Dragon Head the bullet scars in her chest. She then turned around to reveal a track of scars down one side of her back. "He left me for dead!"

"And the part about you trying to kill me?" asked Talanov. "You seemed to have forgotten to mention that detail."

Sofia replied with a savage punch to the stomach that dropped Talanov to his knees. When Sofia started to kick Talanov in the head, Dragon Head stopped her.

"Enough!" he commanded. "Your vengeance is not my concern."

When Talanov climbed unsteadily to his feet, Sofia spat in his face. Talanov wiped off the spit and watched Sofia storm a short distance away, where she began pacing back and forth, glaring at him angrily while slapping the barrel of her pistol in her hand.

"It appears you two know one another," Dragon Head remarked.

"A lifetime ago," said Talanov.

"I have never seen her like this."

"Be patient, you will. One day she'll turn on you the same way she turned on me."

Sofia charged over and jammed her gun up under Talanov's chin. Dragon Head shouted a warning but Sofia didn't budge. Her anger was so intense it was palpable.

After a long moment, Talanov eased the pistol aside. "If you want to settle this some other time, that's fine with me. Right now, your boss and I have business to discuss. And it starts with me seeing Su Yin."

Sofia started to backhand Talanov but Talanov caught the blow in midair and shoved her back. When she started to retaliate, Dragon Head stopped her.

"He *mocks* us!" yelled Sofia.

"I'm here because I'm trying to cooperate," stated Talanov. "But not if Su Yin is dead. Proof of life, that's all I'm asking. A moment to make sure she's okay."

Dragon Head thought for a moment, then nodded to an old *Shí bèi* fighter standing on the far side of the gym. In his seventies, the fighter was fit, as were all the other fighters, but unlike the others, whose expressions were intense, his eyes had a gentle calmness.

The old fighter responded with an obedient bow and disappeared down a hallway. When he returned a minute later, Su Yin was with him. She was wearing the same pink dance leotard she had been wearing when kidnapped.

When Su Yin saw Talanov, she ran across the floor, tears streaming down her cheeks. Talanov knelt and Su Yin flew into his arms and hugged him tightly. "Don't leave me, don't leave me," she kept saying.

After a moment, Dragon Head snapped his fingers and the old *Shí bèi* fighter took Su Yin by the arm.

"I haven't talked with her yet," said Talanov, knocking his hand away.

Talanov was immediately tackled by a swarm of *Shí bèi* fighters.

"*I haven't talked with her yet!*" Talanov shouted over the cries of Su Yin being led away. He tried to elbow his way free, only to be punched to the floor, where he was repeatedly kicked until he curled up tightly in a ball, knees up to his chin, arms covering his head.

After commanding the fighters to stop, Sofia dropped down onto her knees and looked Talanov directly in the eyes. "I *will* have my revenge," she hissed in Russian, her face inches from his. "And that's after I butcher the girl."

"*Touch her and I'll kill you,*" shouted Talanov, also in Russian. He scrambled to his feet, but was punched and kicked to the floor again by Sofia and the *Shí bèi* fighters.

Dragon Head issued a command and everyone stopped.

"What did you say to him?" Dragon Head demanded, pulling Sofia back.

Sofia twisted out of Dragon Head's grasp but said nothing. Dragon Head glared at her for a long moment before ordering his fighters to help Talanov to his feet.

"What did she say to you?" demanded Dragon Head, stepping over to face Talanov. "And what did you say to her?"

"She threatened to kill Su Yin. So I told her I'd send her to hell if she so much as touched her."

"No one will harm the girl so long as you do what I say," Dragon Head replied. "But if I do not get my money . . ."

Talanov gave a start. "Money? Is that what this is about? You want me to give you *money?*"

"Not you, Colonel," said Dragon Head.

"Then who?"

Dragon Head glanced at Sofia, who stiffened for the instant needed for Talanov to discern what was going on.

"My God, it's that bank account, isn't it?" said Talanov, realizing Dragon Head wanted what so many people had wanted through the years: to take possession of a long-forgotten Swiss bank account opened in his name decades earlier by the KGB. The original deposit of seven million dollars was to have funded an espionage program that fell apart with the demise of the Soviet Union. The funds, however, continued to grow because they had been transferred by the Swiss to their investment brokers in Hong Kong, who, since that time, had managed to leverage the original amount into a staggering one point five billion dollars.

Talanov flashed back to his days in Australia, where he had migrated after the Soviet Union had crumbled. Life there had been peaceful until a resurrected Department Thirteen – the KGB's assassination and sabotage unit – came after him for the same reason Dragon Head was after him now: for the money. Their plan had been simple: kill him and take a copy of his death certificate to the bank in Switzerland. That document would have allowed those funds to be released, which almost happened had he not shown up in Switzerland very much alive.

So, why was Dragon Head not attempting the same thing now? Why had he not simply killed him and taken his death certificate to the bank?

The answer brought a smile to his lips.

"Does something amuse you?" asked Dragon Head.

"It certainly does," answered Talanov. "You need me to access my account. That's why you kidnapped Su Yin: to force me into helping you because no one else but me can access my account. Not even my death certificate will allow you access, which means there's some kind of a problem."

Talanov watched Dragon Head's expression harden. A nerve had been touched. So he decided to probe a little deeper.

"But that's not the whole story, is it? I mean, someone at the bank has had access to those funds. How else would they have been able to invest them? But they don't, anymore. What happened?"

"All you need to know, Colonel, is that if you locate and bring me those funds, the girl will live."

"Locate? What's there to locate? I thought they were in the bank."

Talanov saw Dragon Head tense.

"So they're not in the bank?" asked Talanov.

"This isn't a discussion, Colonel. Bring me those funds."

"Is that all you want? Just the money?"

Dragon Head replied with a deadpan nod.

"Are you a man of your word?" asked Talanov.

"I believe my demands are clear."

"Not if you're a liar."

Sofia charged over and again jammed the pistol up under Talanov's chin. "You will do what we say or I will kill the girl in front of you right here and now."

Talanov stared unwavering at Sofia for a long moment before easing the pistol aside and looking again at Dragon Head. "There's only one thing worse than a man who won't give his word. It's a man who doesn't keep it. So, are you a man of honor, or does your word, like hers, mean nothing?"

Sofia started to backhand Talanov but Dragon Head caught

her by the wrist.

"He *mocks* us!" Sofia yelled again, twisting away.

"I don't know what arrangement you two have," said Talanov to Dragon Head, "and I don't really care. She's your problem, not mine. I'm here because I want to make a trade – the money for Su Yin – but I need to know whether or not you're a man of your word. I mean, we hear a lot about the Chinese and their code of honor and how it's a big deal over here, but you're not Chinese, so maybe your word means nothing."

"I was *born* on this island!" declared Dragon Head, his eyes flashing with anger.

Talanov replied with a shrug.

Dragon Head drew to within inches of Talanov's face. His muscles were taut and veins stood out on both sides of his neck. "Do you think I'm a man without honor? Is that what you're saying?"

"I'm not trying to insult you, Mr. Moran, but I don't know who I'm dealing with. And if you're going to kill us anyway, then your promise to let Su Yin go in exchange for the money . . . well, it doesn't really mean very much, now, does it?"

Dragon Head swept his hand in a full circle around the gym, where more than a hundred pairs of eyes were watching. "Do you think these men would be following me if I wasn't a man of honor? They're Chinese, Colonel, every single one of them, and honor means something to them just like it does to me. All *Shí bèi* live by a code of honor."

"If that's the case, then I want you to give me your word that as soon as I hand over the money, you'll release Su Yin, alive and unharmed, and then leave us alone from now on. And that's *all* of us – the three kids, my friends, me – and that's here, in the States, wherever we are."

While Talanov waited for an answer and everyone in the gym continued to watch, Straw Sandal spoke quietly in the ear of her father. When she was finished, Dragon Head nodded thoughtfully.

"What did she say?" asked Talanov, glancing briefly at Straw Sandal, then back at Dragon Head.

"I don't see that it's your concern."

"It is if she's planning a double-cross," Talanov replied.

"I tell my father to be careful what he says to you," Straw Sandal said, "because once a *Shí bèi* gives his word, it is binding on us all to keep that promise."

"Good to know," said Talanov. "So, what's it going to be? Do we have a deal?"

After a moment's thought, Dragon Head nodded. "We have a deal. You've got my word."

"All right. Which bank are we talking about?"

"The Sun Cheng Financial Group, Limited. Straw Sandal will take you there."

"I'll find it," Talanov replied. "I won't risk her or anyone else complicating things at the bank. In the meantime, I need you set up an escrow account and email me the number. Once I get that number and locate the funds, I'll deposit them into the escrow account, then email you a written confirmation. Once I have Su Yin, I'll release the funds."

"You are not in charge!" yelled Sofia, striding toward Talanov with her pistol aimed directly at his face. She stopped with the silencer pressed directly against his forehead, her face livid with anger, her eyes wild with hatred.

A shout from Dragon Head did nothing, and for a long moment, time seemed to stop.

Then came a blur of hand movements that saw Talanov block the gun away from his face while grabbing Sofia's wrist, lifting it upward while sliding deftly beneath Sofia's outstretched arm, then twisting her arm up behind her, where he wrenched the pistol from her hand and shoved her to the floor. By the time Sofia had scrambled to her feet, Talanov had ejected the magazine, cleared the chamber, and handed all of the pieces to Dragon Head.

"If I were you, I'd watch your back," advised Talanov.

Sofia charged Talanov but Dragon Head stopped her. When

Sofia started to protest, Dragon Head stopped her.

Looking back at Talanov, Dragon Head said, "You'll have that number within the hour." He then told Straw Sandal to set up the account.

"Send me a text when you have it," said Talanov.

"What is your phone number?" asked Straw Sandal.

Talanov told her.

Straw Sandal worked the screen of her phone and entered the number into her directory.

"And if I need to reach you?" asked Talanov.

Straw Sandal worked her phone again and sent Talanov a text. She then turned and left the gym.

Talanov started to follow but Dragon Head grabbed him by the arm. "Don't make me do something unpleasant, Colonel. Fulfill your end of the bargain. Find me those funds."

"I'll do my best."

"You will do more than your best," Sofia said, landing a kick into Talanov's ribs, followed by a backfist that snapped Talanov's head back and toppled him to the floor, where he rolled onto his side, gasping, his nose bleeding, one eyebrow gashed. "Or that is just the beginning of what I will do to you and your friends."

After a stern rebuke for Sofia, Dragon Head snapped his fingers and two *Shí bèi* fighters lifted Talanov to his feet, dragged him through the foyer and out the front door, where they tossed him onto the sidewalk.

And with a groan, Talanov struggled to his feet and began his slow walk back to the hotel.

# CHAPTER 55

It was late afternoon when Alpha turned off the mountain highway onto a gravel road that was little more than a pair of weedy ruts that wound their way into the forest. His military GPS indicated it to be a fire road not shown on civilian maps. That meant there would be little risk of civilian interference.

A short way into the forest was a small clearing, where Alpha stopped the SUV and switched off the ignition. It was not as deep into the forest as he would have preferred, but fire roads often grew narrower and more treacherous the higher they climbed, especially when they were not regularly maintained, which this one was not.

Alpha opened his door and got out. "I love the high country," he said, stretching.

"You can have it," Bravo replied. "I'll take tequila with senoritas. Pee break. Back in a minute."

While Bravo stepped away to urinate, Alpha savored the smell of dry leaves and pine needles, which was different than the damp fragrance of the coastal redwoods near San Francisco. Up here, it was drier. Not to mention wild and remote, which meant anyone searching for Babikov would never find his body.

It was a shame that Babikov had to be killed. He admired the former Soviet commando for his fighting skills. All warriors earned his respect, even if that warrior happened to be the enemy.

How Babikov got into the United States in the first place was still a mystery. There was no information on the man apart from some old CIA records from the eighties, when Talanov and Babikov were two of the most feared agents the Soviet Union had ever produced. And whereas Talanov was known for his slick manner and mental prowess, Babikov was known to be a cross between Chuck Norris and a grizzly bear. And whereas Talanov would regularly outsmart Western agents, Babikov would simply break them in half.

Then Babikov appeared to have found God. What a pity. He would have enjoyed challenging the old warrior to a fight, which wouldn't be much of a fight if Babikov had become the kind of man who turned the other cheek. He would much rather fight the grizzly bear. As for "finding God," how did a person find something that doesn't exist? At least he hoped God didn't exist. Otherwise, he was in a shitload of trouble.

What had caused Babikov to change? What would cause a feared commando to become a wimp? Lots of people turned to God when they saw the end of the road. Except Babikov did not fit the image of someone fearing the end. In fact, he seemed to fear nothing.

Seeing Bravo emerge from the weeds, Alpha retrieved the shovel he had purchased from a twenty-four-hour supercenter in Sonora. He tossed it to Bravo, who stuck it in the ground before moving to the rear door of the SUV, where he readied his assault rifle.

Alpha opened the door, grabbed Ginie by the arm, and pulled her out. Her hands were still zip-tied behind her and Alpha made her kneel on the ground a few feet away. He then pulled Emily out and made her do the same.

Babikov would be more difficult. Not only was he solid muscle and a lot heavier, but he was also a former Spetsnaz commando who possessed the capability to kill an opponent with a knee or a foot. So Alpha warned him not to try anything stupid. If he did, Bravo would shoot his wife.

"Why should I make your job easier?" Zak asked. "You're going to shoot us anyway."

"Only if Talanov decides not to cooperate," Alpha replied. "If he does, then all of you go free."

"Not likely, since we've seen your faces and can testify as to what you've done."

"For all intents and purposes, we don't exist. There are no

photos of us on file, so there's no one you can identify."

"Then why are we prisoners? What do you need Talanov to do?"

"No idea. I'm merely following orders and those orders are to keep you safe."

"Is that what you call this? Safe?"

"Get out of the vehicle," said Alpha.

Zak scooted his way out of the vehicle and stood.

"Over there with the others," instructed Alpha, motioning with his assault rifle.

"I need to take a leak."

"Too bad."

"You've got my wife. I won't try anything."

Alpha scrutinized Zak, who did not appear to be feigning weakness with some pathetic stance. He had asked the question simply and respectfully, and he admired that. "Okay," he said, "but if you *do* try something, and I mean anything but watering the grass, I *will* shoot your wife."

"Understood," Zak replied.

"Turn around," said Alpha, "and I'll cut off the zip-tie."

Zak turned around and extended his wrists toward Alpha, who tossed his assault rifle to Bravo, then pulled a military hunting knife from its sheath and used it to slice the zip-ties off Zak's wrists. Stepping back, Alpha replaced his knife and caught the assault rifle tossed back to him by Bravo.

Once Zak had shaken his arms and stretched, Alpha motioned him toward some tall grass near the edge of the fire road. With his back to the others, Zak unzipped his cargos and urinated into the grass. When finished, he zipped up his pants and turned around.

When Zak rejoined the others, Bravo tossed three bottles of water and three energy bars onto the ground near Zak's feet. "Give some to the women," he said.

"Are you going to cut them loose?"

"Nope."

"But they can't eat or drink."

"That's why they have you."

Zak opened the first bottle of water and tipped it to Emily's lips. He then gave some to Ginie. He then unwrapped one of the energy bars, broke it into bite-sized pieces and gave bites to Emily and Ginie.

When Zak was finished, Alpha tossed him the shovel. "Start digging," he said.

# CHAPTER 56

Dragon Head's penthouse occupied the entire top floor of the warehouse. At one end was a living room, with a bank of angled windows in a pitched ceiling that afforded a panoramic view of Hong Kong's majestic skyline. Other windows overlooked the neon bustle of the street below. At the other end of the penthouse was the master bedroom, which included the bedroom itself, a sitting room, dressing room, walk-in closets, and, of course, a spacious master bath. In between these areas was a luxury kitchen, wine cellar, and pantry.

Having stormed upstairs after her encounter with Talanov, Sofia charged into her closet, laid her pistol on a shelf and began undressing. Having followed her, Dragon Head paused in the doorway to admire her lean but muscular six-foot figure. Aside from tracks of scars, her skin was soft and firm, her muscles well defined, her posture erect. Across one shoulder and along the upper portion of her right arm was an elaborate tattoo of a dragon.

"Your hatred for Talanov runs deep," Dragon Head remarked.

"He betrayed me!" was Sofia's reply.

"He said you tried killing him first."

Sofia stepped out of her underwear but did not reply.

"Why would you do that?" asked Dragon Head.

Sofia pushed past Dragon Head, entered the bathroom, and turned on the shower.

"Was it betrayal . . . or rejection?" asked Dragon Head.

Sofia stiffened but did not reply.

"Are you in love with him?" Dragon Head asked.

Sofia's face hardened, and without a word, she stepped into the hissing torrent.

Downstairs, in a long corridor at the other end of the building, the old *Shí bèi* fighter opened the storage room door and looked in at Su Yin. She was seated in the far corner of the room on a slatted bamboo mat, her knees drawn up to her chest. Nearby was a pillow and blanket, and next to these was an empty water bottle.

"Bathroom? asked the old fighter. It was one of the few English words that he knew.

Su Yin shook her head.

The old guard's full head of hair made him look younger than he was. He was still in relatively good physical condition, but was approaching eighty, so the young fighters did not trust him with their lives, especially in fights with rival gangs, where speed and strength were required. That's why he had been relegated to passive duties like guarding Su Yin.

Several young fighters passed him in the hall and he bowed to them. The young fighters simply ignored him.

The old guard watched them disappear down the corridor into the gym. *The highest is revealed in the lowest,* he thought once they had disappeared, which was why he was treating Su Yin with kindness and respect, unlike the arrogant young fighters, who had not yet learned that a man's character is revealed in the way he treats the lowly.

The old guard stepped into the storage room and picked up the empty water bottle. When he did, Su Yin scooted away.

*"Bié dānxīn,"* the old guard said, telling Su Yin not to worry. He smiled and stepped out into the corridor to refill the bottle.

To his left was the wooden stool where he sat while on duty. On the floor beside the stool was a large bottle of water, and beside this was a wooden bowl of *hongshupian,* which were deep-fried sweet potato chips. The old guard used his large water bottle to fill Su Yin's small bottle, then took it back in to her with his bowl of chips. When he approached Su Yin, she looked away. The old guard placed the chips and water on the floor near her feet. Su Yin looked up at him and the old guard made an eating motion with his hands, and with a nod and a smile, he backed out of the cell and locked the door. He then went to the kitchen for more chips.

The kitchen was like most commercial kitchens: tile floor, two stainless steel counters, three large refrigerators, two sinks, and a twelve-burner stove. In the center of one of the stainless steel counters was a basket of fruit containing apples, dragon fruit, jujube, pomelo, and mangosteen.

When the old guard entered, he saw AK standing at the other counter scooping sweet potato chips out of a plastic tub. On the wall nearby was a magnetic strip holding a variety of knives. The old guard crossed the floor and joined AK at the counter. AK nodded respectfully and left just as one of the young fighters entered the kitchen.

"What are you doing here, old man?" the young fighter demanded sharply. "Who is guarding the girl?"

"The girl is locked in her room," the old guard replied, scooping chips out of the tub and placing them in his bowl.

"Go back to your post!"

The old guard continued scooping chips out of the tub and placing them in his bowl.

"You dare ignore me?" cried the young fighter. He strode over to the old guard and knocked the bowl of chips from his hand. The bowl fell to the floor and scattered chips in all directions.

The old guard looked down at the bowl, then at the young fighter.

"Pick them up and go back to your post!" commanded the young fighter.

When the old guard did not reply, the young fighter tried slapping him in the face, which is a blow designed to insult but cause no physical harm.

Without flinching, the old guard caught his hand.

"Better to give honor than have it taken," the old guard said quietly just as the young fighter yanked away.

"If you don't know what that proverb means," Straw Sandal said from the doorway, "it means you have been given the opportunity of saving face instead of suffering the embarrassment of losing it."

The young fighter turned quickly toward Straw Sandal and bowed. But the bow was not only to show respect. It was also to conceal an amused smile.

Straw Sandal walked to the fruit basket and picked out an apple. "Kindness feeds strength while arrogance feeds weakness," she said while turning the apple over in her hand, as if inspecting it. When the young fighter did not reply, Straw Sandal paused and him smile skeptically.

It was an understandable mistake, for the young fighter did not know that the old guard had known Straw Sandal since she was a baby. Nor did he know the old guard had once been the academy's martial arts master. Like most of the other young fighters, he had a dismissive attitude toward the old man, figuring him to be unimportant and slow.

He was wrong.

With his focus on Straw Sandal, the young fighter neither saw nor heard the old guard lift a knife from the magnetic strip. His attention was on the apple that Straw Sandal tossed in a high arc over his head. Turning while watching the apple sail through the air, he saw a blur, then heard the delicate zing of a knife blade before the apple fell into the old guard's hand, apparently still whole. But it was not. It had been cut cleanly in half.

Smiling, the old guard offered one of the halves to the astonished young fighter before replacing the knife on its magnetic strip. He then picked up his bowl of chips and handed Straw Sandal the other half when he passed by her.

"For Sunbird," he said with a smile. And with a bow, he left the kitchen.

The young fighter stared dumbfounded at the chunk of apple in his hand, then at Straw Sandal, whose eyes told him what he already knew, that the old guard was still the master.

When the old guard returned to his post, he thought about Straw Sandal and her father. He would forever be loyal to them, although he disapproved of Dragon Head's criminal activities, especially using a young girl as leverage against the Russian. The young girl, who did not speak Chinese although she was of Chinese ancestry, reminded him of Straw Sandal when she was that age. Same size, same bright eyes, same happy disposition, even though there was little to be happy about now.

He recalled how happy the young girl had been to see the Russian. He could tell that by the way she ran to him, and how they hugged, and the way he fought for her when the order was given for her to be removed from the room. Dragon Head was ruthless in that regard, and did not have the heart of his daughter, who could be ruthless as well, but not with the heartless degree of her father. Dragon Head, he feared, had been lost to his own ego and ambition, now that Xin Li – Sofia, as was her Russian name – had been leading him away from his original purpose of bringing protection and stability to the neighborhoods under his control.

As for the young girl, he would make sure she stayed safe and happy. On several occasions, when he was guarding her door, he had heard her singing. Her voice was innocent and hopeful, even though he knew she was afraid and lonely. What a strong spirit she must have.

Lowering himself onto his wooden stool, the old guard unscrewed the cap on his water bottle and took a drink. He then placed the bowl of sweet potato chips in his lap, and as he started to take a bite, paused and cocked his ear.

And what he heard brought a smile to his weathered face. From inside the room, he could hear the sound of a little girl singing.

# CHAPTER 57

Wilcox was worriedly pacing the floor of the hotel room when a knock sounded on the door. The kids were engrossed in a Chinese action movie on TV and did not hear the knock. But Wilcox did and hurried to the door, and after checking the peephole, yanked open the door and helped a winded Talanov stagger into the room, holding his ribs, bent over in pain. His nose was crusted with blood and the skin surrounding one eye was cut and bruised.

"Alex, what *happened?*" said Wilcox.

After hobbling into the bathroom, Talanov winced while lowering himself onto the floor near the pair of wide steps leading up to the tub. Seconds later, Jingfei and Kai appeared in the doorway.

"Are you okay?" asked Kai.

"Did you see Su Yin?" asked Jingfei.

Talanov leaned his head against a cabinet door. His breathing was labored and shallow.

"Let me clean him up," Wilcox replied, running some hot water in the sink. He nodded for the kids to go back to their movie. The kids hesitated, but when Wilcox smiled reassuringly, they reluctantly obeyed.

After soaking a washcloth in hot water, Wilcox turned off the tap, squeezed out the excess and handed the washcloth to Talanov, who placed it over his face and allowed the heat to soak in.

"Rest there while I call a doctor."

"No time," said Talanov, wiping his face.

"You need medical help."

"I look a lot worse than I am. Help me up."

Talanov returned the washcloth to Wilcox, who tossed it in

the sink and offered Talanov his hand. And with a grunt, Talanov stood.

"You look like crap," said Wilcox. "Which in my book is not a lot worse than you are."

Talanov laughed then winced. "Quit making me laugh."

"I think we could use a good laugh. Now, what happened? Fill me in."

"The good news: Su Yin is okay."

"And the bad news?"

Talanov turned on the tap, splashed some water on his face, then cupped his hand and took several large gulps. When he was finished, Wilcox handed him a towel.

After drying his face, Talanov looked in the mirror. "I do look like crap," he said.

Wilcox continued to wait.

"The bad news," said Talanov, facing Wilcox: "Dragon Head isn't our problem. It's my old KGB partner, Sofia, whom I haven't seen since I shot her twice in the chest at point blank range. Needless to say, I thought she was dead. Needless to say, she isn't."

"I thought Babikov was your partner."

"He was," said Talanov, "but he operated in the shadows while Sofia and I took on the more visible roles." He leaned against the sink. "Years ago, she and I were in Spain tracking down a defecting scientist named Gorev."

"Who was carrying vials of weaponized anthrax, yes, I remember. He and his family wanted to defect, and would have, had you not caught him."

"And I've regretted that day ever since. If I hadn't tracked him down, he would still be alive today. As it was, Sofia and her men executed Gorev and his family, stole the anthrax, then used it to make a dirty bomb that would have killed thousands if I hadn't stopped them. Sofia retaliated by trying to kill me, and would have if I hadn't shot first. How she survived, I'll never know."

"And she's here, now, in Hong Kong, working with Dragon

Head?"

"Yes. And she wants her pound of flesh."

"What does she look like?" asked Wilcox.

"Half Chinese, six feet tall, black hair with some gray."

"My God, she's the one who killed Amber. I remember her from the security footage. And now she's after you? Alex, that doesn't make sense. What's getting even with you got to do with the virus, the hacking, and the midair collisions? How does this all fit together?"

"It's about money, Bill. Getting even is simply a bonus."

"What money?"

"A KGB espionage account opened in Switzerland back in 'eighty-three, which was then transferred by the Swiss to their investment brokers here in Hong Kong. Being KGB, Sofia must have found out about the account and that it was opened in my name, and that over the years, the funds grew from seven million to one and a half billion dollars."

"Did you say b, as in billion?"

Talanov nodded.

"So Dragon Head, or Sofia, or both of them, forced you here because they want that money?"

"Something like that. Dragon Head claims the funds are his, which is why I'm still alive."

"Why does he consider the funds to be his if the account is in your name?"

"Good question," answered Talanov. "I'm guessing Sofia came to Hong Kong years ago with her eye on stealing it for herself, and since Dragon Head controls the island, and since nothing happens here without his involvement, she decided to hook up with him."

"Why didn't he just bribe someone at the bank? Surely he has someone on the inside working for him?"

"Dragon Head said something that makes me think there's a snag. He said I needed to locate the funds."

"So they're not in the bank?"

"That's what I have to find out."

---

"All right, then, what's the plan?"

"I go to Sun Cheng—"

"—which is the bank?" asked Wilcox, cutting in.

"And locate the money," continued Talanov with an affirming nod, "which I will then transfer into an escrow account and later release in exchange for Su Yin. You, meanwhile, contact Alice and see what she can tell us about Sun Cheng and anything that may have happened there."

"As in?"

"I don't know. A banker dying . . . funds being misappropriated . . . anything suspicious. Once we have Su Yin, we can focus on stopping Dragon Head from bringing down any more planes. He's got to have a vulnerability and we need to find out what it is."

"Do you think his weak spot is that money?"

"Judging by how badly he wants it, and that even Sofia has been put on a leash, I'm guessing it is. Trouble is, like I said, Sofia wants more than the money. Which means, the minute I hand over those funds, I'm a dead man."

# CHAPTER 58

The nighttime scene outside the Congressional hearings building was pandemonium. Dozens of floodlights had been set up for news crews and reporters, who were offering somber commentary on the midair collision over the Pacific. Police cars had blocked off streets. The sidewalk was littered with cables. News vans were crammed together at various odd angles. Orange security mesh had been strung up like fences to keep spectators at bay. Shouting protestors were jabbing the air with placards blaming the president, China, and Russia.

Charlie was watching the scene on a series of three monitors set up on her desk in the Naval Intelligence Building. She had been in the office since five o'clock that morning and had no idea when she would be able to leave in light of this escalating crisis. Her eyes roamed from screen to screen and the various talking heads offering commentary on the emergency hearings taking place at this very moment.

"A midair collision between two commercial airliners has claimed more than a thousand lives," a white-haired news anchor droned into a microphone against a backdrop of the hearings building. "Sources inside the intelligence community say hackers in Beijing were able to steal control of the aircraft and divert them onto a collision course over the Pacific. Angus Shaw, Director of National Intelligence, is calling for the resignation of Diane Gustaves, since Chinese agents were able to breeze past her security protocols and plant a virus in her system that led to the hack."

"Are you kidding me?" shouted Charlie, drawing sharp glances from others who were working through the night. "They murdered Amber to plant that virus!" She glanced at everyone looking back at her and sank lower in her chair to hide her embarrassment. She then scooted forward and focused on one of the monitors, where a blonde reporter with lacquered hair was speaking into her microphone.

With an expression of what appeared to be pained sincerity, the blonde said, "The outrage is understandable when a congressional leader like Diane Gustaves helped former Russian spy, Aleksandr Talanov, escape to China in order to avoid questioning by American officials. To quote Director Shaw, 'Perhaps Congresswoman Gustaves is colluding not only with the Russians, but also the Chinese in what is *clearly* an egregious abuse of power.'"

"That is *so* not true!" Charlie shouted, jumping up, then sitting back down when heads again snapped her way with glares of disapproval.

Inside the congressional hearings gallery, Diane Gustaves stood at a wide podium. On the wall behind her was the Great Seal of the United States. Seated before her were nearly two hundred reporters.

After issuing a statement of sympathy for the victims and their families, Gustaves promised to track down and stop the perpetrators of this atrocity.

But when she paused for a sip of water, a reporter shouted, "What do you say to Director Shaw's remark that you abused the power of your office by helping Aleksandr Talanov escape to China in order to escape questioning by U.S. authorities?"

All eyes turned to Gustaves, who set her water glass down with measured control and said, "Colonel Talanov is not a Russian spy, nor was he involved in the airline disaster. In fact, he's helping us find out who's responsible. Beyond that, I cannot speak to who Colonel Talanov is, or where he is, or why, because that information is classified. So to have his name leaked publicly like this, and to have false accusations and innuendos flung recklessly about, *that* is the egregious abuse of power."

"What about the Chinese agents who breezed past your security protocols and planted a virus in your system?" the reporter replied. "How can you accuse Director Shaw of an abuse of power and not accept any responsibility yourself?"

"Because that is not what happened."

"Are you saying Director Shaw lied?"

"I'm saying the two women who planted that virus were not Chinese agents, and I know that for a fact. I also know they did not breeze past my security protocols. They *tortured* and *murdered* my assistant in order to force her to navigate past them. As for me not accepting accountability, I will forever be haunted by Amber's death. Any security protocol, no matter how sophisticated, has weaknesses, and there will always be people who figure out ways to exploit those weaknesses. It's what hackers do. But the fact that none of you bothered asking for my side of this story means you're as complicit in this disinformation campaign as the person who started it. And for that, *you* need to accept responsibility instead of pointing fingers at others. You are here to report news fairly, not make up headlines for the sake of ratings."

A small number of reporters began clapping, then quickly grew quiet when other reporters threw them sharp glances.

"And the accusation that you are colluding with the Chinese?" asked another reporter.

"Just because we're not openly hostile to a foreign government does not mean we're colluding with them. We are, however, cooperating. It's what leaders do, and what I'm doing in order to track down and apprehend the actual perpetrators behind the hacking of our GPS network."

Gustaves went on to ask how many people knew what a ventriloquist was. She didn't pause for responses because she wanted to use the rhetorical question to introduce a principle. That principle was the "throwing" of a "voice" – in this case a hacking signal – to another location in order to disguise its actual point of origin. She elaborated further by explaining what they knew thus far; namely, that while the signal appeared to have originated in Beijing, analysts now believe it to have originated in Shenzhen, which was north of the boundary separating mainland China from Hong Kong and the New Territories.

"To be clear," Gustaves concluded, "contrary to what the perpetrators wanted us to think, we are convinced Beijing was not involved. I know this with a high degree of certainty because signal analysis and sources on the ground are confirming this as we speak."

Dozens of reporters raised their hands and Gustaves pointed to a woman in the third row. The woman, in her forties, stood. She was dressed in a dark blue slack suit, and was known for her popular conservative talk show.

"You mention sources on the ground, Madam Congresswoman," the woman said. "Can you tell us who they are?"

"No."

"Is Aleksandr Talanov one of those sources?"

"Like I've already said, I'm not answering any questions regarding Colonel Talanov."

"Director Shaw has expressed what many think is a valid concern about a former Soviet colonel being involved in our intelligence affairs. What do you say to that?"

"That you should refer to my previous statement," Gustaves said, pointing to another reporter.

"Director Shaw has been especially critical of you lately," the reporter said. "Is it fair to say there's some friction between you two?"

"I certainly hope so."

Polite laughter rippled through the room just as an aide approached Gustaves and handed her a cell phone. "It's Mr. Wilcox, in Hong Kong," the aide whispered in her ear.

Gustaves apologized for having to cut short the Q&A and left the stage with the cell phone to her ear.

# CHAPTER 59

While Wilcox brought Gustaves up to speed, Talanov finished cleaning his face, which was swollen and sore. When he emerged from the bathroom a few minutes later, Jingfei jumped up and ran over to him.

"Su Yin, did you see her?" she asked.

"Su Yin is fine," said Talanov, noticing scrapes on Jingfei's elbows and face, and a blood stain on one knee. He then looked at Kai and saw more of the same. "What happened to you two?" he asked.

Jingfei glanced nervously at Kai but said nothing.

"Did you get in an accident or something?"

Both kids averted their eyes.

"Okay, what gives?" asked Talanov, folding his arms and looking back and forth between them.

The kids said nothing just as Wilcox clicked off from his phone call and joined them.

"What happened to these two?" asked Talanov.

"We had a little . . . problem," Wilcox replied. "The kids thought we were leaving – as in flying back to the States and leaving Su Yin behind – so they decided to give me the slip and follow you to where Su Yin was being held. On the way, they got jumped by one of Dragon Head's men."

Talanov stared at the kids with open-mouthed incredulity.

"We thought you were leaving!" shouted Jingfei.

"Are you out of your minds?" asked Talanov incredulously. "Look at yourselves. Look at what nearly happened!"

"Look at *yourself!*" Jingfei fired back. "You don't look a whole lot better."

"You have got to do what Bill and I tell you. That was part of the deal, remember? It's called responsibility. Want me to spell it out for you? *Re-spon-si-bil-i-ty.*"

"You said the government was making you leave – I *heard* you – and that if you didn't, some guy named Shaw would kill Zak."

Talanov sighed with resignation. "Okay, yes, I did say that."

"See? Someone had to do something!"

"And how did that go for you?" Talanov shouted back. "What happens if you get captured or killed?"

"What happens if *you* get killed?"

By now Talanov and Jingfei were standing face to face, like boxers squaring off.

"I've got it under control," growled Talanov.

"Really? You said you had to go to the bank and put some money into an escrow account, but as soon as you did, some bitch was going to kill you."

Talanov sighed with exasperation. "Okay, yes, I said that, too."

"You *don't* have it under control!" shouted Jingfei, jabbing Talanov with a finger. "So don't expect me and Kai to just sit around while you keep doing dumb stuff that gets you killed. What happens to Su Yin then? So, go ahead and leave. Take the chicken's way out. Me and Kai are staying."

"We are not leaving. How many times do I have to keep telling you that?"

"I heard you!"

"I'm still here, aren't I? So is Bill."

"For how long, though, huh?"

"Until we figure this out. Which we can't do while you and I waste time arguing."

"Come on, Jing," said Kai from the couch. "Maybe we should, you know, give Alex a chance. I mean, he is still here, and all you've been doing is arguing."

"Whose side are you on?" yelled Jingfei.

"I'm just saying—"

"I don't care what you're saying! Su Yin's got no chance with a dinosaur and a moron in charge."

"We are going to get her back," Talanov said gently. "Now,

come on, let's sit down and talk this through." He reached for Jingfei but she batted his hand away.

"Get away from me!" she shouted. "You're the reason she's in this mess."

"And I will do whatever it takes to get her back."

"How can you? You don't know what you're doing. You'll get killed. *Su Yin* will get killed. And none of us will be able to do anything."

Talanov tried reaching for Jingfei again but she knocked his hand away again. "Leave me alone!" she shouted. "In fact, go ahead and leave. Me and Kai will do this on our own."

By now, Jingfei was crying. Talanov tried reaching for her a third time, but Jingfei shoved him back, then kept coming at him, fists flying, enraged, out of control.

Talanov deflected her punches, keeping just out of her range, but the more Jingfei couldn't connect, the more frustrated she became, and the harder she tried, and the more out of control she became as a result.

Finally, exhausted, with tears streaming down her face, Jingfei sputtered to a stop and began crying uncontrollably. Talanov hugged her and Jingfei buried her face against him, sobbing, her back and shoulders shaking, grief and frustration overwhelming her.

"I should have done something when that Chinese bitch took her," Jingfei sobbed. "Ginie tried helping her, but that woman smashed her in the face with her pistol, and I just sat there."

"This isn't your fault," said Talanov.

"Yes, it is! I'm supposed to take care of Su Yin and I didn't. She's my *sister*, and I was right there, and I saw the terrified look in her eyes, and she was looking right at me, begging me to help her, and she was screaming while that woman dragged her to the car, shoved her inside, slammed the door, and drove away, and I just sat *there!*"

"People around you had been shot, which was a calculated act to shock you into submission. It's why she did it."

"I should have done something!"

"If you had, she would have shot you, too. You're alive. Su Yin is alive. And we *will* get her back."

"How?" asked Jingfei, stepping away to wipe her eyes.

"The first thing we do is get you and Kai to safety. Away from this hotel. Out of Dragon Head's reach."

"Then what?"

"Bill and I figure out a way to get Dragon Head his money. Then we figure out a way to keep Shaw from killing Zak and the women."

"I don't see how you can do that. If you don't give Dragon Head that money, he kills Su Yin. If you don't obey Shaw, he kills Zak, Ginie, and Emily. It's a no-win situation."

"We've got time. It's why Bill grounded the Gulfstream for repairs. It buys us some time."

"Time to do what? Don't you get it? You can't do this alone. You need our help."

"Don't *you* get it? If Dragon Head captures you or Kai, it's game over. For all of us."

"If I may?" offered Wilcox. "Right now, we're all we've got. Us four, here, in this room. And we've all got useful skills."

"You can't be serious," said Talanov.

"Very," Wilcox replied.

"They're kids, Bill! Do you get that? *Kids.*"

"And you're a dinosaur," shouted Jingfei. "Want me to spell it out for you? *Di-no-saur.* And we all know what happened to them."

"Come on, guys, not again," said Wilcox, shaking his head.

"He started it," said Jingfei, pointing at Talanov.

"You started it!" Talanov shouted back.

"And I'm ending it," Wilcox shouted in a loud voice that startled everyone. "Now, all of you, just . . . shut up!" He paced back and forth several times, then stopped in front of Talanov and said, "I get it that you want to keep them out of Dragon Head's reach. But we need them, Alex. We need their help."

Talanov started to protest but Wilcox halted him with a hand held up, like a stop sign.

"Do you have the foggiest idea how to access that money?" Wilcox asked.

Talanov shuffled awkwardly and said, "Someone at the bank will help me."

"Really? And if that 'someone' happens to be working with Dragon Head? How can you possibly know whether or not they're actually helping you when you can't understand what they're saying? Dragon Head has friends everywhere and you will be completely at the mercy of whoever the bank assigns to you."

Talanov walked to the window, his frustration evident.

"This is China, Alex," Wilcox continued. "With Chinese banking protocols, language, Swift codes, routing numbers."

"I'll figure something out."

"We've got one shot and this is it. Yes, me grounding the plane may have bought us some time, but Shaw will carry through on his promise to kill Zak and the women if we don't figure this out and do something fast. Jingfei is right. You can't do this on your own." He turned and looked at the kids. "And neither can you. But you've got to quit fighting us at every turn. If you want Su Yin back – and I know you do – then you need to control your emotions and use your skills to work *with* us, not against us. No more tantrums. No more escapes. If you're not able to do that, tell us now."

Jingfei glared at Wilcox for a long moment, then grudgingly nodded.

Wilcox looked at Kai. "What about you? Are you in or out?"

Kai grinned. "I'm totally in."

Wilcox turned to Talanov. "The kids are willing. Are you?"

Talanov continued staring out the window, saying nothing. After nearly a full minute, Jingfei threw up her hands but Wilcox motioned for her to be patient. Finally, with a sigh of resolve, Talanov turned and looked at the kids, eyeing them both. "Are you sure you're up for this?"

"Are you sure *you're* up for this?" retorted Jingfei.

Wilcox cleared his throat.

Jingfei threw Wilcox a sharp glance and Wilcox replied with a warning look.

"All right, yes, we're sure," Jingfei grudgingly replied.

"Then we're in this together," said Wilcox with an approving nod. To Talanov: "What do we do first?"

Talanov thought for a moment. "Call Alice and fill her in," he said. "Then ask if she'll meet us at Sun Cheng. We need her help getting past the front desk."

And with a spreading grin, Wilcox took out his cell phone and dialed.

# CHAPTER 60

Dressed in a black slack suit and white shirt, Alice met Talanov and the others in the giant breezeway of a thirty-story office building. There were tall windows and thick glass doors on each side of the breezeway, and through each sets of doors were banks of elevators. The soaring high-rise had an exoskeleton of titan pillars that resembled ladders. Between these mammoth supports were angled beams and lots of glass. Neighboring office towers were equally artistic and modern, with mirrored exteriors, rounded walls, angled sections, spires, and every size and shape of window.

Alice gave Wilcox a kiss on the cheek before shaking hands with Talanov and the kids, saying she was happy to help. She then turned serious and looked at Talanov. "But I need to confirm that I understood Bill correctly," she said. "Dragon Head wants you to access an account at Sun Cheng that already belongs to you? Is that correct?"

Talanov nodded.

"And the account contains one-point-five billion dollars?"

Talanov nodded again.

"And Dragon Head is extorting you to give him the money or he will kill the young girl he has taken hostage?"

Talanov nodded a third time.

Alice rubbed her forehead anxiously.

"What is it?" Wilcox asked.

"First things first," said Alice, handing Wilcox an envelope. "Your documents came by special courier, which I used to process your entries."

"Thanks, Alice, I owe you," said Wilcox, opening the envelope and distributing the passports.

"Although Colonel Talanov's documents were somewhat unorthodox, I think is the best word to use, since they came in the form of certified copies of an American Green Card based on his Australian passport, which, per the handwritten note from Congresswoman Gustaves, were on file with her office, which she then used to create a temporary American identification booklet – i.e., a custom passport – the likes of which I have never seen. And yet there it was. I have to be honest, Bill, I would not have accepted this passport but for an accompanying letter from the congresswoman – with her congressional seal – verifying the legitimacy of the document. What is going on? Who *is* Colonel Talanov?"

Wilcox opened his mouth to reply but Alice cut him off. "Never mind, I don't want to know," Alice said, then, just as quickly, "Actually, I *do* want to know. Why would Congresswoman Gustaves be issuing a document like this when Colonel Talanov is obviously not an American citizen?"

"We're working on that," Wilcox replied. "I trust it's not a problem, given our longstanding friendship and history of open and honest cooperation?"

"Do not try that on me, Bill. Everything about you is a problem! Which infuriates me in ways I cannot describe in front of these children."

Wilcox replied with an exaggerated smile that showed his teeth, like a small boy who'd been caught with his hands in the cookie jar.

"Don't, just . . . don't," said Alice, holding up a hand, then pacing back and forth, rubbing her forehead and muttering in Chinese while throwing Wilcox angry looks. Finally, after several calming breaths, she stopped and said, "You and I will finish this later."

"I look forward to it," said Wilcox with a smile. "Over a glass of wine, perhaps?"

After a roll of her eyes that said she was both amused and annoyed, Alice said, "I did some digging on the Sun Cheng Financial Group, and two of their bankers died recently from unnatural causes. Their deaths, of course, were familiar to me from police reports that were filed. The CIB considered the deaths of two investment bankers from the same financial institution to be, how should I say, an unlikely and unfortunate coincidence, but not a point of particular concern until your phone call earlier today."

Alice handed Wilcox another envelope. Inside it were several photos, which Wilcox removed while Talanov and the kids gathered around.

"The names of the two bankers were Ling Soo and Wu Chee Ming," Alice continued, "who happened to be the only two bankers approved by the Swiss for the management of Colonel Talanov's account."

"The Swiss?" asked Wilcox.

"They hold control over the account," Talanov explained, "and their governing laws are very strict and specific, which confirms why Dragon Head kept me alive. Aside from those two bankers, no one else can access the account."

Wilcox showed everyone the first photo, which was of a man's contorted body lying on the floor of an office, mouth open, tongue swollen, eyes open and vacant, one hand clutching his throat. When the kids saw it they made squeamish faces.

"Who's this?" asked Wilcox.

"Ling Soo," Alice replied.

While everyone else looked on, Wilcox flipped to the second photo. It was a close-up of Ling Soo's hand, which was grasping a piece of folded paper between his thumb and fingers, almost politely.

Other photos showed Ling Soo's office, especially his desk, which was a mess, with piles of papers on the desk, on the floor, under the credenza, on top of the credenza, and by the window. Pens, pencils, paperclips, and sticky notes were scattered over the desk as well, and there were sticky notes on top of files and on top of other sticky notes.

"The guy's a slob," said Jingfei.

"What's in his hand?" asked Wilcox.

"A suicide note," said Alice. "Ling Soo killed himself."

"Was the note handwritten or on a word processor?" asked Jingfei.

"A word processor."

"What did the note say?"

"Ling Soo apologized for the great shame he brought on his family."

"Meaning, what, exactly?"

"The note doesn't say."

"Are you certain he authored the note?"

"It was composed on his computer, which was password protected, so, yes, we are fairly certain."

"But it's possible someone else could have done it, right? I mean, passwords are so last century, so it wouldn't take much to slip past his."

"Yes," conceded Alice, "that is correct, unlikely as that may be."

"Did anyone dust his keyboard for prints?" asked Kai.

"I am not able to speak to that because it is still an open investigation."

"How did he kill himself?"

"With poisoned tea."

"Did he drink it voluntarily, or was he forced?"

"You kids ask a lot of questions."

"We're the curious type," answered Jingfei. "So, did he drink it voluntarily, or was he forced?"

"Again, I am not able to speak to that because—"

"—it's an open investigation, yeah, I got it," grumbled Jingfei. To Wilcox: "She's a tough nut to crack, but I can see why you like her so much."

"I never said that!" said Wilcox.

"Oh, *please*," said Jingfei, with an impatient roll of her eyes. "It's, like, so obvious there's something going on between you two. Now, come on, what else have you got?"

Wilcox stared with incredulity at Jingfei, then looked at Talanov for help. "You *are* welcome to step in and take charge of these two."

"Why would I want to do that?" asked Talanov. "We're in this together, remember?"

With a growl, Wilcox showed everyone the next photo, which was of a dainty English teacup and saucer.

"The poisoned teacup?" asked Jingfei, and Alice nodded.

The remaining photos were of Wu Chee Ming, the first being a company ID photo, with the next showing his mangled body lying on the train tracks, with his belongings strewn everywhere about.

"Witnesses say Wu Chee Ming panicked," Alice explained, "and that he ran across the platform and leaped in front of the express train."

"Why would he do that?" asked Talanov. "What caused him to panic?"

"Nobody would say, although security footage showed Dragon Head to have been present. Xin Li, too, and Straw Sandal."

"Sounds to me like Dragon Head was chasing him."

"Sounds to me like Dragon Head caught him," added Jingfei. "Or was about to, anyway, but rather than get caught, Wu Chee Ming chose to jump in front of a train."

"Question is, why was he running?" asked Kai. "I mean, Wu Chee Ming would not try running from someone like Dragon Head unless he did something so drastic it put his life on the line."

"I agree," said Talanov, "and we're here to find out exactly what it was he did."

# CHAPTER 61

The Sun Cheng Financial Group Limited occupied the entire twenty-fifth floor of the office tower. It had a spacious lobby with a formidable front counter of polished oak. The name of the company was written on the wall behind the front counter in letters of stainless steel, in Chinese, first, then English.

After emerging from the elevator, Alice led the group to the counter, where she was greeted by the receptionist, a young Chinese woman in her twenties. Dressed in a tailored suit and white shirt, the young woman had spiked hair, a nose stud, and the hint of a tattoo peeking out from the low V-neck of her shirt.

Alice presented her CIB identification while Talanov scanned the lobby. To his left were two ivory-colored sofas and two stuffed chairs with a burnished orange trim in a Chinese motif. The furniture was arranged symmetrically around a glass coffee table. On the coffee table were several financial magazines. Near the wall was a pedestal featuring an ancient Chinese urn, and above it were two framed ink drawings. The first was a vertical column of Chinese characters beside a drawing of a bamboo stem, entirely in black except for one leaf, which was pale green. The second was of a gnarled branch, with delicate cherry blossoms in a slight blush of pink. On another wall was a large acrylic painting that looked like someone had had a good time squirting bright colors onto a canvas. There were splatters and smears juxtaposed in a way that was orderly in its chaos.

Talanov returned his attention to the name of the company in stainless steel letters. Stainless steel, of course, carried a subtext of security, so the company wanted people to feel secure. The quality of the furnishings carried a subtext of success, with the tidiness of the furnishings letting people know that Sun Cheng was conservative and solid.

And yet the modern painting, a striking anachronism, carried a different message entirely. It carried a subtext of boldness and flair, which let people know this company was willing to go beyond the bounds of conventionality.

The mention of his name refocused Talanov's attention on Alice.

". . . and this is Colonel Talanov and his team," Alice was saying in English, obviously for his benefit. "Colonel Talanov has an account here that he would like to access."

The receptionist picked up the intercom phone and pushed a button. When the call was answered, she spoke in an inaudibly low voice, then hung up and told Alice that someone would be with them shortly.

Less than a minute later, a door buzzed open and a short man with oiled black hair appeared. "I am Mr. Song," he said in English after a polite bow. "How may I help?"

Alice, who stood a full head taller than Song, showed her CIB identification. "My friend, Colonel Talanov, would like to access his account. Please give him your full cooperation."

Song bowed again. "Of course."

"Phone me when you are finished," Alice said to Talanov. "If there are any problems, let me know."

Talanov thanked Alice, who stepped over to the elevator and pushed the lighted button.

"This way, Colonel Talanov," said Song. Stepping up to the door, he entered numbers on a keypad and the door buzzed open. Pulling open the door, Song stepped aside and allowed Talanov and the others to enter.

Once the door had clicked shut, Song led the way along a corridor that opened into the company's operations hub, which was a large room with windowed offices located around three sides of the room. The fourth side, a solid wall, featured a line of clocks showing the times in major financial centers. Beneath the clocks were two rows of flat-screen monitors showing real-time fluctuations in various global stocks, commodities, utilities, real estate, and mining resources, along with news headlines and currency rates. The center of the room was populated with back-to-back desks, where brokers were busy at keyboards and phones.

Song led the way around the perimeter of the hub into his office, which overlooked Victoria Harbor. Junks and ferries were visible on the water, along with several cruise ships. The office, with its bookshelves and file cabinets, was neat and tidy because Song was a neat and tidy man. Designer suit. Not a hair out of place. Shoes polished to a shine.

There were two chairs in Song's office and Song gestured toward them while rounding his desk. Once behind his desk, Song adjusted his cuffs, then seated himself with great formality.

"You say you have an account?" Song asked, making direct eye contact with Talanov while folding his hands neatly in front of him on the desk. Song's skin was smooth and unblemished, as if he used moisturizing lotion each morning.

Talanov picked up a pen and wrote an alphanumeric sequence of characters on one of Song's note pads, which he slid in front of the banker, who made the tiniest gesture of disapproval before looking indignantly at the note.

Song's eyes suddenly widened. "You have a double-alpha account?"

Sliding his special passport very deliberately across the desk, Talanov maintained steady eye contact and did not reply.

Song glanced at Talanov's passport, then at Talanov, after which he faced his computer and entered the characters. His eyes then widened even more.

After a nervous glance at Talanov, Song performed a few more commands, then gathered his composure and looked at Talanov with imposed calm and authority.

"We have no biometrics on file for you, Colonel Talanov," Song declared. "Biometrics are required of all account holders. This prevents unauthorized access, you understand."

Talanov picked up his passport and held it in front of Song's face. "It's my account. I'm me. I'm authorized."

"Of course, but this account has been . . ."

Song stopped mid-sentence and struggled for words.

"Has been what?"

"You should contact our legal department."

"Has been *what?*" Talanov demanded again. "If something has happened, I want to know what it is." With a drilling stare, he planted his hands on the edge of Song's desk.

Song tried not to blanch under the heat of Talanov's stare. "Company policy will not permit me to discuss the matter," he said, mustering courage. "You must contact our legal department."

Talanov knew this was not a biometric issue. If that had been the case, Song would have repeated that requirement. But he hadn't. That meant the issue was something else – something Song did not want to talk about – which was why he was trying to hide behind company policy and legalese. It was an obfuscation designed to render the situation bewildering and unintelligible so that what had actually happened would never be known. Even more important, however, it was an effort to get them out of his office and into the hands of the firm's most experienced team of obfuscators, their lawyers. If that happened, he would never be able to access his account, at least not in time to save Su Yin.

*Which meant they could not leave Song's office without getting answers.*

But Song was not about to reveal anything, at least not voluntarily.

Song stood and adjusted one of his cuffs, head erect, shoulders back, an indignant expression that proclaimed Song's belief that he was in charge. "If there is nothing else," he said with a slight sniff, gesturing toward the door.

"Oh, but there is," Talanov replied without moving. He smiled briefly before allowing his smile to morph into a hardened stare. "Have my funds been stolen?"

The question hit Song like a torpedo and Talanov immediately knew the answer, and not by anything Song had said, but by his facial movements. These extremely brief involuntary movements, called micro-expressions, reveal whatever emotions the subject is feeling, such as anger, fear, or happiness, or whether the person is lying or not. Micro-expressions vary for different emotions and situations, so an observer must know which expressions mean what.

Talanov watched as Song stopped breathing for a moment. His mouth was slightly open, his lips were taut, and his eyes were wide open with surprise. In other words, Song was afraid, but why? Whatever the reason, Talanov knew his question had hit a nerve. And what happened next depended on who acted first.

"Call Alice Ti," Talanov said to Wilcox. "Tell her to launch an investigation into my stolen funds. Then phone Dragon Head, since he considers the money to be his, and tell him the funds have gone missing. Be sure to mention Song's name, as I'm certain he'll want to address this matter himself."

Jingfei picked up on the ruse and said, "What about Twitter? There may be restrictions here in Hong Kong, but investors in the West will definitely want to know that Sun Cheng allowed money to go missing, then tried to cover it up, then tried to obstruct the investigation."

"Use the hashtag SCAM," offered Kai. "S-C-A-M, in caps, as an acronym for Sun Cheng Assets go Missing. We could do a series of SCAM alerts. Something like this would go viral in minutes."

"Do it," said Talanov. He tossed his phone to Kai, who began working the keyboard. To Wilcox: "Make the calls."

Wilcox took out his phone and began dialing.

"Wait," cried Song.

Talanov held up a hand, stopping Wilcox and Kai.

"What is it you want to know?" asked Song, his shoulders slumped.

"I want to see my account," replied Talanov.

When Song hesitated, Talanov glanced over at Wilcox and Kai, who were both poised with their fingers over their phones, waiting for the command to continue.

With a defeated sigh, Song sat at his terminal and called up Talanov's account. When finished, he stood and gestured for Talanov to sit. Talanov rounded the desk, but instead of sitting, he motioned for Jingfei to sit. Song moved to object but Talanov stepped in front of him like a defensive lineman protecting his quarterback. Song stepped back, and with a grin, Jingfei sat in Song's chair and began navigating the account. Three seconds later, Jingfei slumped back in the chair, mouth open, staring dumbfounded at the screen.

"What is it?" asked Talanov, bending over her shoulder to look at the monitor.

"Some funds have gone missing, all right. The entire amount, *it's gone.*"

# CHAPTER 62

Talanov stared in shock at Jingfei for a long moment, then turned his focus onto Song, who was staring at the floor. After glaring at Song for a long moment, Talanov looked back at Jingfei and said, "What happened? Where did it go?"

Jingfei began calling up page after page of statements and banking websites. When the screen was full of overlaid pages, she tapped a button and Song's printer sprang to life. Song moved to intervene but Talanov planted his palm in the center of Song's chest, stopping him. With pinched lips, Song again stepped back.

Talanov took one of the statements from the printer. "What am I looking at?" he asked while the printer kept spitting out pages.

Jingfei found a felt-tip marker and drew a circle of twenty-three dots on a blank sheet of paper. She then began labeling the dots: Albania, Cayman Islands, Ghana, Bahrain, Mauritius, Abu Dhabi, Switzerland, Guernsey, Nevis, Thailand, Uruguay, Samoa, San Marino, Marshall Islands, Seychelles, Panama, Djibouti, Vanuatu, Antigua, Singapore, Cyprus, Latvia, and Bermuda. She then began connecting the dots, faster and faster, lines everywhere, crisscrossing the page. When she was finished, she laid down the marker and held up the page for Talanov to see.

A blank stare was Talanov's response.

"It's a global network of banks," Jingfei explained, "twenty-three in all, each linked not only to your account, but to one another with layered passwords so complex it would take a super-computer years to decrypt, which is more time than we have right now."

"Is my money in one of those banks?" asked Talanov.

"That's how it looks. But without a transaction history

– which there isn't – there's no way to tell."

Talanov looked over at Song. "Is my money in one of those banks?"

Song lowered his eyes and shrugged.

"How did this happen?" asked Talanov, stepping over to confront Song, who kept looking at the floor and did not reply. He just stood there, hands folded, eyes averted. Talanov snapped his fingers in front of Song's face and made Song look at him. "Either you tell me or I *will* turn this over to Dragon Head."

Song did not reply.

Talanov looked over at Wilcox. "Get Dragon Head on the phone."

"The account was managed by two bankers," Song said quickly. "Their names were Ling Soo and Wu Chee Ming."

"Who are dead now, yes, I know. Which still doesn't answer my question. Now, how did this happen?"

"Ling Soo stole the money."

"How do you know?"

"Ling Soo confessed in a suicide note."

"Then why kill himself?"

"For the shame it brought on his family."

"Why not return the money?" asked Talanov. "Save himself a lot of dying?"

Song shrugged.

"If he stole it, then, where is it?"

"We do not know," answered Song.

"What's a double-alpha account?" asked Jingfei.

"An investment account for very large sums," explained Song.

"Is Alex – Colonel Talanov – the only signatory to this account?"

"The only one who is alive," answered Song.

"Were Ling Soo and Wu Chee Ming authorized to make withdrawals?"

"No."

"Did either of them hold power of attorney?"

"No. They had authority to invest, but the transactions were strictly monitored, and approval was always required. Plus, our system would have prevented any unauthorized transfer or withdrawal."

"You're talking in circles," said Jingfei. "You say Ling Soo confessed to the theft in a suicide note. You then say there is no way he could have stolen funds because withdrawals are strictly monitored by your system, and that Alex – Colonel Talanov – is the only person who could have made an actual withdrawal. And yet one and a half billion dollars is now gone. Where did it go?"

Song lowered his head and shrugged again. He had no answer.

While the others watched, Talanov began pacing Song's office, back and forth behind Jingfei, thinking, occasionally glancing at the screen. After several moments, he stopped beside Jingfei and pointed at her diagram of dots.

"Any way to check the balances in those twenty-three accounts and see if the money is there?" he asked.

"Not without a PIN for each individual account," Jingfei replied. "Plus, many of those accounts are in countries where banking laws range from sloppy to non-existent. If Ling Soo has hidden the money somewhere in this cybermaze, we'll never find it."

Talanov looked over at Song. "Are you certain the other guy didn't steal it?" he asked.

"You refer to Wu Chee Ming?"

Talanov nodded.

"He had access, of course, but the suicide note . . ."

"Unless Wu Chee Ming wrote the note because he wanted us to think Ling Soo stole the money," Talanov said, then looking again at Jingfei. "Didn't Alice say the note was typed and not handwritten?"

"No one uses typewriters," Jingfei replied. "But, yes, you're right: the note was not handwritten. It was composed and printed by a word processor."

Talanov looked over at Kai. "Where would you hide something that you'd stolen?"

Kai thought for a moment, then said, "In a place where no one would look."

Talanov responded with an annoyed frown.

Kai pointed toward Jingfei's diagram. "Isn't that where everyone's looking?"

Talanov picked up Jingfei's drawing, studied it for nearly a full minute, then looked at Song. "Take us to Ling Soo's office."

Ling Soo's office was two doors down and looked much the same as Song's, with a desk, a chair, some bookcases and file cabinets.

When they entered, a young woman was seated at the desk. Song motioned for her to leave and the young woman did.

"Naturally, the office has been reassigned," Song explained, closing the young woman's laptop.

Talanov asked Wilcox for the photos of Ling Soo's office that had been taken by the police shortly after Ling Soo's death. Wilcox handed him the envelope and Talanov removed the photos and compared them with how things looked now. Whereas Ling Soo's office was shown in the photos to have been chaotic and sloppy, the young woman's office was orderly and clean.

"Would you say these are an accurate representation of Ling Soo's office?" asked Talanov, showing Song the photos.

Song looked at each of the photos and admitted they were accurate.

"What kind of an employee was Ling Soo?" asked Talanov.

"A man of honor," Song replied, handing back the photos.

Talanov stepped over to a bookcase and picked up one of several awards that were on display. The award looked like a small glass headstone mounted on a wooden pedestal. Unable to read its Chinese characters, he replaced it beside the others.

"Will there be anything else?" asked Song.

"I'd like to speak with some of Ling Soo's co-workers."

Song started to object – Talanov could tell by his face – so Talanov responded with a menacing stare. Swallowing his objection, Song grudgingly stepped out of the office and signaled three women from the main floor of the operations hub. Thirty seconds later, the three women had been ushered into the office and introduced by Song.

"Do any of you speak English?" asked Talanov.

Penny Kwan raised her hand. A product of today's fast-food generation, Penny was as plump as she was tall, which was three inches shorter than the five-foot-two-inch Song.

"Thanks, I'll take it from here," Talanov told Song.

Before Song could protest, Talanov led Song out of the office and shut the door. Turning his back to the door, Talanov said, "Anything you say remains confidential."

Penny Kwan translated for the other two women and they all nodded, although all three kept glancing nervously at Song, who was glaring at them through the glass door. Talanov looked at Song and thumbed for him to leave.

Once Song was gone, Talanov faced the women. "Tell me about Ling Soo."

Penny translated and the women made remarks in Chinese.

"Sloppy and arrogant. A rooster," answered Penny.

Talanov responded with a quizzical look.

"Big noise. Small brain. Like rooster."

Talanov glanced over at Jingfei, who nodded discreetly that Penny Kwan was translating accurately.

Talanov looked back at Penny. "He seems kind of messy," he said, showing Penny a photo of Ling Soo's desk.

"He was. He make us keep office straight."

"He made you clean his office?"

"Yes."

"On a regular basis?"

"Yes."

Talanov began casually strolling the office, ostensibly scanning objects on shelves and on the walls, where there were a number of framed certificates, all written in Chinese. "Was Ling Soo good at his job?" he asked.

Penny translated and the women all shrugged.

"He thought so," Penny replied.

"What do you think?" asked Talanov, looking at Penny.

Penny shrugged and did not reply.

"Tell me about Wu Chee Ming," said Talanov.

Penny translated and the other two women offered brief comments.

"Very neat," Penny explained.

"So, the opposite of Ling Soo?"

Penny nodded. "Very quiet. Student of proverb. Always quoting them."

"Such as?"

"Dig well before you are thirsty. A crow cannot be fooled into eating what it does want. One does not seek what one does not see. Last proverb, he say a lot."

"About one not seeking what one does not see?"

Penny nodded.

Talanov thought about that, then thanked the women and left the office. Wilcox and the kids looked at one another before realizing Talanov was actually leaving, and they hurried to catch up with him, which they did at the elevator.

Made in silence, the elevator ride down to the street took just over twenty seconds, and when the doors finally opened, Talanov led the way through the lobby out onto the sidewalk, where he walked to the curb and signaled a taxi.

Wilcox grabbed Talanov by the arm. "Talk to me. What did we learn?"

"More important, what did *you* learn?" Talanov asked in return, his eyes panning Wilcox and the kids.

After exchanging quick glances, everyone shrugged, not knowing what to say.

"I know, it left me speechless, too," said Talanov, "and what a brilliant plan it was. So brilliant, in fact, that, like Kai said, it got everyone looking in the wrong direction, which is good for us, because had it been otherwise . . . well, let's just say, we wouldn't be in the promising position we're in right now, which confirms yet again why Dragon Head needs us. He needs us to do the impossible. He needs us to do what none of his people have been unable to do. Thing is, there's one remaining piece of this puzzle, and it's a big one, and we need to find it, fast."

He waved again for a taxi, but Jingfei jumped in front of him. "Quit messing with us," she said. "What are you talking about?"

A taxi whipped over to the curb and stopped.

"You mean, after all of that, you still don't know? Come on, we're wasting time. Bill, give Alice a call. Tell her we're coming over."

Talanov opened the front door of the taxi and climbed in.

"I want to punch him, I really do," Jingfei muttered, pulling open the rear door and climbing in while Wilcox dialed.

Twelve miles to the west, in a private section of the Hong Kong airport, agents Delta and Zulu climbed out of their helicopter and showed their diplomatic passports to one of the uniformed guards waiting for them on the tarmac. Per instructions issued by Shaw, Delta and Zulu were to look the part of visiting diplomats. That meant dressing in suits, which both agents despised. Manners would also play an important part, so both men bowed politely before Delta greeted the guard in Cantonese.

The guard nodded, then checked the helicopter to make sure it contained no other passengers. Satisfied, he returned their passports. Delta thanked the guard and told him why they were here, which was to inspect the American Gulfstream. The guard informed Delta that clearance for the inspection had been arranged. He then told them where the Gulfstream was parked before escorting them to a limousine with tinted windows.

The guard noticed the small suitcases carried by the two men. He knew not to ask questions about what those suitcases contained. These men had diplomatic clearance, which meant their suitcases were beyond scrutiny.

Once they were inside the limousine, Zulu opened his suitcase and withdrew a handheld RF signal detector, which he moved about the interior of the vehicle to see if any electronic listening or tracking devices had been installed. Nothing registered, so Zulu switched it off.

"We're good," said Zulu, replacing the instrument inside his suitcase.

Delta started the engine, made a U-turn and drove to the hangar where the Gulfstream was parked. Stopping near the nose of the aircraft, Delta took out his cell phone and dialed. Seconds later, the scrambled satellite call was answered by a switchboard operator in Langley, Virginia, who routed the call to Angus Shaw.

After identifying himself, Delta said they were onsite. Shaw replied with instructions to find out what kind of mechanical problem was keeping the Gulfstream grounded.

"I presume you're fully equipped?" asked Shaw.

Delta knew what that meant and gave Shaw the answer he wanted to hear.

"If I give the word, you know what to do," Shaw replied. "Start tracking them now. I'll text you Talanov's number."

"Do these orders include Wilcox?" asked Delta.

"If that's what it takes."

Delta glanced at Zulu and did not reply.

"Will that be a problem?" asked Shaw.

"Not at all, sir. Delta out."

# CHAPTER 63

Talanov tried phoning Zak twice on the way to the police station. Little did he know Zak was waist-deep in the grave he was digging in the mountains of California. Pausing in the wash of headlights, Zak could hear the phone ringing on the floorboard of the SUV. Ginie and Emily looked, too, from where they were seated on the grass several feet away. Their hands were still zip-tied behind them and the smell of freshly dug earth filled the night air.

"Keep digging," said Alpha.

Talanov ended the call when he saw Alice waiting for them in front of a gleaming forty-seven-story skyscraper overlooking Victoria Harbor.

"No answer?" asked Jingfei, reading the worried look on Talanov's face.

Talanov shook his head just as Alice welcomed them to Arsenal House. She gave Wilcox a kiss on the cheek, then shook hands with the others.

"I collected the items requested," Alice said, "but there is nothing there. Our people have examined them numerous times."

"But you don't mind us looking them over?"

"Of course not. I am happy to help. But I think you are wasting your time."

"Cool building," Jingfei remarked, admiring the curved face of Arsenal House, its mirrored surface and ladder-like column of slits. "Looks like a massive computer modem."

Alice said the comparison was entirely appropriate, since battles today were often fought in cyberspace, with stakes that were very real in terms of information technology, identity theft, and funds trafficking for terrorist activities. "The brains behind an attack in one part of the world may be a nineteen-year-old boy in another. National borders are irrelevant, and the criminals do not stake out your house and wait for you to leave in order to steal your jewelry. They hunt you online, penetrate your firewalls and steal not just what you own, but who you are. Like I said, borders today are irrelevant, because you can be living comfortably in San Francisco and be robbed by a thief in Ghana."

"So you track criminals all over the world?" Jingfei asked.

"I've helped cyber investigators - cops, I think you call them - go after criminals in virtually every country on earth. Cyber crime and security is one of my specialties."

After leading the group inside, Alice asked how the meeting went at Sun Cheng Financial Group. Talanov replied that he was able to access his account but that it was empty. No, he did not know where the funds went, nor did anyone at the bank know. That's because the only two people who could have told him - Ling Soo and Wu Chee Ming - were now dead. He concluded by saying he had interviewed several coworkers of the two dead men, but no one knew anything. The money was simply gone.

"How can a financial institution lose one and a half billion dollars?" asked Alice.

"I asked Song the very same question," answered Talanov, following Alice along a corridor, "and all he could do was hang his head."

"How could he not know?" asked Alice. "There has to be some kind of record. Every transaction leaves a trail."

"It baffled me, too," answered Talanov. "And, apparently, everyone else."

"And you found out nothing more?"

"Not a thing."

"I just don't see how this happened," Alice said with a shake of her head. "Someone has to know something."

Jingfei looked inquisitively at Talanov, and when Talanov noticed her looking up at him, intensified her expression as if to say, "Have you forgotten about those offshore accounts?"

Talanov discreetly shook his head.

Alice led them into a stairwell and up two flights of stairs, then along another corridor to a conference room. The room was separated from the hall by a bank of windows. Across the corridor were more windows that looked into a room filled with desks that were typical of police stations everywhere: computers, mugs, stacks of manila folders, papers, sticky notes, pens, pencils, yellow pads with lots of scribbled notes.

Through the window, Talanov could see five men and two women on the far side of the room, huddled around a computer. Several of the men and one of the women were in uniforms of pale blue shirts and dark blue slacks. The others were in plainclothes. Several were armed with pistols.

One of the men in plainclothes was a computer specialist. Talanov could tell because his fingers were flying across the keyboard at an extraordinary speed. He was bridging keys and executing quick successions of commands while everyone else looked on. The specialist, however, was not having a lot of success. Talanov could tell that, too, by the movement of his lips, which were muttering words of frustration. Before stepping into the conference room, Talanov noticed several monitors on other desks. Their screens were all blue, which usually meant a crashed system. The desks had all been abandoned, no doubt by the people who were now huddled around the specialist.

Alice opened the door of the conference room and led the way inside. On top of a worktable was a file box. On top of the file box was a large brown envelope.

"Here you go," said Alice. "The contents of Wu Chee Ming's suitcase."

"Thank you, Alice," said Wilcox. "I owe you . . . again."

"It's a list that is growing," answered Alice with a smile.

An officer tapped on the window and summoned Alice with a wave of his hand. "I'll be right back," she said, stepping into the hallway and closing the door. Because of the window, Alice remained visible while talking to the officer.

"What are we looking for?" asked Jingfei.

"Anything that doesn't fit," answered Talanov.

"What does that mean?" asked Kai.

"It means we take note of everything and how it fits with what we would expect a man on the run to be carrying. We then assess whether or not there is something that doesn't fit. And not just if there's an item that's out of place, but also ordinary items that are not out of place, although something about them is."

"I still don't know what that means."

"Sometimes items can be altered to conceal a message. I know of one instance where a man encoded information on a certain page of a novel using tiny holes above certain letters." He reached into the box and withdrew two mass market paperbacks and a newspaper. The novels were in Chinese and had karate figures on the cover. The newspaper was also in Chinese and was only a few days old. "Are these ordinary items?" he asked. "Or items that a man on the run wouldn't be carrying?"

"They're ordinary items," answered Kai. "Do you think Wu Chee Ming hid his access code in, say, one of those novels?"

"That's what we need to find out," Talanov replied, handing one of the novels to Kai and the other one and the newspaper to Wilcox.

"What about me?" asked Jingfei.

"Go through his clothing. Check hems, seams, and patterns in the material. Look for anything that might conceal or communicate an account number, PIN, or other hidden message, such as the tiny dots and dashes of something in Morse Code."

"What's Morse Code?" asked Kai.

"Don't worry, I got it," said Jingfei just as Alice opened the door and came back into the room.

"Like I said before," Alice continued, "my people have examined those items. They've assured me nothing is there."

"I simply want to get a feel for what Wu Chee Ming might

have been planning," Talanov replied. "I notice, for instance, that he was not carrying any cold-weather gear." He gestured at the various items of clothing that Jingfei had spread across the table.

"Obviously, he planned on buying whatever clothing he needed once he reached his destination," Alice responded.

"Possibly," agreed Talanov, "but if that were the case, why carry anything at all? As it is, we find three changes of clothes, all warm-weather. All I'm saying is that it's a clue about where he might have been going."

"I still don't understand why you are focused on Wu Chee Ming when Ling Soo confessed to the crime."

"I'm not convinced that he did it."

"Do you suspect Wu Chee Ming?"

"Possibly."

Alice scrutinized Talanov, whose expression remained non-committal. "On what basis do you draw this conclusion?" she asked.

"It's not really a conclusion. I guess you could call it a possible hunch."

"A possible hunch?" asked Alice, looking at Wilcox, then back at Talanov. "Is that how the CIA runs its investigations? On possible hunches?"

"I can't speak for the CIA," said Talanov, "since I'm not part of club, but, yes, possible hunches are part of my highly honed set of investigative skills."

Wilcox suppressed a smile just as Talanov picked up Wu Chee Ming's passport and began flipping through its pages.

"There is nothing in his passport," declared Alice. "No visas and no visits abroad, and our computer records concur."

Talanov smiled his thanks and laid the passport aside. He then picked up Wu Chee Ming's toiletry kit.

"We've already looked through those items," said Alice.

"Are these ink dots?" asked Jingfei, who had been examining the hem of a shirt.

The remark drew Alice's attention while Talanov handed

the toiletry kit to Kai.

"When you're finished with the novel," said Talanov, "do the same with everything in this kit."

"I'm done; the novel was clean," Kai replied. He laid the book aside and emptied the contents of the toiletry kit onto the table. There were several throwaway razors, a tube of shaving cream, a tube of toothpaste, a toothbrush, some floss, a tube of ointment, some eye drops, tweezers, a small pair of scissors, and several small bottles of herbal supplements.

While Kai began scrutinizing each item, Talanov opened the envelope of photographs that Alice had supplied. After looking through them, he singled out the one of Ling Soo's desk and held it alongside the photo of Wu Chee Ming's desk. "Wu Chee Ming was neat to the point of being anal," remarked Talanov. "Ling Soo: a dog's breakfast."

"A what?" asked Alice.

"An Aussie expression. Dog's breakfast. A sloppy mess. Which I find very curious."

"Meaning, what, exactly?" asked Alice just as three men and a woman hurried past the window and entered the computer room across the hall. They hurried over to the computer specialist, who began pointing to his screen while explaining something to the new arrivals.

"Computer problems?" asked Talanov.

Alice did not reply.

"If it's a virus, be very careful."

The remark drew a sharp glance from Alice.

"I'm not trying to make whatever's happening over there my business," Talanov explained, "but Dragon Head has already managed to slip a virus into the computer network of Diane Gustaves, as well as on my cell phone so that he could track our movements and record our conversations. Be careful, is all I'm saying. He may come after you."

Alice acknowledged the warning with an appreciative nod just as her cell phone rang. Excusing herself, Alice stepped into the hall to take the call.

Kai was sorting through the toiletries when he picked up the toothpaste, turned it over in his hand, then began examining it more carefully. It was a small travel size, no longer than a man's finger. "Look at this," he said, handing Talanov the tube and pointing to its label.

Talanov was examining the tube when his cell phone suddenly chimed. Handing the tube back to Kai, he fished out his cell phone and checked the screen. It was an email from Straw Sandal. With the swipe of a finger, Talanov opened the email and read it.

"It's from Straw Sandal," he announced. "The escrow account has been opened and she sent me the number."

"How are we supposed to deposit money that we don't have into an escrow account?" Jingfei asked, her frustration evident in the tone of her voice. She tossed the shirt she had been examining on top of Wu Chee Ming's other clothing. "There's nothing here. What are we going to do?"

The door suddenly swung open and Alice stormed into the conference room. "What the *hell* is going on, here, Bill?"

"What do you mean?" asked Wilcox, who had just finished examining the newspaper. "You know why we're here."

"I know what you told me on the phone," Alice replied. "But that's not the whole story, now, is it?"

"Alice, what's this about?"

"You tell me!"

"You know what's going on."

"Do I?"

"Yes!"

"Then why is there an agent downstairs at the front desk – a United Stares Federal agent – who says I'm to hold all of you until he arrives? That's he's taking you into custody?"

Wilcox looked at Talanov with alarm. "Shaw knows. He's shutting us down."

"Shutting *what* down?" demanded Alice. "What are you not telling me? Why would your own government want you in custody?"

"The less you know, the better," Wilcox replied.

"Really? That's your answer?"

"It's for your own protection."

"Then I'm afraid you leave me no choice. I'm placing you under arrest."

# CHAPTER 64

In the darkened computer room of the Zhongzhen Martial Arts Academy, AK was seated in front of his main monitor with Sofia looking over one shoulder and Straw Sandal looking over the other. AK could smell Straw Sandal's subtle fragrance, which was some kind of a nectar-based perfume. Sofia smelled like sweat from her martial arts session.

Straw Sandal's fragrance reminded AK of Straw Sandal's nickname, Sunbird, which was a small, nectar-loving bird, like a hummingbird, although sunbirds were not able to hover like the hummingbird, albeit Straw Sandal was certainly hovering now.

AK had heard how the nickname had been given to Straw Sandal when she was a child by none other than the old guard himself. It was an appropriate name, not only because Straw Sandal was petite, but because Sunbirds represented something good and beautiful in nature, and Straw Sandal was about the only person around here who stood for something good and beautiful.

According to the old guard, the academy had not always been run the way it was now. At one time, it stood for honor, loyalty, and the protection of people in the neighborhood. However, since the arrival of Sofia – Xin Li – Dragon Head's ambitions began to change.

*Which was not all bad,* AK thought.

Or was it? Were things getting out of hand? Was the killing of thousands of people worth the money and stature he would receive? In his own zeal to become the best, had he become the worst kind of human being imaginable?

"You're certain that Talanov read my email?" Straw Sandal asked, causing him to refocus.

AK pointed at the monitor, which not only verified delivery, but how long it had taken Talanov to read it.

"What happens next?" asked Straw Sandal.

"I set up auto-alert. It notify me moment Talanov make deposit."

"And then?" Sofia asked.

"We release the girl. Talanov release funds."

When no one responded, AK looked up at Sofia and then Straw Sandal, who were glaring at each other.

"I presume we release the girl?" AK inquired.

"Yes, she will be released," Straw Sandal declared. "We have given Talanov our word."

With a bitter scowl, Sofia looked away.

"What happens then?" Straw Sandal asked just as her cell phone rang.

"Once Talanov release funds," AK explained, "they will be transferred to our account in Venezuela, then transferred to offshore account of yours. Venezuelan bank will then crash from virus I plant in its system."

"Meaning no record will exist as to where the money went once it leaves escrow?" asked Sofia.

AK nodded just as Straw Sandal turned away and put her cell phone to her ear.

Once Straw Sandal was out of earshot, Sofia leaned down and said in Russian, "Why were you not able to locate the missing funds? We had an agent inside the bank assisting and still you were not able to find out what happened."

"Because Wu Chee Ming destroyed the transfer record."

"How did he manage to do that?"

AK shrugged.

"I must go," Straw Sandal said, returning to the worktable. "Let me know when the deposit has been made."

AK nodded just as Straw Sandal ran from the computer room.

"Back to the Sun Cheng account," said Sofia. "How do we know the funds are in that maze of accounts?"

"Because they are all connected to Sun Cheng account."

"So the funds are definitely in one of those accounts, and all we need do is find out which one?"

"Yes, I think."

"You *think?*"

"There is another possibility."

"Which is?"

"An invisible account, with dedicated number dangling by electronic thread that is visible only to account holder, like a trap door that no one can see unless you know where to look. But because the maze is so complex, like a tangle, it would be impossible to locate the trap door, if one exists at all, even if I had advanced software, which I do not have. Without an account number or an access code, we cannot hope to find it."

"Then where does that leave us?" asked Sofia.

AK shrugged.

"Then how can Talanov possibly succeed where even you have failed?"

"I wonder the same thing," answered AK.

"Do you realize what will happen if we do not get that money?"

AK looked back at his monitor. It was an excuse to avert his eyes from what he knew to be a serious situation.

Sofia grabbed an office chair and wheeled it over, and after sitting, took AK by the chin and made him look at her. "There will be casualties in the wake of such a failure. Do you understand?"

AK stared wide-eyed into the fierce eyes of Sofia staring back at him. His chin was distorted by the squeeze of Sofia's grip.

"I brought you to Hong Kong because I needed you to do what others could not do," Sofia continued. "But everything we have worked for – *everything* – depends on us getting that money. The minute Talanov makes his deposit, you will tell me and no one but me. Do you understand?"

AK nodded.

"You will then transfer everything into the account I had

you set up in Martinique. Do you understand?"

AK nodded again.

Letting go of AK's chin, Sofia stood and shoved the chair away. It spun across the floor and slammed into the front of a worktable.

"And girl? What about her?" asked AK, rubbing his chin.

"Such matters do not concern you," Sofia replied. "Your concern is following my instructions. Do not let me down. That . . . would make me *very* unhappy."

# CHAPTER 65

"Stop what you're doing and step away from the table," commanded Alice.

No one moved.

"Now!" Alice shouted and everyone placed the items they were holding down onto the table. Once they had stepped back, Alice turned to Wilcox and said, "I am sorry it has come to this, Bill, and you yourself are not officially under arrest, but everyone else must be held for the American agent who is downstairs. This has now become a diplomatic issue that is way beyond my control."

Seeing two uniformed officers passing by the window, Alice rapped on the glass and motioned them into the conference room.

"We've got kids with us, Alice," said Wilcox.

"You should have thought of that before," Alice replied just as the officers entered the room and Alice told them to guard the door and wait for an arriving American agent, who would take everyone into custody, except for Mr. Wilcox, who was free to leave.

"Alice, *please*," tried Wilcox.

"My hands are tied," said Alice. "You have stretched this beyond the boundaries of friendship."

"It wasn't his fault. It was mine," Jingfei said, stepping forward.

"Was not," said Kai, stepping in front of her. "It was mine. I snuck us onto the plane."

"Shut up, Kai," said Jingfei, pushing past Kai and stepping up to face Alice. "If you gotta keep someone, keep me. If you keep Alex and Bill, my little sister gets killed."

"She's my sister, too!" said Kai, shouldering Jingfei aside and stepping up to face Alice.

By now, both kids were jostling each other so much that Alice had to step back. The uniformed officers moved to intervene but Alice halted them. Taking both kids aside, she said, "I am sorry about your sister, but you need to let us handle this."

"The way you're handling it now guarantees that she'll be killed," Jingfei fired back. "You police dorks are all the same."

Alice stiffened at being addressed in such an aggressive manner.

"Forgive them, Alice, they're pretty emotional right now because of what's happened to their sister," Wilcox said, easing the kids back a few steps. "And while I admire their willingness to take the blame," Wilcox continued, facing Alice again, "it's me this agent wants. I'm the one who created this mess. So, please, I'm begging you, let them go."

"Shut up, Bill!" yelled Jingfei, stepping in front of Wilcox. "Alex needs you because you've got connections at Langley, and he needs help, because he's a dinosaur, like you, even though I don't mean to make you mad by calling you names, because you've been, like, doing everything you can to try and save Su Yin, which you can't do if Alice keeps you for that agent downstairs, which will really mess things up and keep Alex from locating those funds, which means Su Yin will *definitely* be killed, which Alice doesn't seem to care about, even though I do, so go ahead and tell her to keep me and let the rest of you go, so that you can—"

"Shut up, all of you, just . . . *shut up!*" shouted Alice.

A stunned silence filled the conference room.

Alice glared at Wilcox, then told the uniformed officers they could go. The officers looked at each other, unsure, but Alice told them everything was under control. Once they were gone, Alice said, "End of the hall, down the stairs. You'll see the exit sign."

Wilcox touched Alice on the arm. "Thank you!"

Alice knocked his hand away and pushed him toward the door. "Go!" she said, motioning for them to leave.

On his way past, Talanov took Alice by the hands and rotated her slowly toward the door, saying, "Thank you for giving us this chance to save a little girl's life." He then gave Alice a hug.

Kai started to step past but saw Talanov looking over Alice's shoulder with pointed glances at the toothpaste. Kai responded with a quizzical look, then understood and palmed the tube into his pocket just as Alice broke away from Talanov and turned to see Kai replacing Wu Chee Ming's belongings into the file box.

"I'll do that," said Alice, pushing Talanov and Kai out the door.

Talanov led everyone to the end of the corridor, where they disappeared into a stairwell just as the elevator doors opened at the other end of the corridor and Delta stepped out with an accompanying officer. Fluent in Cantonese because his parents had come from Hong Kong, Delta had been conversing casually with the officer in an effort to build rapport and disarm any suspicions about him being an American agent. He needed cooperation, not confrontation, since his mission was off the books, even though it had the appearance of being official, thanks to a well-placed call from Shaw.

*Quick and easy,* thought Delta.

Which he knew was not the case the instant the accompanying officer threw open the conference room door and he saw Alice alone in the room.

Alice looked up from the file box of belongings when she saw them enter.

"Where are they?" asked Delta. "Wilcox and Talanov?"

Alice shook her head with a sigh. "I stepped away to take a call, and when I came back, they were gone."

Delta glared at Alice for a long moment, but Alice merely looked back at him with a deadpan expression. She knew there was nothing he could say or do. He was, after all, an American agent seeking assistance from the Hong Kong police, and as such, would not make any accusations that might cause him to be detained for questioning on what he knew was an illegal operation on Chinese soil. Controlling his anger, Delta hurried back toward the elevators.

Downstairs, Talanov pushed open a side door and led the way down a flight of steps to the street.

"Where to now?" asked Wilcox.

"Someplace out of reach," Talanov replied while lanes of traffic flowed past in both directions. "So we can figure out what to do."

Across the street was an Esso station set into the corner of a highrise office tower. Talanov waited for a break in the traffic, then ran with the group across the street and along the sidewalk past the station. On each side of the street were more highrise monoliths. Each boastful giant stood proud and erect among other giants testifying to the capitalistic success of Hong Kong.

As they wove their way along through the flow of pedestrians, Talanov knew Alice would be furious once the missing toothpaste was discovered. But if what he suspected were true, it was the missing piece of the puzzle. At least he hoped it was, and he dared not consider the alternative, because right now, that tube of toothpaste was their only hope.

And yet the hope he was feeling on one hand – of saving Su Yin – amounted to a death sentence on the other for Zak, Ginie, and Emily.

A hand touched him on the arm and he looked to see Kai.

"You said to look for something that didn't fit," said Kai, handing Talanov the tube.

"Here's hoping you're right," answered Talanov. "Nicely done, by the way, slipping it into your pocket and covering your action by repacking the file box. You looked like you've done that before."

Kai grinned just as Talanov passed the tube to Jingfei, who was walking beside him.

"What am I looking at?" she asked.

"Remember back at Sun Cheng, when Penny Kwan told us

about Wu Chee Ming's proverbs?"

"Kinda, but how do you even remember Penny Kwan's name, much less a bunch of old proverbs?"

"Because we can't afford to miss important details like that."

"Such as?"

"Dig the well before you are thirsty? A crow cannot be fooled into eating what it does want? One does not seek what one does not see?"

"Stop showing off and tell me how they relate to this stupid toothpaste."

"That's what we're about to find out."

Outside the police station, Zulu met Delta at the bottom of a long flight of steps that Delta had bounded down three at a time.

"Which way did they go?" asked Delta.

"That way," said Zulu, pointing.

They ran across the street and past the Esso station to a tree, where they paused so that Zulu could check his cell phone. On the screen was a digital map of Hong Kong. Zulu touched the screen in a spreading motion and enlarged the map to reveal a close-up of the street they were on. A blinking red dot showed Talanov's position. A blinking green dot showed their position in relation to the blinking red dot.

"They're maybe seventy or eighty yards ahead," said Zulu just as Delta's cell phone rang.

"It's Shaw," Delta said. He took the call and filled him in on how the Gulfstream pilot claimed he saw a warning light and ordered a maintenance crew to check things over.

"In other words," said Shaw, "Wilcox convinced the pilot to ground the plane in order to give them time."

"That's how it looks, because the maintenance crew did not find a thing."

Delta then told Shaw how they had tracked Talanov, Wilcox, and the kids to the Sun Cheng Financial Group, no doubt to investigate the missing funds, meaning Talanov appeared to be cooperating with Dragon Head, after which they followed them to the Hong Kong police station, where they were supposed to have been taken into custody but somehow escaped, although he and Zulu were closing in on them now using the GPS tracking on Talanov's phone.

"They know we're after them," Delta said, "which means if they toss the phone, we'll lose track of where they are."

"I can prevent that from happening," Shaw replied. "Your job is to keep closing the gap."

# CHAPTER 66

Across the street from Esso station on the other corner, Straw Sandal stood in a recessed doorway with her cell held in front of her, her call on speaker so that she could keep watching the blinking green dot showing on the street map on her screen. Dressed in black running tights, a white T-shirt and baseball cap, she was talking with the computer technician who had been working across the hall from the conference room.

The technician described how Talanov and his group had been looking through the belongings of Wu Chee Ming. No, he did not know what they had found, if anything. Alice Ti, of the CIB, had allowed Talanov and Wilcox to look through the belongings, and when it was discovered that an American agent had arrived downstairs to take Talanov and Wilcox into custody, Alice intentionally allowed them to escape.

"Why would she do that?" asked Straw Sandal.

"She and Wilcox, a senior official with the CIA, are longtime friends. What I do not understand is why American agents would be chasing Talanov and Wilcox, especially if Wilcox is himself an American agent."

Straw Sandal knew the answer. The Americans had managed to connect the airline collisions with her father and were doing everything to keep Talanov and Wilcox from locating the money, which the Americans knew would be used to expand his hacking capabilities.

In truth, she did not blame them. At one time, her father was an honorable man. Until the arrival of Xin Li – Sofia – that is, whose lust for wealth and power infected her father.

*Why rule an island when you can rule the world?*

That is what Xin Li had promised him, and this was now his ambition.

Her mother would never have allowed such ambition to

dishonor their family, which is, no doubt, why Xin Li had poisoned her. Xin Li needed a power base and her father was the most powerful man in this part of the world.

It was not a murder she could ever prove, especially when the medical examiner called her mother's death an unfortunate instance of improperly cooked blood clams, which her mother always ordered whenever they dined in her favorite restaurant. She had even gone to the restaurant to question the chef, who had served them faithfully for nearly ten years, only to hear the chef had died suddenly of a heart attack. The manager expressed concern over the incident, saying he had witnessed the chef having an argument with Xin Li in the alley the night before her mother's death. Two deaths within two days. The common denominator?

Xin Li.

It was then and there that she knew Xin Li was guilty of killing her mother, and she would have killed Xin Li in revenge were it not for the dishonor it would heap on her father were she found guilty of such an act without proof that Xin Li had committed the crime. Her only recourse was to —

"Did you hear me?" the technician asked, causing Straw Sandal to refocus.

"Tell me again," Straw Sandal said.

"I asked why the American agents would be pursuing Talanov and Wilcox."

"What did the agents look like?" Straw Sandal asked, spotting two Caucasian men on the corner across the street. Each had short hair and the alertness of men with military training.

The technician described them just as the two men paused in a recessed doorway and Straw Sandal saw one of the men hand the other man a pistol, which he concealed beneath his shirt.

"I see them," Straw Sandal said, her eyes moving back and forth between the two agents and the blinking green dot on her screen. "They are following Talanov."

After ending the call, Straw Sandal clicked photos of the two agents, then dialed a number.

Less than half a mile away, in the Zhongzhen Martial Arts Academy, Dragon Head was in the center of the gym's fight ring, surrounded by four *Shí bèi* fighters. The fight ring was an elevated eight-meter-square platform with a bare wooden floor. The mats from the floor had been removed because Dragon Head said hard wood was a better teacher than soft mats.

The four fighters were feinting and dancing, probing for weaknesses with quick jabs and kicks. Dragon Head moved smoothly and deftly in a small circle, dodging and blocking with quick, fluid movements until he suddenly sprang forward with a leaping kick-punch combination that caused his target to leap back and to the side, avoiding impact. The fighter thought Dragon Head had missed his mark, but the move was actually a feint that enabled him to do a spinning kick into the head of another fighter. Dragon Head controlled the force of the kick to avoid serious damage, yet with enough impact to send the fighter to the floor. Dragon Head then back-kicked the other fighter off of the platform, then danced and punched and kicked his way around the ring, leaving the other fighters lying dazed on the fight ring floor. It was an elegant spectacle that brought smiles and approving nods from elderly spectators, who visited the academy each day, watching the young men and women of the neighborhood train and learn.

Dressed in black yoga tights and a sports bra that showcased her lean but muscular arms, Sofia was sitting on the corner of a wooden table when Dragon Head's cell phone rang beside her. After checking the Caller ID, she took the call.

Straw Sandal asked for her father but Sofia said he was busy. Knowing she needed assistance in preventing the agents from killing Talanov, she reported what was happening, namely, that she was following two armed American agents, who were following Talanov, who had been at police headquarters looking through the belongings of Wu Chee Ming.

"Where are you now?" asked Sofia, jumping off the table.

"Heading east on Lockhart Road, away from Arsenal House. I have the agents in sight."

"Did Talanov locate the funds? Was there a clue that our people missed?"

"Our source did not know."

"Perhaps Talanov is on his way to make the transfer?"

"It is possible," answered Straw Sandal.

"Text me your location," instructed Sofia.

# CHAPTER 67

Talanov stepped between two parked cars and looked behind, as if checking for traffic. Fifty meters back he saw them: two military types, Chinese heritage, pushing their way aggressively through the flow of pedestrians. Even from this distance, he could tell their focus was on him.

"They're gaining, aren't they?" asked Wilcox, winded from the fast pace they had been walking.

"We'll manage. Come on, let's cross," said Talanov, waiting for a break in the traffic before dashing with Jingfei to the median, hopping over a low fence, then dashing to the other side.

"Is it Shaw's men or Dragon Head's?" asked Jingfei.

"Shaw's," answered Talanov. "How did they know where we were?"

"They must be tracking your phone."

Talanov took out his cell phone and began trying to pry off the back.

Snatching the phone from Talanov's hand, Jingfei quickly removed the plate, removed the battery, then replaced the plate and handed it back by the time Kai had helped Wilcox over the fence and hurried with him across the street.

"Good job, Bill, way to go," said Kai, slapping Wilcox on the arm while Wilcox paused to catch his breath.

"We need to keep moving," said Talanov, putting his phone in one pocket and the battery in another.

Fifty meters behind, Delta and Zulu saw Talanov cross the street, and after waiting for a break in the traffic, did the same.

Not wanting to risk being noticed, Straw Sandal did not cross the street as the two agents had done, although she increased her speed so as not to lose sight of them while texting her location to Sofia. Seconds later, her cell phone rang.

"I'm on my way," Sofia said as a heavy metal roller door finished opening. Sofia gunned her motor scooter and sped out of the academy's basement garage into traffic. Following her were six *Shí bèi* fighters, all of whom were armed with pistols in the pockets of their black cargo pants. When the last fighter left the garage, the metal door rolled closed.

Straw Sandal ended the call and touched a button that brought a street map of Hong Kong onto the screen. But there was no blinking green dot. It had disappeared.

A block ahead, Talanov led the way around a corner and along a street bordered by low-rise blocks of apartments with deteriorating plaster walls and air conditioners streaked with rust. Stairwells into the apartments were covered with steel mesh security doors.

"We need to separate," said Wilcox. "I'm slowing you down."

"No way," said Kai, taking Wilcox by the arm. "We're not leaving you behind to get shot and then tossed into some stinky dumpster full of garbage."

"That was . . . graphic," said Wilcox, and Kai grinned.

"Come on," said Talanov, taking Wilcox by the other arm. He could tell Wilcox was hurting. He also knew Wilcox was right. If they didn't separate, Shaw's men would catch them and it would be game over . . . for all of them.

Which it probably was for Zak. He could still see the image of Zak on his knees, hands zip-tied behind his back, staring up into the camera, his face bloody and bruised. Neither he, Ginie, nor Emily had asked for any of this. By all rights, Zak and the women should have been safe by now.

By all accounts, it made sense to send them away to some remote location, except that Shaw had out-maneuvered him. At least Larisa was safe. At least he had done one thing right by sending her away.

Why couldn't life be normal? Why couldn't he just cook veggies for mobs of kids, or go out with friends and eat pizza?

But life wasn't normal, and never would be, and right now

he didn't have time to feel sorry for himself. Right now, his only focus was saving the other lives he had endangered, and that meant Wilcox and the kids.

Ahead on the other side of the street, Talanov saw what looked like a slit between more low-rise blocks of apartments, with people streaming in and out like bees flying in and out of a hive. Quickening their pace, Talanov angled across the street.

"Almost there," said Talanov, noticing how hard Wilcox was breathing.

The "slit" between the buildings was technically a lane, just over one car wide, with clusters of bicycles parked near the entrance.

*A neighborhood bazaar,* thought Talanov, hearing music and the clamor of voices.

Glancing back, Talanov saw Shaw's men turn the corner and come running toward them.

"Hurry!" he said, herding the group into the lane with a stream of arriving shoppers.

The tiny shops lining each side of the lane offered everything imaginable. Roller doors beneath canvas awnings had been raised to expose narrow aisles crammed with colorful merchandise. Goods had been stacked on the floor, shelves, and on tables. Every inch of space was occupied. There were stacks of canned goods, packaged goods, dried goods, bottled drinks, stuffed animals, herbal products, artwork, ceramic bowls, plates, and woks. There were open crates of fresh produce and bins of chopsticks, incense, and utensils. As if that were not enough, there were racks of jewelry, clothing, dried meat, belts, necklaces, handbags, and scarves. There were counters of fresh meat, fish, smoked ducks, hot bread, rolls, pastries, desserts, and candy. Some vendors had deep fryers that were sizzling and popping. Banners hung from ceilings. Red paper lanterns had been strung across the lane. Interspersed between the shops were dumpsters filled with trash.

Because there were so many people crowding the bazaar, the

group had to weave along single-file, like a snake. Talanov was in the lead, followed by Jingfei, Wilcox, then Kai.

Jingfei leaned forward and said, "Bill, he's really hurting."

"I know," Talanov replied, glancing back to see Kai slide his shoulder under Wilcox's armpit to help him walk. "He needs rest and needs it fast. But we have to lose Shaw's men."

Delta and Zulu paused at the entry of the bazaar and Zulu checked his scanner. "The tracking dot's gone. They're definitely onto us!"

A burst of whining engines drew their attention, and the two men saw a pack of six motor scooters racing toward them. The riders were all leaning forward, their black hair blowing in the wind.

Delta and Zulu saw arm movements. Seconds later, bullets began stinging the air next to their heads. One struck Zulu's phone and shattered it in his hand. Delta and Zulu returned fire before ducking into the bazaar. One *Shí bèi* fighter was hit and went down while the others began swerving in a criss-crossing pattern.

Sofia slowed to make sure the injured fighter was alive, then joined the others, who had paused at the entrance, awaiting orders.

"Go after them," Sofia commanded. "But do not kill Talanov or his friends. We need them alive."

Gunning their engines, the *Shí bèi* fighters sped into the lane.

The narrow street was only a block long but that block was the length of a football field. With shots having been fired and people screaming and running toward the other entrance like a runaway herd, Talanov and Jingfei began running with them. A short distance behind were Wilcox and Kai. Kai was helping Wilcox and Wilcox was panting heavily. Farther behind were Delta and Zulu, and behind them were the *Shí bèi* fighters, firing at the agents, into the air, and into shops, in an effort to frighten people out of their way. Bullets shattered dishes and chewed through shelves. Stacks of cans toppled over and spilled out into the lane.

Ducking behind a dumpster, Delta fired over the top of the container while Zulu dropped down onto one knee and fired around the side. Both men hit their marks and two *Shí bèi* fighters flew off their scooters. The first scooter sped straight into another dumpster and exploded, sending a fireball thundering upward, igniting a canvas awning. The other bike cartwheeled into one of the shops.

Falling back to the protection of another dumpster, Delta told Zulu to go after Talanov.

"Copy that," said Zulu, handing Delta a spare magazine. He then sprinted after Talanov while Delta popped up from behind the dumpster and fired, hitting another *Shí bèi* fighter while the remaining two plowed through some racks of clothing before veering back into the lane and returning fire.

Sofia was observing from the entrance when Straw Sandal arrived, winded from her sprint down the block.

"The American agents?" asked Straw Sandal, gulping air while frightened shoppers streamed past.

"In there," Sofia said.

"While you wait *here?*" And after a bitter glare at Sofia, Straw Sandal ran into the lane.

Halfway down the lane, Delta attempted to fire over the dumpster again but his pistol was empty, and with a curse, he ducked back down just as the lead *Shí bèi* fighter opened fire. Bullets riddled the dumpster and made dull thunks. Looking behind him, Delta saw some empty five-gallon cooking oil cans. Grabbing one, he slung it straight at the *Shí bèi* fighter. The spinning can hit the fighter in the face and sent him crashing into a table of dishes. Ducking behind the dumpster, Delta reloaded and fired a quick burst at the remaining *Shí bèi* fighter. The rider skidded into a table stacked with cans and bottles. When the crash occurred, Delta ran after Zulu.

Reaching the other end of the lane, Talanov and Jingfei looked back to see Wilcox hiding behind a shelf of canned goods, bent over, attempting to catch his breath. Kai was beside him, tugging at his arm, but Wilcox was spent.

"Wait here. I need to help Bill," instructed Talanov.

But Jingfei sprinted through the panic-stricken crowd and over to Wilcox and Kai.

"Do you ever listen?" grumbled Talanov, dashing after her.

Jingfei knelt beside Wilcox. "Come on, we've got to hurry," she said just as Talanov arrived.

"I'm finished. I can't go on," Wilcox replied, his brow dripping with sweat.

Talanov peeked around the shelf, then quickly withdrew when he saw Delta and Zulu coming toward him, looking in each shop, pistols in hand. "It's Shaw's men. Stay here, I'll lead them away."

"*I'll* lead them away," countered Wilcox. "You need to find that money."

"Bill, you can't give up," said Kai. "I'll help you. We can do this."

"And I love you for helping me thus far," Wilcox replied. "But I'm finished. You three hide."

"*No*," objected Talanov.

"Su Yin's life is in your hands, now, go!" He turned and gave quick hugs to Jingfei and Kai. "Take care of Alex, okay? He needs you more than he knows." He then handed Jingfei his phone.

"We are not going to leave you!" cried Jingfei.

"It's the only way," Wilcox said. To Talanov: "You're the best friend I've ever had. Tell my son, Danny, that I love him."

And before Talanov could reply, Wilcox ran limping toward the end of the lane.

# CHAPTER 68

Kai started to go after Wilcox but Talanov scooped him and Jingfei into a recessed doorway next to the shop where they had been hiding. With a finger to his mouth, Talanov tucked them into an alcove where a panel of tarnished mailbox doors was mounted in the wall. Talanov stood in front of Jingfei and Kai, his head between theirs, his back to the doorway, like a shield. He knew this placed him in a vulnerable position, but a turned back was more unrecognizable than a face, so he figured the risk was worth it. Seconds later, Delta and Zulu sprinted past.

Talanov waited a few seconds, then slowly turned his head. Frightened shoppers were still running past. Several ran in to escape the danger, saw them hiding, and ran out again.

Telling the kids to remain where they were, Talanov peeked around the corner and saw Delta and Zulu close in on Wilcox. He then glanced left and saw Sofia and Straw Sandal trotting toward him. Sofia stood a head taller than everyone else and Straw Sandal was in a baseball cap, which made both of them stand out. Ducking back into the alcove, Talanov put another finger to his mouth and again shielded the kids in the corner.

Sofia and Straw Sandal bypassed the recessed doorway. Their focus was on the American agents closing in on Wilcox, who had reached the intersection and paused to catch his breath.

Reaching the final shop of the bazaar, Sofia and Straw Sandal stepped behind a display of colorful handbags to watch one of the American agents tackle Wilcox on the far side of the intersection, roll him onto his stomach, then zip-tie his hands behind him. The other agent sprinted short distances in each direction, no doubt looking for Talanov. When that agent returned, the first agent had already pulled Wilcox to his feet.

After watching the two agents lead Wilcox away, Sofia spun around, suddenly alert.

"What is it?" Straw Sandal asked.

"Where's Talanov? You were tracking him."

"The tracking dot disappeared. He must have disabled his phone."

With an angry curse, Sofia began retracing her steps, looking in the first shop, then zigzagging across the lane to the next shop, then back across the lane, then back again, looking in each shop, then angling across the lane again toward the recessed doorway. She vaguely remembered running past it before, although her focus had been on the two agents following Talanov. But since the agents hadn't managed to capture Talanov, she began to wonder if Wilcox had been a diversion. She had promised Dragon Head that she would not kill Talanov until he had transferred the funds, and she would keep her word. The kids, however, were another matter. They would give her the leverage she needed to make sure Talanov complied with their demands. Once he had, she would kill the kids in front of him, then do the same to him.

Readying her pistol, Sofia sprang into the recessed doorway and looked in the alcove. It was empty. She knelt in front of the mailboxes and saw scuff marks in the dust. Three sets of footprints, as if three people had been huddled there, out of sight.

Sofia rattled the heavy security door that accessed the apartments above. It was locked. Turning, she strode back out into the lane and looked left. Police were arriving at the far end of the lane. She could see the flashing lights of their squad cars. Firefighters had arrived on the scene as well and were extinguishing the dumpster fire.

"We missed him," Sofia said angrily. "Talanov is gone."

"What does it matter? We have the girl."

"It matters because the Americans just captured Wilcox and will threaten to kill him unless Talanov complies with their demands."

Two blocks away, Talanov and the kids shuffled along an alley, exhausted and silent. The alley they were in was lined with dumpsters and trash cans. In the center of the alley was a drainage channel, where dirty water trickled toward a drain.

"I gave Bill such a hard time," Jingfei said, wiping tears from her eyes. "I argued with him, was sarcastic and rude, and then he goes and sacrifices himself so that we could get away." She started to cry, and when she did, Talanov paused to wrap an arm around her shoulder.

"What are we going to do?" asked Kai.

Continuing toward the end of the alley, where it met a busy street, Talanov took out his phone. "We've got one play left," he said, removing the back plate, "and I don't know if it'll work, but it's the only play that we've got."

"If you power up that phone again, they'll find us," Jingfei said while Talanov reinserted the battery.

"I know. So what I need you to do is—"

The phone chimed and Talanov looked at the screen and frowned. It was a text message from a blocked number, and after swiping the screen, Talanov saw an image that caused him to stagger back against the wall of a shop, where he was unable to speak.

Jingfei asked what was wrong and Talanov showed her the image of Zak, Ginie, and Emily, their hands zip-tied behind their backs. Taken in the glare of headlights, they were kneeling in front of a large open grave, with piles of dirt and rocks in the background. Zak and the two women had been made to stare up into the camera. Zak's face was swollen more than it had been in the video sent to him previously by Shaw. The two women looked terrified.

But Talanov saw what Zak's captors could not see: the hint of a smile on Zak's face that said, *beaten but not beaten*. The sight of Zak speaking to him that way brought a lump into his throat.

Talanov's phone rang an instant later. Talanov checked the caller ID and saw that it, too, was from a blocked number.

"Don't answer it," said Jingfei.

"I have to," Talanov replied, "or Shaw *will* kill them."

Jingfei grabbed the phone out of Talanov's hand and looked at the image again. "He'll kill them, anyway, won't he?" she asked, wincing at the sight.

Talanov nodded gravely.

"But he's calling to try and force us back onto the plane?"

"With promises to absolutely kill them if we don't."

"Get Shaw to identify himself," Jingfei said, returning the phone. "Get him to state what he's threatening to do."

"Why? What good would that do? We're out of options."

"Just do it."

Talanov stared at Jingfei for a brief moment, then touched the green answer button and put the phone on speaker. "Who is this?" he demanded.

"Like the photo I sent?" Shaw replied. "Open grave . . . Babikov and his lovely wife . . ."

"I don't know who you are or who you work for, but I *will* hunt you down if any harm comes to my friends."

And Talanov hung up.

"What are you *doing?*" shouted Jingfei. "I told you to—"

Talanov held up a hand and Jingfei stopped mid-sentence. Seconds later, the phone rang again and Talanov again put the call on speaker.

"Don't you dare hang up on me again!" yelled Shaw.

"Like I said before, I don't know who you are or—"

"Damn you, this is *Angus Shaw!*"

Jingfei pumped the air with a victorious fist.

"Director Shaw, I didn't realize it was you."

"Shut up and listen or I will put bullets in the heads of—"

"I've found a way to stop Dragon Head!" Talanov blurted out. "All I need is another day."

"Oh, we are *way* past giving you more time."

"I can stop the hacking. I can stop Dragon Head. I've figured out a way."

"You are finished, do you hear me? Finished!"

"Director Shaw, please. A little more time, that's all I need."

"You've got one hour, Talanov, and that's it. One hour for you, those kids, and that Chinese bitch to get back on my plane or I kill your friends. That's Babikov, his wife, your girlfriend . . . and Wilcox. That's right, Wilcox dies, too, if you do not stop what you're doing and get back on my plane. One hour. Or all of them die."

# CHAPTER 69

After the mechanized gates closed slowly behind him, Shaw continued along a curved driveway bordered by hooded lights. Across the spacious lawn, floodlights illuminated the tops of numerous trees. The wooded property was once part of a large Southern plantation. In fact, several Civil War relics had been found on the grounds, including a rusty .58 caliber rifle and bayonet.

Shaw drove into the first of three garages and switched off his engine, and after pushing a button, the garage door behind him rolled down with a creaking hum.

Sitting in his car, Shaw thought about what Talanov had just told him. Was it possible the man had found a way to stop Dragon Head? Even if Talanov had, he, Shaw, would make sure that Talanov was deported if not sent to prison.

He had never liked Talanov or the idea of bringing a former KGB colonel into the intelligence community. Obviously, Gustaves favored the move, which was why he had tried to get rid of her at the Monocle and make it look like the Chinese were responsible. She, like Talanov, possessed a working-business-model view of government that cluttered the landscape. Checks and balances, oversight, accountability, transparency: he would be glad to get rid of such clutter.

After climbing out of his car, Shaw walked over to his workbench, which was a platform of seasoned lumber beneath a row of overhead lights. The work surface of the bench was a sheet of one-inch-thick marine plywood, which was totally unnecessary but which Shaw paid to have installed because the carpenter who built the workbench told him it was the best. The legs of the workbench were seasoned four-by-fours, and there were eight of them, which meant the workbench could support a small truck. On the wall was a large sheet of pegboard holding various hand tools and chrome wrenches. Nearby was a chop saw, which Shaw never used because he didn't like dust.

When he was stressed, Shaw often came out to the garage and rearranged the screws and nails in the drawers of his bright red, solid-steel roller cabinet. It calmed him down and made him feel useful and in control.

Shaw surveyed his workbench kingdom. It was efficient and clean, and everything was just where he wanted it. He lifted a thirty-two-ounce framing hammer off its pegboard hook and hefted it in his hand. He never understood why there were waffle-like grooves in the face of the head. No matter, he just wished he could smash Talanov in the forehead with it. Babikov, too. Like Talanov, he was a loose end that needed to be dealt with. Same with the two women. If he let them go, they would talk, and if they talked, questions would be asked. That's why Alpha and Bravo had standing orders to kill them as soon as Talanov and the kids were in custody. Then Talanov and those miserable kids would be dealt with in the same manner.

Spinning the hammer in his hand like a tennis player spinning a racket, Shaw smiled. Everything was falling into place.

Shaw replaced the hammer just as the door into the house opened and Shaw's six-year-old daughter, Abby, ran out. "Daddee!" she squealed, leaping up into his arms.

"What are you doing up so late?" asked Shaw, kissing his daughter on the head.

"Mommy said I could stay up!"

"Oh, she did, did she?" asked Shaw, smiling at his wife, Olivia, who was standing in the doorway.

"Movie night," Olivia explained.

Shaw tickled Abby and carried her into the house.

"Want to come and sit with me?" asked Abby. "I'm watching a magic horse!"

"Daddy's tired," Shaw replied, carrying Abby into the kitchen. In the center of the kitchen was a large island of polished black granite. Above it was a metal rack festooned with an array of skillets and pans. To the left was a six-burner industrial stove. To the right was a counter of more black granite, with a stainless steel sink beneath a window that overlooked a turquoise swimming pool.

"If you're tired, you should take a nap!" Abby declared. "Mommy makes me take a nap when I'm tired." She wriggled out of Shaw's arms, ran across the kitchen floor into a wide hallway, where her footsteps echoed off the polished oak floor while she ran to the end of the hall and turned left, into the television room, which was furnished with couches and stuffed chairs and a giant flat screen television that filled one wall.

"Where in the world does she get all that energy?" asked Shaw. He walked around the island to a gigantic stainless-steel refrigerator.

"I could ask you the same thing," Olivia replied. "I don't know how you do it."

Opening the refrigerator, Shaw grabbed a beer. It was a European variety in a fat green bottle. Shaw popped the cap and loosened his tie and paused to look out the kitchen window at the pool, which was illuminated by underwater lights.

"Sometimes I don't, either," he replied, taking a drink.

Olivia stepped to his side and rubbed his back. "How was your day?" she asked.

"It was a good day," Shaw replied, taking another swallow. "I'm getting rid of some excess clutter. Now, come on, let's go watch a magical horse."

# CHAPTER 70

Jingfei was literally jumping in place, unable to contain herself while turning tiny circles and pumping her fists.

"What is wrong with you?" asked Talanov once his call with Shaw had ended.

"You mean, what is *right*," Jingfei replied with a grin.

When Talanov responded with a clueless expression, Jingfei snatched the phone from Talanov's hand and held it up for him to see. "Whose phone is this?" she asked.

Talanov responded with an impatient sigh. When Jingfei kept waiting, he said, "Okay, I'll bite. It's mine."

"Ah, but it's not," she said, working the screen. "It's Emily's. Which means . . ."

Jingfei finished working the screen and again held up the phone, this time while it replayed Shaw's words: "Like the photo I sent? Open grave . . . Babikov and his lovely wife . . ."

Talanov's mouth fell open while Jingfei told Talanov about the spyware. She then fast-forwarded the recording to where Shaw bellowed, "This is *Angus Shaw*," then, after another quick fast-forward, "You've got one hour, Talanov, and that's it. One hour for you, those kids, and that Chinese bitch to get back on my plane or I kill your friends. That's Babikov, his wife, your girl-friend . . . and Wilcox. That's right, Wilcox dies, too, if you do not stop what you're doing and get back on my plane. One hour. Or all of them die."

"That's why I needed Shaw to identify himself and vocalize his threats," said Jingfei, returning the phone. "I needed Shaw to incriminate himself. Which we now have on tape."

"I didn't know spyware could do something like that."

"Mine can. Uploaded automatically to the cloud for all of posterity."

"And I know just what to do with it," Talanov replied, dialing a number.

Half a world away, Diane Gustaves was asleep in her upstairs Georgetown bedroom when her phone began vibrating on her bedside table. The blackout curtains were drawn and the room was in absolute darkness save for the glowing red numbers on a digital clock.

The repeated, intermittent vibrating finally awakened her and she leaned over and switched on a lamp, annoyed at having been yanked from one of the best sleeps she'd experienced in months. The wood of the bedside table amplified the vibration and made it sound like a woodpecker.

Gustaves picked up the phone and touched the answer button. "This had better be good," she said.

# CHAPTER 71

Zak loved the mountains. He had spent a lot of time in the mountains and loved everything about them. The fresh air. The changing seasons. The remoteness. The fragrances of early morning, before the sun had risen, while mists still hung in the air. Yes, he loved the mountains because the mountains had always represented freedom. They made him feel alive.

Except now. Now they were his prison, and they would be his final resting place.

Although Zak was at peace with God, which meant he was at peace with the idea of dying, he was not at peace with what these beagles would do to Emily and Ginie. When they had beaten him the first time, it had been for the video camera . . . for effect. Then they saw him praying and began beating him more savagely while mocking him about turning the other cheek. *"Where's your God now, Pilgrim?"* they would ask before punching him in the face or hammering their rifle butts into his stomach. Eventually they grew tired of his quiet acceptance and retired to the front of the SUV to eat energy bars and tell crude jokes about what they would do to the women.

Through swollen eyes, Zak could see the beagles had relaxed. Their assault rifles were standing at their sides and there was no expectation of trouble.

*If your enemy has a weakness,* he thought, *it is in the blind spot created by their weapons.* It was an axiom he and Talanov had used many times through the years. He just hoped it worked for him now.

While kneeling on the pile of rubble he'd dug from his grave, Zak had been discreetly but steadily sawing the strap of his zip-tie on the edge of a rock. The beagles had been careless in positioning them facing the SUV, where they could see their faces whenever they switched on the headlights. That carelessness would cost them, because it had enabled him to keep working the zip-tie without being noticed.

Zak felt the plastic snap.

With his wrists now free, Zak knew he needed a diversion, and Ginie would be a natural choice to help him create one. Fearless and smart, she had an instinct for spontaneously going with the rhythm of a situation. She also had a flair for the dramatic. Emily, on the other hand, would need everything spelled out for her, and even then he was not sure she could carry it off. Violence was abhorrent to her – as it was to most people, himself included – but Emily had the naiveté to believe it should never be employed. Which worked so long as someone else was willing to pay the price. Without doubt, Emily was fearless in a courtroom, especially where social injustice was concerned. This, however, was not a courtroom. This was an execution site in the mountains, where the victors would live and the losers would die.

The headlights of the SUV were off now although its parking lights were still on, which Zak knew afforded him a measure of protection, but not total. He still had to be careful with his movements.

Bowing his head, Zak breathed a silent prayer for help. He needed to speak with Ginie without the beagles overhearing him. He knew the beagles were planning to kill them.

*If now is my time to reap what I have sown, so be it,* Zak prayed. *But I ask you to help me stop these men.*

Moments later, a cool evening wind began blowing through the trees.

With the sound of the wind masquerading his voice, Zak leaned slowly to the side and whispered in Ginie's ear. It was important that Emily did not hear them, and it was doubtful that she would, being three feet on the other side of Ginie, her chin to her chest, sobbing, her long hair draped like curtains on each side of her face.

"Zak, no!" Ginie whispered back. "If something goes wrong, they will kill us."

"They will kill us, anyway," Zak replied. "This hole that I dug is our grave."

"They said they wouldn't hurt us."

"If that were true, then a grave would not be necessary. They are going to kill us, Ginie."

"I can't risk losing you. You're like the father I never had."

"And I love you like a daughter, which is why I will do anything to keep these men from violating you and Emily. But to do that, I need your help."

Ginie fought back tears. Fought the overwhelming urge to keep pleading with Zak. But she knew Zak was right. The hole in the earth behind them *was* their grave. "Okay," she whispered. "What do you need me to do?"

"This could hurt. Your head . . . your nose . . ."

"I'll be okay. What do I do?"

Zak told her and slowly straightened. Fifteen seconds later, Ginie began to cry, and before long, her wails grew louder.

"Shut up!" commanded Alpha from the front of the SUV.

"I'll try and calm her down," Zak called back, then turning to Ginie and saying in a loud voice, "Ginie, please, settle down. We're going to be okay."

"Settle down? They're going to kill us, Zak!"

"It's not us they want," said Zak. "They said they wouldn't hurt us."

Ginie's wails grew louder.

"I said, shut *up!*" Alpha shouted. He reached in through the open window of the SUV and switched on the headlights. They bathed the area in a wash of brilliance. Zak and Ginie both squinted and turned their heads. Emily, whose chin was still resting on her chest, hardly moved.

"I'm so sorry I got you into this," Zak said, his hands still behind him.

Ginie's wails diminished to intermittent sobs. "It's not your f-fault," sniffed Ginie, rivulets of tears now streaking her face. "But p-please don't tell me to settle down when you know what those monsters are planning to d-do."

"Our lives are in God's hands," said Zak, his head bowed, as if in prayer.

"And you actually *believe* that shit?" Alpha called out with a laugh.

"Zak is a good man," Ginie called back defiantly. "You pick on women. You tie them up and then beat them when they can't defend themselves. I really don't have words to describe the kind of cowards you are."

"Watch your mouth," snarled Alpha. He started toward Ginie but Bravo held him back.

"Ignore her," Bravo said.

"It's not me you need to worry about," said Ginie. "Our lives are in God's hands. Yours . . . I'm not so sure."

Alpha and Bravo both laughed.

"I take it you don't believe me," said Ginie.

"You got that right," Alpha replied.

"Yeah, well, you may not believe in gravity, either, but take a swan dive off a cliff and see what happens."

Alpha and Bravo both snorted their derision.

"Go on, give it a try, since you're such know-it-alls!"

"Don't antagonize them," said Emily, looking over at Ginie. "Don't make things worse than they are."

"Worse than they are? They're going to kill us, Emily. How much worse can it get?"

"You don't know that."

"Yes, I do. This hole in the ground behind us isn't a barbecue pit. It's where they're going to bury us."

Emily did not reply, and after a long moment of silence, Alpha switched off the headlights.

"Zak, I'm sorry about not supporting you more," said Ginie.

"It's okay," Zak replied. "If I'd been more proactive, you wouldn't have had to get all the grant money we needed to fix up the community center."

"Yeah, but I could have done more to help those kids. And I'm really sorry about that."

"I'm sorry I didn't encourage you more."

"For God's sake, *shut up!*" yelled Bravo. "Enough with all the confessions."

"I'm also sorry about those oranges," continued Zak. "I know you said you wanted them, but we just didn't have the money."

"I'm sorry, too," said Ginie. "I know I overreacted, but those kids needed oranges, even though Emily said they didn't."

"What are you talking about?" said Emily.

"Oranges," Ginie replied. "Two lousy crates. I don't know why you made such a big deal out of it. They would have cost, what, five bucks? Five dollars for two crates of oranges, but you had to go and raise a stink. Maybe it's the lawyer in you. I don't know. Maybe you don't like oranges. But you know what? This isn't just about you. Kids need oranges, although you probably think five dollars is way too much to spend."

"I have no idea what you're talking about," cried Emily.

"Yes, you do," Ginie replied. "You just can't admit it. Why do you have to turn everything into an argument?"

"I said, *shut up!*" yelled Alpha, switching on the headlights again.

"Quit arguing, Emily," said Zak, "or Ginie will do something impulsive and the guards will have to step in before one of you gets hurt. Just . . . quit arguing, okay?"

"I'm not the one arguing," yelled Emily defensively. "I'm not the one making up this nonsense about oranges."

"What have you got against oranges?" Ginie shouted back. "We were talking five dollars, Emily. *Five lousy dollars.* But you had to turn it into an argument, and now you're doing it again. Why is everything an argument with you? I am sick of it, do you hear me, sick of it!"

The high beams of the SUV were lighting up the area like a Friday night football field, with long shadows behind each of the three kneeling figures. Zak had his head turned away from the light, while Ginie was shouting at Emily, who was shouting back at Ginie.

Suddenly, with a scream, Ginie rammed her shoulder into Emily, and the two women slid down the embankment into the grave, one on top of the other, where they began screaming and kicking.

Alpha and Bravo moaned with irritation before walking over to separate the two women. Bravo had his assault rifle in hand but Alpha did not. He'd left it standing against the front bumper of the SUV.

Arriving at the open grave, Alpha jumped down into the pit and began separating the two women. Neither he nor Bravo were expecting any serious trouble because the hands of the women were zip-tied behind them.

Standing on the rim of the grave, Bravo was actually grinning at the sight of Alpha trying to wrestle the two screeching women apart. But they were rolling around and kicking, and separating them was proving difficult. If only he had his cell phone with him to record a video for future enjoyment.

Suddenly Alpha's phone started ringing from the hood of the SUV. At first Bravo did not hear it. But eventually he did and turned to go answer it.

And that's when Zak made his move.

# CHAPTER 72

Dressed in a green and blue track suit made of lightweight parachute material, Gustaves ran down the steps of her brownstone and out to a waiting black Suburban, whose rear passenger door was being held open by Grady. With her cell phone to her ear, Gustaves nodded her thanks before sliding into the back seat, where her new assistant, twenty-three-year-old Becka Ford, was waiting with a notepad and several manila folders. Becka was dressed in jeans and a jacket. On her head was an OU baseball cap.

After the call from Talanov, Gustaves had phoned Becka and told her to be ready in five minutes. Four minutes after that call, Becka was waiting at the curb for the two black Suburbans, which came roaring down the street. Both had emergency light bars concealed in their grillwork. Both light bars were flashing red and blue. Ten minutes later, the Suburbans picked up Gustaves and squealed off down the street.

Gustaves was speaking with the president, and the president was doing most of the talking. Was Gustaves absolutely sure the recording was legitimate? The president had asked the question a total of seven times, and each time Gustaves repeated her affirmative answer before reiterating her trust in Talanov and Wilcox. Even so, the president found it hard to believe that Angus Shaw, the Director of National Intelligence, was involved in something like this.

"Then please tell me how Shaw's net worth, since his appointment by the previous administration, had climbed from less than a million dollars to more than *forty* million." Gustaves paused briefly to let her words sink in, then continued. "Sir, I've known you for more than thirty years, and you and I both know a public servant does not make that kind of money in Washington unless favors are being sold. Obviously, I'm not in your shoes, so I don't know what kind of pressure is on you to keep him in that position, but I've been locking horns with Angus Shaw for nearly a decade. Don't get me wrong. A lot of that is to be expected. He's a Democrat and I'm a Republican. We lock horns for a living. However, I know for a fact that Shaw lied before Congress about spying on American citizens. I know for a fact that Shaw sells protection and quid pro quo to certain foreign nations willing to pay and play by his rules. I also know that Shaw personally ordered the assassination of Saya Lee, the young woman who tried to kill me at the Monocle."

*"What?"*

"Yes, sir, who we released from custody, ostensibly on a legal technicality in order to bait the people who hired her."

Gustaves then briefed him on the sting and how Federal agents, who were waiting in Saya's apartment, apprehended the assassin sent to kill her late one night.

"The assassin, of course, was more than happy to make a deal in exchange for his testimony on who had hired him, which was Shaw's chief-of-staff, Adam Schiller. Once we hauled him into custody, Schiller was happy to make the same kind of deal. Want to know who he said ordered him to set up the kill?"

"My God," was all the president could say.

"That's right, sir: Angus Shaw. That aside, right now we're in an emergency situation. Shaw will have Wilcox and the other hostages killed unless we take him into custody, and I mean tonight. Give me the authority to do that."

"You've got it, Diane, so long as you realize that you, personally, do not have the authority to arrest him. For that you'll need the FBI."

"Of course, Mr. President, and I took the liberty of arranging that. Don't worry, we'll handle this by the book."

"Give Shaw the respect his deserves."

"Of course, sir, even though you and I may define that differently."

After Gustaves clicked off, Becka showed her the screen of her notepad. "Here are the phone numbers you requested from Charlie, in descending order, with the relevant code-names, security questions, and responses."

"Thank you, Becka," said Gustaves, who dialed the first of the numbers.

"Does Charlie ever sleep?" Becka asked. "She sounded wide awake when I called, and she managed to get everything you asked in thirty minutes. I mean, some of this material is top secret. How does she do it?"

"Charlie is Charlie," Gustaves said with a smile, "although you may want to exercise caution around her with that base-ball cap."

"Ma'am?"

"OU . . . Oklahoma. Charlie and I are from Texas, although Charlie is a lot more rabid than I when it comes to football." Gustaves suddenly turned serious when the phone she had placed was answered half a world away, in Hong Kong, by Zulu, who was seated in the passenger seat of a van parked near the Gulfstream. Behind the wheel was Delta.

After identifying herself, Gustaves told Zulu to switch the phone to speaker, which Zulu did. A conversation then took place that lasted roughly thirty seconds. The call contained a series of questions and answers that were exchanged for secu-rity reasons. Gustaves then cited a special codeword that had just been sent to Zulu's encrypted phone from the office of the President of the United States. That codeword allowed Gus-taves to speak on behalf of the president.

"Do you recognize that codeword and the office from which it originated?" asked Gustaves.

"Yes, ma'am," Zulu replied.

"It's been assigned for purposes of this particular situation as it relates to the removal of Angus Shaw as the Director of National Intelligence. As such, I have been granted the au-thority to overturn any and all orders issued to you by Mr. Shaw, either directly or indirectly. I am also authorized to issue new orders, which you will be expected to carry out. Do you understand and accept what I am telling you?"

"Yes, ma'am."

"Is Mr. Wilcox in custody?" Gustaves then asked.

Zulu looked nervously over his shoulder at Wilcox, who was seated in the back of the van. The van was a commercial variety, which meant the entire space behind the front seat was empty and available for freight, which in this case was Wilcox, whose hands were cuffed to one of the metal struts, with a piece of duct tape covering his mouth. When Wilcox heard Gustaves ask the question, he smiled beneath the tape.

"Yes, ma'am," answered Zulu. "He's with us."

"Is he alive and unharmed?" asked Gustaves.

"Yes, ma'am."

"Is he being restrained against his will?"

Zulu did not reply.

"Is this Zulu or Delta I'm speaking with?" Gustaves asked in the absence of a reply.

"It's Zulu, ma'am," he replied, glancing uneasily at Delta.

"Well, Zulu, I have your entire profile right here, complete with military history, family history, bank records, phone records, credit card statements, gun registrations, martial arts training and ranks earned, educational history – my goodness, another Sooner from Oklahoma, with a three-point-nine GPA – plus photos of your gorgeous wife, Ashley, and your two adorable children. Rest assured, Major, I know everything about you, and your future at this moment, whether as a free man or an inmate of Leavenworth Federal Penitentiary, quite literally rests in my hands. So if Mr. Wilcox is not released within the next sixty seconds, and if he does not give me a glowing report about how wonderfully he's been treated, a court martial will be the least of your worries. Am I clear?"

"Yes, ma'am," he said, handing the phone to Delta, then quickly climbing over the seat back and hurriedly cutting Wilcox loose.

"Excellent. I'm going to hang up now and make another call.

When I phone again, Wilcox had better be the one who answers. Is that understood?"

"Yes, ma'am," Zulu called out just as the connection was terminated.

Gustaves closed Zulu's profile and opened the master list of phone numbers again. "God, how I love Charlie," she said to herself while the Suburban sped along a dark, curving rural highway. Behind them now were two more black Suburbans with flashing lights in their grills.

The second vehicle had joined them at the last intersection. Inside that vehicle was Ed Purdue, the newly appointed Director of the FBI, whom Gustaves had phoned earlier. Purdue was a retired Army lieutenant-general who was forced to retire by the previous president for challenging Angus Shaw's "naive and dangerous" sanitizing of intelligence reports coming out of Afghanistan and Iran, which Purdue knew to be false because on-the-ground intelligence reports said the exact opposite. So Purdue was not about to surrender this opportunity to place handcuffs on Angus Shaw.

After dialing the second number on Charlie's list, Gustaves put the phone to her ear and listened to it ring and ring.

"Where are you Alpha?" she said as the phone kept ringing and ringing.

# CHAPTER 73

At that very moment, two incidents were unfolding simultaneously. The first was in a clearing in the forested California foothills of the High Sierras. The other was in a Hong Kong restaurant called Vincenzo's.

In the forested California foothills, Zak had chosen his moment carefully. Thankfully, Ginie had taken his hint and created a scene, which hooked the involvement of the two beagles, and like dogs on the scent of a rabbit, the beagles had taken the bait.

Alpha had already hopped down into the grave to pull the two women apart. For him, it had been an amusing sight, watching the two women grunting and thrashing, unable to do any real damage because their hands were zip-tied behind them. But enough was enough.

The grave was roughly three feet deep, six feet long, and six feet wide. The SUV, with its headlights illuminating the area, was about twenty feet from the grave. Because they had been waiting for further orders from Shaw, Alpha and Bravo had laid their cell phones on the hood of the SUV, then stepped away to halt the wrestling match. Then Alpha's phone started ringing, which neither of the beagles heard, at least not initially. That's because there was so much enjoyable commotion happening down in the grave.

By now, Zak's knees were aching because he had been kneeling for so long. When he was twenty-five, he could kneel all day long. He wasn't twenty-five anymore and his knees were screaming with pain.

But Zak was accustomed to pain. He knew how to inflict it and he knew how to take it, as his mentor's words from his military training came back him. *Channel your pain. Let it empower you.*

And that's exactly what Zak did when Bravo turned toward the SUV.

Using his arms as counterweights, Zak rocked back onto his feet, which put him in a crouched position, and with two mighty steps, launched himself at Bravo in a flying tackle. Alpha saw Zak's sudden movement, but it was so unexpected, his brain did not have time to react before Zak landed on Bravo's back and dragged him to the ground.

Alpha grabbed for his sidearm but Ginie kicked him in the groin. But because Ginie was lying on her side, the kick was not powerful enough to do any serious damage. It was, however, accurate enough to drop Alpha to his knees. Ginie then began kicking Alpha in the stomach with both feet, her legs pumping furiously like a piston engine at full throttle. Fighting his way free, Alpha climbed out of the grave and paused on all fours to catch his breath.

Seeing Alpha pause on the rim of the grave, Ginie scooted her zip-tied hands down over her feet and up in front of her. She then scrambled to her feet, climbed out of the grave, and jumped on Alpha's back just as he once again reached for his sidearm.

*"Meurtrier!"* shouted Ginie in French, calling Alpha a murderer while circling her zip-tied hands around his neck.

Arching backward and falling onto his side, Alpha grabbed at the plastic strap cutting off his air.

"Emily, help me!" shouted Ginie while Alpha thrashed left and right, trying desperately to shake free.

Emily continued to stare absently down at the dirt.

While Alpha fought for his life, Bravo found himself trapped in a bear hug that had pinned his arms at his side. He tried a backward head butt, but Zak tucked his chin and the head butt missed.

Zak knew he could not defeat the beagle with a bear hug. The beagle was twenty years younger and twenty years stronger, which meant there was no way he could squeeze hard enough to defeat him, which in turn meant they would roll around on the ground until Zak grew tired and the beagle broke free. He needed to deliver a knockout blow, but in order to do that, he needed to first let go.

That moment was coming soon whether he liked it or not, because Zak could feel his arms weakening. He glanced over at Ginie, who had the other beagle in a chokehold. Sooner or later she, too, would grow tired. He had to act now.

Zak saw Bravo's assault rifle laying in the dirt four feet away, and Bravo was trying desperately to roll near it. So Zak log-rolled Bravo in the opposite direction. Over and over they tumbled, kicking up dirt until Bravo stuck out a leg and stopped them.

Bravo then did something Zak did not expect. He curled up in a fetal position, tightly, like a knot. But it was not a position of surrender. It was designed to break Zak's bear hug.

And it did.

Breaking free, Bravo hammered an elbow into Zak's face, then scrambled on all fours toward his assault rifle, twelve feet away.

Inside the grave, Emily blinked several times at all of the grunting and fighting. She heard Ginie screaming her name and looked up to see Zak and Ginie locked in battles with the two guards. An image came to her mind – of Ginie sliding her zip-tied hands down over her feet – and Emily instinctively did the same. With her hands now in front of her, Emily clambered up out of the grave just as Alpha head-butted Ginie in the face. When Ginie let go, Alpha climbed to his feet just as Emily ran over and punched him in the groin. When Alpha again fell to his knees with a moan, Emily repeated what she had seen Emily doing and looped her zip-tied hands around Alpha's neck and yanked back.

With her nose bleeding from Alpha's head-butt, Ginie struggled to her feet and wobbled unsteadily for a moment. In the harsh wash of the SUV's headlights, she could see a rifle laying on the ground, with Zak and Bravo fighting to reach it with a crawling, punching, tug of war.

Ginie ran over, picked up the rifle and jumped back, wondering what to do. She had never fired any kind of a weapon, much less an assault rifle.

Nearby, on the hood of the SUV, a cell phone kept ringing and ringing.

Ginie looked toward the phone just as Bravo elbowed Zak in the face, rolled free, and pushed himself to his feet. When Ginie saw Bravo charge toward her, she lifted the rifle and pulled the trigger.

*Click.*

Ginie looked down at the rifle in her hands. What was wrong? She tried pulling the trigger again.

Nothing.

Bravo arrived and punched Ginie in the face. Blood flew from her nose and she fell backward to the ground, leaving the rifle in Bravo's hands. Flipping the safety, Bravo spun to his right and fired a sweeping burst of gunfire at Zak, who was rushing him like an angry water buffalo.

Most of the fusillade missed.

Some of it did not.

And with a gargling gasp, Zak collapsed to his knees and toppled facedown into the dirt.

# CHAPTER 74

"Why isn't Alpha answering?" muttered Gustaves, ending the call. "Keep trying while I try Bravo," she instructed Becka while dialing Bravo's number, which was the third number on Becka's notepad screen.

"Yes, ma'am," Becka replied just as the motorcade of black Suburbans sped around a corner.

Using the Suburban's scrambler phone, Becka dialed Alpha again. Moments later, in a clearing in the California foothills of the high Sierra mountains, two cell phones began humming and vibrating on the hood of the SUV.

No one heard the vibrating hums amid all the noise. That's because Ginie was crying from having just had her nose broken again, while Emily was screaming with rage, and Bravo had just gunned down Zak.

Bravo could see Alpha struggling to break free. He was thrashing around on the ground and Babikov's wife was behind him with her zip-tied hands around his neck and her knee jammed in his back, pulling with all of her strength. Without a doubt, Alpha was stronger than Babikov's wife. But Babikov's wife had not only punched him in the groin, but had the additional advantage of position and adrenalin. Alpha was in fight-or-flight mode. Babikov's wife was in an I-will-kill-you-at-all-costs mode, with the added anguish of having just seen her husband gunned down powering her like a locomotive.

Having used all of his ammunition on Babikov, Bravo popped the empty magazine from his M4A1 assault rifle, which was an upgraded lighter-weight version of the M16A2. Capable of firing over nine hundred rounds per minute, the M4A1 could empty its thirty-round magazine in two seconds, which is what had just happened with Zak.

Bravo began fumbling for the spare magazine located in the pocket of his cargo pants.

Seeing Bravo having trouble with his rifle, Emily released her chokehold slightly. This allowed Alpha to yank forward in an attempt to throw Emily off his back. But rather than yanking back again, Emily allowed herself to be flipped. When she did, she looped her wrists up off his head, clenched her hands into fists, and began hammering Alpha in the nose. Blood burst from Alpha's nostrils and he grabbed his face.

And in one smooth motion, Emily unsnapped the strap on Alpha's holster and yanked out his pistol. Jumping to her feet, she took aim just as Bravo cocked his weapon and pulled the trigger, cutting Emily down where she stood.

With more echoes of gunfire echoing away into the night, Emily wobbled for a brief instant before collapsing like an imploded building.

"*No!*" screamed Ginie. She crawled over to Emily and began cradling her bleeding body.

Gasping for air, Alpha grabbed his pistol out of Emily's hand and staggered to Bravo's side just as Bravo took aim at Ginie.

"You okay?" asked Bravo.

Alpha nodded. "Get rid of the bitch."

Calling on every ounce of strength remaining in his body, Zak climbed awkwardly to his feet.

The sound of gunfire had snapped open Zak's eyelids and he had raised his head in time to see his wife fall to the earth in a hushed moment of silence. The shock, the horror, and the agony of seeing Emily gunned down filled Zak with uncontrollable rage. It was a rage he had vowed to leave behind when he asked God to forever change him from a man of violence to a man of peace, and over the years, he had been privileged to experience God's answer to that prayer at the Quiet Waters community center. Lives had been saved, a community had been revived, the poor had been fed. What a joy it had been.

But men of peace sometimes needed to become men of war, and now was one of those times.

*Give me strength this one last time,* Zak prayed.

Bravo did not see Zak coming. He was focused on Ginie, who was sitting in the dirt, sobbing, with Emily's head in her lap.

*Fish in a barrel,* thought Bravo just as Zak drove his shoulder into the small of Bravo's back, sending both of them sprawling to the ground.

The blow caused Bravo's spine to bend forward, which meant his upper body arched backward, which caused his aim to lift just as he pulled the trigger and sent a blast of gunfire singing harmlessly away into the night.

Alpha didn't see the incident. His back was to Bravo because he had stepped over to the SUV to see who was calling. But he did *hear* the incident when Bravo pulled the trigger, and, spinning around, he saw Zak and Bravo tumble into the open grave, where Zak reared up and began punching Bravo in the face. Tears were streaming down Zak's face and his chest was saturated with blood.

The first of Zak's blows caught Bravo by surprise. He had landed on his back and Zak had landed on top of him, where he began punching Bravo in the face. The first blow broke Bravo's nose in one direction. The second blow broke it in the other direction. But Zak was exhausted and weak, and Bravo quickly threw him off, grabbed his assault rifle, and fired.

"Bravo, don't!" shouted Alpha, running toward Bravo with the phone just as Bravo pulled the trigger for a quick burst before Alpha's shouting caused him to stop. And with the acrid odor of spent ammunition hanging in the air, he hopped up out of the grave.

"It's Congresswoman Gustaves, on behalf of the president," Alpha said, holding out the phone. "We're to release our prisoners immediately."

"Call Shaw. Ask him what's going on."

"I think you should take this call."

Bravo hesitated, then accepted the phone and put it to his ear. "Who is this?" he demanded.

From the back seat of her Suburban, Gustaves identified herself, then recited the same codeword she had used with Alpha and Zulu. She then asked him if he recognized that codeword. Bravo said that he did. Gustaves told Bravo that if her new orders were not obeyed to the letter, or if a call was placed to Angus Shaw, whose telephone lines were being monitored, Bravo would spend the rest of his life in prison. Was that clear? Bravo said that it was. Gustaves then asked for an update on the status of their prisoners.

Bravo took a deep breath and said, "Two dead, ma'am. One alive."

"Babikov?"

"Dead, along with his wife. The girl, Ginie Piat, is alive."

A long moment of silence ensued. Finally, Gustaves told Bravo to lay the bodies together in a secure location, covered and protected, along with his cell phone, which would guide a clean-up team to their exact location. She then ordered Bravo and Alpha to escort Ms. Piat to the Marine Corps Mountain Warfare Training Center south of Lake Tahoe.

"When you get there," said Gustaves, "ask for Major Patterson. Disobey or try and run, and things will get very nasty."

"Yes, ma'am. Understood."

After clicking off, Gustaves stared out the window of her Suburban. The headlights of the three speeding Suburbans illuminated the grass along each side the pavement, making the scenery appear as little more than a blur, although Gustaves was not paying attention. Her attention was on the tragic and pointless deaths of Babikov and his wife at the hands of Angus Shaw. She had never met Babikov, but had heard Talanov speak fondly of his oldest and dearest friend.

The loss of a best friend was up there with the loss of a spouse, which she knew all too well. She thought briefly of her husband, Master Sergeant Mike Gustaves, who died years ago in a firefight with the Taliban while trying to keep a girls school from being overrun. He had ordered his unit to get the girls to safety while he held off the enemy. His men came back for him, of course, but it was too late. One dead Marine. Nineteen dead Taliban. Twenty-three girls and two teachers, alive. Seven of the girls – all young women now – attended university in the United States, and not a week went by that one of them did not text or email to ask how she was doing.

The thought of Mike's sacrifice brought a tear to Gustaves' eye. It was an ache that never went away.

"We're here, ma'am," the driver said as the Suburban began to slow. Visible in the high beams ahead was a wall of shrubbery and trees. In a gap in that wall of green was a decorative wrought-iron gate.

Gustaves knew Shaw had his own team of security guards. They were housed in an annex at the far end of the garage. Two of the guards were always on active patrol, while a third guard slept, and a fourth guard watched over a bank of monitors connected to security cameras and other electronic sensors blanketing the grounds.

Becka entered an override code on her notepad that remotely opened the gates. Seconds later, the motorcade raced up the curving drive and stopped in front of Shaw's mansion. When they arrived, motion sensors were triggered and floodlights illuminated a wide verandah and soaring white Colonial columns.

The doors of the Suburbans flew open and more than a dozen heavily armed agents spilled out just as one of the security guards hurried out of the darkness with his gun drawn. When he saw the agents were FBI, he dropped his gun and raised his hands.

The agents commanded him to move away from the gun and lie face down in the grass, where he was quickly zip-tied and hoisted to his feet.

Purdue got out and used hand signals to direct half of his agents to secure the perimeter and confine all of Shaw's guards to the guard house. Taking the zip-tied guard with them, the agents disappeared into the darkness. Seconds later, confirmation of containment was received.

Stepping out of her vehicle, Gustaves joined Purdue at the bottom of the steps leading up to the verandah.

"Madam Congresswoman, the honor is yours," said Purdue, gesturing Gustaves toward the front door.

With a smile of satisfaction, Gustaves led the way up the steps to the front door, where she began ringing the bell.

Inside the house, Shaw cinched his bathrobe and descended the curving stairs. He had been awakened by the activated porch lights and presence of three government Suburbans parked outside with their light bars flashing. He had received no word of an emergency and wondered what was going on. Surely the president would have let him know if another midair collision had occurred. Whatever the reason, it was important, although the incessant ringing of the bell meant someone was going to get fired.

Approaching the door, Shaw punched several numbers on a keypad and opened the door. "What the hell do you think you're—" he began, then stopping when he saw Gustaves, Purdue, and four heavily armed agents staring back at him. "Diane? Ed? What's this about?"

"Honey?" Shaw's wife called out from the top of the stairs.

Shaw didn't answer or even look up at her. He was watching Gustaves work the screen of her cell phone. When Gustaves was finished, she held it up for Shaw to hear. On the screen was Shaw's photo of Zak, Ginie, and Emily kneeling before an open grave.

"Like the photo I sent?" the recording began. "Open grave . . . Babikov and his lovely wife . . ."

By the end of the recording, the color had drained from Shaw's face.

"I'm also here to inform you," Gustaves said, "that your chief-of-staff, Adam Schiller, has been taken into custody on charges of organizing the assassination attempt on me at the Monocle. Mr. Schiller, who himself recorded his conversations with you, has furnished proof that I think a jury will find very interesting at your trial, which, when taken in concert with what we just heard . . ."

Gustaves looked over at Purdue and nodded.

Purdue stepped forward with a pair of chrome handcuffs, took Shaw by the arm, and rotated him around. "Angus Shaw, you have the right to remain silent . . ."

# CHAPTER 75

The second unfolding incident involved Talanov, who was seated at a table in Vincenzo's Ristorante in Hong Kong. Wilcox had just called to say he had been released and that Shaw was now in custody. Talanov asked how Zak and the women were doing but Wilcox said he didn't know, that Gustaves told him she didn't have time to talk, although presumably they were okay. Wilcox then informed Talanov that the kids were safely with Alice and that his plan was being implemented.

*Here's hoping I can pull this off,* thought Talanov just as Sofia and Straw Sandal stormed in.

The Italian restaurant Talanov had picked was clean and contemporary, with lots of wood paneling and small tables covered with white tablecloths. To one side of the restaurant was a bar, with shelves of liquor bottles set against a mirrored wall. On the other side was a staircase that led to a second floor dining room. Beneath the staircase was a section of crisscrossed shelves filled with bottles of wine. At the rear of the restaurant was a door that led into the kitchen.

The restaurant was mostly empty, and Talanov was casually looking over a menu when Sofia and Straw Sandal strode over to him. Straw Sandal was holding her phone in front of her. On the screen was a blinking dot.

"I love Italian food, don't you?" Talanov asked rhetorically. "Olive oil and fresh herbs in a thick tomato sauce that's been cooking all night. Beats the hell out of watery noodles." He smiled up at Sofia, who was scanning the restaurant, her pistol held discreetly by her thigh. "I presume you're looking for the kids? They're smart, those two, so I thought it best to send them away since we did indeed find your money and they alone have the PIN."

Straw Sandal and Sofia exchanged glances.

"That's right," said Talanov in a friendly tone. "I found your money, but, like I said, the kids have the PIN. If that confuses you, allow me to explain. No PIN, no transfer, simple as that. For the record, the kids have instructions not to make that transfer until they know I'm safe."

Sofia aimed her pistol directly at Talanov's face just as a waiter came out of the kitchen, saw what was happening, and vanished back into the kitchen, where it suddenly grew quiet.

"I should probably remind you what Dragon Head said," Talanov remarked. "I give you the money. You give me Su Yin. And you leave us alone and unharmed. That was our deal." He moved his focus to Straw Sandal. "I presume we still have a deal?"

"No deal until we get our money," snapped Sofia.

"Which I am about to give you," Talanov replied. "But not until you lower that gun. Unless, of course, that famous *Shí bèi* code of honor is nothing but a lie."

By now, Sofia's hand was quivering with rage.

Straw Sandal placed her hand on Sofia's gun and lowered it. "Keep your word," Straw Sandal said curtly. "We keep ours."

Talanov smiled and stood. "Then it looks like everybody wins," he said, nodding respectfully at Straw Sandal, then looking coldly at Sofia. "Except you, perhaps. But we can always settle that later." To Straw Sandal: "See you in an hour, when I pick up Su Yin."

"Where is money?" Straw Sandal demanded.

"If I told you that, you wouldn't need me, now, would you? Don't worry. I'll make the transfer."

"Make transfer here."

"I don't think so. Once the transfer is complete, you'll get an email confirmation."

After dropping some cash on the table, Talanov left the restaurant.

With her breaths coming out as angry gusts, Sofia stormed after Talanov.

Straw Sandal caught her at the front door. "Let him go. We keep our word."

Sofia pushed past Straw Sandal and out the front door in time to see Talanov disappear around a corner. Running after him, she reached the corner just as Talanov climbed on the back of a motorcycle that had been waiting and raced away with an accelerating whine.

Sofia ran back to where Straw Sandal was waiting. "Do you still have him on GPS?"

"Yes," answered Straw Sandal, showing Sofia the blinking green dot.

Grabbing the phone, Sofia ran to her motor scooter parked near the entrance to the restaurant. Two boys were admiring it, but when they saw Sofia's pistol, they hurried away.

By now, Talanov was more than two blocks away. "They won't be far behind," he told Liena Zhang, the driver. A young officer with the CIB, Liena was dressed in black leather riding gear and a shiny black helmet.

"No worries," said Liena. "Hang on."

When Liena accelerated, Talanov tightened his grip on her waist. At the end of the block they banked right and took the corner, then banked left and took another corner before Liena opened the throttle up all the way, sending them forward like a bullet between cars that were speeding along the street.

"Does Alice know you drive like this?" yelled Talanov over the sound of the wind rushing past them.

"You should see the way *she* drives. And you had better not tell her I said that."

Within five minutes, Liena downshifted and paused briefly in front of a twenty-story apartment building.

Talanov jumped off and handed Liena his phone. "Thanks for helping me out."

"I'll take them on a wild tour of the city, then remove the battery and return the phone to Alice," Liena replied, slipping the phone in her pocket. And with that, she roared away.

Alice was already holding the door open for Talanov when

he arrived, and once he was inside, ran with him to the elevator, which Kai was holding open. Once they arrived on the third floor, Alice led the way down the corridor and into her apartment, where Jingfei was seated at a glass dining table, working at a laptop. Visible on the screen was a live image of Charlie, who was wearing an orange University of Texas beanie. The beanie was barely able to restrain Charlie's mane of thick raven hair.

The apartment was a two-bedroom contemporary unit that overlooked a park surrounded by more highrise apartments. A dining table was positioned near a sliding glass door that led out onto a small balcony, where Wilcox was talking on his cell phone. Along the railing of the balcony were some potted plants.

"Did you get the file I sent?" Charlie was asking just as Talanov entered the apartment and came into view. "Alex! Glad you're okay."

"Charlie, how are we looking?" asked Talanov, looking over Jingfei's shoulder.

"It's all there, right where you said."

"So you were able to do whatever it is you hackers do?"

"Yep. The deposit's been made, so we are ready to rock and roll. I was just asking Jing if she got the file I sent."

"Which I did," Jingfei replied.

"Then we're set to go," said Charlie. "Step one: take a screenshot of their escrow account page. It will verify the deposit. Step two: embed the file I sent you in that image and email it to them."

"That's it?" asked Jingfei.

"That's it. I will take care of the rest. Call me when you get to DC. We'll go out on the old man's dime."

"I heard that," shouted Wilcox from the balcony.

With a grin, Charlie clicked off.

"I trust what you're doing is legal?" asked Alice while watching Jingfei work the keyboard.

"Absolutely," Jingfei replied.

Alice frowned at her warily. "Are you telling me the truth?"

"Absolutely," Jingfei replied.

Alice looked over at Talanov. "Is she telling the truth?"

"Absolutely," Talanov said.

Alice looked suspiciously at Talanov while Jingfei continued to work the keyboard.

"Will someone please talk to me?" asked Alice.

"What do you want to know?" asked Talanov in return.

"How did you locate the money? The original account was yours – this I know – so you already knew the account number. But the account had been emptied of its funds, which you discovered had been placed in a secret account that no one knew about, which could be accessed only by an access code and PIN that no one knew about. How did you do it?"

"I guess we just got lucky."

"I don't think luck had anything to do with it. You and your *team,* as you now call them, came to the station, rummaged through a file box of evidence, then miraculously figured out what none of my people could figure out. I demand to know how you did it."

"Are you sure you want to know?"

Alice replied with an exasperated sigh.

"If I explain, you're not going to turn cop on us, are you?"

Alice folded her arms impatiently.

"Okay, okay," said Talanov. He looked at Kai and gave him a nod.

Kai arched his eyebrows in response. It was a gesture that asked, "Are you sure?"

Talanov nodded again, so Kai reached into his pocket and withdrew the tube of toothpaste that he had palmed from the box of Wu Chee Ming's belongings. He handed the tube to Talanov, who handed it to Alice.

"What is this?" asked Alice, examining the tube.

"Aside from it being the secret to whiter teeth, it was Wu Chee Ming's way of safeguarding his account number and PIN."

"So you *stole* this? From one of my evidence boxes?"

"Technically, it was Kai, so if someone's in trouble, blame him."

"You *told* me to steal it!" exclaimed Kai, punching Talanov on the arm.

Talanov recoiled and laughed.

"Enough, both of you!" cried Alice. "Tell me what this is."

"Am I in trouble?" asked Kai.

"No, you're not in trouble," Alice replied, glaring briefly at Talanov, then looking at Kai and gesturing with the toothpaste again. "But I need to know what this is."

"His PIN is in the barcode," explained Kai, "which Wu Chee Ming designed and then printed as a customized label."

"How did you know that?" asked Alice. "Lots of products have barcode labels."

"True, but of everything that Wu Chee Ming was carrying, that tube of toothpaste was the only item with a printed label. The other items, like the books and other toiletry items, had no added label. Those barcodes had been produced as part of those items."

Alice shook her head, partly in admiration of the teenager who had figured out what her people had missed, partly in frustration because a teenager had figured out what her people had missed. "I still don't see how you did it," she said. "Why did you suspect Wu Chee Ming when we were certain it was Ling Soo? The money disappeared right before Ling Soo committed suicide. He even wrote a suicide note confessing to the crime. How did you know?"

"Yeah," agreed Kai, looking at Talanov. "How *did* you figure that out?"

"Dinosaur technology," answered Talanov.

A blank stare was Kai's reply, while Alice's glare was more menacing.

Still working the keyboard, Jingfei chuckled and said, "Old school detective work. No way could Ling Soo have managed to hold onto a suicide note after writhing in agony. That meant the whole scenario had to have been staged, including a typewritten, not handwritten, note that had obviously been planted in his hand. That left one man with motive, opportunity, and access to all of that money."

"Wu Chee Ming," stated Alice.

"Not only that," added Talanov, "but Ling Soo was a slob, whereas Wu Chee Ming was the meticulous one. Plus, it was Wu Chee Ming, not Ling Soo, who was fond of saying one does not seek what one does not see. But I have to admit, I didn't realize the full impact of that proverb until I asked Kai where he would hide something important, like a PIN."

"And I said, in a place where no one was looking."

"Exactly. That's when I began to suspect Wu Chee Ming might be our culprit."

"So he was running off with the money when he got caught?" asked Alice.

"Yes, and rather than face Dragon Head's torture, threw himself in front of the train. Who knows, at one time he may even have been working with Dragon Head, but for whatever reason, decided to run off with the money."

"What I still don't get," said Jingfei, "is how you knew the money was in another Sun Cheng account. The PIN doesn't tell you that."

"Again, like Kai said, we needed to be looking where no one was looking."

"So he hid the money right under everyone's noses and got them looking in the wrong direction with that crazy maze of his?"

"Yes," answered Talanov. "And he made it so confusing and impenetrable that no one would be able to figure it out."

"And yet you did."

"Dinosaur technology," said Talanov with a grin.

"Stop saying that."

"You're the one who called me a dinosaur. But what *I* don't get is how Sun Cheng could have missed an account that huge. How could they not see one and a half billion dollars?"

"Because it was in a trapdoor account," explained Jingfei.

Talanov responded with a clueless expression.

"A digital safe deposit box."

"A what?"

"Digital safe deposit box. If I had a bunch of money inside a physical safe deposit box, that money would not show up on the bank's record of assets. Same with a digital safe deposit box, which is a separate account within an account. No one knows what's in that account, or even that it exists, because it's behind a digital trapdoor that's not publicly linked to the world of electronic banking. This makes it totally invisible, like a website on a dedicated server that is non-indexable by search engines and, therefore, invisible to everyone unless you know its specific address, or, in this case, an account number and a PIN. It's a complicated arrangement, but since Wu Chee Ming worked at Sun Cheng, he would have known how to set it up and conceal any record of its existence."

"O-kay . . . I think."

"So, are you ready to do this?"

Talanov looked over at Alice. "I am. Are you?"

Alice did not reply and Talanov could almost read her worries about the legality of what they were about to do.

"This gives all of us what we want," said Talanov, reading her indecision. "It saves Su Yin. It stops the hacking. No more planes go down."

Alice continued deliberating for several more seconds, then finally nodded.

A moment later, Jingfei tapped Send.

# CHAPTER 76

While Jingfei told Alice what would happen next, Kai drew Talanov aside. Wilcox was still on the balcony talking on the phone, although the slider was open.

"Are you really a secret agent?" asked Kai.

The question gave Talanov a start. "Where did that come from?" he asked with an amused smile.

"Bill said you were, like, this badass Russian spy for America back in olden days, and that he was the guy who recruited you, and that he taught you the ropes and turned you into this super-agent, and now you're going to be working for him in this new task force that he's heading up in DC."

"He told you that? That he taught me the ropes?"

"Yeah, and that is, like, *so* cool! He made me promise I wouldn't tell anyone because it was, like, you know, top secret."

Wilcox had been listening from the balcony, and when Talanov looked his way, replied with a sheepish smile.

"So, have you ever, like, killed anyone?" asked Kai, leaning close and lowering his voice.

"I'm thinking of doing so right now," said Talanov, his glare still on Wilcox, whose smile broadened into an exaggerated grin.

Kai laughed and punched Talanov on the arm. "For an old dude, you're not so bad."

"You're not so bad, either . . . for a kid," Talanov replied. "A kid I might have to strangle if he keeps calling me an old dude."

"But an old dude who rocks," Kai said, extending his fist.

And with a chuckle, Talanov bumped fists with Kai.

Across town, in the computer room of the Zhongzhen Martial Arts Academy, AK motioned his three visitors to chairs.

Two were young men and the third was a young woman, all Chinese and in their early twenties.

"AK, this here is Krait," the young woman told AK, nodding to the first young man, who was chewing gum, "and this here is Z-Qi," she said, introducing the other. "Guys, meet AK. The one and only."

"Dude, you're a legend," said Z-Qi in English.

Krait sniffed indifferently at the remark "Your stuff is shit, you know that, don't you?" he remarked while surveying the room. "If you expect us to hack anything more than a Gameboy with this junk . . ."

The pong of an email drew AK's attention and he looked at the monitor dedicated to the handling of the escrow account. Because the escrow account was such a priority, AK had been instructed to sit by the monitor until the deposit had been made and verification had been sent.

AK opened the email, then the attached screenshot image of the escrow account's online banking page, which showed a deposit of just under one and a half billion U.S. dollars.

"Wait in gym," AK told the others after switching off his monitor.

"I thought we were here for an interview," Krait replied. "To build an army of hackers for some secret project you couldn't tell us about."

"You are," AK replied, motioning them toward the door. "I call you when I am ready."

With a snort, Krait stood and left the room, followed by the others, then AK, who ran past them with a lanky stride into the gym, where Sofia was practicing roundhouse kicks on one of the *muk yan jongs*.

While he was gone, his monitor's built-in camera was activated, which was noticeable when its tiny LED, no larger than a pinhead, came on briefly before being switched off by Charlie. Twenty seconds later, AK re-entered the computer room with Sofia, in whose hand was a silenced pistol.

AK slid into his chair and switched on his monitor, and with

Sofia looking over his shoulder, pointed to the verified deposit that had just been made into the escrow account. Sofia smiled and left the room without saying a word. Slouching back in his chair with a contented sigh, AK popped open a can of milk tea and took several long swallows.

In her cubicle at the Naval Intelligence facility, Charlie took a bite from an organic apple while watching AK on her computer screen. "Did you know commercially grown apples are sprayed more than thirty times?" Charlie asked rhetorically. "That's why people today get so sick and that's why I buy organic, not that creeps like you care about people getting sick, because you are sick in the worst way possible. You kill people in airplane crashes without so much as batting an eye." Charlie took another bite, her anger rising. "So let's see what you do with *this.*"

Charlie worked her mouse and took a screenshot of AK's face, which she forwarded to Zulu, who was sitting in his van a block from the Zhongzhen Martial Arts Academy. In the seat beside him was Delta. Zulu heard his cell phone ding and read the message from Charlie.

"This is our man," said Zulu, showing Delta the image.

"Funny how things change," Delta replied, opening an energy bar. "A few hours ago we were hunting Talanov. Now we're on his side."

Inside the stairwell leading up to the penthouse, Sofia paused to make a call. The walls of the stairwell were covered with silk wallpaper that featured a bamboo motif. The steps themselves were made of polished mahogany, and at the top was a landing featuring a shiny black credenza, which had brass hinges and white lotus flowers. To the right of the credenza was a large red door. Black metal straps with heavy carriage bolts gave it an impenetrable appearance. On the wall beside the door was a lighted keypad.

Sofia had just begun to dial the number when she heard a noise at the bottom of the stairs. She turned to see Chao. The door was normally locked but Sofia had left it ajar.

Putting a finger to her lips, Sofia motioned for Chao to join her. Chao closed the door while Sofia finished dialing and put the phone to her ear.

On the second ring, her call was answered by Talanov.

"Come and get her . . . alone," Sofia replied. She clicked off, then led the way up to the landing, where she entered a code on the lighted keypad and the red door clicked open.

Chao withdrew a pistol from where it had been tucked near the small of his back just as Sofia pushed open the door and gestured Chao to enter.

"He's all yours," Sofia said.

# CHAPTER 77

At the bottom of the stairs Sofia paused to dial another number. It was answered on the first ring by Penny Kwan, at the Sun Cheng Financial Group Limited. Penny had a desk near Song's office, and hers was one of sixteen desks that filled the main floor of the operations hub, which was humming with the noise of a busy office. Phones were buzzing politely over the cacophony of brokers buying and selling, mostly in Chinese, but a few in English.

"The money's in escrow," Sofia said.

Penny hung up the phone. The moment had come. All she had to do now was hack that account and transfer the funds into Sofia's offshore account.

The plan had been Sofia's brainchild and the reasons were obvious. First, Sofia wanted the money for herself. Second, she wanted to take possession of it *before* Talanov picked up the girl. Dragon Head had foolishly given his word that he would release the girl and that no harm would come to any of them. Penny snorted. Dragon Head and his code of honor. Sofia, of course, had no such morals.

To his credit, Talanov had been crafty to use the funds as a bargaining chip, and it had almost worked. Sofia, however, was always one step ahead.

With her fingers working the keyboard, Penny instinctively glanced around to make sure no one was watching. She had already made several practice runs hacking the account, and on each practice run, she had come and gone without anyone knowing. Thankfully, Straw Sandal had handled the opening of the escrow account, which had been set up with minimum security, as if she were buying a house. Obviously, she had not been savvy enough to order extra security protocols, nor had Talanov been savvy enough to demand them. His only interest had been the safety of the girl. To him, the money was unimportant. *What a fool.*

As on each of her practice runs, Penny easily bypassed the firewalls and accessed the escrow account. But when she tried making the transfer, her keyboard froze and the webpage began to dissolve. Penny hit the Escape button repeatedly and tried every emergency measure she knew. But the webpage kept slowly dissolving until she was looking at a bright blue screen.

Penny was stunned and all she could do was stare at the screen. What had just happened? Had she inadvertently caused a crash? *Had she inadvertently just signed her own death warrant?*

Grabbing her handbag, Penny hurried to the elevator, where she pushed the call button repeatedly. She had to get out of here. Where she would go, she had no idea. She just knew she had to run.

A ding sounded and Penny readied herself to step into the elevator and disappear forever from the Sun Cheng office. She had been wise enough to stash a supply of cash at home for emergencies, and this qualified as an emergency. But when the doors opened, Penny was met by Alice Ti and three uniformed officers.

Startled, Penny stepped back.

"Going somewhere?" asked Alice, who nodded to one of the officers, who took Penny into custody.

The operation center grew quiet and everyone turned to watch.

"Ms. Kwan, let's take a ride," said Alice, gesturing toward the elevator.

Back at the Zhongzhen Martial Arts Academy, AK finished his milk tea and tossed the can into the trashcan near his feet. It slid off the other cans already filling the receptacle and landed on the floor, where it rolled to a stop.

AK was about to wheel his chair over to the refrigerator for another when his monitors winked black for several seconds before rebooting with live-feed images of himself. Leaning forward with a frown, AK stared back and forth at all of his monitors, unable to figure out what had just happened. Why was he seeing himself?

Finally, it hit him: his monitor camera had been switched on. But by whom? Had he been hacked?

AK began furiously entering commands but nothing happened. He wheeled over to another keyboard and attempted the same thing. When that failed, he wheeled to yet another keyboard and tried accessing the system from there. Again, nothing.

During the next ten minutes, AK entered every imaginable command that he knew while repeatedly hitting the ESC key, trying desperately to escape. Nothing worked. Exhausted, he finally slouched back and stared at the multiple images of himself on all of his screens.

"Hello, Bogdan Kalashnik," said Charlie's voice. "Aka AK," she remarked, then laughed. "How funny is that? Aka AK. Hilarious."

AK looked around. The voice was coming from everywhere, which meant someone had taken control of his entire surround-sound system. A second later, Charlie's smiling face appeared on all of his monitors.

"I'm Charlie," the smiling face said, "and as you can see, you've been locked out of your system. That was necessary in order for me to copy all of your files, including your external hard drive, before deleting them from your system. Hacking is *so* treacherous these days, don't you think, especially when you're about to get blamed for the *very* nasty virus I placed in your system, which, when you think about it, is really Dragon Head's system, so I doubt your boss will be pleased. With that in mind, I'm going to make you this one-time offer, unless, of course, you prefer a slow painful death at the hand of Dragon Head. If it were up to me, and I'm not a violent person, I would let him go for it, because you deserve something like that for what you did to those innocent passengers and their grieving families. But it's not up to me. I'm merely the messenger. And the message is this: get out of your chair right now and leave by the side door. Once outside, you will look for a black van that's parked nearby and get into it." Charlie leaned forward with a hardened expression. "Take my word for it, you son of a bitch, there is no escape. Now, what's it going to be? My offer? Or whatever Dragon Head decides to do with you? You've got ten seconds to give me an answer."

AK took only four. Ten seconds after that, he rushed past the old guard sitting in front of Su Yin's room.

The old guard watched AK hurry down the corridor and disappear out of sight.

At the bottom of the stairs, AK was about to push open the door when it was pulled open by another of his hacker recruits, a young woman who went by her avatar name of Jiàntóu, which meant "arrow." Dressed in jeans and a T-shirt, she had a leather satchel slung over her shoulder.

"AK?" Jiàntóu asked in English, surprised to see him. "I thought we had —"

"I am going outside," AK cut in. "Need sun. Wait in gym." He pushed past her and disappeared.

Jiàntóu watched the door ease closed, and with a shrug, continued inside and climbed the stairs.

Outside, AK was barely able to see because of the blinding sunlight. He spent most of his time in a darkened computer room, so stepping out into the daylight made him squint and recoil. Attempting to shield his face, he nearly ran into an old couple. They scolded him sharply and AK fumbled past them, looking in both directions for the black van Charlie said would be waiting.

Across the street to his right he saw it, parked in front of a repair shop. The roller door of the repair shop was open and several old men were servicing bicycles that had been mounted on racks.

AK dashed across the street and approached the van from the rear. In the outside mirror, he could see someone behind the wheel. The driver looked to be a man and AK could see the man watching him.

One car away from the van, AK stopped. Should he turn and run? If he could just make it to Shenzhen . . .

Who was he trying to fool? And after a steadying breath, he continued forward. When he drew near to the van, the side door slid open.

Alice was the first to step out, then Wilcox, who was still in his Hawaiian shirt, then two uniformed officers. When Alice held up her badge, AK held out his wrists. One of the officers snapped on handcuffs and placed AK inside the van.

"As promised," Wilcox told Alice. "The hacker who brought down those planes."

"And the software he used to accomplish this?"

Wilcox smiled but said nothing.

"I can force you to surrender it," said Alice.

Wilcox continued to smile but said nothing.

With a shake of her head, Alice stepped inside the van and sat down opposite AK. "We are looking for a young girl who is being held against her will. Where is she?"

AK said nothing.

"It will go easier if you cooperate," said Alice.

AK said nothing.

Alice nodded and her officers removed AK from the van and escorted him to an unmarked squad car half a block away. In the back seat of that car was a handcuffed Penny Kwan.

"Smart move, placing Kalashnik and Kwan in the same car," said Wilcox as he and Alice stepped onto the sidewalk. "Whoever talks first gets the deal."

"Now, about the second part of your plan," said Alice. "My men and I will wait in front of the academy to assist. However, I must remind you that we still have no proof that Su Yin is even there, which is why I cannot raid the premises. Mr. Kalashnik gave us no cause."

"Understood," Wilcox replied. "Alex is on his way and will negotiate her release."

"Assuming Alex is successful and does not get himself killed, then I will escort all of you to your Gulfstream so that you can go home."

"Including my men? The ones driving this van?"

"They weren't always your men," Alice replied. "Prior to the call from Congresswoman Gustaves, they were your enemy."

"True, but that has changed."

"I'm inclined to lock them up. Do you know how much havoc these men have caused? They killed people, Bill."

"They killed Dragon Head's men, who were trying to kill us."

"It was a *gunfight*. In a neighborhood bazaar. I have no doubt they would have killed you, too, if Congresswoman Gustaves had not intervened."

"And we will deal with them. Look, we can go back and forth about who gets to punish whom and miss the greater victory that we should all be enjoying. No innocent bystanders were killed. The violence and the hacking have stopped. You and your department will get all the credit for stopping a major threat to the national security of both our nations."

"Boy, do you know how to rub it on thick."

"It's true, Alice. I came to you, and you helped arrange all of this. Yes, I was involved, and so were Alex and the kids, but I mean it when I say you were the catalyst. Please, accept the fact that we worked together to stop further catastrophes from happening. I promise, these men will be dealt with."

Alice deliberated for what seemed like forever, chewing on her lip, wrestling with indecision.

"All right," she finally said. "In the interest of cooperation and our longstanding friendship, I will release your men into your custody. I know they are part of your military, which means they will no doubt avoid prosecution, but you need to appreciate what I am doing here, Bill, and the bullet these men have dodged. I do not use the metaphor lightly."

"I know," said Wilcox somberly. "God willing, we're nearing the end."

"Will Dragon Head honor his word?"

"Alex thinks that he will. However, the real problem isn't Dragon Head. It's Sofia and her vow to kill Alex. She feels that he betrayed her."

"How so?"

"Years ago, they were partners in the KGB. She fell in love. He didn't. She tried to kill him. He shot first."

"And now she wants revenge?"

Wilcox nodded. "And she won't rest until she gets it. Let's hope Dragon Head keeps her in line."

# CHAPTER 78

Upstairs in the penthouse, Chao screwed a silencer onto the barrel of his pistol. He was in a small foyer inside the front door and could hear the distant hissing of a shower. Soon, this would all be his. He would finally have his revenge.

He held no illusions about Xin Li, or Sofia, or whoever she was. She was a ruthless opportunist whose loyalties were to whomever was in power. At this very moment, it was Dragon Head. That was about to change.

Chao took a moment to appreciate the luxury of the penthouse. Straight ahead was the living room. It was a large room, with gossamer curtains and large windows that overlooked the stunning Hong Kong skyline. Chao remembered the derelict building that used to stand outside those windows. Rusting fire escapes. Rattling air conditioners. Lowlife residents. He himself had put in an offer to purchase the building, but Dragon Head found out and bought it for himself, or, technically, for Sofia, who wanted the building demolished in order to improve her view of the skyline. Hundreds of residents had been displaced, but Sofia got what she wanted, which he, Chao, would now inherit.

The furniture was likewise to his taste, so no change would be needed there. The wall on the right was covered with textured cream fabric. Mounted on the wall were some framed drawings of Chinese women, with demure poses, delicate features, and small blushes of red on their lips. Beneath these was a long white sofa. The ceiling had beams of polished hardwood, while the wall on the left was of reflective tile on which was mounted a large flat screen television. Below the flat screen was an ornately carved credenza. A throw rug added accents of color.

He wished he had the time to stroll through the lavishly

furnished kitchen. If he knew Dragon Head, it would be equipped it with every conceivable appliance and gadget, not that he or Sofia ever cooked.

Moving quietly toward the bedroom while the shower continued to hiss, Chao peeked around the corner and saw the bedroom to be empty, although Dragon Head had already laid his clothes out on the king-size bed he shared with Sofia. Crossing the carpeted floor, he peeked into the bathroom. It had a tile floor and two polished sinks with stainless steel fixtures. On a rack near a window was a folded towel. To his left was a walk-in shower with a long wall of frosted glass. Steam could be seen rising above the top of the wall.

Holding his pistol in a braced, two-handed position, Chao positioned himself in front of the frosted glass wall and fired a rapid burst. The glass shattered into a thousand pieces. Chao stared in shock at the empty stall and the hissing spray of hot water.

"Your ambitions betray you," said a voice from behind. "Do you think I did not know?"

Chao whirled around to see Dragon Head pointing a pistol directly at him. It, too, was fitted with a silencer that almost doubled the length of its barrel. The bare-chested Dragon Head was dressed in boxer shorts that accented his rippled abdominal muscles and sculpted, tattooed arms. Chao was dressed in baggy slacks and a large black shirt that accommodated his belly.

"And your ego betrays you," Chao replied with a sneer. "The great Dexter Moran."

Dragon Head responded with a quizzical frown.

"Who do you think unlocked the door?"

The remark stunned Dragon Head for the brief instant needed for Chao to front kick Dragon Head's pistol upward at the same moment he raised his own gun and fired. The bullet punched through Dragon Head's chest and sprayed blood on the wall behind. Dragon Head tried to comprehend what had just happened but the circuitry in his brain flickered for a confusing moment before he collapsed to the floor, where he twitched several times before sighing a final time.

*The empire is mine,* Chao thought with a smile.

Downstairs, Sofia charged along the corridor with her pistol in hand. Ahead, on his wooden stool, was the old guard. He had his ear cocked toward the door and was smiling at the singing he could hear.

"Bring out the girl," Sofia commanded, stopping near the old guard.

When he stood, the old guard looked warily at Sofia's gun.

"Hurry up!" Sofia barked.

The old guard unlocked the door and stepped inside. Su Yin was seated on the floor in the far corner of the room. Her knees were drawn up to her chest, and when she saw the old guard, she smiled. She then saw Sofia pacing back and forth outside the door and instinctively drew herself into a tighter knot. The old guard smiled and motioned for Su Yin to stand. Su Yin looked again at Sofia pacing back and forth in the corridor. The old guard motioned again and Su Yin finally stood, and at his coaxing, walked tentatively to him.

With a reassuring hand on her shoulder, the old guard led Su Yin into the corridor, but when Sofia reached for Su Yin, the old guard stopped her. "No harm must come to the girl," he said.

"The girl is not your concern."

The old guard glanced down at Su Yin , who was staring up at him with frightened eyes.

"Stand aside," Sofia said.

The old guard looked back at Sofia and did not move.

"*Stand aside,*" commanded Sofia.

The old guard still did not move.

Sofia and the old guard locked eyes. Sofia was a full head taller and she stepped up to the old guard and drew her face to within inches of his. "I said, stand aside," she commanded a third and final time, jamming her pistol into his stomach.

The old guard bowed, and when he did, Sofia instinctively

retracted the gun only to see the old guard spin away in a smooth pirouette that was as graceful as it was shocking when he blocked her pistol to the side, and with his following hand, landed a lightning punch into Sofia's face, which knocked her backward into the wall. Sofia tried to fire, but the old guard grabbed her wrist, wrenched it to the side, slid under her arm and spun in a full circle, twisting the gun away.

"*Păo!*" the old guard yelled, telling Su Yin to run.

Su Yin ran toward the end of the corridor.

Sofia gabbed the old guard's arm and yanked it around her, pulling the old guard with her and tilting him off balance. Planting her foot, Sofia hammered a knee up into the old guard's ribs, and with a gasp, he fell to his knees. Sofia then punched him in the face, grabbed her gun, then stepped back and shot him three times.

The sound of a door slamming echoed toward Sofia, and with a curse, she hopped over the old guard's body and ran after Su Yin.

# CHAPTER 79

The red and white taxi stopped in front of the Zhongzhen Martial Arts Academy, and after paying the driver, Talanov got out to see Wilcox, Alice, and six uniformed officers waiting for him on the sidewalk. Forming a protective wall in front of the entrance were Straw Sandal and a small army of *Shí bèi* fighters. The policemen with Alice were in flexible body armor and carried semi-automatic rifles. The barefooted *Shí bèi* fighters were in loose-fitting karate clothing.

"The hacker, Bogdan Kalashnik, is now in custody," said Alice, "so there isn't much time. Once Kalashnik's apprehension is discovered, or that we have stopped Penny Kwan from hacking the escrow account, your life may be in danger."

"Then I guess we'd better hurry," said Talanov, and with a wave of his hand, he led the detail toward the entrance.

Straw Sandal and the *Shí bèi* fighters came forward to meet them.

"How do we do this?" asked Talanov once he was face to face with Straw Sandal.

"You come. Others stay," Straw Sandal replied. "When you release money, I release girl."

"Other way around," Talanov replied. "Once Su Yin is safely with me, I send a code to the escrow company and they release my hold over the funds. That was our deal, and the funds are already in escrow. I sent you a confirmation and our records show that email was opened."

Straw Sandal replied with a look of concern.

"Don't tell me you didn't know," said Talanov. "I did warn you about Sofia, so if she's pulling something, don't blame me. I kept my end of the bargain. Release the girl."

Straw Sandal's eyes flashed briefly, after which she nodded for Talanov to follow.

Inside the academy, Chao opened the stairwell door and peeked out. The gym was empty except for some young people sitting along the far wall, working their phones. After quietly closing the door, he looked in the kitchen. Where had everyone gone? More importantly, where had Sofia gone? She was supposed to meet him here with the girl. The girl, he knew, was being held in a storage room. *Maybe she's with her now,* he thought, hurrying along the corridor toward the storage room.

When he turned the corner, he froze at what he saw.

Lying in a pool of blood was the old guard. With his pistol still in hand, Chao knelt beside the body and felt for a pulse. The old guard was dead. Standing, Chao looked into the storage room. No girl. He then saw bloody footprints leading along the corridor toward the exit.

It was easy to see what had happened. Sofia had come for the girl but the old guard had put up a fight, which allowed the girl to escape before Sofia shot him and ran after the girl.

Chao started to go after Sofia, then hurried into the computer room to see if the funds were in escrow.

The computer room was typically dark, like a cave, except for vertical rectangles of light in the center of each of the monitors. The room also smelled stale and sour, like a boy's bedroom that hadn't been cleaned. AK may be a genius but AK was a slob. That would have to change.

Walking over to the worktable, Chao switched on a lamp. When he did, AK's monitors lit up with the same image on each of the screens. Chao leaned forward and stared at the images.

*These monitors are a live feed . . . of me.*

In her cubicle in the Naval Intelligence building, Charlie sat forward when she saw the face of a man she did not recognize. She then saw the gun in his hand. "What have we here?" she said to herself, and was about to take a screenshot of the man when the lights in the room came on.

And what Charlie saw next made her smile.

When the lights came on, Chao turned to see Talanov and Straw Sandal standing in the doorway. Talanov was not armed although Straw Sandal was, and Straw Sandal's pistol was aimed straight at his chest.

"Old guard, did you kill him?" asked Straw Sandal in English, obviously for Talanov's benefit while the *Shí bèi* fighters entered the room and fanned out on each side of Talanov and Straw Sandal.

"It wasn't me," Chao replied, laying his gun carefully on the table and holding up his hands. "He was already dead when I found him."

"And girl?"

"Gone. It looks like she escaped and Sofia went after her."

"If Sofia harms her," Talanov said quietly to Straw Sandal.

"Go," Straw Sandal said.

Talanov ran from the room just as another *Shí bèi* fighter arrived and whispered in Straw Sandal's ear. Chao and Charlie both watched Straw Sandal's face morph from disbelief to an angry glare directed at Chao. She stepped forward and pointed her gun at Chao's face.

"Your pistol, has it been fired?" Straw Sandal asked in Chinese.

Charlie activated a program that translated the conversation into English.

"I don't know what you mean," Chao replied.

"It's a simple question, Chao. Has your weapon been fired? Shall we go ask my father?"

Chao stiffened.

"We cannot ask him, can we?" Straw Sandal continued. "Because he is dead on his bathroom floor. I wonder whose bullets we will find in his body."

Chao and Straw Sandal locked eyes, neither one blinking until Chao finally lowered his head with a sigh.

Such a response can mean two things. It can indicate capitulation and surrender. But it can also be a gesture designed to masquerade a preemptive blow. In Chao's case, Straw Sandal knew which it was, and she was ready when Chao unexpectedly ducked right and grabbed for his gun.

In her monitor, Charlie saw Straw Sandal's pistol kick smartly. Saw the spent cartridges tumble through the air. Saw Chao jerk like he'd been shocked by high voltage before collapsing to the floor.

"Holy shit," Charlie whispered, sitting back, stunned. She grabbed her phone and dialed Wilcox. "Where are you?" she asked once Wilcox answered.

Wilcox told her.

"So you're in the middle of this?"

"In the middle of what?"

"So you're not in the middle of it?"

"In the middle of *what?*"

"The attempted coup. Dragon Head's dead and so is his rival, some guy named Chao. Straw Sandal just shot him and I saw the whole thing."

*"What?* How do you know this and I don't?"

"That's what I'd like to know. I thought you'd be right behind Alex."

"Where's Alex?"

"He ran after Sofia, who's chasing Su Yin, who apparently escaped."

"How did she manage that?"

"Why don't you know any of this? You're not just standing around outside, are you?"

"We were waiting for Talanov! He went inside to make the trade. To get Su Yin."

"They're gone – both of them – along with Sofia, who's no doubt trying to kill her."

"Where did they go?"

"I don't know, Bill, I'm not there. But you are and you've got to find them. Before Sofia kills them!"

"What about the money?" asked Wilcox.

*"Go!"* shouted Charlie. "I'll finish things up from my end."

Straw Sandal was standing over Chao's body when the monitors on AK's worktable suddenly began flashing and buzzing. She stepped over to the worktable, her eyes darting back and forth, wondering what was happening and what she should do. She yelled for AK but none of the *Shí bèi* fighters knew where he was. Straw Sandal reached for a keyboard, then withdrew, not knowing what to do while the buzzing grew louder and the flashing grew more intense.

"Does anybody know what to do?" Straw Sandal screamed in Chinese, with Charlie's translation program giving her an instantaneous translation.

Within seconds, Jiàntóu ran into the room.

"Who are you?" shouted Straw Sandal.

"One of AK's recruits."

"Where is he?" demanded Straw Sandal.

"I passed him in the corridor twenty minutes ago. He said he needed some sun."

"AK *hates* the sun!" shouted Straw Sandal, kicking AK's chair and sending it across the floor.

Jiàntóu recoiled at the outburst and turned to leave.

"Can you fix this?" Straw Sandal demanded while pointing at the flashing monitors.

"I do not know," Jiàntóu replied.

Straw Sandal commanded her to try, so Jiàntóu rolled AK's chair over to the worktable and began entering commands, while large red letters flashed VIRUS WARNING on each of the screens.

In her cubicle in the Naval Intelligence building, Charlie saw the young woman furiously entering commands on AK's keyboard. "Time to turn up the volume," she said with a mischievous smile, her fingers flying across her keyboard. Seconds later, she tapped Enter, which triggered an electronic siren on AK's sound system. It was an escalating siren, beginning low and climbing to an ear-piercing crescendo before repeating itself again and again.

"Do something!" shouted Straw Sandal while the *Shí bèi* fighters watched.

Jiàntóu was trying, and wanting to state the obvious, that there was nothing anyone could do, but knew better than to infuriate Straw Sandal more than she already was.

Charlie watched Straw Sandal pacing angrily back and forth behind the young woman, her hands over her ears while the siren blared.

Finally, exhausted, Jiàntóu slumped back in her chair.

"Why are you stopping?" Straw Sandal shouted.

"I'm locked out. Nothing works."

"How could this have happened? *Where is our money?*"

Jiàntóu shrugged and shook her head.

And with an angry scream, Straw Sandal stormed out of the room.

In her cubicle in the Naval Intelligence building, a smiling Charlie took another bite of her apple.

# CHAPTER 80

Su Yin had no idea where she was running. She just knew she had to keep running and not let the tall woman catch her.

She had seen the tall woman run out the door after her. That meant the old guard was now dead. She remembered the tall woman shooting people back at the pizza parlor. Never had she seen such a cold and cruel look in anyone's eyes.

The sidewalk where she was running was clogged with people, which was good in one way but bad in another. It was good because she was only half as tall as everyone else, which meant the tall woman wouldn't be able to see her very easily. But it was also bad, because so many people meant she couldn't run very fast, and if she tried running in the street, she'd get hit by a bicycle or a car. She needed a place to hide.

Su Yin ran past a store called the East-West Market, and when she did, she saw that it was full of people. Doing a quick U-turn, she ran into the store, which was not only full of people, it was filled with tables full of merchandise.

Two main aisles stretched the length of the store. On the outside of each aisle were shelves and racks crammed with clothing and colorful goods. In the center, between the aisles, were wide wooden tables stacked with more goods. At regular intervals were crossovers connecting the aisles.

Su Yin threaded her way along one aisle, ducking and weaving and sidling between shoppers examining jewelry, clothing, handbags, herbal remedies, and dishes.

Suddenly, she heard people screaming behind her. Looking back, she could see the tall woman pushing shoppers out of her way. Many were falling to the floor. Others were stumbling into shelves and spilling cans and clothing onto the floor.

Su Yin ran around a cluster of women examining placemats.

The tall woman pushed through them and sent hundreds of placemats flying in all directions. Pans and dishes crashed to the floor.

Dropping down onto all fours, Su Yin crawled under one of the center tables. With a diving slide, Sofia reached under the table and caught Su Yin by the ankle. Su Yin kicked Sofia in the face and broke free. Screaming curses, Sofia crawled after Su Yin, who was small enough to move between the legs and over the struts to the other aisle. Sofia was unable to fit through the same tight spaces and backed her way out.

Sofia and Su Yin jumped to their feet at roughly the same time. Su Yin was in the other main aisle, and Sofia saw her run toward the front door. Sofia did the same, paralleling Su Yin but unable to see her because of the high shelves full of merchandise. Sofia shouted for everyone to get out of her way and people moved aside, giving her a clear path. But when she reached the front door, Su Yin was nowhere to be found. Sofia looked outside. No Su Yin. She looked down the second aisle. No Su Yin. She then looked back down the first aisle. Halfway to the end of the store, she saw Su Yin dash across the aisle into an open corridor.

The little monster had doubled back!

Using her pistol to wave people out of the way, Sofia raced along the aisle to the corridor where Su Yin had disappeared, which was a walk-through into a neighboring department store, which was densely packed with racks of clothes and glass cases filled with cosmetics. Punctuating these displays were small stages featuring sleek mannequins dressed in the latest fashion. Above were banners portraying chic models in designer labels. Aisles zigzagged all over the place, with the front entry of the store like an airport duty-free zone of brightly lit fragrance counters. In the center of the floor was an escalator leading to the floors above.

Sofia cursed to herself. *Where was that wretched girl?*

Crouching while she ran, Su Yin threaded her way among the racks of clothing toward the front door, which was a soaring opening with overhead banners and floodlights. She made a point of avoiding the larger aisles, but wherever she ran, people were pausing to stare. What was wrong? Why were they looking at her?

Near a circular rack of jeans, Su Yin saw herself in a mirror. Her arm was bleeding.

"Are you all right?" an old woman asked, handing her a tissue.

Su Yin took the tissue and hurried on.

With her pistol held discreetly at her side, Sofia stood on her tiptoes and scanned the busy store. A normal kid would be running for the door. But this kid was not normal. She was clever, and she had already doubled back on her once.

To her right was a small platform. On the platform were two fashionably dressed mannequins. Sofia stepped up on the platform, which gave her another twelve inches of elevation. She looked left. No kid there. She looked straight ahead, toward the escalator. No kid there. She looked right and saw an old woman staring . . . at a small girl moving among the racks.

*Got you*, Sofia thought just as Talanov entered the East-West Market, where a small crowd of spectators had gathered inside the door. Beyond, he could see merchandise littering the aisles and people climbing slowly to their feet.

"What happened?" asked Talanov, hoping someone spoke English.

"Tall woman chasing girl, hurt people, cause much trouble," answered a college student with long black hair. She was dressed in frayed jeans and had been texting her friends about the incident.

"Where did she go?" asked Talanov.

"There," the student replied, pointing down the aisle and to the right.

# CHAPTER 81

Su Yin saw the tall woman jump off the platform and start running toward her. Dashing between several racks of glittery T-shirts, Su Yin pushed past a group of shoppers and out the front door, where she turned left and began running as fast as her legs would take her, wishing – praying – she could somehow get away from the tall woman.

Ahead, an old woman had just placed her bicycle in a rack. Su Yin ran up to the old woman, grabbed her bicycle and raced away. Waving her hands, the old woman shouted after her.

Sofia backhanded a passing cyclist with her pistol. The young man fell and skidded off his bicycle. Sofia jumped on the bicycle and raced after Su Yin.

The lane was full of cyclists coming and going in both directions, sometimes two abreast, which made the bicycle lane a moving obstacle course. The only clear riding area was in the dangerous narrow strip of space between the clogged bicycle lane and the lanes of moving traffic. It was dangerous there, but Su Yin knew it would allow her to faster.

But it would also allow the tall woman to go faster, and because the tall woman was faster and stronger, sooner or later she would catch up.

But faster and stronger did not always win the race, at least not in BMX.

Increasing her speed to that of the traffic, Su Yin slid between two cars, then cut between two other cars to the median, which was a low barricade made of concrete, where she sprang upward with her legs and jumped the median. Landing at full speed to the honking horns of oncoming traffic, Su Yin hit the brakes, skidded her rear tire a quarter turn to the left, then began pedaling again on the inside lane, near the median. When she reached full speed, she merged between two moving cars, then through two others to the other side of the street, where she began pedaling furiously.

Su Yin glanced back and saw the tall woman scream. She couldn't hear what she said because of traffic noise, but she saw the tall woman pound a fist on her handlebars before cutting out into traffic.

What to do? The tall woman would eventually make it to the other side of the street and come after her. Whipping down a side street was certainly an option. She could then look for other side streets to turn down. But she was also growing tired, and her legs were burning, and side streets were always less busy. What she needed was another place to hide.

Talanov was running along the sidewalk when he saw Su Yin racing in the opposite direction across the street. He yelled and waved his hands frantically, but Su Yin didn't see him. He then saw Sofia racing after her.

Increasing his speed to a sprint, Talanov did what Su Yin had just done by cutting between the moving lanes of traffic and leaping the median barrier, where he held up his hands as cars skidded and honked and finally slowed long enough for him to sprint to the other sidewalk, where he began running after Su Yin and Sofia. He, too, was winded, but he could not let Sofia catch Su Yin, not without giving it all he had.

A block ahead was an intersection, where cross traffic had the right of way. Reaching the intersection, Su Yin turned right, then made a quick left through a gap in the oncoming cross-street traffic into the lane of bicycle traffic coming toward her. Cyclists dinged their bells and shouted, while Su Yin weaved back and forth, avoiding head-on collisions with the river of cyclists coming toward her. She sped past an open arcade of boutique shops, then flipped around in a skidding turn and raced into the arcade. When she did, she saw the tall woman crossing the intersection behind her.

Dinging her bell as a warning, Su Yin zigzagged from one side of the arcade to the other, avoiding people, benches, and planters filled with palm trees and flowers. She raced past an escalator, then more planters and benches until she shot out the other end of the arcade onto the sidewalk, where she hit her brakes, looked both ways, then pedaled across the street toward an electronics store. And while she could not understand the name of the store, which was in Chinese, she recognized many of the logos. In the store's front windows were displays of laptops, cell phones, game consoles, cameras, and flat screens of all sizes. Ditching her bike, Su Yin ran into the store.

The entire length of the store was dotted with display cases and counters. To her right was an escalator leading up to a mezzanine dedicated to video games. It was filled with teenagers trying out the latest consoles to the sounds of roaring monsters and electronic machine gun fire.

Running past the display cases, Su Yin headed toward the glass door at the other end of the store, where she could see cars and pedestrians moving past in both directions. When she reached the door, she pushed it open and turned right, then flattened herself against the wall to catch her breath. After a few seconds, she peeked around the corner in time to see the tall woman stride into the store and pause, her angry eyes sweeping left and right.

Still panting, Su Yin ducked out of sight. Now where? She had seconds at most until the tall woman came outside.

Across the street was a grassy park, and beyond this, a construction site where a new highrise apartment building was going up. Separated from the park by a chain link fence, the building was the newest in a complex of highrise apartments being erected along the edge of the waterfront. Beyond the building was an offshore elevated expressway that ran parallel with the north shore of Hong Kong island.

In its present state, the newest apartment building was little more than a skeleton of thick concrete wafers on giant pylons. The upper floors had metal scaffolding supporting the floors above. The lower floors were full of building materials and pallets of supplies. On the barren earth in front of the site were forklifts and piles of debris. Towering overhead was a giant crane, which was silent, its boom extending out over the top of the construction site toward the harbor.

Feeling a burst of hope, Su Yin ran across the street to the park, which was crisscrossed with sidewalks and dotted with trees. There were people in the park. Some were holding hands. Others had paused to look up at the new building. Others were focused on their cell phones. A few were walking their dogs.

To Su Yin's left was an occupied highrise apartment building, which faced the water. To her right was a similar building. Even if she could reach one of those buildings, the doors would no doubt be locked. But even if someone tried helping her, the tall woman would simply shoot them as she had shot those people at the pizza parlor. The construction site was her only chance.

Su Yin ran up to the gate of the chain link fence surrounding the site. It was locked. Workers were gone for the day and the building site was empty.

Sitting on the ground with her feet braced against a metal post, Su Yin tried prying the gate open at the bottom in order to squeeze through. It wouldn't budge.

Glancing over her shoulder, Su Yin saw the tall woman running across the street toward her. Jumping up, she grabbed the fence and looked up, wondering if she could climb it. It was too high and she was too tired. She looked both ways for some kind of an opening. To her right was a damaged section of fence that had been repaired with large sheets of plywood. Graffiti had been spray-painted on the panels.

Su Yin ran alongside them, looking for an opening. Nothing. Ahead was another gate.

When Su Yin reached the gate, she saw that it was padlocked with a heavy chain. She started to run on but stopped when something caught her eye. Like the other gate, the frame of this gate was made of galvanized pipe. Unlike the other gate, the bottom corner of this gate was bent and a small flap of fencing had come loose.

With her heart pounding, Su Yin sat on the ground as she had before, braced her feet, and pulled at the flap.

By now, people in the park had stopped to look. A little girl had been running frantically beside the fence, looking for a way to get into the construction site. Now she was pulling at the fence. What was going on? Who was that woman chasing her? Was that a *gun*?

Su Yin fitted her head and shoulders through the opening, then used her feet to try to push through. But the sharp ends of the wire had snagged the pink cloth of her leggings. She pulled and yanked, but her legs were caught. She was trapped.

Exhausted and panting, Su Yin collapsed back onto her elbows, wanting to cry but knowing she couldn't. She looked up. The tall woman was almost upon her. She saw the tall woman's enraged eyes. Saw the tall woman's bared teeth. Saw the tall woman raise her pistol.

An old man with wispy white hair shouted something. Sofia paused and shouted back at him, and when she did, her sharp voice jolted Su Yin, who began pushing and twisting until she finally pulled free.

And jumping to her feet, Su Yin began running for her life.

# CHAPTER 82

A winded Talanov ran out of the arcade and saw two bicycles laying on the sidewalk in front of an electronics store. Traffic was intense, so he paused at the curb and waited until there was a break so that he could dash across.

He had seen Su Yin and Sofia ride into the arcade, and now, judging by the two bicycles on the sidewalk, Su Yin had run into the electronics store and Sofia had run in after her.

Entering the store, Talanov paused to calculate probabilities. Where would Su Yin go? To his right was an escalator that led up to a mezzanine. One way up. One way down. Su Yin would not go there. She would run straight ahead, toward the other door at the far end of the store. With shoppers pausing to stare, Talanov ran the length of the store and out the other door onto the sidewalk, where he paused and looked both ways. What would Su Yin do next? Would she go into another store? There were many from which to choose, but calculation and probability told him she would try something different since she had not been able to ditch Sofia in stores thus far. She may not be consciously thinking that way, but her instincts would guide her that way.

Across the street was a highrise construction site. The chain link fence fronting the site was too tall for Su Yin to climb. In fact, it was too tall for most people to climb, save teenagers like Kai and Jingfei. Instinct would tell Su Yin to run for that fence. To find a gap in the fence where Sofia could not go, assuming, of course, that such a gap existed, and assuming further that Sofia had not already caught her.

Calculation and probability. Right now, it was all he had.

Across the street, Su Yin paused to catch her breath in the damp stairwell between the second and third floors of the new highrise. The walls of the stairwell were raw concrete, and the steps were littered with nails and debris. Wind was blowing up the shaft, and it was cool.

The tall woman would be here soon, and Su Yin was not sure how much longer she could keep going. She didn't know why she had chosen the stairwell. It was just something she felt she should do, because remaining on the ground floor meant she would have to keep running until she found a way out, and she was tired of running. At least up here, among the equipment, pallets, stacks of lumber and other supplies, she could find a place to hide and rest.

Su Yin looked down at her leg. It was bleeding from where the fence had cut her. The bleeding had mostly stopped but it still hurt.

She wondered if Alex would be able to find her. He had said he would come for her, but that was at the academy, and now she was here, in a construction site a long way from the academy. She knew Alex would never desert her, but how could he keep his promise when he didn't know where she was?

Su Yin climbed another switchback flight of steps and emerged on the third floor. Apart from the concrete walls of the stairwell and the elevator shafts, the third floor was a vast open space. There were no exterior walls. Just unimpeded views in all directions.

The floor was full of construction supplies. There were stacks of lightweight ceiling tiles and piles of steel "jack posts," which had been used to reinforce the concrete floors above while the concrete hardened and cured. There were piles of studs, both wood and metal, which would be used to construct interior walls. There were pallets of paint in forty liter metal cans, which had been shrink-wrapped together. Other pallets contained bundles of insulation, sacks of plaster, mortar, and boxes of electrical supplies. Nearby were numerous large spools that contained miles of electrical cable. In the middle of the floor were piles of pallets in jumbled disarray. Suspended from the underside of the ceiling were dozens of plastic sheets. The sheets had been fastened to lightweight metal channels that would eventually hold acoustic ceiling panels.

While the sheets of plastic flapped in the wind, Su Yin ran from pallet to pallet, looking for a place to hide.

One floor below, Sofia stepped out of the concrete stairwell and listened. She could hear no footsteps, which meant the girl had found a place to hide. She had seen her run into the stairwell, so that meant she was somewhere on one of these upper floors. The question is, which one?

Outside, Talanov ran alongside the fence, looking for a way to get into the construction site. To his right, he noticed an old man with wispy white hair. Dressed in a white tank top and baggy black slacks, he had been practicing tai chi. Running up to the man, Talanov said he was looking for a little girl. The old man didn't understand what Talanov was saying but did understand his hand gestures about a little girl of a certain height. Talanov then made a hugging gesture that let the old man know she was dear to him.

The old man motioned for Talanov to follow and led him to the padlocked gate, where he pointed at the bent flap of fence.

Talanov knelt and saw a bloody piece of pink fabric caught on the bottom of the fence.

*Su Yin had entered here.*

# CHAPTER 83

The old man grabbed the fence flap and pulled it back, then made a gesture for Talanov to scoot through, which Talanov did. The old man told Talanov to hurry and pointed in the direction of the new highrise apartment building. Talanov replied with an appreciative smile and ran toward the building.

When Talanov entered the cavernous first floor, the temperature dropped immediately, and the damp air smelled of seaweed and fish.

Running to the far side of the building, Talanov looked over a temporary fence of orange mesh. The seawall on which the highrise was being constructed fell away into the sloshing brown water of Victoria Harbor. Multiple signs fastened to the mesh warned of deep water in both English and Chinese. In the near distance was the elevated expressway and Talanov could hear the whoosh of traffic. Across the harbor was the densely packed skyline of Kowloon.

Talanov looked both ways for any signs of Sofia or Su Yin. Nothing. He ran back to the center of the floor and looked around. What would Su Yin do? The cavernous space of the ground floor was nearly three stories high. The ceiling, also of concrete, was supported by dozens of huge columns that supported more than a dozen other floors. There would be stacks of supplies on those floors. Su Yin would be tired and scared. She would want a place to hide. Calculation and probability told him Su Yin was up there somewhere.

*And so was Sofia.*

Up on the third floor, with her knees drawn up to her chest, Su Yin sat huddled beneath a lean-to of pallets piled against one of the walls of an elevator shaft. After crawling into the cavity, she had scooted two boxes in behind her, one on top of the other. Sitting in the darkness, she thought of Zak and how he had taught her to pray whenever she was afraid. She was afraid now, but what should she say? She wished Zak was here with her right now, because if he was, he would know what to say.

Leading with her gun, Sofia emerged from the third floor stairwell and paused to listen. The only sound was of the wind flapping plastic.

She crept toward a pallet of shrink-wrapped cans of paint, but with so much debris on the floor – nails, cans, scraps of metal – making noise was unavoidable. But the wind was also making noise, so it was unlikely the girl would hear her.

Sofia looked behind the pallet. Nothing. She then moved to the large spools of wire and checked behind them. Nothing. She crept ahead, her eyes and ears peeled, looking and listening for any sign of the girl. Ideally, she would like to shoot her in front of Talanov and make him suffer the anguish of watching her die. But Talanov was not here, so she would have to let the media feature gruesome photos of the girl's body on television. Talanov would still see what had happened, and still suffer, and forever live with the knowledge that he had been unable to save Babikov's kid.

If Talanov had a vulnerability, it was Babikov. The two were close, like brothers, so making Babikov suffer would make Talanov suffer, and making Talanov suffer was almost as important as seizing control of Dragon Head's empire, which included Talanov's old KGB bank account.

Still leading with her gun, Sofia turned toward the elevator shafts, which had been designed in pairs of two, facing each other. There were no elevators yet in the shafts, nor were there any doors. Just gaping openings fenced off with waist-high orange mesh. The perfect place to hide? The girl was resourceful, so hiding in one of them, as dangerous as it would be, was a distinct possibility.

Sofia glanced down into the first shaft. Nothing. She then did the same with the other three. Again, nothing.

Moving left, Sofia saw more pallets of supplies. Some were

shrink-wrapped and some were banded together with metal straps. Beyond these pallets, at the other end of the floor, was another stairwell. Had the girl—

A sharp crash snapped Sofia's head to the right.

Su Yin gasped when one of the boxes she was trying to scoot closer fell over and burst open with metal brackets. She could see the shiny metal brackets scattered all over the floor. The tall woman would know where she was.

Sofia circled quickly around the sheets of flapping plastic and paused. She could see an overturned box of metal brackets next to a pile of pallets. The pallets were leaning against the back wall of an elevator shaft. Was the girl hiding between those pallets and the wall? By the sound of it, the girl had knocked over that box of brackets. Had she then scrambled out of her hiding place and hidden somewhere else? It was hard to tell because the flapping sheets obscured a clear view of the rest of the floor.

Creeping over to the pallets, Sofia peeked inside the cavity. It was empty.

Backing away from the pallets, Sofia turned a full circle. The girl had been here, she was sure of it. Where was she now?

"You can come out now," Sofia called out, then pausing to listen.

Nothing.

"Talanov is not a nice man," Sofia continued, ducking beneath a sheet of flapping plastic and looking behind a pallet of boxes.

Nothing.

"I want to help you. Hong Kong is a dangerous place. Come out. I'll take you to safety."

An empty can clanged in the direction of the other stairwell and Sofia ran between several sheets of flapping plastic. She paused at the sight of a can rolling slowly across the floor. The girl must have accidentally kicked it while running for the other stairwell.

Sofia sprinted to the other stairwell, then suddenly stopped.

*The little monster had already doubled back on me in the store. Was she doing the same thing again? Had she rolled the can across the floor as a diversion?*

Sofia thought about that for a moment. Judging by the girl's behavior, it made sense.

Doubling back by circling wide around the perimeter of the room, Sofia ran past numerous spools of wire, pallets of shrink-wrapped paint cans, and bundles of ceiling panels. She then made a quiet approach toward Su Yin's original hiding place along the backside of the elevator shaft.

And there the girl was, crouching behind the pallets, her back to Sofia, looking and waiting.

Sofia smiled and raised her pistol.

# CHAPTER 84

Su Yin cautiously stepped from behind the pile of pallets. She had seen the tall woman run in the direction of the far stairwell, then lost sight of her behind the sheets of flapping plastic. She just hoped the tall woman was heading upstairs or downstairs by now.

"Looking for someone?" asked Sofia.

Su Yin jerked around and gasped at the sight of the tall woman and her gun.

Sofia smiled at the horrified look of shock on Su Yin's face that slowly became what appeared to be a wide-eyed . . . smile? Why would the girl be—

Talanov's roar reached Sofia's ear a full second before his shoulder met her lower back with the force of a locomotive. The blow arched Sofia's back and lifted her arm just as she fired.

The bullet hit the ceiling and spit chips of concrete down on Su Yin.

"Run!" Talanov shouted while driving Sofia across the floor into a pallet of ceiling tiles, where they crashed to the floor, causing Sofia's pistol to bounce free.

Frightened but unwilling to leave, But Su Yin remained standing where she was.

Sofia hammered a knee at Talanov's head but he rolled away. Sofia sprang on top of Talanov him and began smashing him in the face. Talanov grabbed Sofia around the waist and log-rolled away with her, where they began a close-quarters punching contest on the dirty concrete floor, inches from one another, growling, grunting, thrashing, trying desperately to land a disabling blow.

Talanov suddenly broke free, kicked his legs up over his head and sprang to his feet just as Sofia scrambled to her feet.

Talanov flew toward her with a leaping front kick that Sofia blocked to the side before launching a fierce counterattack, which Talanov blocked. Back and forth they fought, advancing then retreating, the gun between them on the floor, neither one able to grab it.

"Run!" Talanov shouted again, but again Su Yin refused.

"I won't leave you!" Su Yin cried.

"You've got to!" shouted Talanov. And when he pointed to the stairwell, Sofia drove a roundhouse kick into his side.

Talanov heard his ribs crack and fell to his knees, doubled over with pain, unable to breathe.

When he fell, Sofia sprang for the gun.

The sight of Sofia lunging toward the pistol triggered an automatic reflex in Talanov that overrode the pain he was feeling. There was no time to think, no time to breathe, no time to do anything but keep Sofia from reaching that pistol.

Exploding to his feet, Talanov made a desperate dive for the pistol. He missed but slid into Sofia's ankles, felling her like a tree. Sofia rolled quickly onto all fours and lunged again for the gun. Talanov grabbed her by an ankle and began dragging her away from the pistol.

Sofia kicked Talanov in the head, rolled on top of him again and began punching him in the face with one fist then another, back and forth, again and again. Blood was flying everywhere.

With shaking hands and tears in her eyes, Su Yin grabbed the gun and pulled the trigger. The bullet hit the stairwell wall and spit chips of concrete onto Sofia.

Sofia jerked back to see a frightened Su Yin holding the pistol in her two quivering hands. With an angry curse, she jumped to her feet just as Su Yin ran beneath a sheet of flapping plastic. Sofia batted the plastic away and chased Su Yin around a pallet of floor tiles. When Su Yin turned and tried aiming again, Sofia grabbed her hand and wrenched the pistol away. Su Yin screamed and began punching Sofia, who used the pistol to backhand Su Yin to the floor.

Panting with hatred, Sofia straddled Su Yin and took aim at the crying little girl.

"I've had enough of you!" yelled Sofia.

Like a runaway dump truck, Talanov charged into Sofia, again causing her shot to miss. With an angry scream, Sofia began smashing her pistol against the back of Talanov's neck. But Talanov's head was tucked beneath her arm while he powered them forward through one sheet of plastic after another until they hurtled off the edge of the floor, where they flailed apart while plummeting downward three stories into the sloshing brown water of the harbor.

Talanov and Sofia hit separately with huge splashes. Sofia landed on her side and Talanov on his bottom, bent at the waist, legs in the air.

Su Yin ran to the edge and looked down at the water, which slowly subsided until Talanov finally thrashed to the surface, gasping and coughing. With a scream, she ran to the stairwell and down the steps to the ground floor, where she raced to the water's edge just as Talanov paddled awkwardly to the wall, wincing and gasping and clawing for some kind of handhold.

But there was nothing to grab . . . no handholds, no ladder, no anything to keep him from going under from exhaustion and pain.

Looking desperately around, Su Yin saw a loose board, ran over and grabbed it, then ran back to the top of the wall and extended it down to Talanov, begging him to take it.

Talanov tried, but Su Yin could not hold on and the board slipped from her hands. When the board hit Talanov in the head, he went under again. Screaming and crying, Su Yin prepared to jump into the water.

Kind hands pulled her away from the edge.

"*Zài zhèlǐ!*" the old man with wispy white hair shouted to Jingfei and Kai, who were running toward him. Police officers had cut the chain on the gate with bolt cutters and the kids had sprinted past them. Farther behind were Wilcox and

Alice, with other officers following, along with an ambulance and three police cars.

While Jingfei and Kai hugged Su Yin, the old man extended another board down into the water for Talanov, who thrashed to the surface and grabbed on until police officers arrived to pull him up out of the water and lay him gently on the concrete.

Talanov kept looking out into the brown water of the harbor, searching for Sofia. But there was no sign of her anywhere. No body. No one swimming. Nothing.

Su Yin broke away and ran over to Talanov. "13:5," she sobbed, hugging him tightly.

Talanov winced at Su Yin hugging his cracked ribs but he held her close. "13:5," he whispered hoarsely just as a medical team arrived.

When he was being lifted onto a gurney, Talanov looked out into the water a final time.

Sofia was nowhere to be seen.

# CHAPTER 85

The next few days flew by in a blur. Talanov was admitted and released from a Hong Kong hospital with three cracked ribs, a broken nose, and some lacerations and abrasions. He was told he would heal just fine. Su Yin was also admitted and released. She had lost several pounds but was told she would recover quickly. Gustaves phoned Wilcox to say Charlie had dissected AK's virus and been working with the appropriate agencies to make sure nothing like this would ever happen again, especially since the Chinese would no doubt pressure AK to reveal his hacking secrets.

Gustaves then broke the tragic news about deaths of Zak and Emily. She relayed how she had tried to get through to Shaw's men and countermand the termination orders, but the phones kept ringing until it was too late. A clean-up crew was sent to the site, but when they arrived, they found no bodies, and what had once been an open grave had been filled in. Gustaves ordered the grave reopened, but when it was, it was found to be empty. The explanation given was that wires had gotten crossed and another clean-up crew had arrived first and removed the bodies. Her suspicions: the anonymous powers of the Deep State did not want their agents prosecuted and had stepped in to remove the evidence.

Wilcox asked Gustaves whether or not charges would be filed against Shaw's men. Gustaves said she was looking into that, which Wilcox knew was code for, "I doubt it." He then asked about Ginie, and Gustaves said she was a remarkable woman who was understandably grieved over the deaths of Zak and Emily, but had the discipline and clarity to describe in detail what had happened.

That night in their hotel room, Wilcox gathered everyone together and made the announcement. As expected, the kids reacted differently. Jingfei stormed out of the room, Su Yin cried, and Kai didn't make a sound, but simply fell onto the couch and curled up to stare bitterly at the floor.

The next day, Wilcox concluded his business with Alice, who escorted them to the airport and saw them safely off as promised. When the kids all hugged her, Alice was touched. She was not affectionate, as Americans so often were, but found the warmth of these children especially beneficial at this particular time. It had been a time of great strain and uncertainty between China and the United States, and she hoped this burst of affection was an indicator of what was ahead.

As for Sofia, police divers searched the waters around the construction site for three days but came up empty. The currents of Victoria Harbor had obviously carried her body away.

As for the money, the escrow account was inexplicably empty. Where the funds had gone, no one knew. That's because Charlie's virus, which she had emailed to AK, had obliterated the money trail. Apparently, her virus struck after the account had been emptied but before the destination account could be identified, so it would take years before the maze of offshore accounts could be untangled and finally searched.

After they arrived home, the next week also flew by in a blur. There were debriefings, medical exams, meetings and more meetings, and more meetings on top of those. On Friday, Wilcox arrived at the Rayburn Office Building, where Gustaves had her office. Wilcox saw Talanov, Ginie, and the kids waiting for him at the top of the steps, near the elevated entrance, and after climbing out of the taxi with his phone to his ear, he paused on the sidewalk and waved that he would join them momentarily, then turned away to finish his call.

"Where are you now?" Wilcox asked.

"Leaving airport," Larisa replied, walking with her roller suitcase toward a line of taxi cabs. Her long blonde hair had been pulled back in a ponytail and she was wearing a short summer dress, denim vest, and cowboy boots.

"We're going into our meeting with Congresswoman Gustaves," Wilcox said, "so wait across the street on the Capitol grounds. There are some benches beneath the trees. I'll come and find you."

"Does Alex know I am coming?"

Wilcox did not reply.

"He does not know I am here, does he?" asked Larisa.

Wilcox did not reply.

"You invite me to come from Australia, and you buy me a ticket – which is very nice of you – but you do not tell him that I am coming? This puts me in a very difficult position."

"I know him. He wants to see you."

"How do you know that? He sent me away, to *Australia*, to other side of planet. I know he thinks he did it for my protection, but he never returns my calls, or my emails, or my texts. Is that the behavior of someone who wants to see me?"

"Don't worry, I know him. He will."

"You lied to me, Bill. I should get back on airplane and go home."

"Please be there, okay? Sorry, I've got to go." And without waiting for Larisa to reply, he ended the call.

Inside Gustaves' outer office, Becka was working at her desk when Gustaves opened her door and said, "Amber, will you – "

Gustaves stopped mid-sentence and put a hand to her mouth.

Becka smiled and waved it away.

Gustaves came over and gave Becka a hug. "I am *so* sorry," she said.

"It's fine, ma'am," Becka replied. "Amber was a huge part of your life."

"You're very kind."

"If you'd like, one night I'll stick around and you can tell me all about her."

"I'd like that," Gustaves replied, noticing the small tattoo of a dot above a comma on the inside of Becka's wrist. "Is that a semicolon or a winking symbol?" she asked.

"Both," Becka replied. "I'm a grammar nerd who winks a lot."

Gustaves laughed just as the door opened and Wilcox stepped through. He was dressed in a suit and Talanov was right behind him, dressed in slacks and a sports jacket, followed by Ginie and the three kids. Ginie was wearing a blue slack suit, while Jingfei was wearing a dress, as was Su Yin. Kai, as usual, was in baggy jeans.

With a sad smile, Gustaves gestured them into her office. "Hold my calls," she told Becka.

"Yes, ma'am," Becka replied.

After shutting her office door, Gustaves walked over to Talanov and took him by the hands. "I am so sorry about Zak," she said with genuine empathy. "I didn't know him, but wish that I had. There are very few people in this world with the integrity of you and Bill, and from everything Bill has told me, Zak was one of them."

Talanov nodded but did not reply.

"I understand he was a true man of God," Gustaves said.

"He was, ma'am," said Ginie, "and he didn't just preach the gospel, he lived it. Forgive my interruption, but Zak gave his life for me. He embodied 13:5."

"13:5?"

"From the Bible, ma'am, Hebrews 13:5. 'I will never desert you.' It's how Zak lived."

Gustaves nodded sadly and looked back at Talanov. "You were right, by the way, about the assassination attempt at the Monocle. I thought there was a connection with China. We've since confirmed Angus Shaw to have been responsible."

"He was only the tip of the iceberg," Talanov replied. "Your Deep State opponents will stop at nothing to get rid of you."

Gustaves nodded somberly. "And you," she said, stepping in front of Wilcox and taking him by the hands. "You put everything on the line for your convictions. Your career, your life . . . I owe you."

"You owe me nothing," Wilcox replied. "I simply did what had to be done."

With an appreciative nod, Gustaves moved on to Ginie, who still had scabs on her face. "The sacrifices of Zak and Emily will not be in vain, Ginie. I promise you that."

"Thank you, ma'am."

"I hear you're going back to the community center to continue their legacy."

"Yes, ma'am."

"Let me know how I can help. And I mean that. Whatever it takes."

"Thank you, ma'am."

Gustaves gave Ginie a hug before moving on to Jingfei and Kai. "I . . ." she began, then looking away, unable to complete her sentence, her eyes welling with tears.

Su Yin looked up at Talanov and saw him nod, and with a smile, she stepped over to Gustaves and gave her a hug.

Gustaves wrapped her arms around Su Yin and hugged her tightly.

And they both began to cry.

# CHAPTER 86

The meeting did not last much longer because there was not a lot more to say beyond what had already been said. The business talk would come later.

Talanov led the way outside and down the steps to the sidewalk, where he told the others to go on ahead, that he wanted to talk with Ginie.

Once the others were gone, Talanov took Ginie by the hands.

"You don't need to say it," said Ginie.

"Say what?" asked Talanov.

Ginie linked her arm through Talanov's and began walking with him along the sidewalk. "You need to heal, Alex, and you need to decide what you want, and who you want, and I need to let you do that, because I have a lot of healing to do myself in light of what Zak did for me. And right now, I'm not sure how to do that."

"I'm glad you're taking over the community center. I know Zak would want it that way."

"You don't have to do this, you know."

"Zak and I were the only family each of us had, and he left the building, so I'm turning it over to you."

"Are you sure?"

"I'm sure."

"Well, thank you, and if you're ever in a mood to get your ass whipped again in basketball, you know where to find me."

Talanov laughed and gave Ginie a hug. When Ginie hugged him in return, Talanov flinched.

"Sorry," Ginie said with a grin. "I forgot about the ribs." She gave him another hug, this one gentler.

"Much better," he said. "Much better."

Downhill, across the street on the Capitol grounds, Larisa

shook her head angrily. *I am such a fool,* she thought when Talanov and Ginie hugged. Bill had been convincing, that was for sure, but what she was seeing right now spoke more truth than Bill would ever admit.

Turning away, Larisa ran downhill through a small stand of trees and along a curving sidewalk that took her to a line of waiting taxi cabs.

Uphill, Wilcox led the kids along a sidewalk on the western side of the Capitol. "The center of freedom and democracy," he said proudly, pointing at the majestic dome silhouetted against a bright blue sky.

"How about power and corruption?" asked Kai. "And we can't forget duplicity and greed."

"Cynic," muttered Wilcox, and Kai grinned.

"You do know the CIA is a globalist cabal bent on taking over the world?" Kai stated more than asked. "Did you know those fake Russian hackers were really CIA? It was a false flag all the way, which makes you more than a little suspect as far as I'm concerned."

"Is there, like, someplace I can ship you back to?"

Kai grinned again and punched Wilcox playfully on the arm. Wilcox rolled his eyes and began looking around. He turned a full circle – twice – looking in all directions.

"What are you looking for?" asked Kai.

"Someone I told to meet us," Wilcox replied.

"Who?" asked Jingfei.

Wilcox did not reply, and with a shrug, Jingfei kept walking.

"Wait up!" yelled Talanov.

Wilcox looked back to see Talanov dash across Independence Avenue against the light.

"You can get ticketed for jaywalking in this town," Wilcox called out.

"That's why I keep you around," answered Talanov. "To take care of things like that."

Wilcox shook his head, then looked down the hill toward Garfield Circle, where he could see a blonde woman getting into a taxi. But she was so far away he couldn't tell for sure who she was.

Taking out his phone, Wilcox quickly dialed Larisa's number, and with his phone to his ear, he watched the blonde pause to retrieve her phone, look at the screen, then put the phone in her handbag and climb into the taxi just as Wilcox heard his call go to voicemail.

"Who was that?" asked Talanov, looking in the direction Wilcox was looking.

"Where's Ginie?" asked Wilcox in return.

"We hugged and said goodbye."

Wilcox looked again in Larisa's direction just as the taxi drove away.

"Is everything all right?" asked Talanov.

"Peachy," Wilcox mumbled, and without another word, he marched off toward the Capitol.

"What's up with him?" asked Talanov.

"I think I may have upset him," Kai replied. "I was joking around about him being in the CIA and I don't think he liked it very much."

"Go show him some love," said Jingfei.

Kai responded with a dubious frown.

"Come on, Kai, don't be a jerk."

Su Yin grabbed Kai by the hand. "Come on, Kai!" she exclaimed, grabbing Kai by the hand and tugging him into running with her. "Uncle Bill, wait up!" she called out.

Once Kai and Su Yin were gone, Jingfei stepped in front of Talanov and looked him directly in the eyes. "Are you sure you want to do this?" she asked.

"Absolutely," Talanov replied. "I want you three to come live with me. We'll get a new house. File the legal paperwork. Make this official as far as me being your legal guardian. No need to change your last name or anything like that."

Jingfei gave Talanov a hug.

"Just to be clear, I'm not trying to replace your parents," said Talanov. "Or Zak. Those people are irreplaceable. I just want you to know I'm here for you, that my home is your home, and that any guy wanting to date you will be thoroughly background-checked."

Jingfei punched Talanov on the arm and he laughed. She then took a tiny flash drive from her pocket. "Okay, then, here you go," she said. "One and a half billion and change."

"The money's here, in this little thing?"

"Not physically, of course, but, yes, as far as electronic codes are concerned."

"How did you manage to steal it?"

"Technically, I didn't steal it," answered Jingfei. "I simply returned it to its original owner, which I was able to do with Charlie's help by hacking the escrow account, which was a breeze, then creating a phantom duplicate of the account webpage, which showed your deposit, then embedding that page with an executable virus, which I then juxtaposed over the original, which I'd already emptied before Dragon Head's stooge clicked the link that I sent him, which nuked everything at his end, which, of course, was just how I—"

Jingfei stopped when she saw the blank stare on Talanov's face. "Forget it, you don't want to know," she said.

"Probably not," Talanov replied. "Where's the money now?"

"In a trap door account inside an offshore bank that I created using a circular blind."

"What does that even mean?"

"It means no one can find it unless we want them to."

"And it's all in here?" Talanov asked, holding up the flash drive.

"Every number you'll ever need."

Talanov nodded, then turned to watch Su Yin doing the happy dance for Wilcox, who was laughing and shaking his head while Kai was trying to get him to do the happy dance with her.

"I wish Zak could be here to enjoy this," Talanov said, smiling at the sight. "He was the best friend I ever had."

"He said the same about you," Jingfei replied. "He told us

stories about when you were young and stupid and how you'd get in all sorts of trouble. How he was constantly bailing you out."

Talanov laughed, then looked away, fighting back emotion.

"Don't worry, old man, you've got us," Jingfei said, linking arms with Talanov. "13:5, remember?"

"13:5 to you, too . . . kid," responded Talanov. "But there's one thing I still don't get."

"What's that?"

Talanov looked at the flash drive quizzically. "How do I upload – or is it download – music onto this thing?"

Jingfei grabbed for the flash drive but Talanov yanked it away. "It's not a toy!" she yelled.

Talanov darted ahead and turned, holding the flash drive high in the air.

"You need to grow up!" yelled Jingfei, racing after him. "It's called responsibility. Want me to spell it out for you? *Re-spon-si-bil-i-ty.*" Catching up with him, she punched him on the arm. When Talanov grabbed for Jingfei, she ducked aside with a girly scream and began making faces and dancing around, taunting Talanov to try to catch her.

With a laugh, Talanov glanced upward toward the sky. *"Kak odin,* my friend. I'll take care of them," he said before racing after Jingfei.

# EPILOGUE

Located on a neon strip of Bangkok, the nightclub was vibrating the night with synthesized music that spilled out into the street, where surges of partygoers drifted past in slow currents, drinking and laughing while eyeing the enticing array of teenage prostitutes loitering around the entrance. The enticements of a good time intensified inside, where a strobes of pulsating green laser lights kept beat with music so loud it made conversation all but impossible. But no one was interested in conversation, at least not on the dance floor, where a packed crowd of more than three hundred partygoers were dancing with their hands in the air.

Carrying a small handbag and wearing a shimmering black micro-dress that showed every curve of her statuesque body, a woman smiled her way past the bouncers and entered the club, where she paused to survey the layout. To her left was a lengthy bar of gleaming liquor bottles. To her right was a darkened mezzanine of tables and chairs. At the far end was an elevated platform, where a caramel-skinned DJ operated a vast electronic console from behind a glass partition.

The DJ pumped his fist in the air several times, then flipped a switch that turned the green laser beams into a rotating red and blue light show that bathed the dance floor from numerous angles.

None of this interested the woman. Her eyes were on a guarded staircase to the left of the elevated platform.

With beams of red and blue flashing across her face, the woman made her way through the crowd to the four guards who were stationed there. Wiry and thin and dressed in suits that concealed their pistols, all of them were a full head shorter than the woman.

"I'm here to see Chakrii," the woman said.

The men all glanced at one another before one of them waved her away.

"No speak English?" the woman asked.

With one hand on his pistol, the man pushed her away.

With a patient smile, the woman repeated her request in Chinese.

"Chakrii does not accept visitors," the man replied, also in Chinese. "Go, and do not come back."

"He will want to see me," answered the woman, handing the man her clutch handbag and nodding for him to open it.

The man hesitated, then accepted it, then looked at the woman, still unsure, then guardedly opened it. Inside was a Ruger SR40c semiautomatic pistol, which was a compact handgun, in matte black, loaded with fifteen rounds of forty caliber ammunition, which packed more stopping power than nearly any other compact handgun on the market.

The men drew their weapons when they saw the pistol.

With a smile, the woman casually held up her hands. "It is a gift for Chakrii," she said, "and there are more where that came from. I thought he might be interested in acquiring some for himself."

While keeping the woman covered, the men gathered together to look at the pistol. Very few handguns were forty caliber, and none of the men had ever seen such a weapon.

"I will get you one as well," the woman said. "Provided you show it to Chakrii."

The man looked back and forth between the handgun he was holding and the beautiful woman.

"What is your name?" asked the woman. "I am here to help. Not to cause trouble."

"Mongkut," the man replied. "Where did you obtain this pistol?"

The woman smiled but did not reply.

Mongkut thought for a moment, then motioned for the woman to follow him up the stairs. When one of the other guards asked if that was a good idea, Mongkut rebuked him, then motioned again for the woman to follow.

The other men watched them climb the stairs, mostly to see the woman's long slender legs and shapely figure.

At the top of the stairs, Mongkut led the way to a black door at the end of the corridor, where two more guards were stationed. Both were short and thin, like Mongkut, and both had black hair tied back in ponytails. On the wall beside the door was a lighted keypad.

Mongkut told the woman to sit on a bench while he presented the pistol to Chakrii. The woman smiled and sat, and when she did, her micro-dress slid up her thighs.

Both guards brightened with interest, especially when she smiled back at them.

Mongkut entered a series of numbers on the keypad and the door clicked open. An instant later, the woman sprang from the bench and punched the other two guards in the throat, dropping them to their knees, gasping. Mongkut did not have time to react before the woman pushed him through the door, grabbed the Ruger from his hand and closed the door behind them.

With Mongkut in her grasp, the woman approached the seven men seated around a polished mahogany table, playing cards. All had drinks in glass tumblers and several were smoking cigars. In the center of the table was a pile of poker chips. Across the floor was a pool table brightly lit by three conical billiard lamps suspended from the ceiling. On the green felt of the table was an assortment of eight pistols normally carried by each of the players.

Three of the men lunged for their weapons.

"Sit down or I will kill you," the woman said in Chinese.

The men grudgingly obeyed.

After shoving Mongkut to the other side of the poker table, the woman said, "Which one of you is Chakrii?"

The men instinctively looked at one man in particular, and the woman smiled.

"Do you know who I am?" said Chakrii.

"Do you know who *I* am?" asked the woman.

"I don't care who you are," Chakrii replied. "When my men get through with you . . ."

"Do you really want to finish that sentence?" asked the woman, stepping forward and pointing the Ruger directly at Chakrii.

Chakrii averted his eyes.

The woman stepped over to the pool table, picked up the eight handguns and carried them to the table, where she dropped them on top of the poker chips, which scattered them in all directions.

Chakrii and the others exchanged surprised glances, then backed away from the table instinctively.

"You want an excuse to kill us," Chakrii said, commanding the others not to move.

"I am not here to kill anyone," the woman replied with a smile. "Especially not you."

Chakrii looked quizzically at the woman.

The woman tossed her pistol to Chakrii. "I am here to apply for a job."

Chakrii caught the pistol, then jumped up and pointed the Ruger at the woman while everyone else grabbed their pistols just as the door flew open and Chakrii's guards swarmed into the room with guns drawn.

The woman raised her hands. "If I had wanted to kill you, I would have. The pistol in your hand holds fifteen rounds of forty caliber ammunition . . . enough to have silenced everyone in this room while still allowing me time to escape. Like I said, I am here to apply for a job. But I needed to get your attention."

"Well, you've got it. But you may not like what happens next."

"Are you sure? Look how easily I bypassed your security."

Chakrii glared at his guards, then licked his lips. An indication that what he had just heard had grudgingly piqued his interest.

The woman lowered her hands and approached the poker table, where the others backed away while keeping her covered. She placed her hands on the edge of the table and looked directly at Chakrii. "Someone like me could have prevented this from happening," she said. "Like I said, I am here to apply for a job."

Chakrii stared at the woman for a long moment, noting how she was stronger and more agile than any woman he'd ever seen. "What kind of a job?" he asked.

"Bangkok is full of gangs," the woman replied. "Ever wondered what would happen if you could unite those gangs? Get them to quit fighting each other over who controls which prostitutes on which corner? Get them to channel their resources into a cyber army that can steal anything from anyone on earth?"

"Is that what you're offering?" asked Chakrii.

"Is that what you want?" asked the woman.

Chakrii grinned a mouthful of yellowed teeth. "When can you start?" he asked.

Sofia smiled. "I already have."

# PUBLISHER'S NOTE

Thank you for reading *Dragon Head*. Please take a moment to leave a rating and/or comment on the site where you purchased this book. Our hope is that that you were treated to a few enjoyable hours with Talanov and his friends, who will return soon in a new adventure.

CPSIA information can be obtained
at www.ICGtesting.com
Printed in the USA
LVHW010922290620
659221LV00008B/472